MR FRIEDMAN'S FIRESIDE TALES

*Seven Adventures From
Parallel Dimensions*

A.L. Bell

Book Guild Publishing
Sussex, England

First published in Great Britain in 2012 by
The Book Guild Ltd
Pavilion View
19 New Road
Brighton, BN1 1UF

Typesetting in Meridien by
Norman Tilley Graphics Ltd, Northampton

Printed and bound in Great Britain by
CPI Group (UK) Ltd, Croydon, CR0 4YY

A catalogue record for this book is available from
The British Library

ISBN 978 1 84624 786 6

Contents

CONTENTS

The First Tale

A middle-aged lady was hunched over the fireplace, stirring a hot soup. Wisps of vapour flowed up the chimney and a magical warm air filled the old kitchen. Colourful Christmas stockings were hung up on the mantelpiece; there were twenty-seven in all.

A slightly older man sat muttering cheerfully to himself on an armchair nearby, sucking on a pipe, and in front of him were toys that would make any child's eyes light up and their cheeks glow; a wondrous collection of this year's stocking fillers. It was already the morning of Christmas Eve, and as usual there never seemed to be enough time to do everything; and yet the same procedure went like clockwork every year. Mr Friedman couldn't help thinking that perhaps this efficiency was down to the aid of some Christmas angels. The house was often filled with unexpected blessings and gifts would appear, and he would not always know by whose hand. But the children were getting used to that; being blessed and having their hearts filled with joy, and never once taking it for granted, either.

'Let's hope he'll come late this year.' He was joking about Father Christmas's arrival for the benefit of his hard-working wife.

'Mr Friedman, they're expecting you again!' She laughed, straightening up excitedly. 'You know it's that time of year. They'll want to hear some more of your wonderful stories. You do tell them so well.'

A look of delightful remembrance tempered with complete astonishment crossed his face; that he should need reminding of his most cherished duty was a surprise to him. Yet it was understandable in the circumstances – he was so preoccupied with considering what present would bring the biggest smiles to their faces, a prospect that filled him with joy to the brim.

'Right!' He stood up in a businesslike way. 'They await me.'

'You know how much they adore it,' she said, giggling with glee and giving him an affectionate hug and kiss. 'Where you get the inspiration for your stories, God only knows.'

'Yes,' he replied, with the twinkle in his eyes she always loved. 'My dear Evelyn, indeed He does.'

A few magical moments later, there he sat in the lounge, surrounded by the children he had come to love and cherish, and they all stared up at him in silent awe. You could have heard a pin drop. The candlelight and the Christmas lights on the tree added to the atmosphere of the occasion. They sat snug in the heat of the log fire, which seemed to crackle appreciatively.

'Now, listen children... and you older ones as well!' He turned to the adolescents who, although they were sitting further back than the rest, were no less engrossed in his every word. 'It's that time of year again, indeed it is, and as an extra special treat I have discovered some new adventures which, once told, will help you go to sleep so that you don't hear *him* or his reindeer...'

'He doesn't exist!' piped up a little voice.

'Quiet, Judah! We need to listen,' hushed another.

'But Mr Friedman told me himself. *He* is just another fairy tale.'

'A fairy tale he may be,' went on Mr Friedman, winking affectionately at little Judah, 'and that is for you to decide.

But each and every one of you will also have to decide if the stories you are about to hear are *true*, or if they are *part true*... As usual, you are to guess who the character of the story is, and the special meaning of each story, but most importantly, just sit back and enjoy the telling.'

'I wonder if we'll be in this one,' Russian twins Salomya and Simira whispered excitedly, hugging each other in delight. They were both twelve years old, Simira just the eldest.

Mr Friedman leaned towards them, a sparkle in his eyes.

'You know what, daughters? I think you may well be... Wait and see!'

'Will there be one for me this year?' an older male voice sounded humorously from the adolescents in the back row. He was the musical one, who would put some of Mr Friedman's tales to song, and on these special occasions he always sat with his guitar close at hand, ready to inspire the imaginations of those gathered with some background music.

'Well, David, that will be for you to decide,' went on Mr Friedman with his mysterious air. 'As you know, everyone gets to be in a story at some point, or if they are especially imaginative, they get many more turns than one – indeed, some of you have been in all my stories, for you were surely there, entering into these other worlds, even more involved than I was! And you came out again quite changed people.'

The children loved it when he got really into the act of the telling. And he was quite right; as they watched him and listened to his voice, other worlds and dimensions would come alive before their eyes. So, they all sat back for the first tale to be told.

He told them its title. It was called...

The Rose that Bloomed

The Searching of a Princess

In a tall tower of a castle in Igniteland, a princess was writing a page of her memoirs...

'One day, perhaps a prince from a faraway land will rescue me, a knight in shining armour will climb my tower and take me away to live with him.

'Yet I feel that there is more for me to do here first. There is a time for everything and often I wonder if my time in this castle will last a lifetime.

'Somehow, I need to break free and I know that it is not the knight in shining armour who can truly save me. I can only do that myself, with God's help. Even in an attitude of mind. The situation may stay the same but maybe something inside me can change. I will no longer be a victim of my environment, but secretly a rose that is waiting to bloom from a stony bed. Waiting for the rain, the Great Awakening.

'But until that time a part of me must sleep on, and yet in the present time I must choose to live.'

I laid down my pen and waited. The frost on the window pane seemed to echo my state of mind; glistening yet still, as if expectant of a miracle that could break the spell of winter.

I saw my rose outside standing ruby red and pure, majestically enthroned on its bush of thorns, the only beauty left alive by the frost. I often pondered on how wonderful it was that the rose had managed to survive all weathers, as if by a secret magic, never withering completely before blooming again.

I had lived a relatively comfortable life in the castle with my adoptive parents, the king and queen, and my brothers and sisters, yet still it seemed that something vital was missing. I felt unable to break into full bloom; it was as if something unseen wished to diminish my progress.

I heartily hoped that I did not seem ungrateful for all the love and care with which I had been reared, yet burning inside my soul ever so deeply and constantly was the awareness that I was an adopted child. I was therefore not a natural heir to the throne, which had been in their family for thousands of years. I was not theirs and never truly would be; I did not belong here.

The thirst to know my true roots once again sprung up within me as I fanned my tired hot face with the paper onto which I had just poured a few heartfelt thoughts. This action did not seem to help me much and certainly did not answer any more questions, although I soon decided that the expression of my thoughts on paper was at this time enough. They were a record of my progress and discoveries and I could only console myself with the idea that one day some answers would be added to help resolve the thought-provoking mysteries that made up my life.

Fuelled by my parents' over-protective efforts to cover up all traces of my past – in effect, by informing me of as little as possible – I became more determined to learn of my true identity.

In truth, I did know some small details which preyed on my mind at such times as this, and these were that the king and queen's eldest son, Prince Ernest, had found me as a two year old hidden in a basket hanging from an oak tree in the nearby forest. At this time, a fierce and greedy people called the Tikes had invaded our land and attacked the forests where the ancient peaceful race known as the Tree People lived. The Tikes mercilessly marched throughout the forests, cutting down great trees, the homes of the Tree People, and creating burning altars to honour their lord, a spirit who was said to appear in the form of a terrifying great dark panther to devour any of his people he desired.

Of course, the hope of our nation, and particularly the Tree People, was that if so many Tikes were devoured by their dark lord, there would be none of them left to cause havoc and suffering. However, there were also rumours that the Tikes who were devoured by the panther often did return, in spirit form, and were far more frightening than ever before, rendering the forests places of unrest and danger.

Many preferred not to consider these more sinister aspects, and either assumed that the panther was fictional nonsense, or that he was not nearly as great and terrifying as the rumours gave him credit for. I, on the other hand, believed firmly in the existence of such a beast. It seemed to explain something of all the suffering in the world; somehow, that the fallibility of man himself had given permission for the entrance of the beast in the first place. For when man turns away from the light, there is only one direction in which he can walk, and that is towards the dark side, the side of all opposite power and nature to that of his creator. Yet more importantly, I believed that no matter how great the power of the dark beast, this was insignificant in relation to the almighty power of God, who I knew only waited for the time to bring all wrongs to right.

Moving aside from the dilemmas of the present world, I turned back to the question of my identity. Of course, I knew that God who created me knew the answer, and in fact, He held my ultimate identity; I was His child above everything else. That was all that should have mattered. But the more I questioned my past, the more I desired to unravel its mystery, and nothing could push away the thoughts that came as sturdy as steel, marching further and deeper into my mind in a rhythmic procession: WHO AM I?

I closed my eyes as if in a trance, trying to grasp all my parents had implied about my true heritage over the years. It felt like clutching at straws in the dark. Sometimes my mind made up possibilities of its own and often the hardest task was discerning which ideas were imagined presumptions and which ideas were real.

I was more certain of this: that there were two possibilities for my origin; either I was from the race of the Tree People, or I was a child of the tribe of Tikes. Of course, my parents always objected to the latter connection by pointing out that I bore no resemblance to the Tikes, with their characteristically mean and heavy features and stocky frames. I was far more like the tall, slender Tree People. I was rather pleased and relieved that everyone around me agreed and never associated me with the Tikes.

One story my parents often told about me, on festive occasions, concerned my finding. The world learned that I had been hung in a basket high in the oak tree for my own protection from the Tikes. Whether I was from the Tree People, or from the folk of the land or the sea that surrounded the hills beyond our castle, remained a mystery. The invasion had caused such chaos that many folk fled from their homes to take refuge in the forests, which turned out to be the most unsafe part of the land. Somehow, the peaceful Tree People managed to bring an end to the short reign of the land-greedy tribe, by fighting back for the first time in centuries. And, taking the Tikes by surprise, they used their wily forest ways to entrap and repel them, and in so doing saved many lives, including the lives of the few trees left in their forest.

Miraculously, it seemed, luxurious woodlands soon grew up again around the country, making it appear as if there had never been any devastation. People said that the Tree

People had their strange ways; some grew suspicious of them as they lived their secret lives once again, and trees around them bloomed and grew. Some said that they practised dark magic and should never be conversed with (not that many people ever saw them to converse with, as it was said that the Tree People tended to keep all their activities minimal until after dusk). This spreading of hostility and suspicion seemed an unfair way of repaying them after all they had done for the land, in sending the Tikes out defeated.

My fascination and empathy for these mysterious folk had increased over the years and I longed to know more about them and even liked to imagine that I was one of them. Yet my true identity had never been revealed in all the years in which I had grown up amongst the royals as my family, and due to my parents' protective natures and household rules I had never set even one foot into the forest that surrounded our grounds.

Recently I had turned eighteen years old, and I reasoned that my coming of age must bring with it a time of great discovery and the permission to live in true independence as an adult.

My watchful eye had witnessed, however, my parents' attitudes concerning their true heirs, and there did not seem to be much hope for my aspirations, for my brothers and sisters were also greatly over-protected. From observing this, I knew that as the youngest addition to the family, it was unlikely that I would ever be allowed out of their sight. Many times I became highly frustrated with these limitations and at such moments I would go to my room in the tower that overlooked the beautiful lake where swans bathed, and I would sit at my lonely desk and attempt to write myself into a point of acceptance.

So here I sat with my head in my hands, until a familiar voice stirred me back into this world, the only voice that could.

11

'Salomya.' The inquiring voice rang in my ears, interrupting my train of thought.

I looked up quickly to see the brightly lit countenance of my eldest brother, Ernest, as he gazed fondly across at me. I quickly pushed my writings aside and ran to the doorway where he stood patiently, and greeted him.

'How is my favourite sister this morning?' he asked, surveying me carefully. 'Is anything troubling you? Nothing terrible to write about, I hope?' He searched the desk where my writings lay.

'Everything is fine,' I replied quickly, with bright but still slightly tearful eyes. 'How could I describe my situation any differently?'

My brother's searching face was not entirely convinced of my happiness, and he continued, 'Has Mother had her chat with you yet?'

My eyes fell to the floor, for her morning chat with me had been the reason for my writings, and Ernest knew that all too well. 'She's perfectly determined to marry me off today at the ball,' I replied slowly, 'and I just want to enjoy the dancing!'

Ernest took my hand gently and whispered, 'And dance you shall, if I can possibly help it. Why, if I don't see my little sister happy on my birthday then I shall not be happy!'

I smiled at his jovial words and remembered the present I had set aside to give him. 'Wait,' I said, and quickly went to the wardrobe and withdrew the cross-stitch picture which I had been working on for many months, a design of my own imagination. Now it was perfectly complete; the baby in the basket shone with eyes full of joy at her rescuer, a young boy.

As I placed it in his hands, I could see Ernest was delighted with it, and it was also evident that it touched him deeply. As he continued to survey the cross-stitch picture with warm admiration, tears filled his light blue eyes and for a moment I thought that he was going to cry.

'This is the best birthday gift I have ever had,' he whispered, in a voice of awe. 'I am so glad that I found you there, Salomya.'

Ernest's Birthday Ball

It seemed just a moment later that we were walking arm in arm down the grand staircase to find a crowd of guests awaiting the arrival of the prince. Standing at the front of the crowd were our father and mother and our two brothers and two sisters. Beside them were our aunts and uncles, cousins and second cousins, dukes and duchesses and lords and ladies, our two living grandparents and our resident great-grandfather. All of our relatives were present, giving bows and curtseys. My father stepped forward and warmly greeted his son with an enthusiastic handshake.

'Many happy returns, dear Ernest.' His rich voice filled the grand hall with a warm and noble air. 'You are now a quarter the age of your great-grandfather, Joseph, who is pleased to still be around to celebrate this joyful occasion with you.'

With this, our father turned to assist a very elderly man who hobbled on a golden stick towards him. For a moment Ernest and I were quite taken aback as we were used to seeing our great-grandfather Jo in much more simple, humble attire; he always made it plain that he had no use for the luxuries of life. He was, as he often pointed out, our mother's grandfather, and merely a lord of a manor who had trained to be a vicar and just so happened to marry a duchess, and had never intended to have any royal connections if he could possibly help it. Obviously, on that front he had failed entirely, but we never pursued the point; only our mischievous twin brothers, Charlie and Cecil, did so for their own amusement, and often got a heated response.

Seeing Grand Jo, a little man at one hundred years of age, freshly robed in a new sparkling array baffled me and Ernest so much that we simply stared at him with our mouths wide open.

He evidently found this to be somewhat disagreeable, and instantly attempted to change the expressions on our faces with a quick flick of his new golden stick, which he had acquired especially for the occasion. We closed our mouths without any hesitation. Satisfied at the triumph of his new implement, Grand Jo then proceeded to prod Ernest rather hard on the shoulder and say in a rough, gravelly voice, 'Straighten up! Look your best, that's it.'

Ernest politely obliged, although he obviously did not fully appreciate Grand Jo's insistence on good posture, as if that alone would make us into the best examples of royal rulers in the kingdom.

'Really, grandfather,' cried our father, laughing heartily, 'don't you think that the young fellow is far too tall for all that?'

In response Grand Jo coughed and spluttered, apparently perplexed at being interfered with by an over-protective parent.

'And who helped him to grow so tall?' Grand Jo challenged the king. 'I did! And who made him eat all his greens? I did! And who gave him the height he has inherited?'

He waited, as if expectant of a certain response, and turned and looked the king up and down as if to suggest that Ernest certainly could not have inherited his height from him. My father, as it happened, was not as tall as Ernest, but was by no means short, and certainly stood a good few inches taller than Grand Jo. I could see Ernest smiling at this remark, but then he turned to address Grand Jo with a wonderfully polite and serious expression and said, 'Indeed, I am sure that your height was of greater stature in your youth, great-grandfather.'

Now it was Grand Jo's turn to appear surprised and he did this rather well. After muttering his indignation his mouth hung open in exasperation. Before he could muster up a verbal response, my father patted him jovially on his back and called out with an air of jollification, 'Come, come now, grandfather; you're only young once. Shall we allow Ernest this one piece of impertinence on his own birthday?'

'Well...'

The old man looked thoughtful. He leaned on his golden stick, attempting to straighten his back as much as possible and propped himself up quite effectively in this manner until my mother broke out in her chirpy laugh and made him jump in surprise. Clapping her hands together, she called out, 'Come; let us have music and dancing!'

At once the musicians began to play the latest dance movement composed by the king himself. He always took pride in adding another ten instruments to his symphonies each time he composed; the difficulty was finding enough players to join the court orchestra. As children we had all been strongly encouraged to sing and to play at least one instrument each. I had taken to it naturally, as my parents often commented with some pride, 'like a fish to water'. I most enjoyed playing the harp and singing and, much to my concern, my parents had always claimed that they would hold a concert when we were all good enough to play, which would be attended by all the highest standard professionals in the country. As neither I nor any of my siblings had achieved such an impressively high standard of performance, I think my parents had decided to leave that agenda dormant for a while. However, in the meantime they still continued to mention the idea of me doing solo performances on my harp, singing some of the songs which I had written. I did not mind singing in itself, even in front of a group of people, but I knew these occasions would call forth the multitudes, as well as men with notebooks who would mark my music as a performance rather than an expression from the heart.

The dancing began and I stepped back as my mother eagerly took hold of Ernest, kissing him warmly and whispering something sweet in his ear. Then she swooped around to me in her flowing cream garments, took my arm and sung in her sweet voice, 'Well, dear, you are nicely dressed for the occasion.'

I noticed, however, that she surveyed my favourite rose-coloured dress with some incomplete satisfaction as she took me aside.

She continued in a quieter voice, 'But I had rather hoped that you would dress in the latest addition to your wardrobe. Now that you have recently come of age, my dear, may I suggest that next time we have a ball, the rich ruby-red ballgown which was handmade for you and sent all the way from Perusia may be a more fitting item?'

The king and queen of Perusia had been considering me as a bride for their son for some years. 'Besides, the Prince of Perusia himself is present, and you are of the age when new alliances between countries can more easily occur.'

My mother seemed rather overcome suddenly, as she dabbed her nose with her golden-embroidered pocket handkerchief.

'Really, mother, wouldn't you be better off pairing me with a young suitor who is not from such a distant land?' I quickly suggested.

She looked at me for a second with a certain amount of empathy, but then the look faded as her gaze fell on the handsome young princes who were waltzing across the hall with exquisitely dressed, elegant women.

'My dear child.' She lowered her voice. 'Don't you think I desire what is best for you? Our country is well aware that you are not really of noble blood. Don't you think that you should marry an heir to the throne to secure the best future for yourself? Here we have the perfect opportunity.'

I knew that my mother's reasons were more complex than this; she wished to do all she could to maintain the peace between our nation and the Perusians, for there had been outbreaks of war in previous centuries when the Perusians did not gain what they desired from our nation. That was generally more connected with the underground seams of gold which had been discovered on our shores at that time than with arrangements of marriage between our nations. Furthermore, the then Perusian king and queen had been unseemly characters of unfortunate temperament who liked to have everything which they desired and were willing to destroy lives to accomplish this. I often thought that my mother was over anxious on such matters and read the history books with too much concern. She was convinced that as the blood of the spoilt king and queen was still in the veins of the present king of Perusia, then it was inevitable that at any point his placid personality could change into the temperamental nature of his ancestors, if relationships with our kingdom in any way displeased him. From what I had gathered of the Perusian king, however, he was unlikely to become my parents' enemy, even if I denied his son's hand in marriage. He appeared to be a contented man who was generally good-natured, despite being rather indulgent at feasts and a little lax when it came to organising anything. I had no intention of marrying his son whatsoever, and I would continue to make this as clear as I ever had done, without any fear at all of the consequences.

'Hush!' My mother interrupted my train of thought as if I had spoken these words to her. I noticed that she appeared to be composing herself to introduce me to one of the handsome foreign princes.

She drew me close to her as we moved slowly across

the hall together, and at this moment none other than the prince of Perusia himself stepped forward. He was olive-skinned, with eyes that contained light amber flecks, and his smile was rather dashing, yet something appeared to be hiding behind that smile and I did not feel safe with him. All the same, I took his hand boldly as we exchanged our introductions.

'I am Prince Vicoro, son of Filio, king of Perusia.' He spoke with some command in his voice.

'Prince Vicoro, it is my pleasure to introduce my youngest daughter, Princess Salomya.' My mother curtseyed to him, and I followed suit.

'It is my pleasure to meet you properly at last, Princess Salomya.' His voice became smooth and airy. 'May I have the pleasure of this dance?'

'You may,' I replied, as duty required of me.

We danced around the room breezily, and a little idly on my part, as I was just trying to pass the time away. I saw my brother Ernest's watchful regard from the crowd, carefully checking the countenance of my dance partner as if attempting to discern his character from afar. Even my brother became protective over me at times like these, and especially when I was dancing with a prince from another land who could be a prospective marriage partner.

The waltz ended and Prince Vicoro seemed pleased with it. He took my hand, kissed it, and bowed low as I curtseyed.

'It has been an honour, Princess Salomya,' he said in his honeyed voice.

I returned the appropriate comment, and then I left him rather carelessly, with little concern as to whether we would meet again.

Next, my mother came to introduce me to another prospective partner. She had the tendency to whirl me around all the royal single men present regardless of their age or odd dispositions and she claimed to do this in order to ensure that I had higher chances of finding a match. This time, a younger prince stood before me and he appeared to be very amiable, although it was evident that he was vastly uncertain of himself. He had a boyish, clumsy frame and a well-featured, pleasant face which lacked the maturity and refined appearance of so many of the elder suitors I had met. However, I preferred him to anyone else due to his genuine glow of warmth and cheerfulness. He was like a breath of fresh air.

'This young man–' Mother paused a little uncertainly '– is Prince Derek, of Tunamasia.'

For some reason this name jarred with me, and then I recollected that some of our family had taken a snobby dislike of the small, insignificant kingdom. I felt myself fighting the instinct to turn my head away at the mention of the place which our nation criticised for the simplicity of many of its inhabitants. I tried to see the best in my dancing partner, despite all that had been said of his race.

As we proceeded to dance (or stumble around, for he kept treading on my feet), Prince Derek stuttered a few nervous statements.

'This is… my first dance, Princess… er…'

'Salomya,' I prompted him graciously.

'Princess Samantha,' he continued.

'Salomya,' I repeated in surprise.

'That's what I said.' His voice became indignant. 'Princess Samantha. What a lovely name. Why, that's the name of my cousin!'

'No,' I corrected him again, 'I said Salomya. Sal-om-ya.'

For a moment he gave me a quizzical stare, as if I was joking. It appeared that my dance partner was rather hard of hearing.

'Very well, Princess Samantha,' he said rather foolishly; and this time I did not bother to correct him. 'As I was saying, you and my cousin share a lovely name. How did your parents come to name you?'

'It's quite an unusual story, actually,' I replied. 'They did not name me themselves. I was wearing a golden necklace when they found me. It was engraved with the name *Salomya.*' Then I added with a humorous smile, 'So how were you named, Derek? I don't suppose your name appeared in gold writing?'

He looked momentarily stunned. 'Actually, yes, it did. That is how I got my name. My father wrote it on the wall in gold pen; he spelled it out for my mother because she did not know how to spell.'

I felt totally taken aback by this unexpected irony. It was not the fact that Prince Derek's mother could not spell that surprised me the most; it was the fact that I had such little awareness of his customs. In his country all names were chosen in a sacred manner and were always written in gold ink, I later learned.

At a point in the dance when the music faded away and Prince Derek referred to me by the wrong name once again, I felt it right to correct him one final time. In response he appeared very puzzled indeed. He stood with his hands on his hips and his eyes bulging.

'Well!' he said very slowly. 'Why didn't you say so before?'

His hearing had evidently improved on the background music's fading. And as we continued to stumble around the dance floor like some of my parents' more drunken guests, I fervently wished to be rescued.

My brother Ernest was quick to see a damsel in an awkward situation and stepped out in front of us on the dance floor. Unfortunately, he had over-estimated Prince Derek's ability to stop dancing quickly or, in fact, to stop at all. Derek tripped over one of his own feet and fell, nearly taking me and Ernest with him, and he made quite a rumpus. He looked fairly shocked lying down there, staring up at us, and Ernest immediately apologised profusely.

21

'Dear, dear!' he cried, stooping to help Derek up to his feet. 'I am awfully sorry, old boy! I simply thought that it was the perfect moment for a dance with my sister, if that is agreeable with you.'

Prince Derek blinked at Ernest in some astonishment then gave a strange high-pitched titter. It was such an unusual sound that all the gentry standing nearby turned and gave Prince Derek perplexed stares, and his ears went rather pink.

He then proceeded nervously. 'I was... wondering... whether I might be permitted to ask Princess Salomya one question?'

'Yes, certainly,' my brother replied warmly. 'What will it be?'

'Am I...' Prince Derek stepped back a little and drew his breath. 'Am I... er... going to be the ideal suitor for her ladyship – I mean Her Highness? You see, my mother said that...'

'My dear boy,' Ernest quickly said, his face filled with great surprise, 'this isn't the done thing at all, you know. I really can't stand matchmaking of any kind at the best of times, but, sad as it may be, the decision really isn't ours. Our parents have their own requirements in a suitor; for one, I believe they expect a suitor to be around a decade my sister's senior.'

This statement alone would have been a kind enough way of informing Derek of the unlikelihood of any union occurring between him and myself. Already, his face and neck had started to turn a rich crimson colour. However, it was not enough for our great-grandfather Jo, who, being as timely as ever, happened to be standing close by and, most uncommonly, had actually been able to hear some of our dialogue.

He took his golden hearing horn out from his ear and jumped in a surprisingly sprightly fashion between myself and Prince Derek. His former limping with the golden stick now appeared rather unconvincing. He even went so far as to grab Prince Derek roughly by the collar and raise his gravelly voice several decibels higher.

'Why, who do you think you are?' he growled indignantly. 'You ought to know your place amongst your elder and betters. To think that the child decides who they are to be betrothed to on only one meeting... Why, you are but a child, and the only suitors appropriate for my great-granddaughter are probably a good decade older than yourself.'

Prince Derek looked momentarily speechless and, interpreting this response to be one of submission, Grand Jo suddenly became somewhat fatherly towards him and he lowered his voice a little, placing his hand on Derek as he continued, 'Well, I am sure you could see this as a bit of practice for when you join the realm of adulthood.'

Prince Derek drew back in dismay as he cried, 'But I am not a child! I reached adulthood seven years ago.'

'And how old exactly does that make you now?' questioned Grand Jo suspiciously.

Mathematics was clearly not his strong point.

'I am five and twenty,' declared Derek in a rather hurt voice. 'That makes me seven years the princess's senior. Won't that do?'

Ernest and I glanced at each other in further disbelief. Grand Jo was repositioning his hearing instrument in his ear, to check whether he had heard correctly.

'I am ever so sorry,' Ernest said in an apologetic tone, 'I took you for a boy! But as I said before we cannot decide whom we are to marry. There must be a consultation between our parents, but I ought to tell you now that Princess Salomya is likely to be destined for another suitor. Of course, we cannot say whom. Maybe there is a princess closer to home who will take your hand, near to – what do you call it – Tunamasia?'

'No, no,' objected Derek, 'you haven't pronounced it right at all!'

Then he pronounced it again, exactly as my brother had done. Grand Jo, who appeared rather taken aback by this last exchange of information, butted in. He hit the floor sharply with his stick rather close to Derek's feet, who jumped in fright.

'Tunamasia, eh?' shouted Grand Jo. 'Now tell me, boy, what is your commonest food out in that odd country? Would it be tuna and mayonnaise, perchance?'

Suddenly all the gentry present let out a strange guffaw in unison, and so it was Grand Jo's turn to jump. He had not been humouring Derek; his innocent question was just his attempt to make polite conversation, but as always, his odd remarks led to the end of all chances of normality. Grand Jo merely pouted at the laughter, particularly at Charlie and Cecil, who were half hidden behind a pillar, their hands covering their mouths and going as red as two beetroots.

'Why, yes exactly, sir,' Derek continued with a strange jolly smile spreading over his young face. 'Tuna and mayonnaise is the only food we eat, that is with the exception of a few vegetables here and there.'

The gentry present flung their heads back and laughed once again, and Derek merely smiled at them all, wondering what the joke was, and even started tittering away to himself. This was too much for Charlie and Cecil, my elder twin brothers, who could be heard laughing above the rest. As they were nearer than most, Grand Jo turned around and chased them out of the grand hall, waving his stick.

Ernest quickly swept me off around the dance floor, which I suspect was an act to disguise his great amusement. Neither of us could wipe off the smiles that had spread across our faces as we danced lightly around the room, our relations and friends watching us. I decided that perhaps balls could be rather fun, even the waiting on ceremony and the warding off of inappropriate suitors. I noticed Prince Derek standing beside Prince Vicoro, both looking on in apparent awe as we danced, just as precise and practised as a pair of experienced dancers of royal heritage. I was enjoying this dance vastly more than the previous ones, but my mother stepped in all too soon to end it.

'I can't expect you to be the only one of my three daughters unable to find a suitor because you dance a whole evening with your brother,' she whispered, looking in an unimpressed fashion at Ernest. Then she added in a louder voice so that he could hear, 'And likewise, it's not surprising that my Ernest does not find himself a wife as he only likes to dance with his sibling. Things must change!'

'Mother, really,' he replied in a disapproving tone, 'I think a future king has the right to choose his future wife in his own time. Besides, in his one moment of great wisdom, Grand Jo advised me to wait for whoever was worth waiting for rather than rush into things merely for the sake of ceremony. I can assure you the matter is in hand; after all, I am hardly getting on at twenty-five, mother. Whatever is the rush?'

'*Wisdom?*' replied my mother, looking dumbfounded.

'Yes, wisdom,' repeated Ernest. 'Let me enjoy my birthday!'

Mother could say nothing more to convince him. She merely sighed and looked on as he danced up to our sister Liliana, who had just finished a dance with her husband. He started to spin her around, making her squeal with surprise and delight. Liliana was often quite a serious girl, but Ernest had the ability to charm her into spontaneous fun. Our eldest and most serious sister, Petrovka, who was currently standing beside our twin brothers trying to encourage them to exercise restraint in their wine drinking, looked on in some bemusement. The twins were as happy as larks, laughing at everything that passed them. They had already guzzled countless glasses of wine, much to mother's dismay. Father, who was game for anything, was in the most jovial of moods as he came to join them. I wondered what had happened to Grand Jo, who normally would have been chasing them back out of the hall. Perhaps he had fallen prey to yet another of their tricks. They could be rather frivolous, but never in a way that risked causing harm to others. Well, not much. Mother generally disapproved of their antics yet, for a change, she started to speak rather highly of them.

'Ernest is not like his younger brothers Charlie and Cecil,' she murmured, still tutting at their jovial parade. 'They have already found wives, and only at the age of nineteen. You do know that boys progress slower than our gender, of course, so the twins really are still boys. Unlike you, for you are already a *lady*. I think you need to reason with your brother, for time is getting on and he confesses to having a complete disinterest in marriage. I am sure that even you are more interested in that subject than he is. Oh! Here is another opportunity, my dear…'

With little warning, she pushed me towards another prince who took my hand very promptly. I looked at him in surprise, for I found him stunning; he happened to be attractive in every possible way, being tall, dark and handsome. Something had to be wrong, I found myself thinking, for things are never as perfect as they seem. Yet I could not help being rather taken with his beauty and charming, mild manners, and it soon appeared that he was very much taken with me.

'Prince Sean Healy has the honour,' he sang in a smooth, soft voice, bowing ever so low as he did. 'And with whom do I have the pleasure of dancing?' He was evidently humouring me, for all who were present must have known who I was.

'You are assuming that you have the pleasure?' I attempted to humour him back.

His face fell a little at this, but then he smiled again quickly.

'May I, then, have the pleasure of your name?'

I could not deny him that. 'I am Princess Salomya.' Then I added, 'And as it happens, I am most obliged to dance with you on this occasion.'

He laughed in apparent surprise at my show of reluctant willingness as he led me to the dance floor. Then he whispered in my ear, 'And on what occasions would you *not* be obliged to dance?'

I returned his intent gaze, and replied, 'If, perhaps, you were to tread on my foot, I would find it necessary to establish a non-dancing acquaintance between us. You wouldn't be offended?'

Prince Sean had begun to whirl me around in perfect time.

'But I am,' he cried, 'that you would think me clumsy enough to hinder your steps – although I am quite certain that no one could hinder them more than Dopey Derek, standing in the corner there next to the Prince of Perusia.'

'He means well,' I replied in Derek's defence, 'even though he does step on my feet. But you must respect him as your equal, for I am sure that he is equal to you in years.'

'By the lion's mane!' cried Prince Sean. 'How old can he be?'

'Twenty-five,' I replied, seeing his face fall in astonishment, then brighten up again.

'Your countenance changes,' I continued. 'What were you thinking?'

'He is older than I expected,' replied Sean in amazement, 'but he is not quite my age, for I am twenty-eight, and I can tell from your face that you took me for being a few years younger, a compliment of my eternal youthfulness which I find strangely agreeable, for you are not twenty yourself?'

'Quite right,' I replied. 'I am eighteen.'

'Eighteen?' His eyes looked delighted. 'So young a maiden.'

At this moment I fell silent, quite unable to think of

another thing to say. I found myself considering what Ernest had said in trying to discourage Derek. Perhaps ten years' age difference was not a bad idea. Sean was ten years my senior exactly, but he looked younger, and to top it all off, he was the only dance partner with whom I had exchanged more than a handful of words that made some sense, that is with the exception of my brother Ernest, of course. Thinking of him, I searched around for him as I danced, wondering what he would make of Sean. My eyes found him standing alone by a rose bush under the arched doorway that led to the gardens, his eyes directly fastened on me. I sensed that he was giving me space to be with my new acquaintance, to experience these new interactions without his interference.

Sean quickly noticed that my eyes were not on him and he suggested that there was another suitor whom I preferred in the hall.

'How about Prince Vicoro?' he questioned. 'Do you not want to have another dance with him?'

I turned to see Prince Vicoro speaking to one of my countess cousins, Rosamund, whilst staring fixedly at me and carefully scratching his chin.

'Well,' I replied, 'I doubt that there is any need to go through the same routine again, where conversation has dried up, merely for the sake of ceremony.'

'Did Prince Vicoro not have much to say to you?' he questioned. 'He looks at you often.'

'So do all prospective young suitors,' I replied.

'And you think the same of me?' he asked rather quickly.

This was unexpected. I bit my lip a little uncertainly.

'You ask very direct questions for a new acquaintance,' was all I could think of saying at that point and I motioned that I would prefer to sit down for a while and rest.

As I reclined in a chair at a white table, I looked over at the archway where I had seen Ernest standing, and saw that he had gone. Perhaps he had thought that a breath of fresh air would benefit him for a while, away from all the jovial chatter and our matchmaking mother.

'Mind if I join you?' Prince Sean asked.

'Not at all,' I replied, although I was not entirely sure whether I really wished to continue in dialogue at this moment.

He reclined in a chair opposite and sat a little forward, watching me thoughtfully. His face was filled with eagerness.

'Ah,' he sighed, 'that was a fine dance.'

He waited on my response. I was not unimpressed with the dance, although I had not enjoyed it as much as when I danced with my brother.

'Yes,' I replied, 'it was very enjoyable.'

His searching expression relaxed as he continued.

'You move as gracefully as a swan. Everyone watches you.'

I could not help blushing slightly at these compliments, and I certainly felt a little uncomfortable so I tried to diffuse them.

'I hardly know whether a swan dances gracefully,' I replied in a dismissive way, 'or, in fact, whether it dances at all.'

'Well, of course, they could not look slender besides you,' he said.

'You are quite a charmer, Prince Sean,' I replied with a smile.

He suddenly took my hand, looking quite serious.

'I mean every word,' he whispered, 'I can't take my eyes off you.'

I felt rather taken aback but I let him continue.

'You are like a rose among thorns.'

I took my hand away quickly. 'You obviously haven't seen any of my lovely cousins.'

'No, I haven't,' he continued in a love-struck voice, 'for you have become like the sun shining so brightly that I haven't seen anything else. You cast out the moon and the

29

stars and exile them into darkness. You light up my path to lead me straight to you.'

Quite forgetting myself, I held my hand out to stop this flattering but monotonous prose.

'Prince Sean,' I declared boldly, 'you are painting a picture which I cannot recognise. From this wonderful poetry, it is perfectly clear to me that you do not know me at all. You cannot, for we have only just met.'

In response he drew me closer, evidently not getting the hint.

'You speak so modestly!' he cried. 'You are perfection itself.'

'No!' I cried out, for I could bear this torture no longer. 'That proves that you have not even laid eyes on me yet!'

'But beauty can only be seen in the eyes of the beholder,' he replied as if in a trance, 'and true beauty is in the one who is modest.'

I had started to become impatient.

'Likewise, empty-headedness may be perceived by the beholder who is unwillingly confronted with it.'

His look of awe suddenly changed to one of disbelief. He was silent for a moment, and then he continued, 'Are you really suggesting that an angelic creature such as yourself could possess such a terrible thing as empty-headedness?'

At this gross misunderstanding I arose from my seat.

'You consider yourself a poet, but you don't seem to understand simple meanings. For I was not referring to myself when I mentioned the subject of empty-headedness.'

With that I picked up my skirts and moved quickly to the arch to find my brother. Surely his perceptive eye could have quickly rescued me from such an ill-fitted suitor, whose glamorous looks merely seemed to mask the emptiness beneath. I thought maybe I had helped to shift his world of clouds. Surely on one's first meeting, one could not proclaim such undying sentiments, the very renderings of which still made my stomach churn. I turned back to see what his response was; he merely sat looking rather thoughtful. Perhaps our exchange had done him some good, I hoped. However, just as I was leaving the grand hall from the archway, I turned again to see him stooping to kiss the hand of my fair but empty-headed cousin Georgiana, whose gold ringlets no doubt filled him with a new sense of rapture, and whose stunning blue eyes were like misty pools into which he could sink. She seemed quite taken with him and I could see that before too long, she would be swept entirely off her feet on the dance floor.

I stepped outside into the dusk and the singing of birds, calling Ernest's name. At first all else was still, except for the rippling of swans in the lake and the sound of children running around the grounds. I wondered where Ernest could have disappeared to, and where his walk of escape had taken him. So I waited, wondering how I was to begin to tell him about my rather empty encounter, or whether I should pain him with it at all.

It was not long before I could hear his familiar tuneful whistle, and I was most surprised to see him emerging from behind a tree towards the edge of the forest. I surveyed him with some disapproval, for I had never been allowed to venture into the forest where the terrible war had once raged. In fact, this was the forest in the very depths of which my brother had first found me. He too, despite his heroic discovery, had been frequently discouraged from taking a walk there.

Impatient to meet him and inquire about the cause of his disappearance, I called out to him. 'Ernest! Where have you been?'

Ernest's Secret Meeting

Ernest lifted his head in a dreamy way and saw me, and his face filled with joy. In his eagerness he hopped over the bushes that walled our grounds as if he had invisible wings, then he skipped up the path towards me like an excited lamb.

'Oh Salomya!' he cried breathlessly before he had quite reached me. 'I have seen such a sight that you would never believe.'

He stopped as he came to my side, and looked around to check no one else was present, as if he wished to share a deep secret with me.

Satisfied that no unwanted ears listened, he continued. 'It was all so sudden. I was standing at the archway, wishing for some fresh air and escape from the din within the hall, and I noticed you with a particularly slimy individual – of course, my normal procedure would have been to whisk you off for another dance, but then something happened to stop me. A beautiful sight appeared before my eyes; she stood there like an angel. She was a woman of the woods, a fine majestic lady of the trees. I have never seen a Tree Person before, but why didn't Mother ever say they looked so beautiful?'

I shrugged, thinking that perhaps Mother would not wish to encourage any union between their people and ours.

'The strange thing is, she did look rather like you, my fair sister. Your rare looks have always been complimented by all who see you, and if you were a child of the Tree People, then perhaps that would explain your appearance.'

'But Ernest,' I replied, 'are you saying that you actually saw a Tree Lady in this wood opposite? I thought Mother and Father said they no longer lived there, that they had fled from the Tikes to some secret place deep in the heart of the forest. And appearing in daylight? All the books that I have read about them say that they only appear after dark, or they don't appear at all, or at least, not so that country folk can see them. In fact, we know so little about them, I've come to think that maybe the Tree People must have written the books themselves, in ancient times.'

'But Salomya,' he continued, 'they do appear and they speak, too, in voices like the eternal midsummer song. I do believe she quite sang me to sleep. Oh, Salomya, she is *wonderful*, such a graceful, tender spirit, and her name... her name is Simira.'

I shuddered at the sound of this mysterious lady's name, as if a long-distant past had been awoken from within my spirit.

'Simira?' I asked slowly. 'Did she say anything else about herself?'

'Oh yes, we spoke for a long time.' Ernest, I noticed, had begun to speak almost as if in an echo of a dream. 'She has put quite a spell on me.'

'Surely, Ernest,' I said, frowning with concern, 'that isn't such a good thing. Who knows what magic these Tree People do?'

Ernest seemed to wake up and he stared at me with large blue eyes that danced with strange new life.

'But Salomya, surely you've read in those books of yours how harmless and peace-loving these Tree People are, or have you been influenced by Mother's words of caution? I know for a fact that the Tree People whom I met today intend only good to others and Simira truly is a God-fearing maiden.'

I looked into his eyes and could see that they were in no

way entranced by magic, or anything else that denied reality. He was speaking from the heart, and in fact from the soul.

'Why, their very voices convey only goodness itself, and their appearance surely captures some of the beauty of God's angels. Simira is the only woman I will ever desire to be with for life. We had the rare occasion of two souls meeting on the same level. Never have I met a woman to whom I can relate so completely. Soon we shall become joined as one...'

His voice tailed off as he lay down on the steps beside me and he seemed to drift off into a trance-like state. As he leaned his head against my shoulder, the concern I had previously felt slipped away with his consciousness; his description of the encounter had sent a shiver down my spine, but I knew somehow it was a good shiver. As I watched him sleeping I saw how his mind was rested, his burdens lifted and his whole countenance had a new glow, as if he had received an angelic visitation.

I felt happy for my dearest elder brother, to see him in love at last. If one woman could have such a positive effect on him, surely this was a good thing. I had always trusted Ernest's instincts from an early age, perhaps partly due to his heroism in my rescue as a young boy, and his general level-headedness. I was merely rather worried as to the nature of my parents' reactions once they should discover the reason for Ernest's new happiness; if they would not permit a son of theirs to marry a lady of the trees, I supposed he would be forced to renounce his right to the throne, as the first born. For the Tree People, as graceful and noble a race as they evidently were to Ernest, had no titles that I was aware of and were counted as common people. The irony that although it was likely that I was of the same race as them, every royal suitor seemed to be quite forgetful of this possibility.

A Night of Mysterious Events

As I lay in bed that night, recovering from the eventful day, I could not stop thinking of Simira, and the reason her name should send a strange shiver down my spine. Could it be possible that she was a key figure in my previous life, and in fact held the key to the mystery of my existence? Maybe she had hung the basket in the oak tree to rescue me. I wanted so much to meet her and to see if she could tell me the secret of who I was. I could not sleep, for my mind was active and excited about Ernest's new finding, and so I decided that as he had trespassed into the forest of discovery, so would I.

The time was now midnight. Normally guests stayed at our parties until several hours into the morning but due to my brother's dreamy eyes for the remainder of the day, Mother had cut the party short, demanding to know which girl he had set his eyes upon. Ernest had not replied with a name, but merely described to his mother the rare beauty which had captivated his heart that late afternoon. So frustrated was she with the lack of useful information on his part that she sent a servant to attend to him all night long, lest in his sleep the name should slip out from his lips.

I realised that I could not take Ernest into the forest with me for this reason, so I reached for my candle and put on a thick shawl, and nimbly crept from my bedroom with the flickering light, leaving it in darkness.

At first, I thought I heard the pattering of footsteps from behind me as I went along the dimly lit corridor that led to the winding staircase. I turned quickly, but found that there was not a soul to be seen, so I continued walking until I reached the bottom of the staircase, still not entirely convinced that no one followed. I was aware that my mischievous brothers Charlie and Cecil only too often liked to play pranks on me in the night if I should happen to pass by their rooms. After gallivanting around all day in celebratory moods they sooner or later turned to mischief.

Mother always liked to remind me and Ernest that in spite of their behaviour they still somehow managed to attain strong admiration from Princesses Carmella and Cordelia, the cheerful and beautiful twin daughters of the king of Brozalanda. My parents were quite taken with them both, though evidently not half as much as Charlie and Cecil were, and were delighted that their future in-laws were keen to set a wedding date as soon as possible. Much to Charlie's and Cecil's delight, the girls had a great mischievous streak and more often than not were known to encourage their future husbands to further extremes of hilarity, unless, of course, their pranks were played on them. Together they all made a terrible team and I already had some concern for their children. I also knew that as much as my brothers adored these young girls (who were but sixteen), I could see that they were most definitely not ready to settle down to a solid state of matrimony, a restraint which I thought could not bode well with the height of their jovial youthfulness.

However, of course, being a year their junior, it was not my place to reproach them for their childish pursuits. I knew all too well how children in our situation were made to grow up sooner than was truly possible; ironically, this expectation only kept us back, ensuring that we would hold on to all we could from our childhood as long as possible. Charlie and Cecil were prime examples, as I often witnessed their chameleon natures; the forced mask of conformity when in elder company and their mockery of it when in the company of those with whom they could relax.

Yet this night I heard no sign of them sneaking around the corridors, although a few odd noises did surprise me on my way. Shadows seemed to flicker and move by themselves and even my footsteps seemed to have their own extra echo. Finally I passed Ernest's bedroom, where I was sure I could hear him sleeping deeply with a multitude of snores. I was surprised to hear him so loudly, and wondered if perhaps the wine had truly taken its toll, alongside the incredible events of the day. However, then I remembered that he had not touched a drink since his return from the forest. I decided to check Ernest's room and opened the door very slightly, as noiselessly as possible, expecting to find the servant sitting there with him. To my surprise, I found that a candle still flickered in the large dark room and the silhouette of the servant propped up in a chair, his chest rising and falling noisily, was all I could see. In disbelief, I moved to the bed and without a sound I gently pulled the covers back to find Ernest had gone. My mind raced to where I knew he would be and instantly I pictured him with his secret maiden amidst a gathering of leaf-covered people, enjoying a wonderful party in the middle of the forest.

Forgetting myself and overtaken with the idea of finding the mystery people of my dreams, I picked up my skirts and ran from the room, leaving the servant sleeping quite undisturbed. I rushed down the next corridor and then down another set of steps to the staircase that led to the now empty grand hall. I was just making my way to the archway at the entrance to the castle when I was stopped most abruptly. A strange small figure shot an object in my direction, pulled me forwards and by the light of my own candle started to examine my face.

'So! Who is this snooping around the castle in the dead of night?'

The gravelly, rough voice filled me with a sense of relief.

'Oh, hello great-grandfather,' I said pleasantly, and in a playfully stern voice added, 'Really, I wonder how you ever get any sleep at all!'

Grand Jo was known to roam the castle at night like a guard dog and he was very good at it.

'Well!' His eyes squinted. 'It's *you*! Bless me, I can't see anything these days.'

'Yes, well it is the night, great-grandfather,' I replied, 'and I am not surprised you cannot see without a candle.'

'The best way!' he cried. 'It catches them unawares, you know. It's just as well you spoke, or I might have taken you for a common trespasser – or worse still, one of those *Tikes*!'

Grand Jo always got overly concerned with warding off all unknown visitors with the assumption that they were spies for the Tikes. I supposed that he must have been involved in the war against them, although their invasion was more during the early years of my father, and he may have been too old to fight. All the same, dear old Grand Jo always liked to think he did his bit for our country, and was in fact very much still doing it.

'So what do you think you are wandering around for at this time of night?' He suddenly cross-examined me, looking attentively at my face.

'Well, really,' I pretended to be slightly offended. 'One might very well ask you the same question.'

'Preposterous!' Grand Jo raised his voice, then quickly smothered his mouth with his hand, gazing up at the banisters as if concerned he had disturbed the sleepers of the castle.

At that moment, a clear deep giggle was heard, penetrating and echoing down the staircase. After this, some suspicious shuffling followed and in response, Grand Jo quickly raised my candle and moved to the bottom of the stairs. Squinting up at the curtains which covered the hall landing window at the top of the stairs, we noticed two pairs of feet sticking out at the bottom.

'Aha!' cried Grand Jo, quite forgetting his rule of being quiet after bedtime.

He became as springy as a wild cat chasing its prey, running two steps at a time with no need for his stick. In no time at all, he had pulled the curtains apart and seized the two unfortunates behind them.

'What do you think you're up to?' he cried, shaking them.

Charlie and Cecil stood a little awkwardly and it was evident that they were trying hard not to laugh. They were shaking considerably and had gone an interesting shade of red.

'Enough!' barked Grand Jo. 'This won't do at all, you know. Your duties are to protect the castle you grew up in, not create havoc within its walls. Come, I shall take you both to your rooms, and shall ensure that you don't step another foot outside them without my stick.'

With that, Grand Jo took them by the collars of their dressing gowns and attempted to lift them up the remainder of the stairs to the passageway on the right that led to their rooms. I knew that in no time Grand Jo would forget all about me, having a memory like a sieve, so I took this opportunity to escape from the castle unnoticed.

As I stepped out in the pure moonlight, I marvelled at the many stars that lit up the sky. They very much reminded me of the white specks of foam reflecting the sun on a watery canvas of dark sea at sunset, which I had often seen at the end of family outings to the beach. I loved these times; this was when I felt most like I belonged and I loved the sea air and the deep turquoise colour the sea turned in the midday sun. Ernest and I also enjoyed waving at large boats that drifted by, which sounded their horns in return to salute the royal family on the beach.

The moon was reflected in a bed of liquid before me where swans still moved and held secret conversations. The lake had often inspired me to write. I drew in a breath of awe as I took in the holy night and cast my eyes on the forest ahead.

Wrapping my shawl around me tightly, I began my journey into the unknown. I walked as if on padded feet towards the nearest opening of the forest. As I entered the first trees, the night became yet stiller, almost as if the nocturnal creatures were hushed at the newcomer's approach. I continued to walk straight ahead, feeling slightly fearful lest a wild beast should suddenly appear, or a monster should swing around a tree, one that no humans had ever heard of or written about in the books about forest life; or worse still, I feared being confronted by the great dark panther of the Tikes. However, silence continued to surround me and all I could hear was my own heart.

As my eyes adjusted to this dark veil, I became aware of a mysterious flickering of lights in the distance. They rose up in colours like sparkles of smoke; green, pink, purple and blue. As I approached these strange but wonderful arrays of colour, I sensed that I was about to enter a wondrous party of forest folk.

So I moved nearer to the life of the forest with the sparkles of lights as my guides. All of a sudden, I started to hear faint echoes of ethereal music drifting from branch to branch, and singing more beautiful than I had ever experienced washed over me in small pure waves. As I ventured closer to the gathering, I started to decipher that the music came from harps and woodwind instruments, and also the beat of drums, and that the majority of the singing came from one solo female. I thought that I could hear words which I recognised at times; the words which most overwhelmed me were 'God' and 'blessing', and the music appeared to grow more enchanting the nearer I strode.

Finally, I saw the silhouettes of people dancing to the beat of the drums. All was jollification and much celebration filled the air. I moved cautiously as close as I could without being seen, and had just stationed myself behind a large oak tree when I was stunned by the beautiful singing voice I had heard previously; this time I could hear the words clearly.

'I pronounce Blessing of Life on you, young tree;
Grow to the height that God made you to be.'

The singer repeated these lines several times, in the midst of wondrous varying harmonies sung by other nearby folk. I turned and glanced around the tree to see a beautiful Tree Lady who had flowing wavy hair as golden as the sun and wore a lovely green dress of leaves. She was leaning gracefully over a small budding tree in the centre of a ring of mushrooms, in the midst of a large gathering of Tree People. Her hands gently lifted a slender silver jug which contained a liquid that glistened like the stars, and she let it slowly pour onto the young tree. The drops appeared to be clear until they touched the tree, at which point wonderful sparkles of colour were emitted and floated upwards in smoke puffs; these were the very same ones which had guided me through the forest. At this moment a beautiful red apple sprouted from one of the tiny branches, glowing supernaturally with rich life.

It became evident that the elegant lady had completed her God-filled blessing and she cast her head back, her veil of fair hair flowing in the breeze. She turned to look at one other who stood near to her in the gathering.

'Ernest,' she called softly. 'Come, if you desire it; take and eat, if it be thy will.'

My heart filled with joy as I saw my dear brother step forward with boundless energy, clothed with a fine leaf garment that left part of his noble chest bare, with the exception of a golden necklace that had been placed upon it. His eager blue eyes were brimming with indescribable joy and his whole face was a vision of serenity. Shining boldly in the moonlight which fell through a parting in the trees to the mushroom ring, he echoed in a sing-song voice, 'Oh, yes, Simira. I am willing to do whatever thou desires, sweetest maiden.'

It seemed to me that these words had been previously set out in text, as if they were like the vows of marriage.

The lady, Simira, walked gracefully to meet him and took both of his hands. They were nearer to where I was now and I could see her captivating deep blue eyes filling with tears of joy. Then, in the moment of silence they turned one at a time to take a bite from the sacred apple and after they did a new music filled the air; the entire forest of Tree People appeared to be singing a song of great celebration:

'Man unites with Woman; conquering the disunity of the
    fallen one,
Revealing a part of God's love; His marriage with all
    mankind,
May God bless you and keep you and make you strong in
    unity,
May you grow closer together and in Him as you bless
    nations.'

In the midst of the joyful song, I felt overwhelmed. Yet it was more than music that moved me; it was her face, her deep kind eyes, a look that I felt uncovered a long-forgotten past. I could do nothing but move towards her, my hands reaching out, my throat so tight I could not speak. As I entered the circle of dancers, all the music died down and all the eyes of the Tree People were on me. Ernest gazed at me with eyes full of delight but said nothing as he waited to see what Simira would do. Simira looked back towards me in surprise and as our eyes met she visibly shuddered in awe.

She released Ernest's hands and slowly turned and moved towards me. It felt rather like I was confronting a mirror image; only the figure before me was taller and more slender, and she moved more gracefully than I knew how. Shadows seemed to pass from her eyes as she searched me, her lips moving but making no sound. All her face seemed to fill with a new light as she moved closer still, noiselessly, and reached out her hand to touch my face. At that moment I felt the life of the forest enter me as if an eternal flame had been lit. Then she held both my hands in another moment of silence. Ernest was also by my side and I could hear him breathing in deep anticipation. Then, all at once, Simira broke the silence, with such grace as only a noble Tree Lady could.

'You are my long-lost sister, *Salomya.*' Her lilting voice sounded mournful yet her face was filled with hope.

I stared back in amazement as my heart raced ahead of my mind.

Ernest spoke next. 'Simira, are you certain? Your sister was so young when you left her in the tree basket.'

'Many babies were strung up in tree baskets,' she continued softly, 'but I can recognise my sister's features instantly. And what about this golden necklace that hangs around her delicate neck? It bears her name, *Salomya*, given by her father and mother, clearly set into it. This is a mark of the rulership of our tribe.'

I glanced down at the golden necklace which I had worn as long as I could remember. I marvelled that it bore the name given by my Tree People parents, who were the rulers of this tribe. I wanted to greet my new-found sister, but was not sure what to say or where to begin, even though I knew that it was more than enough to her that I had returned.

'Simira,' I began, my eyes filling with tears, 'I did not know I had a sister…'

I could not contain my tears now, and in response my sister took me in her arms and whispered in my ear, 'I will never let you go again, my little sister.'

I could hear the wind singing in the trees as if in honour of this reunion. We stood holding each other's hands for some time.

'I cannot describe how wonderful it is to have found my home!' I said, with great joy.

Then, everyone gave a shout of glee and several Tree People started chanting:

'The princess has returned! Salomya is alive!'

'Princess?' I whispered to Simira.

In the midst of the joyous sounds, Simira gently told me, 'Yes. Our parents are king and queen of the entire forests of this land. You are the missing piece of our lives and hearts. Through your return, Ernest and I can enjoy our union more fully.'

I drew in a sudden breath. 'Your union? Do you mean to say...'

'We are married,' Ernest completed my sentence smiling and he stooped to kiss my forehead. 'This tree-blessing ceremony you witnessed was the finale of our marriage festival. Now we have shared the red apple all I need to do is to find Simira a rose; the eternal rose that grows somewhere hidden in the depths of the forest.'

I remembered the rose that grew without withering outside my tower at the castle, and I wondered if the eternal rose in the forest was its long-lost sister.

'My Ernest,' Simira responded with grace, 'why, we have already found the rose. My little sister is the most precious rose in all the forest!'

She took some of the leaves that decorated her hair and placed them lovingly in mine, smiling down upon me in sisterly delight.

'Thank you,' I whispered, for I could barely speak. 'My dear Ernest, this is wonderful news for the two of you. But what would father and mother say?'

Ernest chuckled in delight, far from the response I expected. 'My dear sister,' he said jovially, taking me by the arm, 'or shall I call you also "sister-in-law", as now you have become so? If my parents could see how happy I am, they would be perfectly content for me to rule with my new wife. Besides, you and Simira really are of royal birth.'

'Where are my parents?' I asked the question which had been bursting to come from me. 'Are they still alive?'

'Very much alive,' answered Simira, 'and they will be very happy to see you.'

'So,' Ernest continued, 'it turns out you really are a princess and the next in line after Simira as heir to the throne. And I figured as Simira is joining me in our castle, you could one day rule as queen of the forests.'

Whilst he was still speaking in this manner, I saw a great man and lady step forward to greet me. He was covered in a heavenly robe of leaves and carried a great stick of gold and on his head was set a golden crown, glowing with jewels. His deep, warm brown eyes were filled with mirth and humbleness and he greeted me with a noble kiss on my hand. His lady, who was dressed in splendour, lifted her great decorated green dress to curtsey in respect and lowered her jewel-decorated hand, her fair hair shimmering like shooting stars. Her beautiful blue eyes rested on my face with gentle longing and her arms eagerly reached for me. I took both her hands and realised how like mine they were; small and petite with nails like cream-coloured seashells. I searched the contours of her face and could see how like mine her face was, with its high cheekbones, long, straight nose, rose-tinted lips and graceful jaw set on a slender neck. My mother also had wavy, golden hair that fell to her waist. I hugged both my parents together and nestled into their rich garments of leaves for some time as Simira and Ernest beamed on.

After all had been said that needed to be said at that moment, my father turned to face the gathering of tearful onlookers, some of whom were wiping their eyes with hanky-leaves, or something of that description. As I stood between my new-found parents, my father looked down on me fondly and addressed the crowd.

'Tonight is to be a night of much celebration! Not only have we the union of marriage to sing about, but we have the return of my second daughter, Salomya; for my daughter was lost, but now she has been found. God Himself has returned her to us... and through the marriage of her adopted brother to our people, two peoples can be once again united.'

The Tree People gave a great cheer and two Tree Maidens took my hands and began to dance with me in the centre of the mushrooms.

And so the night went on, and we enjoyed a splendid dance where I believe I danced with every person present during the entire course of the night. And the night danced on and on and I felt so full of joy that I was able to skip and dance and bound about as if I had endless energy. It seemed that as if to fulfil my discovery of my heritage, the wood itself filled me with eternal strength. Here, I felt I belonged at last, and here I would always stay.

The dances and the singing and other customs of the Tree People were restored to my memory in one night. I learnt fast and made an exciting discovery; I could understand the ancient and poetic language of the Tree People as if it was my common tongue. In fact, when I had heard Simira singing the tree-blessing song, I had understood the words, not knowing it had been in Tree-Maiden Tongue (which differs slightly to Tree-Man Tongue). Simira, who was surprised to hear me repeating the song later, informed me that Ernest had not understood their language and that I must have known it simply because it was in my veins and it would have been sung to me frequently from the moment I was born. Knowledge had begun to dawn on me that the song was sung not just to bless the trees but also to bless the people who lived among them.

Later in the night, just before the dawn chorus began, we

participated in a traditional forest circle dance. I danced next to a tall Tree Man who was more handsome and gentle than any man I had ever seen. He stared down at me with warm amber eyes and he smiled. After he had twirled me around according to the pattern of the dance, it came to an end, all too soon. I turned away from him for a moment to applaud the musicians, who applauded us in return. As I turned back towards my dance partner, to my surprise I realised that he had vanished into the night. Puzzled by his sudden disappearance, I looked about me, but could not see him anywhere in the crowd. Suddenly, Ernest was standing beside me, and his face was rosy with the excitement of the dance.

'How goes the dancing, sister?' he inquired jovially.

'Very well,' I replied with a rather faraway expression, 'although now it has ended, I don't know quite what to make of it.'

'And how goes it with the *dancing partner*?' he continued, raising his eyebrows suggestively.

'I hardly know,' I replied, meeting his meaningful gaze, 'for he disappeared right after the dance ended. I would wonder if it was past his bedtime!'

At this remark, Ernest gave a deep, hearty laugh.

'Well,' he replied, 'I shouldn't think so, for he is quite capable of staying up into the early hours, from what I have gathered. I believe he is a year your senior. Besides, you ought to know, he's become like an adopted son to your true parents, as his own parents were killed by the Tikes many years ago.'

'Oh.' I became quiet as I searched my thoughts.

'And I suppose you have noticed already that he is rather shy.' Ernest looked quite serious for a second.

That was all Ernest could say at that moment, as the mentioned individual returned to the scene just as the next dance was beginning. It was just as if he could only be present when there was music in which he could hide, I considered. He came straight towards me, bowed and took my hand, and we danced again.

And so the wondrous night of dancing continued. My dance partner spoke few words and I still did not have the pleasure of learning his name. It occurred to me that perhaps some Tree People were so accustomed to dancing that they were quite unused to normal conversation. As it happened, I noticed that quite a lot of the conversations between others on the dance floor were sung in time to the music. I knew they were not singing pre-written songs, as some of the dialogue consisted of phrases quite unrelated to the dance, such as 'Did you remember to put up the laundry, dear?', which one mother sang to her daughter.

Another more unusual phrase was actually spoken in my tongue (not Tree Tongue) in a strange gruff voice, quite unlike the musical voices of the others: 'I fancy a bit of nosh.'

There followed a deep, throaty chuckle and to my surprise, another incredibly high-pitched voice joined in and cried, 'Here, shove this pizza in!'

I turned to see two young Tree Men dancing in a rather humorous and idiotic way, quite out of character with the other graceful dancers. I saw one quickly ram some food in the other's mouth and they were both grinning at me and my dance partner with highly mischievous faces. What I also noticed about them was that they were covered in more leaves and twigs than any of the others. Furthermore, they wore the strangest moss-coloured paint on their faces, with warlike black markings, as if they were attempting to camouflage themselves in a foreign setting. They were starting to get strange and confused looks from those nearest to them on the dance floor. Then an enlightening thought crossed my mind, but I decided to ignore it for the time being, as I preferred to enjoy the dance and dream. I barely noticed when they left the group with the most peculiar strides that only seemed to have the purpose of drawing attention to themselves, as they certainly succeeded in doing. The Tree People watched them as they left with knowing faces and they exchanged subtle smiles, as if to inform one another that the wool had not been pulled over their eyes.

As the dawn chorus began and the sun rose higher in the sky, Ernest became suddenly purposeful, and without any warning he took my hand and Simira's and together we took leave of the enchanting gathering. I looked back at my dance partner as I ran and I noticed how forlorn and lost he suddenly appeared to be as he gazed after me. I tried to smile back at him, but I had to mind all the trees and look where I was going, for Ernest was desperate to return home with the call of the dawn.

'I must tell my parents!' he cried in a new sing-song voice.

So we ran through the forests as light-footed as elves, and I knew that our three hearts leapt within us even more joyously, filled with new magic. I was almost as certain that as we passed the trees, several times I caught sight of a small something, dressed in tree-coloured garments, darting away to avoid contact. They were so very little, and particularly sprightly in their step, that in fact I began to suppose they were figments of my vivid imagination; hallucinatory products of a night without sleep and lungs filled with the strange colourful mist of the forest. It seemed that as quickly as they passed us I forgot them, as if they had turned to cover my memory with a puff of smoke. Ernest did not even notice them; his eyes were fixed straight ahead as he and Simira were in one mind and purpose, and I did not think about these sights any more.

Finally, we danced through the last tree before our castle grounds, and as soon as we had come in to sight of the castle we found a line of expectant and slightly grim faces stood in waiting. With the exception of Charlie and Cecil, who seemed as if they were trying to look as straight-faced as possible, but failing miserably, the rest of the company appeared to be bemused and perplexed. But none so much as Grand Jo and our parents, who held particularly strict countenances to hail our arrival.

The Second Wedding Ceremony

Our father, the king, greeted us at once in a rather sombre tone. 'My dear, dear children! Whatever possessed you to run into that accursed forest? And who is this fair maiden whom you have witlessly taken from it?'

Then his tone quickly changed as he regarded the forest specimen in wonder. 'Why, she looks rather like you, Salomya.'

'Upon my word!' cried Ernest eagerly, his face still glowing and fresh from the dance. 'This forest is blessed mightily by its inhabitants. They live by the great love and power that only comes from one source: the pure source of all love, none other than our Almighty God Himself. And this lady with whom I have joined under sacred vow before the most high King is actually my wife.'

The king drew back in astonishment as if a bow had fired an arrow straight into his chest. My mother looked like she was about to faint. I wondered if there could have been an easier way of informing them. There were several shouts of dismay from those gathered. Charlie and Cecil for once were not laughing but stood in uncertain silence.

Finally my mother spoke, in a rather weak voice. 'Married to a *Tree Maiden*?'

Ernest realised that he had to subdue the effect of this unexpected information and he ran to his mother, sweeping her fondly into his arms.

'Dear mother,' he whispered, 'I can assure you that this

fair Tree Maiden is the loveliest lady I have ever met, apart from my immediate family of course, and she is of royal forest blood. Not only is she daughter of the king of the Tree People of this nation, but she is none other than Salomya's long-lost sister. And her name is Simira.'

My mother was soothed slightly by his words but was at that moment quite unable to speak. Ernest took her by the hand and led her to his wife, and lifted the necklace that hung around Simira's neck.

'See, the necklace that Salomya has always worn is almost the same as Simira's. It was given to her by her royal tree parents.'

My mother silently held Simira's necklace in her hand and my father leaned down to examine it. On seeing the golden gleam of the necklace, they both appeared to calm down, although they continued looking from me to Simira and back to Ernest in disbelief.

Finally, Charlie broke the ice by shouting rather abruptly, 'Salomya, I always knew that you were a Tree Maiden!'

Cecil echoed, 'Yes, you were always rather too excellent at shinning up and down trees when we used to chase you. It was most irritating, actually.'

At this Grand Jo yelled in his gravely voice, 'Quiet, buffoons!'

With a swing of his sceptre, he managed to straighten the backs of the twins, who were nearly doubled over with laughing.

'This lunacy is beyond reason,' he barked. 'You could have made yourselves a lot more useful by following Salomya to see what she was up to rather than hiding behind that curtain like two ninnies.'

'What?' our mother the queen suddenly found her voice. 'You mean to inform me that Charlie and Cecil knew all about Salomya's disappearance and did nothing to stop her at all, and did not even come and inform me? And you, grandfather, really should have informed us if you knew that something irregular was going on.'

Grand Jo fell silent as Cecil quickly tried to explain. 'We tried to follow Salomya,' he muttered, 'but Grand Jo found us behind the curtain and sent us straight to bed.'

'Lifted us up there,' continued Charlie. 'Literally.'

'By our dressing gown collars,' added Cecil with a pained smile.

Mother turned to glare at Grand Jo, who looked rather submissive.

'I thought they were up to no good, as usual,' he went on to explain. 'They totally distracted me so I forgot all about Salomya and what her business was downstairs at night.'

For some reason my father seemed to find this amusing and started to chuckle, but a glare from my mother soon stopped him.

'Perhaps you can explain what the joke is,' she cried.

'Ahem!' The king cleared his throat nervously, before continuing. 'But surely between the two of you, you are more than a match for Grand Jo?'

Charlie appeared to be relieved to see that our father had begun to feel more at ease with the situation and he laughed in return.

'Well yes, father,' he replied, 'you are quite right. In fact, no sooner had Grand Jo gone than we slipped out of our bedroom window and ran towards the forest straight after Salomya. It turned out to be quite a wild party and...'

Here Charlie broke off abruptly, for Cecil had given him a kick.

'Trust you to get us in trouble with mother,' he murmured.

Now it was mother's turn to take them both by the collars of their dressing gowns; she was fuming.

'You mean to say that you two saw everything?'

Then, Ernest remembered the strange uninvited guests who had gatecrashed the party. 'I swear I did not see head or tail of *you* – unless, of course, you came under camouflage. How about you, Salomya, with your hawk eyes?'

'Well,' I said in an amused tone, 'I certainly had my suspicions.'

'Of course, Ernest,' replied Charlie, mischief spreading across his face. 'We were the ones dressed in leaves. I believe you danced with us several times.'

'Too besotted with his lady to notice,' said Cecil with a smirk.

'It took ages to get that moss off my face,' remarked Charlie.

'But you've obviously forgotten to wash your hands,' Mother snapped.

Ernest, who was still humouring them, said, 'Of course, if you were dressed in leaves you would have looked like everyone else, so how on earth was I to notice you?'

'Well, they did stand out quite a lot, actually!' Simira spoke for the first time in the present company. 'All the Tree People knew.'

The queen interrupted. 'Why did you both keep this information from me?'

Charlie and Cecil stopped still and stared at the ground.

'I can't bear to think that I missed out on all that fun,' Mother said in a put-out tone, but then her face brightened.

In response to this, the gathering cheered all at once and the king said with a sigh of relief, 'Why naturally, my dear. Next time there is to be a forest gathering let us be the first to hear. If our dear adopted daughter is descended from this tribe, then they can't be a bad lot, can they? Let us ignore the old books on folklore and magic practices and give our woody neighbours the benefit of the doubt. And if my wisest son Ernest wishes to marry one of them; well, they must be of the most royal blood, mustn't they? But let our newly-weds hear this – they must now remarry under our approval. Let us set a date!'

The king beckoned to his servants and butlers and directed them, 'Begin the wedding preparations right away. We shall arrange for the nuptials to take place as soon as possible.'

'My son, Ernest.' Mother became as warm as a dove, taking him under one arm and Simira under the other. 'I am so glad that you are happy and have at last found a wife. After all my worrying, now I can rest assured. And you are a very gentle and graceful dear, aren't you?'

Simira, who had not lost any peace during the previous exchange, had the same relaxed countenance as ever as she gazed at my mother with her warm, wise eyes.

Taking in all these changes, I began to feel once again as if I was in a dream. My thoughts returned to the forest where I knew a Tree Man whom I had met at a dance in a singing forest patiently waited for my return. As I thought of the night's wonderful adventure, I felt my eyelids closing. Ernest carried me up to my tower bedroom and laid me down.

There, I dreamt of a hunt for a rose. As the dream unfolded, it became apparent to me that the Tree People would never hunt a living animal, but only search for what is sacred. Then a disturbing element entered my dream; the forest rose was encased in a glass box and could not breathe. It began to wither. I felt a sense of urgency to go and free the rose, as if it had become a living being that was as dear to me as my own brother, and I spent what felt like hours pursuing something dark deep into the forest with a band of forest folk. Just as we were despairing of ever finding the rose, a new mighty leader emerged on the edge of the horizon, a great warrior knight with an army of men, coming to the rescue of the sacred being. I watched as he continued to ride towards me from out of the dawning sky, and the closer he got, the more certainly I felt that he would be willing to give up his life for the sacred rose which he loved so dearly.

When I awoke, it was under new morning light. A strange glow surrounded me and as my misty eyes adjusted I recognised the glowing veil to be the flowing white curtains decorated with ruby red roses that hung around my large bed.

I had half expected to awake to the song of the forest under the bough of an oak tree. All of a sudden, I remembered another strange dream I had had; strange faces had entered my mind, ugly fierce creatures with long spears. My elder sister was also there, as a much smaller girl, leaning forward to bid me farewell. I noticed one other child was strung up alongside me; I peered into his face and saw familiar large eyes that were just turning from blue to warm amber. He smiled and we chuckled, thinking what a fun game it was, to be swinging from baskets in the trees. I held out a hand to clutch at his but just as our fingers touched, to my horror, I felt the sensation of falling fast through the air, as if something had just disturbed our joyful union. Instead of an abrupt landing, I found myself in the lap of a boy who had earnest eyes that were as pure as gold. He sat on some kind of fast-moving beast, and he rode us away as quickly as he could, away from the fierce faces that drew in on all sides. I could not see where the other child had fallen and I peered back to the forest, calling after my new friend. But I saw him no more.

I was stirred from these heavy thoughts by the entrance of Ernest, who had been watching me for some time from the doorway.

'Sister,' he called gently, 'I see you have slept for a whole day and a night. You obviously needed sufficient rest from such dancing as the night before.'

I sat up slowly, rubbing my eyes.

'Or perhaps,' he continued, 'your memory needed some stirring. I saw that at times you slept quite fitfully, for you talked out loud and once you sat up in bed out of sheer terror. Most of the time, however, you slept soundlessly and in apparent bliss. Let me assume that you had found wonderful solace at last in those moments; who knows who may have entered your dreams at such a point?'

Having said this he tilted his head slightly and regarded me quizzically. I merely returned his stare in a bemused way.

'I am not sure of whom you speak, Ernest.' I tried to conceal the pink shade which I was sure my cheeks had turned by pulling my bed covers slightly over my face, for I had begun to remember new elements to my dream. 'But the fretful sleep you refer to, I can only presume to be the result of the terrible Tikes who invaded my pleasanter dreams.'

He breathed in wonder as he walked over and sat on the edge of the bed. 'So you remember them?'

'Yes,' I replied eagerly, leaning forward, 'and I remember you; the hero of my dream, alongside the warrior knight.'

Ernest smiled modestly then continued. 'I wonder who the warrior knight is. Was I a warrior too?'

'No, you were just a little boy,' I replied, 'like when you first found me. I am sure the warrior knight will be revealed in time. But he seemed to remind me of someone. He was probably God Himself.'

'What about Simira?' asked Ernest. 'Was she in your dream?'

'Oh, yes,' I replied. 'She was stringing my basket up in the tree.'

Then I remembered something else.

'Another child was with me in the tree.'

Ernest suddenly looked very serious and, I was surprised to see, downcast.

'Yes,' he murmured, 'I didn't manage to save him. The Tikes were too quick and he landed straight in their hands. What do you remember of him in your dream?'

'We had a close bond. He had warm eyes and a great chuckle. I didn't see him again.'

Ernest looked at me with new interest.

'That child,' he said slowly, 'was the very same Tree Man who paid you special attention at the dance two nights ago.'

I sat up in amazement and nearly knocked Ernest off the bed.

'So he's still alive?' I cried, my eyes welling up.

'He lived as a slave for the Tikes for many years,' continued Ernest. 'One day he managed to escape them. He was a boy in his early teens, growing in strength, as if the life of the forest still breathed in him. Yet he returned to his people emotionally scarred and mute.'

For a moment we were silent, reflecting on the atrocities that he must have suffered.

'Did he have no speech at all?' I asked. 'For I am sure that he spoke to me last night, at least a little.'

'A very little,' replied Ernest, 'for that is all he can manage. Yes, the forests have helped to breathe some words back into him, but something needs to be done. It is likely that one of the Tikes put a curse on him, perhaps as a punishment. All the Tree People have tried to break the spell, but none of them have succeeded. We have little idea of what he encountered there in the enemy camp, but there are rumblings amongst the wood folk that the Tikes plan to return, for they were thwarted in their plans by the wise rulership of your parents, the king and queen of the forests, and they have a few things which they intend to pursue, including vengeance for their previous defeat.'

The news of these rumours seemed to confirm my restless dreams.

'If the Tikes should return,' I pondered, 'perhaps this Tree Man could tell us a few things about them to aid us, if only we could get him to speak. I still do not even know his name.'

'His name–' Ernest paused '–no one knows, as his parents along with many were taken by the Tikes. He did not have a necklace on him when he returned. The Tikes just called him Slave. Currently, the Tree People call him Shyman because of his nature. It is suspected that he comes from Treeland, the vast land full of nothing but trees, from where all Tree People originated. This is due to his tall stature and the colour of his skin; more olive-coloured than you and your fair sister. This is typical of the Treeland folk. Of course, this is just a rumour, as no one can locate his family. Many Treeland folk came across to our country to help the forest folk to fight the war. The great king and queen of Treeland themselves even came to our aid. These are the rulers over all Tree Peoples of the world.'

'If only Shyman could discover his true identity, just as I have mine,' I cried, 'then maybe the past could unlock his voice.'

'I am sure that he longs to know his real name,' Ernest replied quietly, 'but this cannot be done without the necklace. There are no living relatives to claim him. He was thought to be about three years old when he was taken; Simira remembers putting him up in the basket next to you, and he certainly remembered it, for it was he who helped jog her memory by drawing a picture of himself in the basket up in the tree. Simira would have only been seven then. What a brave girl she must have been.'

As I gazed up at Ernest, he seemed to go into a trance-like state for a moment. His eyes then returned to the present.

'But here we are!' He spoke with a tone of triumphant certainty. 'And we are all well and not a scar to show for it all. Well, sister, is it now an appropriate time for me to change the subject? For a long awaited time has come upon us. You are to be my bridesmaid.'

I leapt out of bed for sheer joy.

'You are to be married today?' I cried.

'Or remarried,' Ernest said with a laugh. 'Yes! Today, in the castle.'

Presently there came a knock at the door.

'Is my favourite daughter ready yet?' rang my mother's expectant voice. I practically jumped into my large amber wardrobe to grab a dress.

'Mother, she is barely out of bed,' Ernest sang, running out to the landing in joyful bounds. 'Allow the servant to attend to her and she will be ready in no time.'

'My dearest!' Mother's persistent tone rang, and she entered the room, looking at first perplexed that she could not see me.

I slowly stepped out of the wardrobe and she looked shocked. She was holding a garment she had chosen specially for the occasion and she nearly dropped it on the floor.

'Really!' she cried. 'You did not sleep in there, I hope? You know there are strange stories about people disappearing into wardrobes and never coming out again...'

'Yes, but my wardrobe is perfectly safe, mother,' I replied. 'Nothing inside it but clothes. I have just checked.'

'Yes, well, never mind,' my mother retorted a little impatiently. 'You never know what could be hiding *behind* those clothes; a few of those creepy crawlies and who knows what else.'

'I have no fear of anything of that sort, mother,' I sighed.

'Anyhow,' my mother continued abruptly, 'you must put on your choicest of dresses for the occasion that awaits us.'

I held the luxurious ruby-red garment against myself and gazed in my long gold-framed mirror whilst my mother placed a pair of matching petite ruby shoes by my golden hatstand.

I looked just like a rose, I thought, ready to bloom.

'My dearest, make haste,' came my mother's anxious voice, 'for we have summoned all the princes from their travelling across the country. Is it not fortunate that this wonderful event is so close to Ernest's birthday party? For they will still be able to attend his wedding. It is also particularly fortunate that the prince of Perusia is but a few miles away. And you, dear rosebud, must look your best!'

I knew that now she was more eager than ever to find me a suitor.

'And are the Tree People also invited?' I questioned.

'Why, of course!' Mother exclaimed. 'To think that I would permit a wedding to take place without the bride's parents being present.'

I realised that this was exactly what the Tree People had done and mother probably felt a little slighted by it. The fact was that the Tree People had previously held their own perception of other folk in the land and it had not been, until that point, entirely favourable. This was partly due to their own ill-treatment by other races that they had come into contact with in past times, and who viewed them with the highest suspicion and contempt. This was partly the reason why Tree People only tended to come out after dusk and rarely mixed with outsiders to the forests. Through the trees, I discovered later, Simira had often watched the parties of guests arriving on special occasions at the castle, longing to find a way for her people and this nation to unite again. It was on one such occasion that she had met Ernest and from that moment on, the views of the Tree People about the land folk had started to change.

'Will the bride's other friends and relatives be present?' I asked my mother.

'Why, you are going to be there, of course,' chirped Mother, 'along with the bride's adopted brother. That is all. Now make haste!'

I was just about to request that more of the Tree People should attend when I remembered that they were generally very shy. I began to wonder how Shyman would manage in the rather eccentric company of my family. The rest of the Tree People had already witnessed a wedding ceremony in their own setting and surely that was enough for them.

The day went on gloriously. I was totally astonished by the amount of preparation which must have been accomplished only the day before. Beautiful golden strips of material draped the entire interior of the castle and a tall white cake that gleamed like pure snow sat in the main dance hall waiting patiently for someone to cut and taste it.

I watched the guests arrive in their array of luxurious robes and ballgowns. Prince Vicoro of Perusia wore a ruby-red cloak and ruby shoes tied with gold lace, on which bells jingled as he walked. This sight amused me particularly, so much that I had to swing round and hide behind the banister to avoid his puzzled stare. I was not aided by the arrival of Prince Sean immediately afterwards, who strode in to the hall in a most important fashion in a deep velvet-green gown which was covered with floral decoration, his hair swept back off his face without a strand out of place. He came in with my cousin Georgiana on his arm and in fact it would not have surprised me if she had attended to his hair that morning; it seemed to display the woman's touch and I had to cover my mouth once again to keep myself from laughing. Prince Sean noticed, however, and he turned and bowed in his elegant way and straightened up to give me a sickly gleam of a smile, pulling Georgiana even closer to him as she peered up at me and giggled foolishly.

All the guests had arrived, some in finer attire than others, but none surpassed the hand-woven gowns of the three splendid Tree People who came to witness the occasion. The king and queen of the forest and their adopted son stood back in deep respect as they saw me coming down the stairs to meet them. All three gave a humble bow and I curtseyed accordingly. My parents took both of my hands, pressing them affectionately, and my tree mother kissed me.

'You look like a true forest rose,' she sang in my ear.

'We are very proud of you,' joined my tree father's mellow tone.

Behind them both, looking as timid as ever, came Shyman. His warm eyes immediately lit up on seeing me and he spoke one word of greeting, which appeared to take him great effort.

'Blessings,' he said, bowing respectfully.

I delighted in hearing his voice; it was so pure and it resonated deep within me like a new note. I held my hand out to him and he took it. We stood for a moment in silence, then, as the queue of guests pushed us on, he released me.

Of course, the bride looked more than beautiful on that day, and instead of wearing her wondrous green dress she had decided to follow the tradition of the land folk in wearing a flowing ivory dress richly patterned in gold embroidery. With this she wore a light veil that, as Ernest later informed us in the speeches, 'covered too much of her beauty'.

The wedding ceremony itself went quite smoothly, until it came to the reciting of the vows. Grand Jo, who had formerly trained as a vicar, conducted the ceremony, and he kept on stumbling over the words. There was most unusual scope for laughter for such an occasion, and a surprising lack of it came from all those present, with the obvious exception of the twins. I kept trying to suppress the peels of laughter that came upon me whenever I saw Charlie and Cecil shaking all over, their faces as red as my dress. They were being nudged into silence by our two older sisters, Petrovka and Liliana, who I thought always tried to be too serious. I decided that in order to help maintain the peace, I would turn away and avoid all eye contact with the twins, and I tried my best to concentrate on the vows with all the gravity I could summon. It did not seem to help the following events much, however.

Grand Jo managed to get through the introduction, which was rather long and drawn out. I realised that he had added a lot of unessential parts. For example, he included bits about war history and how vital it is for men to stand and fight together. He also took the opportunity to give a small lecture on how to make the ideal marriage; at this point he nodded at a picture of his deceased wife on the wall opposite, as an example. After this, Grand Jo began to inform us all of the best parenting techniques, which he indicated by waving his sceptre around. I noticed my grandmother nudging my grandfather (who was his son), and the pair, who wore hearing aids and were nearly deaf, started shaking their heads and signing to each other in a furious fashion.

I breathed a sigh of relief when this unwanted speech came to an end. The vows would have gone favourably enough if Grand Jo had not given Simira the wrong name or referred to her as the groom and Ernest as the bride.

'I, Ernest,' barked Grand Jo, tapping his stick on the ground, as if to keep time.

'I, Ernest,' Ernest echoed in a trance.

'Take thee, Marmaduke,' continued Grand Jo.

'Ahem!' Ernest cleared his throat loudly. 'Take thee, Simira...'

There were some titters from Charlie and Cecil and a few growls from other relatives. Marmaduke, our second cousin, had once been a possible wife for Ernest, and she was the one of whom Grand Jo most approved. It had taken him too long to accept that Marmaduke was by far the least appropriate of all partners. She married a clumsy duke from another land who just happened to be the cousin of Prince Derek, my ungainly dance partner. Grand Jo had liked her bold nature, which in some way was quite similar to his own, despite the fact that he would normally have considered it mere impertinence. Besides, Marmaduke had tended to make an exhibition of herself in public, firstly by having the loudest voice and most dramatic nature of all our relatives, and secondly due to sheer awkwardness. She always knocked into things and broke many expensive items in this manner. Everything of delicacy or value was removed and hidden in the cellar store whenever she came to visit. I should imagine that she and her husband got on very well; I had heard that he had a lovely, calm and placid nature even when amongst the most stormy of characters. Fortunately, Marmaduke had not been able to attend this ceremony and therefore was not present to be distressed by Grand Jo's mistake.

So the ceremony proceeded and I had just managed to contain my amusement when Grand Jo did something else that caused another eruption of laughter from the twins.

'Now, then,' uttered Grand Jo. 'Who gives this woman to this man?' (He should have asked this at the beginning.)

On looking down before him he came face to face with a dog, the constant faithful companion of my father, known by our family as Chewie; only on this occasion the dog had chosen a new friend. He had set his eyes on the bride's tree father, and had been dragged down the aisle with his teeth firmly clenched in the flowing green robe of the king of the forest. Unfortunately, Chewie had a very strong grip and had managed to pull the tree king right down to the ground, and so Chewie stood further up the steps than he should have been. The tree king was under his robe, as the dog had pulled it over his head.

Grand Jo coughed and spluttered and had to rub his eyes several times in order to clearly study the canine that stood boldly before him. Finally, he cried out in sheer frenzy, 'A *dog* gives this woman away?!'

The twins laughed without restraint, even when they were nudged fiercely by their elder sisters.

'Well!' growled Grand Jo, with a greatly vexed look. 'Never before have I heard of a dog giving away a bride in a marriage ceremony! It simply isn't the done thing and it won't do at all, you know.'

He leant towards the dog and began to prod him with his stick, at which Chewie snarled in fury and snapped hold of the stick, and then held on for dear life even as Grand Jo started to swing it in the air. In the middle of this fiasco, the tree father of the bride emerged from under his robe, having just managed to untangle himself, and he extended his hand, calling out, 'I do! I give the bride away!'

Grand Jo stopped swinging father's dog around his head on his stick and peered down at the tree king rather suspiciously.

'And who is this?' he demanded. 'Snooping in on a private royal wedding like a spy? On guard!'

He aimed his stick this time at the tree king, who held his hands out with a slightly bemused smile on his face.

'This is surely a hanging offence,' Grand Jo went on. 'This is treason!'

Ernest quickly stepped out and said in his matter-of-fact way, 'Grandfather Jo, you need your eyes adjusting. And you need to keep up to date with present events. Surely you know that a law was passed to ban hanging from this country at least thirty years ago.'

'And more importantly,' added Simira, showing an exceptional talent for maintaining a respectful composure, 'this man is my father, the king of the forest, and he is here to give me away.'

'Well, bless me,' the old man continued in a much quieter voice. 'These Tree People really are quite as mad as we make them out to be, aren't they? She suggests that this dog is her father. More than that, he is KING. Now, we all know that my granddaughter's husband is the only true king.'

Simira sighed in slight desperation and merely stared up at Ernest, who tried to smile encouragingly and turned back to Grand Jo.

'Great-grandfather,' resumed Ernest, 'the father of the bride is no dog. I'll have you know that you should bow to him as king.'

Grand Jo looked more perplexed than I had ever seen

him. 'You as well? Deranged! My great-grandson is deluded by his Tree Maiden. I told you never to trust these Tree People. In league with the Tikes, they were. You mark my words.'

'Enough!' The king of the castle silenced him, and came to stand beside the tree king and helped him up. 'Forthwith, let the myths of this persecuted people be forever more abolished. Under my command we must all bow before this noble and worthy tree king, for he is every bit a king as I am. In fact, I believe that he is more of a king!'

At this moment the king kneeled before the tree king, my true father. In response, everyone in the hall went down on their knees and the tree king and tree queen stood before us with gracious smiles. I could also see that both of them were deeply moved. We stayed on our knees with our heads bowed for a sacred moment when we could have heard a pin drop.

Then the tree king instructed us all to arise and the king of the castle cried out in joy, 'Let the dancing begin!'

And so it did, and continued all through the day and all through the night. At an unsuspected moment, after I had danced with all of the available princes in the room (and Prince Vicoro had paid me special attention), a tall man gently tapped me on the shoulder and asked, 'May I?'

I nodded quickly in delight and curtseyed low as he bowed in humbleness before me.

That dance was the most wonderful of all the dances in the evening; it brought me back to the forest in my mind as I closed my eyes. All I could hear was his tuneful hums. All I could feel was his warm breath against my cheek, and I drifted into another world. I remembered the little child beside me in the basket and once more I could hold onto him and did not have to let him go. He was alive and well and unharmed. And he had returned to me. We could have grown up together as brother and sister, but somehow I could see more clearly than ever that this path of life simply had not been our destiny. I had been taken from him and he had been taken from me, so that I would be Ernest's sibling and Simira would be Shyman's sister. Our new partnership was meant to be different to that of siblings, and I felt that although hardly any words had passed between us, I could understand his thoughts. It was as if we were connected by a strange tree telepathy, but not telepathy by any dark magic source. All was right and sound; all we now needed was a voice to express our thoughts. But for the time being, I was content to be silent and enjoy our time together, communicating through tree dance movement. The experience was timeless, and I was unaware of all the onlookers who must have stared at us whilst we rotated round and round. I felt like I was floating and all I needed was his arm to steady me and keep me from falling. I kept my eyes closed and I did not realise how far we had danced from the hall until a long time later. When I opened my eyes, I was amazed to find myself lying in the forest, stretched out on a large silver mushroom in the ring of mushrooms at the centre of the forest.

The Return of Shua

I turned to see Shyman sitting on the next mushroom and I sat up quickly.

'I must have fallen asleep,' I whispered.

I noticed how thoughtful he looked; his head rested in his hands and his eyes looked sad. To my surprise he started to speak. Each word came slowly yet with so much energy.

'I... know... you... Salomya.'

'I know you too,' I answered straight away. 'You were the boy strung up in the basket next to mine, but you were cut down by the Tikes and taken away.'

I stopped speaking for he winced at the mention of his enemy's name. His warm eyes grew cold as they filled with tears. His memory of me seemed to be healing his soul. Tears poured down his face and I watched them soak the ground beneath us where a young apple tree stood. We were sitting in the same ring of mushrooms where we had witnessed Ernest and Simira making their first tree marriage vows. As I gazed at the apple tree, I was surprised to see a new apple start to grow.

I went to sit beside him and put my hand gently on his shoulder.

'Listen,' I whispered, 'you are going to be all right. Whatever happened, whatever they did to you, you can be restored; it can be used for good.'

'By... what... power?' He began to sob quietly.

I paused, hoping that he would believe me.

'By the power of the Great King on High.'

As I said this, an unnatural light shone through the parting in the trees, hitting the mushroom circle, and suddenly Shyman collapsed and fell to the ground. A warm glow continued to fill the blessed circle, and it grew ever brighter. To my amazement, I realised that we were not alone; a great shining being stood before us in the centre of the circle, beside the apple tree. Looking down, He spoke to the tree and His voice was as clear as crystal and as warm as a flowing spring on a hot day. He awoke Shyman, who sat up and blinked in awe.

'I pronounce blessing of life on you, young tree. Grow to the height that God made you to be.'

The tree suddenly blossomed and grew up, sprouting many rosy-red apples. The first one fell to the ground.

'Take it and eat it,' the divine being instructed Shyman, giving him the apple, 'for it is food for your soul.'

Shyman was so overcome by the presence of the being that he quivered in fear.

'Do not be afraid,' the being continued, 'for greater is He that is in you than the enemies that invade the world.'

He leant over and lifted Shyman's head with a strong arm and Shyman willingly took the fruit and ate it. As soon as the fruit had entered his mouth, his cheeks began to glow with fresh colour and he closed his eyes, as if meditating on new words that affirmed him and filled him with strength.

'Your faith increases,' said the being, 'and now you are ready to receive this blessing. As Father God blessed the tree, so He blesses you. For you must reach your full stature in order to face the coming battle.'

With this, the being placed his hand on Shyman's head and said in a voice filled with divine power and authority, 'I pronounce blessing of life on you, man of trees. Grow to the height that God made you to be!'

There was a great flash of white lightning and then the being disappeared.

I blinked as if awakening from a powerful dream and I saw a new man before me, stretching to his full height with strength inhabiting every corner of his being. I saw him standing in the glory of God, for the great light stayed with him, shining all around him. As he took in deep breaths of new life, it seemed for a moment that the moonlight itself formed a sparkling crown on his head. Suddenly, the Shyman I had briefly known was gone and existed no longer, and instead a new kingly ruler had taken his place. He spent many minutes standing in this way, with his back towards me, as if looking out at a heavenly place in the distant trees. He continued to breathe in the forest air deeply, and I could see his lungs were greatly expanding his rib cage, and his entire frame seemed to grow stronger by the second.

When he finally turned round to face me, I was nearly knocked over by the zeal and electricity that shone from his blazing eyes. They were lit like two amber flames and his thick dark hair had a flame-like life that moved out from it, into the surrounding trees. When he spoke, it was with a voice of power and authority.

'I have been given a new name, and I have found my true identity. It is the true name which I was given by my parents, the great high king and queen of Treeland, under God's instruction, and it is the name I will take once again. I am Samson the Stronghold-Shaker. My elder brother is Shua, the saviour of all. His birth was prophesised by our people. He is sent to us from God to save all from death, and He has appeared to me today. Our tree parents are ruling in Heaven alongside God on High now, and one day we will join them, but first we have a great mission to fulfil on earth, under God Most High's command.

'The time is coming very soon when our land will yet again be invaded, but it is by a greater evil force than the Tikes, who act merely as puppets.

71

'From land to land, and across the seas, great armies are coming to take our country and our lives. But all those who call on the name of the Lord Most High shall stand. *We must brace ourselves for battle! We must shout out the war cry! We must summon all the company of heavenly hosts to come to our aid!'*

Samson cried out these final words in our own tree tongue and he stood up on one of the mushrooms with his arms lifted high and the entire forest suddenly stirred with life. All of the surrounding trees opened out like doors, and Tree People emerged from them, dressed for battle, armed with bows and arrows, swords and shields. I turned to see many other beings leaving their homes in the forest; little elf-like creatures hopped from branch to branch, raising a war cry and waving their spears.

Samson continued to prophesy: 'Even now as I speak, the Tike armies are invading the castle and making prisoners out of royalty. It is our mission to rescue our friends and free the captives from their chains. Let us march on, now!'

So we marched on, a vibrant army that was united in its cause. Samson and I walked at the head with the finest men of the forest following, and the women walking alongside. The women with children stayed behind in the trees. Behind them came the elf creatures with their nimble frames, quick-footed and alert.

As we came to the clearing at the end of the forest, we were joined by a group of men who looked like woodland folk, all dressed in the finest leaves. Their leader was tall and astute, standing at least a head and shoulders above the rest, even greater in stature than Samson, and he carried a great resemblance to him. The most unusual thing about him was the light that radiated from his being, lighting up the forest all around him like a strong flame. Samson went forward eagerly as if he had been waiting to meet him for a long time. I could feel our people were relaxing in the stranger's presence as if he was familiar. I could feel it, too; somehow I felt that I knew him and that he seemed to know me, as he smiled out at the crowd.

Samson and the stranger greeted each other with a firm embrace.

'Greetings, Samson, and greetings to this noble people.' The stranger spoke in a rich voice that warmed my soul, in the same way as the divine being had done. 'I am Shua, high king of Treelands, Samson's elder brother. I have come to save our world from the enemy.'

On hearing this news, the crowd cheered and waved their swords and spears in the air.

'It is my Father's will that we join forces to succeed in battle and conquer the Tikes. Yet it will require greater sacrifice than you think.'

Shua's face became serious as he lowered his head to contemplate the forthcoming events, and the crowd fell silent. In the hush, I felt my heart beating stronger and faster, as I wondered what the sacrifice would involve. A moment later, Shua lifted his head in an apparent new exuberance of spirit, and he extended his hand.

'I have appointed these Tree Men, my disciples, to impart to you wisdom and understanding. They will be a great strength to you.'

Samson fell on his knees before Shua, and the crowd did the same.

'My brother, you are the leader, the king of all kings. We will follow you wherever you go.'

Shua gazed down lovingly at his brother with tears filling his eyes.

'You may have to follow me through all the pain and even the sacrifice; the cost will be great for both of us, but the enemy's work will all be undone.'

Shua took a sword from the sheath on his belt and knighted Samson with great reverence.

'You, my strong knight, will help me to deliver my people from their oppressors. Rise again, Samson the Stronghold-Shaker.'

All the people were bowing down again before the high king.

'Now, we march onwards!' commanded Shua, and everyone obeyed, knowing that the words came from a being that was far greater than a man.

We moved on, pressing into the castle noiselessly from all sides, until finally Shua cried out, 'People of the forest, blow your trumpets!'

I heard the noise of a vast army, as if the heavenly armies joined us in the cry of battle. As I turned, I could see many angels of light closing in around us, also blowing horns and singing with beautiful crystal-clear voices. The ground around us began to shake as we continued to march around the walls of the castle, whilst the Tree Men cheered in Tree Tongue: 'Let the king of glory enter!'

Finally, Shua himself let out a cry of power and authority that made the crowd draw in a deep breath. As his cry echoed in the air, the very foundations of the castle trembled and we could hear a mighty stirring from within. A few minutes later we turned to see terrible dark creatures fleeing at the sound of his voice. They were exiting the castle in the most disorderly fashion, through the archway entrance and through side doors; one even came from a window, high up in one of the castle's towers. As the voice of Shua continued to resonate, the creatures still inside the castle could be heard giving ear-splitting screams. Soon their dark forms appeared, their ugly, cruel faces filled with terror, for none could hide from him. Indeed, it seemed that nothing on earth could stand against the authority of Shua.

I was in the midst of rejoicing with all the Tree People at our quick victory when a sight that terrified our troops sprang from the main archway of the castle. I recognised the giant dark panther from descriptions in books regarding the

Tikes' first invasion, and I had never imagined any being as terrifying and evil as he. His claws were the size of swords which were drawn as if ready to capture his victims. I shivered when I saw his eyes, which blazed like green fire in the moonlight. They seemed to burn right through each one of us, and he displayed a great deal of contempt for the company which he beheld, snarling and spitting in distaste. He gave a particularly fierce roar when he saw Samson in the crowd, but he stopped still when he came face to face with Shua and looked visibly shaken.

'You?' he growled in horror and hate. 'The Son of God?'

'Your time is nearly up, Azriel,' shouted Shua, raising his hand.

I saw that Azriel, as Shua had called the panther, could come no closer and seemed to find Shua too bright to look upon, as if it was a strain for his eyes; he even backed off towards the archway from which he had come.

'You cannot reclaim that old ground,' continued Shua, in fearless authority. 'This castle is used to honour my name and it has done so for some time. This land is mine and the people in it submit to me. Therefore, you have no claim here.'

'They are all *MINE*!' snarled Azriel. 'All are guilty for the times each went his own way. Now give me the boy – *HE* made a pact with me. Even you cannot alter that. Return him to me and I will be gone.'

'The boy you speak of is now a man,' replied Shua, 'and he has submitted his life to me. You have no hold over him any more.'

Azriel moved towards Samson, his eyes flaming with fresh hate.

'NO!' howled the demon. 'He is my slave. He gave his life to me and he belongs to ME! Is this not right, slave?'

Samson looked suddenly weakened. The creature drew away from him and stared at Shua with eyes of terrible victory and vengeance.

The crowd started to murmur in fear. I reached out to Samson but he only looked away; a very lost expression was returning to his face. The new bold warrior had started to tremble.

'Samson?' I called out to him, beginning to feel like I was withering inside. He did not answer but only gazed at the ground, his eyes welling up with tears. Surely something could be done, I thought; after all, Shua had much more power than the panther.

The creature roared. 'He signed a pact whilst he was dying and agreed to be my slave for life if I let him live. You cannot undo the pact. It was signed with his *blood.*'

The crowd gasped and several people stepped forward, waving their spears at Azriel, but he merely laughed at them and continued, 'As he has betrayed me, there must be a sacrifice tonight under the moonlight in the mushroom circle. Our law requires it.'

All eyes were on Samson, who held his face in his hands. Suddenly Shua turned to him, and spoke quietly. 'This matter will be settled between me and the panther. You cannot do anything about it; just trust in me.'

He lifted Samson's head and almost immediately the light that came from Shua's eyes seemed to be reflected in Samson's, and I could see that he was both comforted and strengthened by these words.

The panther became strangely quiet at this point, as if he was revelling in a new evil plan and he lashed his tail impatiently from side to side.

'There will be a meeting tonight at the mushroom circle,' instructed Shua. 'It will be done in the way my Father has willed it.'

'The sacrifice will take place?' questioned the panther, leaning closer to Shua, as well as he could manage. 'You keep your word?'

'Do not question God's word!' commanded Shua. 'Now be gone!'

I will never forget Azriel's howl as he turned from us and ran quickly to the forest, for in that howl there was a sort of terrible vengeance. And as he turned to glare at us with his glowing green eyes, I could hear an evil laugh come from his soul, and his foul sounds continued to echo long after he had disappeared, leaving a sense of unfinished business in the air.

As he left, I saw Samson clutch his chest in great pain. I turned and held him in my arms and Shua rested his hand on his shoulder.

'All evil that was done against you will be undone.'

Only we could hear his words over the wild talking that had started after the panther's departure. Samson's pain seemed to subside momentarily and he straightened out to his full stature. But he had lost some of the life that had entered him in the forest earlier and everyone was very concerned for his well-being.

Presently Shua turned our minds back to recent events. 'Come; let us unbind those who are in chains within the castle.'

He led us into the castle archway and we ran into the main hall. Almost straightaway I saw many people chained to the walls and gagged. As Shua entered the dark hall (for the Tikes had eliminated all sources of light upon their entrance), light shone all around him so that the place seemed very bright, and the terrified people in chains began to calm down. At this instant, Shua turned to me and gave me a small sword from his belt.

'Go, daughter!' he commanded. 'Set free the captives!'

I saw my father and mother and ran to their side and undid their chains by one stroke of the powerful sword in my hands, and I did the same with my tree parents, who lay beside them. They all thanked me and, getting up, went straight to Shua and bowed down low. He looked delighted with them and raised them up, then held them close to him for some time. I could hear his warm voice say, 'I know you well, my sons and daughters. Go now, and release others, just as you have been released.'

I moved quickly to release Ernest and Simira, and then they held me close to them, and Ernest whispered fondly in my ear, 'I always knew you were sent to save our family.'

'I'm simply returning the favour you did me all those years ago, brother,' I replied, smiling at him.

'They were going to hold us hostage to demand the nation's surrender,' said Simira softly, 'but at the sound of Shua's voice, the Tikes could no nothing but tremble and then flee for their lives.'

I turned and saw Charlie and Cecil, still looking quite shaken, but they both attempted to muster a mischievous smile for me. I undid their chains and as soon as they were un-gagged they both talked non-stop.

'Well!' cried Charlie. 'That was rather exciting, wasn't it, Cecil?'

'Certainly!' replied Cecil. 'You missed a capital adventure there, Salomya.'

'I just wish I had given him a bigger clout over the head,' went on Charlie, giving me a merry wink, which could have easily been mistaken for a nervous twitch.

'I would have if the heavy ape hadn't sat on my head and chained me,' continued Cecil, laughing as heartily as he could manage, whilst clutching his side, which appeared to be sore.

'You are not too badly hurt, I hope?' I questioned in concern.

'No, no!' cried Cecil, suddenly sitting up with forced energy. 'Nothing that nature can't fix. I think we put up rather a good fight, that's all.'

'Well, you are very brave, both of you,' I told them. 'And I'm proud of you.'

I gave them both a hug, quite forgetting their bruises, and they winced a little, but this did not seem to bother them too much; under the circumstances they felt their bravery had gained them high approval. As usual, they were putting brave faces on, and even competing with each other to see who could recover quickest. It was good to see them being their familiar jovial selves. It was the way in which they always survived; if either boy ever became withdrawn, which rarely happened, there was reason for concern.

'Goodness!' Charlie cried suddenly. 'Did you see that? What are those funny little imps running around, dragging those chains and hopping from one person to another?'

I was just going to say that they were our woodland allies whom I had only just met, when a strange high-pitched voice answered for me. 'Those "funny little imps" are actually called Help Elves, and you had better get used to it because we are helping you too!'

Charlie and Cecil both gasped, then started chuckling foolishly as the said Help Elf jumped on top of them and held a strange stick over them, out of which poured sparkles of colour that vanished into the twins. After this, I noticed that they became calmer and breathed a lot more easily. Their faces filled with colour and their eyes twinkled.

'Ah!' said Charlie. 'That was nice; I feel like sleeping now.'

He actually yawned and stretched and began to close his eyes.

'Thanks, Help Elf,' continued Cecil. 'I believe you've healed my bruises; you are very helpful indeed. May I know your name?'

'Jabez at your aid, sir,' replied the elf. 'And some of those bruises were actually broken ribs, my dear prince. Glad to be of service.'

And with that, he bowed and hopped away to the next person.

After all had recovered and the castle was full of chandelier light, everyone was drinking cups of hot chocolate and merriment had returned. I found Samson sitting alone at the archway, looking out towards the forest, which was strongly lit by the ever-present moonlight. He still appeared to be thoughtful and concerned.

'Samson!' I cried. 'We have nothing to worry about; Shua said himself that he will resolve things, did he not?'

'Yes, he did,' replied Samson quietly. 'He is going to settle the matter tonight. I fear he will leave us for a while and we will be alone.'

His shine was dimmer and he seemed to be carrying a burden too big for a man. I rested my hand on his shoulder and he took my hand in his and pressed it to his face. I knew my presence comforted him. He remained silent.

'Surely Shua's power is greater than Azriel's,' I continued, softly. 'Samson, we have nothing to fear.'

'Something terrible is going to happen tonight,' Samson replied, 'I can feel it in the air. A storm is brewing, hell is waiting. I can't do anything to stop it, and *I* have brought it on us, and on Shua.'

I waited with him, watching the moon, until all the people in the castle were falling asleep. Then Shua came to our side.

'The panther and his army await me.' He spoke quietly, filling me with a sense of calm. 'Walk with me to the forest, but you must not go as far as the mushroom ring. You must keep out of sight.'

We both nodded solemnly.

'What is it you are going to do, my lord?' asked Samson, trembling with fear.

'A terrible thing,' answered Shua. 'But through it all mankind will be saved.'

Together, we headed to the forest. The night was unusually quiet, with the exception of the occasional scuttling of tiny feet, which I presumed to be that of the Help Elves' wives and children. As we passed their residence, one of them suddenly appeared in a ray of moonlight before us and bowed low at Shua's feet and offered him a gift.

'Your Majesty,' she said in a reverent voice.

The gift was the rose which Ernest had mentioned; the sacred flower from the heart of the forest for which the Tree People often searched. It was said that it could cheer a sad heart and that it was found where the strongest love ruled and where peace and harmony existed. Shua took it with deep gratitude.

'This gift has given me much comfort,' he said. 'Your people have always been loyal to mine and for this you will be paid in full. I am in need of such consolation tonight.'

The Help Elf bowed low again and said, 'It has been a pleasure, master. It's the least we can give you.'

Then she bounded away and I saw Shua gaze longingly at the beautiful rose that shone with his glory, and as I looked closer, I noticed that the petals of the rose had started to wilt. As he leaned over it, tears filled his eyes and flowed over onto the rose, and almost immediately it became brighter still and new leaves were restored to it.

'My children will bloom again,' he said, so softly that Samson and I could hardly hear him, and he held the rose so tenderly that I felt his heart almost breaking. 'If there is another way, Father, please lead me there.'

'Never leave our side, lord,' pleaded Samson. 'We cannot live without you.'

Shua turned to face his brother.

'I will never leave you,' he replied, 'even when you think I am not here, I will always be here.'

After a few more minutes of silence, Shua paused in his steps.

'I have appreciated your company tonight. There is little time left and I must leave you just for a while. Then I will return to you. Promise you will stay hidden here and not fall prey to the enemy.'

We both agreed that we would do so, and not let ourselves be harmed. Then he threw his arms around both of us and wept. I felt my heart breaking for him, and from that moment Samson and I were certain of the terrible thing that Shua was about to do. In the distance was the sound of drums. When we came into sight of the mushroom circle, I felt suddenly cold and I shuddered. Shua turned to us.

'Now I must go on alone.' His voice sounded sorrowful but resolute. We let him go on with heavy hearts and were overcome by a feeling of helplessness. He moved slowly through the trees that led to the clearing where the mushrooms lay. The moonlight shone onto the mushroom circle the moment that Shua entered the ring and by this time the drumbeat had stopped and suddenly there was Azriel, the dark panther, pacing around the mushrooms, snarling at Shua, just as a predator regards its prey.

'So, you have come instead of him? Don't you see that you are not saving him by dying in his place? For I will kill him after I have killed you.'

Shua was silent, and he stood still in the centre beside the tree from which red apples still shone.

The panther seemed irritated by his silence and continued, 'The slave owes me *his* life, after all, and your death will not change that.'

Shua remained quiet, and a calm serenity shone from his being as Tikes emerged from the shadows and bound him with chains to the tree; it was a lot taller and stronger now than any normal apple tree, and they evidently trusted its sturdiness. Shua still held the rose close to his heart and they mocked him with it. Azriel snatched it from him, and observing the thorns attached to its stem, he wrapped it around Shua's forehead until large drops of blood fell to the ground.

I could feel Samson's hand clutching mine tightly as we watched from behind a huge oak tree. We both sensed some of Shua's pain and I could hardly bear it. I saw the drops of blood soak into the earth and as this happened some fresh apples grew from the tree. Disturbed by Shua's power even when in deep suffering, the panther responded with a cruel jibe. 'Isn't it fitting,' he snarled, pacing closer to Shua, 'that the very place which is meant to be blessed with life should become the place of your death? Do you really think that one death will absolve all crimes against me? Samson was not the only one to stray into my territory and make a pact with me. There have been others; many, many others...'

Suddenly I felt my heart grow very cold, and Samson noticed.

'Salomya,' he whispered, 'don't let his words fill you.'

A strange wind was rushing around my head; it was the wind of realisation. My heart was throbbing and tears poured down my face. I let go of his hand and fell against the tree, feeling very faint.

'I need to sit down,' I said. 'I am the rose thorn that has pierced his head. I have done wrong to Shua in my life, in thought, word and even in deed, and therefore I too have entered into enemy territory without even knowing it. We are *all* to blame for Shua's impending death.'

Saying this, I fell into a sort of faint, but I was even more aware of what was happening to Shua, and a hot sweat filled my whole being. Samson could do nothing to comfort me, and he too joined me in his own agony; his own terrible realisation of the price that had to be paid.

The panther was still snarling and his voice filled my being with anguish. 'But, the victim must be prepared for his death. We have waited for this moment for countless centuries.'

One of the Tikes started to sharpen a terrible great dark knife, whilst Azriel sprang upon Shua and dragged his claws through him as deeply as they could go. I saw that as the blood poured out of fresh wounds it soaked into the earth, feeding the apple tree just as before, and new apples that were larger than ever sprung to life all over the tree. But the most amazing thing was not this; as soon as the new wounds had formed, Shua gazed up to the heavens and his face shone more brightly than ever before.

'AAH!' The panther cried out as if in pain. 'Stop the SHINING! I cannot bear the SHINING! If we are going to torture and kill our number one enemy, we are going to enjoy doing it. Judo, cover him with a cloak and sharpen your knife to get ready for the killing.'

Even the great cloak of Azriel's chief Tike could not cover the multitude of light rays that were shining out from under it.

'NOW DO THE DEED, JUDO!' roared the panther, with such momentum that several of the surrounding Tikes were blown across to nearby trees in the ghastly wind of his breath.

Judo quivered in his boots so much that he nearly dropped the heavy dark knife.

'Why the wait, slave?' snarled the panther, lashing his tail out angrily.

'I... I... can't do it,' cried Judo. 'He... Shua... does not deserve this.'

'SILENCE!' bellowed Azriel, bristling in complete fury. 'What have I asked of you? To obey me! Have I not granted you a high place in my kingdom, when I come to reign? And how do you repay me? By using the name that is detestable above any other name. You know what the penalty of using his NAME is; instant death! Do you want to die with him? If you do not kill him, you certainly shall die.'

Judo trembled even more and bowed down so low that he nearly sat on the ground. 'I wish I hadn't brought you here to him,' he continued to mutter, 'his death may be the worse for us.'

'AAAAH!' Azriel looked so terrifying at this moment that Samson and I nearly stood up and ran away; instead, we stayed hidden by our tree.

'Do you DARE to cross me, Judo?' the great panther

bellowed, pulling Judo down to the floor and clawing him until he squealed. 'You who sold your soul to me? Is this your Tree Man leader, whom you followed around with those disgusting Tree People disciples, claiming to be there as my spy? I often wondered if you were going to change sides. Now I see that you have – very well, I will kill him myself.'

'No!' cried Judo. 'He is a good man. I have seen since I followed him that he really is the Son of God, and he is *good*. I was wrong about him.'

Suddenly Shua spoke and his voice was like new daylight. 'Judo, one day you will be with me in my Father's house.'

'Give me the knife!' snarled the panther. 'Get out of my way; I will KILL you!'

Roaring in fury, the panther grabbed the sword from Judo and threw him aside with one swipe of his great claws. Judo fell weeping, and then ran for his life before anyone could grab hold of him.

'Go after him!' cried Azriel. 'When you catch him, kill him.'

Several Tikes ran after him, hurling abuse at him and looking back at their master eagerly, as if not wanting to miss anything.

As the panther started to circle the centre of the ring again, this time with the gleaming dark knife, the rest of the Tikes began an eerie chant that seemed to subdue all life in the forest; even the trees seemed to wither as the drums began to roll again.

Finally, the drum roll came to a stop just as the panther raised the knife high in the air. The panther brought the knife down with a mighty roar, but at this moment, a stronger voice echoed all around the forest: 'IT IS FINISHED!'

As the knife plunged into the cloak that was draped over Shua, we could see blood soaking it, and as it did, many more apples came into fruit on the tree, and it grew taller than ever and shone like a great lamppost in the sky. I wept on Samson's shoulder as he held me close and he too wept.

'This is all my doing,' he whispered.

'Mine too,' I replied through my sobs.

'Shua said he would return,' Samson continued. 'How can he save the world when he is dead?'

'Because he has died for the crimes of the whole world,' I replied. 'He said that all evil that has been done will be undone.'

At this moment I noticed something strange. Judo's cloak, which had been stained with blood, had turned pure white and a strong piercing light came from the place where Shua was chained; the source of light to the tree. Suddenly, a rumbling occurred deep within the ground beneath us and with a great roar, the earth split right through the mushroom circle. With a cry of terror, Azriel froze and stared in disbelief at the cloak. A strange music started to come from it and it seemed that once again all the heavenly host could be heard with voices as clear as crystal, amidst a giant storm that hurtled through the skies. Azriel turned to look at the sky above, and to his horror, he saw what looked like a giant tornado; a vacuum in the sky waiting to take him. Howling in despair, he fled, and the Tikes fled with him, screaming in fear.

As we stood up to watch, the great tornado followed the dark creatures further away from us into the forest, sucking up some of the trees as it went, until finally we saw it lifting them clear off the ground and they disappeared entirely into the great hungry vortex. Soon after this, the storm subsided almost as quickly as it had come and we were in a strangely calm and serene place once again. The great apple tree glowed and the cloak shone beneath it and a greater music filled our ears. The dawn had started to colour the sky and rejoicing birdsong soothed our souls. We watched the sun rising across the horizon and found ourselves falling into a strange deep slumber.

*

When we awoke, the sun was at its highest point in the sky and we remembered all the events of the night before. In deep longing, we got up and went over to the apple tree. Slowly and sorrowfully, we lifted Judo's cloak from its place, and to our amazement we found that Shua had gone. Light still shone where he had been chained, and the cloak was still pure white. As we pondered on the mystery of our finding, we found a brighter light shining down on us, which was stronger than the light of the sun, and we gazed up into the branches to see a dazzling being observing us. He must have been there for some time, but we had not noticed him.

'Please,' cried Samson, 'we do not know where Shua has gone.'

'Shua stands before you,' replied the being. 'And now He lives within you, and He always will do, just as He said.'

'Shua?' I cried, knowing at once the voice that brought music to my soul. He rested His hands on my shoulders.

'Rose that has bloomed,' he said tenderly, and gazed into my eyes for a moment, 'go and help others to bloom.'

Then he took Samson in his arms and said, 'Can you see the light shining within?'

He laughed as we embraced Him. 'I am in your hearts for all eternity. Go now, and take my presence with you, to the ends of the earth.'

We stepped back in awe, as the light that shone from Shua warmed our hearts. And as we left that place together, we knew that new music played within us. As the bright midday sun continued to shine, we realised that the message of hope and forgiveness which we were to take to our people and the nations beyond was a truly great one.

*

The Tikes never returned to our land; it seemed that the story of the giant tornado had spread far and wide and stopped any more Tikes from returning. That is, with the exception of Judo, who had been Azriel's chief Tike, and who came to the woods to seek the forgiveness of the Tree People disciples.

He gained a gracious welcome, and the words of Shua's disciples stayed in my mind forever more: 'What you once intended for bad, God has changed for good.'

He changed and started to glow like the other disciples. But he never ventured near to our castle by the wood, for fear of Grand Jo, who had wanted to behead him on the spot the first time he attempted to do so.

One night, three years after these happenings, Samson took me for a moonlit walk in the forest. As we walked hand in hand in peaceful bliss, I noticed that he had a fresh glow in his face, as if he knew that an exciting forthcoming event awaited us. When we reached the mushroom circle, he led me to the apple tree, which was bursting with luscious fruit. Not just apples grew there now – there were all manner of fruit such as oranges, plums, bananas and berries, and others I had never before heard of or seen. Knowing that this tree had become a prophetic tree, I started to wonder what its bearing new fruit meant. A moment later, Samson plucked one of the largest apples and kneeled down before me, holding out the apple to me with glowing eyes. In complete humbleness he made a vow and offered me his love for the rest of our lives. It was a Tree People tradition to use fruit to seal an engagement and I accepted instantly.

Like Ernest, I had two weddings; one in the castle and one in the forest, and when the Tree People tradition to hunt for the eternal forest rose came, a strange light shone pink into the depths of the forest, and a new mystery filled the air. The rose had been with Shua in his death, and many people wondered if it had grown to become a part of the apple tree.

Others thought that perhaps Shua had taken it with him to his Father's house. A long exciting search for the forest rose took place; however, none could be found. After we consulted the leader of the Help Elves, who held some ancient forest wisdom, he replied in surprise:

'Did you not know what the rose represents? When it was not in full bloom, the rose was the buried Lord Shua, whose death has been prophesised for centuries. When it came into full bloom, one of our people knew that the curse of the panther was to be broken and we took it out to Shua on the night he was to be sacrificed. In full bloom, the rose represents the risen Lord Shua, and now that we know he came to live and die among us and to rise again, we know that we do not need to look for him any more. Yes, we have found him! Likewise, the eternal forest rose has risen and it grows in Heaven under the care of our Father. Of course, that does not mean to say that the forest rose tradition needs to come to an end – far from it, for the rose is a constant reminder of the conquering power of our risen Lord.'

Then I remembered the rose that grew outside my bedroom, and Samson and I went out to find it blooming more radiantly than I had yet seen it. That night we used the rose for the forest search; the leader of the Help Elves hid it where they had previously found its sister and the first person who found it gave it straight to Samson and I, and Samson lovingly placed it in my hair as Ernest and Simira looked on in admiration, and I could just hear Simira saying fondly, 'She is the forest rose.'

The rose brought a fresh fragrance to the dances of the night, even after I had given it to the leader of the Help Elves who went to plant it in a secret place deep within the forest, awaiting the next rose hunt. On this dancing occasion, my twin brothers, Charlie and Cecil were dressed in smart suits (with an absence of leaves) and yet they still managed to bring great humour to the dance floor. For on this occasion, they were able to be themselves with the full approval of the Tree People, alongside their fiancées, who danced the night away with them full of boundless energy and laughter.

After a night of celebration and the fulfilment of our marriage union, I closed my eyes on the leaf-filled cushion next to Samson, in the basket-bed which had been made for us especially by the wood folk and elves to celebrate our marriage, and partly to honour our first meeting in the trees as infants. I sank into a sleep of beautiful dreams, and I later discovered that exactly the same dreams entered Samson's mind on that starry night.

Shua returned in my dreams sometimes as a mighty knight warrior, and at other times he appeared as a bridegroom coming to meet his bride, dressed in radiant splendour, with all his followers giving him a great homecoming welcome. Trumpets were sounding, angels were singing joyfully and people everywhere were cheering as he approached in a blazing chariot of fire. In one version of the dream, he reached out his arms, and filled with an irrepressible longing, he drew us all up in the air to be with him for eternity.

The Second Tale

Mr Friedman breathed a sigh of relief. He gazed fondly at the twins, Salomya and Simira, wondering what they would make of it. Throughout the tale, both pairs of eyes had been fixed on him and he could see they were gripped to the core.

'So, who was the rose that bloomed in the story?' asked Mr Friedman.

'I was the rose in that tale,' murmured Salomya in great awe. 'I was a *princess.*'

'Yes, that's right,' continued Mr Friedman. 'Yet there was also another rose. Can anyone tell me who that was?'

'The eternal rose in the forest, which represented Lord Shua,' replied Nehemiah, an older youth who rarely spoke.

'Yes!' cried Mr Friedman, watching the twins. Salomya seemed to be deep in thought.

'I'm used to Simira getting the attention in our lives,' she murmured, 'because she is the cleverest and the most out-going, and I always live in her shadow. But this time, I got the star part!'

Simira frowned at this comment. 'You know that we are equals. Surely you have seen that by now. Look at your musical ability. You can play at least five instruments, and you can pick up any tune you hear. And when you sing, everyone listens.'

'Yes,' whispered Salomya dreamily. 'When I sing.'

'Talking of music, brace yourselves for the next two tales,' went on Mr Friedman, 'for both are all about the powers of music, and perhaps these two tales come as a pair, for they may be not too unlike each other, perhaps a little like our Russian twins, although of course they are also quite different as well.'

The second tale was called...

Harpist's Haven

The Discovery of the Tunnel

He watched the birds spread their wings and fly to the sun, as he sat high up on the large oak tree. They encircled the great light until they became like dots on the horizon. How he wished he could too. He threw a few broken twigs after them, as if in a vain attempt to do so. But he was only reminded of his own mortal imprisonment.

David was in hiding, from an angry uncle who had been chasing him for most of the day. He had been caught letting the hens go free that morning and his Uncle Saul had taken a stick and shouted a threat that made David run fast. His uncle was never the kindest of farmers and David was not always the most obedient of children (although any disobedience was usually more down to absent-mindedness on David's part), and so they got on very badly.

David had never got used to farm life. His father died when he was five years of age and he had been taken to live with one of his few living relatives, Uncle Saul. The connection was Saul's late wife Carolina, who had been an adopted sister of David's father. David had to rise early in the mornings to escape a beating, and work hard all day long on the farm. He loved the country; just to sit and stare at the bubbling brook, or to play with the barn cats and dogs, or follow the call of the tawny owl. He enjoyed fishing, if there was ever any time for such leisure pursuits, but then he always let the fish go.

He was a rare child, exceptionally gentle and caring

towards animals, yet he also had a hidden talent. He could see realities that others could not foresee. He had wisdom and understanding for all that lay beneath the surface in social situations. He was so discerning that sometimes he could read between the lines even before the lines were written. His gift was displayed mostly in his musicality, and his as yet unsung ability manifested when he was alone with the birds in the wood, when he understood their conversations and even joined in their song. Not only did David possess a rich understanding of music, but also an awareness of its powerful effects, for he knew that music had healing properties that penetrated the soul. His gift was an unusual one that required a genius to use it, and he was certainly that.

Sadly, Uncle Saul had little time for David, and seemed to be hardly aware of the gift he possessed. Neither did Saul appreciate David's clever mind, and if he caught him daydreaming on the farm, Saul did not hesitate to send him to the farmhouse cellars, which David called the 'Dragon's Dungeon'. Sometimes, Saul would leave David down in the Dragon's Dungeon for a full day at a time without food. However, while Saul was not looking, Gretela, the kindly Italian cook, would come down to visit him with freshly squeezed orange juice, chicken legs and chocolate cakes. It was on one of these long days in the cellar that David discovered his gift of song. He improvised long passages of his own grief and isolation and would hear the walls of his dungeon sing it back to him in a slightly eerie echo. This echo helped him to realise that there was someone else who at that moment was going through exactly the same thing as him.

These thoughts cheered him even more when they were met with the merry whistle Gretela brought on her brief visits to the dungeon. Known to David as Grettie, this warm, stout and bubbly Italian cook conveyed everything of what motherhood should be to David, of which he had been deprived. Hired by Saul to bring some variety to his diet since the death of his wife, her kitchen was the best part of the farmhouse, always full of wonderful aromas. Saul never said a kind word about her cooking; in fact, he ate in sullen silence, and he would stare at the fire, drinking bottles of ale each evening. Despite his coldness, Grettie's warmth and joy was relatively unaffected while David was around. All Saul managed to do was make her lavish her affection even more on David. As far as Saul was concerned, she was there just to make food and keep the farmhouse tidy. All he chose to understand about David was that he was a difficult child who often needed to be locked in a cellar.

The story of Saul's wife, Carolina, was a tragic tale. She had suffered terribly with nerves, and her temper worsened as the years went by. Like Saul, Carolina turned to alcohol as a way to cope with hard farm life, and this habit resulted in her premature death. Deeply grieved, and struggling under the increased strain of work in her absence, Saul took out his bitterness and despair on the newcomers to the household.

'I'm going to run far, far from here,' David retorted, as he began to climb down the boughs of the tree. He knew that Saul and his searching hounds were far away in the woods and were returning home. The sun had nearly set, so David realised that he needed to find somewhere safe to settle in for the night, and he knew that there was no safer place than Selina's sturdy tree house. Selina's father, Eric Woodman, who owned the farm at the other side of the wood to Saul, had built this tree house for Selina's seventh birthday, and David often went to visit her to share a cup of lemonade and a tea cake with jam. Like him, she was very clever, and she spent all the time she could find in books when she was not helping with farm duties. Fortunately for her, she also had an older brother, Samuel, who carried a lot of the weight of the farm work alongside their headstrong mother, Leah.

Selina had first spied David when he was running away from his uncle – he had been caught having a quiet read in the haystacks when he should have been helping the farm workers with the hay. She had quickly rushed down and smuggled him into her tree house, where they hid until Saul and his hounds had passed. Although the hounds had stopped by the tree house at David's scent, causing Saul to peer up into the tree suspiciously, Saul had thought twice about his own climbing ability and moved on with a weary growl.

And so, David approached the well-loved tree house, hoping that Selina would be inside with a book; maybe *The Voyage of the Dawn Treader*. They had acted out parts of the story last time, pretending that the tree house was a boat. He also hoped that there might be a cup of lemonade or even a tea cake waiting for him. As he climbed the sturdy boughs of the oak tree, he felt a shiver of cold and began to long for a hot chocolate. Grettie always made him a cup at eight o'clock in the evening, just before his bedtime. However, a dark, cold, empty room awaited him as he climbed to the tree house and pushed the little wooden door open.

He pulled out his torch. Selina kept a thick duvet in there for when she stargazed late into the night. She, like David, was ten years of age, but was older than her years, and would certainly stay up later than her bedtime if she could manage it. They would watch the stars together and throw breadcrumbs to them, making wishes. One of David's wishes was that he and Selina would always be able to meet together in the tree house, and he knew that Selina wished for the same. It was a safe haven from the tyranny of Uncle Saul, and David lived for their times there, where he grew in wisdom and understanding. In his own home, he would dream of the haven and eagerly await the next tree house meeting.

With a feeling of deep satisfaction at having returned to his haven, David got into the small bed that was in the tree house, lay his heavy head on the pillow, and drew the thick covers over him. Soon he felt warmer, and fell into a deep pleasant slumber...

He thought he was still dreaming when a fair face with vivid sea-blue eyes surrounded by wild blonde curls approached and kissed his face. Then he felt the warm rays of the morning sun soothe his face as the bed covers were lifted.

'David, surely you haven't been here all night?' Selina's song voice echoed.

David blinked in the light and smiled. 'It was too late to disturb you, Selina. I thought you wouldn't mind me sleeping here.'

'Of course not,' she said, and smiled sweetly. 'What is your uncle upset about this time?'

'I let the hens go free again,' he replied.

'Good!' she cried. 'I'm glad. They'd be much better off on our farm. He's cruel to them, keeping them all cooped up like that. Oh, I do hope they find their way here.'

'Don't worry,' he reassured her, 'I left a trail of chicken food all the way up to your backyard the previous night. That should help them find their way.'

Then they reverted to discussing the ways in which Uncle Saul's farm could be run more effectively if Uncle Saul was not running it. They talked on in this way until finally they were interrupted by Selina's father, who came by to offer them her mother's teacakes. He was pleased to find David in the tree house, and kindly offered him his own teacake.

'No, father,' objected Selina. 'I will give him half of mine.'

Selina's father laughed a jolly chuckle and accepted this arrangement, then with a merry whistle and a kind of dance he skipped back to duties on the farm.

'Perhaps we'd better help,' suggested David.

'You are a guest,' Selina objected firmly. 'Besides, our farm doesn't run to strict slave rules like your Uncle Saul's farm does. There is always time made for relaxing and jovial discussion. So eat up.'

'Thanks, Selina,' said David, full of gratitude and admiration for his angelic friend.

It was on this day that David found a small harp which belonged to Samuel. After watching workers do their duties from a haystack, under the midday summer sun, David picked up the harp and began to play all the joy he was feeling to the animals and the workers, who whistled along. Eventually, as he played the harp and expanded his melodies upon it, he remembered the songs he had sung in the cellar, and started to put them to the notes on the harp. He realised that he had managed to get a perfect fit; the melody from the time of loneliness and the one from his happiness somehow went together like a hand into a glove. And, in turn, the perfect harmony sent an air of freedom to the surrounding farm. The workers were very happy to have such pleasant background music to work to, and as the day went on and her duties were done, Selina came to visit David on the haystack and fell into a trance. As he raised his voice in his wordless song, he knew that all creation was somehow lifting up its voice to join him. It was then that he became aware of a higher purpose in his life. It seemed to be that heaven had come to earth as he played, and that the birds that came to listen were really pure white angels with rich melodies.

A few hours later, most of the workers were resting around the haystack on which David sat, having managed to do their work unusually efficiently, due to the music of the harp. Selina's father Eric had even merrily stated that David's playing had helped the work on the farm and that he was more than welcome to play there all the time, if only his uncle would allow it.

And so, in this way, David enjoyed his day on the Woodman's farm. However, things began to change tune later that evening. He and Selina were stretching their legs by the fire with a warm cup of chocolate when suddenly there came a sharp knock at the door. Uncle Saul's loud, hoarse voice came bellowing through the letter box, and the door rattled ferociously on its hinges.

'Eric! It's Farmer Saul here. Open up! Let me in!'

Eric, who had also been relaxing by the fire, swinging in his beautiful wooden rocking chair, jumped up so quickly that the chair flung backwards and practically landed in the fire.

David whispered fearfully, 'Why does he think I'm here?'

All Eric could mutter was a nervous 'Oh dear!' as he clasped his little silver bell which he kept on the mantelpiece and normally used for getting his children out of bed in the morning. He started to ring it with a shaking hand, calling out, 'I'm on my way, Farmer Saul! I'm on my way! Just finding the key.'

The banging on the door stopped and Eric urged the children, 'Quick! Hide yourselves. I don't mind where you go as long as it's far from here.'

'I'll hide you, David!' cried Selina. 'Now follow me.'

Just as Uncle Saul was starting to bang on the door again, Selina took David by the hand and led him up a winding staircase, until they reached the landing. Then she took him up yet another even more winding staircase, which led them to a small, lonely room filled with cobwebs. David shuddered as he heard Uncle Saul's loud voice enter the kitchen below; it was evident that he was in a fit of rage.

'That boy let my chickens escape again and this time they fled through the woods. Oddly, I've noticed that *you* have acquired some extra chickens on your farm. What do you have to say to that, Eric?!'

Eric's nervous, high-pitched voice could just be heard: 'W-well, now you mention it, Saul, I did think I spotted some recent additions to my group of hens. But I just assumed I must have counted 'em wrong. I did also chance to notice that they had peculiar red rings on their feet that I'm sure I never put there...'

'Don't play games with me, Eric!' snarled Saul. 'They're my chickens, and I'm here to get them back. Hand 'em over!'

'Certainly, Saul,' cried Eric. 'I hope you realise that I would never take anything of yours.'

'Wouldn't you, now?' retorted Saul, through gritted smoke-stained teeth. 'If it weren't for you, this whole stretch of land would be mine, and the entire forest would turn into farmland. But of course, that mayor, while he lived, imposed such laws that removed my rights altogether.'

'Are you talking about Mr King, David's late father?' Suddenly Eric's voice gained in strength. 'I hope you can also recall that he saved you from impending imprisonment, Saul, and that you have your farmland thanks to him.'

'Why, you side-taker!' spat Saul. 'I knew it wouldn't take you long to show your true colours. That man was nothing but a weasel and a traitor. What did he do for his sister, my wife Carolina, when she got ill? Nothing! She died because her family did nothing to help. She was only adopted, not like their favourite son. Expected me to take on the burden... aaah, poor Carolina...'

Saul appeared to be breaking down in a moment of recollection. Eric's voice softened as he attempted to comfort the stricken man.

'Saul, I don't think you realise what they tried to do for Carolina. Joseph King had special musical powers – but he did not realise soon enough what he could do for Carolina. It was too late. She had shut her brothers out. She was going through a terrible mental breakdown and refused to see anyone... you did all you could, Saul.'

'Don't you tell me what my wife went through!' snapped Saul violently. 'As if I didn't know it. And are you telling me that Joseph singing a little ditty over my dying wife was really going to cure her? Ha! Now get me my chickens right now, or you'll feel my whip just like his son David does.'

'Certainly, Saul, certainly. Follow me.' Eric's voice faded, and David and Selina heard the back door slam. Selina, meanwhile, had led David into a large cupboard built into the wall at the back of the lonely room. David's head was reeling from the conversation they had just heard.

'My father was the mayor of Jonastown?' marvelled David, and Selina touched his arm, nodding.

'I guess there are lots of things Saul hasn't told you,' she went on, 'and I wish my father could tell you more, but there isn't time. Soon they may be returning to the house, as I'm sure Saul didn't just come for the chickens, David.'

'The hounds know my scent well,' he assented, nodding fearfully, 'and they start howling in a certain way whenever I am anywhere near them. He knows.'

'David,' she went on, 'there's a secret passage in this cupboard. It leads to two places; upwards goes to the attic and downstairs goes to our cellar. In the cellar, there is a shifting stone, from which another passageway leads you underground, but I don't know how far it goes, as I'm not allowed to go down there. I've often imagined it goes on forever.'

'Forever?' David echoed, feeling a cold shiver.

'Well.' Selina looked slightly uncomfortable in the dim light. 'You know my imagination, David. I really want to go down and explore it. But you have a chance now. I'll have to stay in the house in case Saul returns and they wonder where I've gone.'

'Has your father been down there?' whispered David, uncertainly.

'No, I don't think so,' she replied.

'Then how does he know it's really a passageway?' asked David.

'He found the shifting stone a few days ago, by accident,' she explained, 'but he was meaning to check out the passageway with torchlight this evening.'

Suddenly, both of them froze in terror, for they could hear Uncle Saul and Eric returning to the house, as the sound of howling hounds entered the kitchen downstairs.

'Quick!' cried Selina. 'You must go. When you find the loose stone that reveals the passage, don't go too far. Wait for me to let you know when Saul has gone. Farewell!'

And she gave him a light kiss on his cheek.

'Farewell.' David nodded, feeling suddenly light-headed.

And with this, he walked further into the cupboard, turning on his torch as she closed the door behind him. There was a passageway to the left and steps going down to the right. He walked quickly down the cobwebbed stone steps to the cellar. His torch flashed across a face staring out of the wall, and he shuddered in terror. He soon realised, however, that the face belonged to an old painting that hung there and, catching his breath slowly, he continued down the seemingly never-ending steps until he entered a cold cellar. He shivered, and longed for a log fire to keep him warm during the anxious waiting. He ventured up to a fireplace which lay ahead of him. *Please reveal your hiding place, shifting stone,* he thought. At this moment, he heard the pattering feet of the hounds, and an eerie echo of Saul's voice started to fill the cellar walls with a fiery vengeance, which put out any desire for lighting a fire.

'Now I've got me chickens,' the echo said, 'I'm gonna search your house for that wretched boy! Ooh, when I get my hands on him, he'll have some explaining to do.'

'Er, Saul,' the echo of Eric's voice brought a fearful tremor to the cellar. 'What makes you think that David is hiding in my house?'

'Eric!' yelled Saul. 'I know when David is nearby. My hounds are onto something. And they won't stop searching until they find him.'

Suddenly a high-pitched scream resonated through the walls.

'Now, then!' Saul's victorious voice boomed out louder than ever. 'I've found a child hiding in a corner. But... but... the boy wouldn't wear girl's clothes, would he?'

'That's Selina, my daughter! My poor girl is scared out of her wits. She doesn't like your hounds. And all this racket dragged her out of bed...'

'Doesn't like me hounds?!' said Saul, suspiciously.

'Do put her down, Saul,' commanded Eric, sounding a lot bolder.

'Not until she tells me where David is,' growled Saul. 'She spends so much time with him – I'm quite sure about that. In fact, I wouldn't be surprised if they lived in each other's pockets. Where is he, little girl?'

'I don't know.' Selina's sweet voice was firm, as it bounced off the cellar walls. 'That is – I don't know... exactly.'

'What do you mean, you don't know exactly?' Saul's voice was in harsh contrast to the sweet sound of Selina's.

'Well, I saw a boy who looked like David in the woods yesterday. But, as you said, David always runs from your hounds.'

'So, you don't know where he is?' He was stamping his feet in fury.

'Precisely!' replied Selina, sounding very self-assured.

Some muttering was heard, and then everything went deathly quiet for a few minutes. Then, the sounds of scuffling and howling came, accompanied by heavy footsteps running up the stairs. David began praying under his breath that Saul would not find the cupboard in the lonely cob-webbed room. David frantically searched for the shifting stone in the cellar floor with his torch. In dread, he started to hear the echoes of the hounds' feet pattering down the stairs that led to the cellar. In greater panic, David poked around the fireplace, and then stood up quickly, knocking a large picture from the wall above. It fell with an awful clatter and created shivers of excitement from the hounds in the passageway, which began to howl even louder. As David pushed the picture aside, he noticed a large crack that had formed between two paving stones directly beneath it. The picture's impact seemed to have caused a stone to shift place, and David found that he was able to move it, with great effort, leaving a large hole just big enough for a small person to fit through.

In a few seconds, he had squeezed through the gap and lowered himself into the underground passage. As soon as his feet hit the top of the steps, he hauled the shifting stone back overhead as well as he was able, just as several hounds ran into the cellar. Uncle Saul stormed in soon afterwards, as the rest of the hounds poured in, and David put out his torch and waited. It became evident that the time had come to move swiftly on, for Saul started to create quite a rumpus above, and it sounded as if he was destroying the entire contents of the cellar in his fury. This seemed to be a good moment to start running. His torch went on, and he ran as fast as his legs could carry him, down many steps, until he approached a wide entrance to a mysterious passageway. It looked like an ancient tunnel which seemed to go on for miles, or even, as Selina put it, forever.

'He's been in here; they are picking up his scent!'

He continued to hear that booming voice that filled his being with dread, and with it, the sound of claws scratching away at the cellar floor, as if digging for certain treasure. At this moment, David stumbled across a large rock and, using all his might, he erected it in the entrance of the passageway, hoping that it might block Saul from getting further than the steps, if only temporarily. Then he picked up some smaller rocks and piled them on top of the large rock, knowing it would take time for Saul to remove this obstacle. He realised that it was time to run again when he heard Saul lifting the paving stone and entering the tunnel. And so he ran and ran, deep into the unknown, hoping his torch would sustain him so that he would not run into a wall, or worse still, someone else.

Suddenly he heard his uncle's booming voice. 'I can hear him! I know he's down there. We need light. Get me some light, man!'

That rock should slow them down a little, thought David in some relief. But he kept on running, his heart pounding in his chest, until finally his limbs became painful and he could run no more. He walked on for some time, exhausted and almost ready to collapse, when all of a sudden he heard the howling hounds once again. His heart filled with panic, and once more he took to a sprint, ignoring the pain in his legs. On and on he ran until his legs could take no more, and they gave way beneath him as he collapsed to the tunnel floor.

It was then that David noticed something rather unusual hovering in a recess in the tunnel wall. At first, he thought he could see a black huddled shape that was moving slowly towards him. He could see the flicker of a candle directly behind the rim of a hooded cloak. A face slowly emerged from the cloak. David found the features unusual, for the being had a rather large, knobbly nose, and a greatly protruding chin, unless this was a trick of the candlelight. He lay, frozen to the spot, keeping his eyes on the hooded figure. Perhaps it was sizing him up, preparing to pounce on its victim and make itself a decent-sized meal. Hopefully it only liked vegetables or, better still, perhaps it did not like to eat at all. It was then that the creature chose to speak.

'Halt! Who goes there? Is it friend or foe?'

David paused uncertainly; this could be a coded language for the creatures of this underground world, he considered. The former word might mean the latter, and vice versa.

'Is it friend or foe?' the creature repeated, shining its candle into his face.

'Er... friend... if that's what you are,' David replied quickly.

'Ah! A friend!' The creature sounded delighted, as it clapped its hands together. 'Friend, he says. How wonderful that is! For we haven't seen a friend in this tunnel world for a long stretch... if even at all. Ah, but wait!'

The creature reached out its hands, which were long and thin, and pulled David towards it, so that he could now see its eyes clearly. They shone like turquoise stones and light actually poured out from them onto his own face. He swallowed and blinked nervously.

'But what if he is a deceiver dressed as a friend?' he heard the creature murmur.

The creature's eyes started to pierce his own with their light and as it poured into him, it became almost unbearable. Finally, the creature pulled away and he was surprised to see its eyes light up even more brightly.

'Ah, so you are *him*?' Its voice was full of awe.

Seeing David's puzzled look, the creature continued, 'I am your guide. I have been looking for you for a long time. We are the creatures of the tunnelled worlds. One tunnel always leads to another. The underground is a maze and some from above manage to find their ways here. And you have arrived! So, it must be *time*.'

The last sentence was spoken with a sense of certainty and great significance. David could feel his heart flutter with excitement as he heard the words. Yet he longed to understand what they meant.

'So, who am I?' he asked quietly.

'Who, indeed, are any of us?' This was not the reply he had hoped for, but it made him ponder for a while. That is, until the creature gave a loud, hearty chuckle and slapped him on the back with a surprisingly heavy hand for one so slight and thin.

'That, my boy,' it continued in a mysterious whisper, 'is

something you must find out for yourself. For you have a share in a kingdom that you know nothing of yet. I am here to guide you to it.'

Suddenly, the guide pushed David into the recess in the wall of the tunnel.

'I hear danger in the footsteps of Saul. David, you must hide in the place where you awoke me. Now!'

'You know Uncle Saul?'

But the creature put its finger to its mouth and threw its cloak over them both, blowing out the candle. In a few moments, David could hear the sounds of pattering feet. Then Saul's growling voice followed. They were racing straight towards them. At this moment, David was sure he could feel the guide's eyes piercing into his soul again. And, instead of feeling panic, he became aware of a strange sense of calm.

Soon they were surrounded by the hounds, followed by Saul, who shone a light directly onto them.

'There are so many rocks in here. I wouldn't be surprised if he's hiding behind one of them, just like he moved that big rock to stop us getting in.' Then he raised his voice, 'I'll find you, boy! I didn't train these hounds for nothing, you know. You can run, but you can't hide from Uncle Saul.'

To David's surprise, Saul moved to a rock standing next to them and started searching the recess in the wall where they stood. It appeared that he had not seen them, even with the torchlight directly on them. After searching the recess, Saul said, 'Well, I know that boy's been down here. But somehow he's got past our noses. Eric's in on this, for sure. He and that squealing girl of his have done a dirty deed on me if they have been hiding that boy. We've come to a dead end, boys. The tunnel goes no further. Heel boys, heel!'

The Master

Saul gathered the hounds with a whistle, and David could hear him muttering under his breath, 'What's the point of an underground passage that doesn't even lead anywhere?'

David waited as the footsteps gradually died down. A few lingering echoes bounced off the walls. He could still hear Saul's mysterious words: *the tunnel goes no further.* He thought to himself, *I never noticed an end to the tunnel.* As if in response to his puzzled thoughts, the guide slowly shuffled, seeming to awake from a deep sleep, giving a mighty stretch and a yawn.

'My, that was a pleasant dream,' it sighed. 'I was riding a grand sea horse across the ocean, as in the days before man took over the world and ruined it. But then, of course, we could not tamper with free will, hence evil advanced when the door was opened to it.'

'How could you sleep?' cried David in astonishment. 'Weren't you afraid Uncle Saul would find us?'

On hearing this, the guide let out a hearty chuckle.

'Uncle Saul? Find us behind the cloak? Ha! This cloak is adapted too well to its rocky environment for that. It turns into whatever is around it, as long as you cover yourself with it.'

'I wondered why Saul could neither see nor touch us,' whispered David. 'But now where can we go? For the tunnel has ended.'

He was just about to step out of the cave when the guide

pulled him back and said, 'How do you know the tunnel has ended?'

'Saul himself said so.' David frowned at his guide. 'I guess you were asleep.'

'Did you see the end of the tunnel?' asked the guide.

'Well,' replied David, 'no, I did not. I was pretty certain it went on indefinitely. But when I was running just before I met you I was worn out, and not really looking where I was going. On the other hand, why would Saul see an end if there wasn't one?'

'Or, you could ask why would you *not* see the end of the tunnel if there was one? Who decides where the end really lies? This much I can tell you; this tunnel goes on as long as you want it to, and to wherever you want it to. For you created this tunnel, David. All the years that you wanted to escape from your uncle and be with Selina and her happy family, you built this tunnel in your deepest wishes and dreams. This tunnel brings you escape from the tyranny of Saul.'

The guide let these wonderful insights seep into David's mind.

'Realise that only because you actually came here did you make it real. It is now a tunnel you can walk in physically, not just in your imagination. Until you entered, it was all in your imagination.'

David thought for a moment.

'I often dream of a tunnel of light; an escape route from Saul. But then, Selina knew about this tunnel, as did her father, Eric.'

'That is because it was in their imaginations, too; their escape route from Saul. Great minds think alike, as the Above World saying goes. Of course, we guides of the tunnels have our own saying – great minds think alike, but dreamers think greater still. This ancient proverb reminds us to practise our dreams in reality. You practised your dreams by believing. You believed, therefore you entered.'

The guide paused again to let these enlightening words take root. David was so baffled that he was unable to speak for some time. Finally, he remembered an unanswered question.

'But how did Saul get in?' he asked. 'Does he also wish to escape from something?'

'You have good insight, David,' his guide commended him, 'for Saul does, in fact, run from something which he fears; a monster deep within himself. Yet he does not realise that he can never defeat the monster by running from it, only by confronting it. But this is not the reason for him entering into your tunnel, David. He came in because you did. You had to enter first, because it was your dream. Then in doing so, you made it real for others. But, of course, Saul could get no further than you as you hadn't traversed any more of the tunnel after you fell; hence, for Saul, the end of the passage-way appeared.'

The guide walked out of the cave and beckoned to David, who followed behind. Then, it relit its candle. David surveyed the tunnel and realised that it extended much further than Uncle Saul had been able to believe; in fact, he was convinced it would not come to an end.

The guide continued to speak, 'You may not find Saul much changed by this experience. His type is stubborn and impatient, and his mind is much altered by his drinking.'

'You know about that?' David questioned.

'I told you, I am your guide. And I have long known about your struggle with Saul. So I have been appointed to lead you from the dark pit, to wake up your imagination and many other things. You have a gift which is most rare, and your good nature has been unaltered by the oppression your uncle inflicted on you all these years. If anything, you have learned from it, to cling to what is good. Your joyful times in the tree house will always be remembered by Selina, and will be fresh in her memory by the time you both meet again. But it may not be for a very long time.'

David felt crushed. 'A long time?'

'Alas,' the guide sighed, 'we know how much strength you drew from your friendship with Selina. But you must draw strength from another greater source now.'

'Selina is my closest friend,' continued David, sadly. 'I was hoping that one day I would be adopted by her family.'

'Ah!' cried his guide, clapping his hands together with joy. 'And so you will be one of their family... one day! But first you have another path to pursue. My Master has asked for it, for you are to follow Him.'

'You mean to say that you are here at another guide's bidding?' David was astounded. 'I did wonder why you kept saying "we" rather than "I". Who is your master?'

The guide paused, in deep reverence for the one it spoke of. 'My Master is not of this world. His kingdom extends further than the Above World, so far that it envelops all created things throughout eternity. All is in His hands. Time is man's measure. The sun was our measure before man existed here. But my Master is *without* measure. His power is limitless.'

'Will I come to know your master?' David said, with a shiver.

'You have always known Him,' the guide replied softly. 'You just haven't let Him into your world yet. You used to hear His voice in the soothing of your troubled soul whenever you escaped the tyranny of Saul, as you imagined fresh sea air, even as you stood in your room looking at a picture of a boat on the sea. For you knew your mother was lost at sea when you were just a baby, and found great comfort in imagining that someday you would find her there.'

'*The Voyage of the Dawn Treader*,' David whispered, gazing upwards. 'Selina and I used to imagine we would enter it together in the tree house. I had a picture of a boat in my room which I used to gaze at, but then Uncle Saul destroyed it because he disliked having pictures in the house. But I still imagined it was there, and pretended to enter the picture and breathe its fresh sea air.'

The guide's voice became softer as it continued.

'You used to see His hands blessing your breadcrumbs as you threw them up to the stars with Selina, to make wishes come true. Sometimes you noticed the bread did not return from the stars, for they became your prayers to the listening heavens.'

'He heard my prayers?' marvelled David.

'He hears and knows everything. You heard His voice even in the thunder, taking your part in anger against all Uncle Saul said and did against you. The raindrops were tears from heaven that gave you great comfort as you cried into the night. And the dawn chorus was full of His sunshine and His kind cool breath on your forehead as you awoke with new strength with which to enter the next day.'

'He saw my tears?' David spoke very quietly now.

'He keeps them safely with Him, so He can use them to bring you complete healing one day. For He has cried over them many times.'

The creature paused, looking downcast. It appeared to be clutching its chest in pain. David became aware that its face was wet with tears, and he felt his own eyes welling up as he remembered his lonely times in the Dragon's Dungeon.

As his guide started to speak again, David felt warm tears flowing down his own cheeks and dropping to the ground.

'The Master's singing voice anointed you through the music of the harp, and He listened in pleasure to your song on the farm today.'

'So it *was* Him!' David's voice brightened. 'I thought it was. I *do* know Him!'

'Yet now you must accept Him,' his Guide replied. 'Believe and trust Him and let Him into this tunnel, and all the tunnels of your making, all the rooms of your heart.'

David paused uncertainly.

'You mean I need to ask Him to come into this place? I will see Him face to face?'

'This tunnel is a part of you, for you made it. You must let Him into every part of you. Then His radiant light can flood through your soul and guide you to the way ahead. You will not see me for much longer. I was merely appointed to guide you to the way of life.'

Before the guide had finished speaking, David already found himself on his knees in the tunnel. Preparing to meet with the Creator of all, he felt rather nervous.

But then, in a whisper that was filled with certainty, he said, 'Come in, Master of all things.'

As soon as he had said this, a penetrating light flooded the passageway, and soon he felt a wonderful peace enfolding him. The creature threw itself face down and sang songs of worship to its Master. The rocks trembled as a beautiful melody moved through the passageway, and David could feel His presence, sure and certain. It filled him with complete comfort and assurance. And, as David stayed in the warmth of this heavenly radiance, he felt as if this was where he had been all along. It felt like coming home. By this time, the light was becoming so strong that it was overpowering. And in the blinding light, all David could do was cover his face in wonder as he heard the strong, warm voice of the Master singing over him:

'You are my son.
I am completely delighted in you.
Stay in My ways, for My ways are higher than your ways.
You know only from the beginning of time; My eyes see
      beyond eternity.
Everything is of Me, originally made beautiful.
All have choice, but some have chosen darkness.

But know in Me, you are made whole,
For I knew you before you entered this world,
When you were pure and blameless,
And only through Me can you become
Pure and blameless again.
Dwell in Me, look to Me, My son.'

David stayed that way for a very long time, and he never looked back in the tunnel after that. His spirit was so uplifted, he could have soared as if he had new wings, and he held a new glow of joy that seemed to light up the passage as it shone from his face. He no longer felt fear of Uncle Saul, for he knew that with his all-powerful Master on his side, nothing could harm or conquer him.

The Make-believe Cottage

In that timeless moment, the Master had taken David back
to the pain of the dungeon and removed the loneliness of it
by standing there with him. Somehow, he knew he would
never be alone in his suffering again. David slowly raised
himself to his feet, feeling as if he had just awoken from a
heavenly sleep, and looked around him. He realised that his
guide had disappeared. But in its place was its cloak, lying on
the tunnel ground. He picked up this garment of protection,
and put it on with a new sense of purpose and certainty as
he continued moving down the long passage that lay before
him.

After walking for a while he started to wonder how far his
imagination had extended the passage, for he was beginning
to feel rather hungry. His meeting with the Creator had been
timeless, for the Master was one of eternity, and therefore
David did not know whether it was day or night. He checked
his watch; it read six, and he presumed it must have been six
in the morning. He started to wish more than ever for some
fresh eggs and a cup of something hot.

At this moment, he realised he could actually smell cooking eggs, and all of a sudden some rocks in the wall to the
left started to turn and move aside with a great tremor.
Daylight fell through the gap and the rocks took turns to
move so that they jutted out, forming steps going upwards.
With an eager heart he skipped up through the narrow
opening and met the warmth of the sun. He also came face

to face with a crowing cockerel, standing on a scarecrow. The cockerel received quite a fright when David emerged from the passageway and it let out a loud squawk, falling off its perch.

'Sorry!' cried David. 'Do start the dawn chorus again, you poor thing.'

To David's utter amazement, the cockerel swiftly replied, 'Well, of all the cheek! I shall jolly well do as I wish, for I rule the roost here, David.'

'You can talk!' David exclaimed. 'And you know my name!'

'If I didn't know your name,' continued the indignant cockerel, 'then I wouldn't think you were worth speaking to.'

'In that case,' David replied with a smile, 'I shall take that as a compliment. But I'm really sorry to have caused you to fall off your perch.'

'Well, as it's you, David,' the cockerel's tone softened a little, 'I'll let you off this time. I must say that few people I have met emerge from the ground in that undignified fashion. I suppose you are only new; the latest talk of the Tunnel World, and the Above World. Saul's been stirring a hornet's nest and believe me, I don't like hornets.'

Before David could respond to this, the cockerel hopped back onto its scarecrow perch and restarted its strident crowing. David stood back with his hands on his ears and even made faces, but the cockerel paid no heed and merely carried on louder than before, though with some strain on its part. So David thought it safer to move away, and he moved towards a lovely little cottage that stood further down the path.

It reminded him of the cottage made of sugar in the fairy tale *Hansel and Gretel*. It looked like a delicious cake with thick icing as its roof. The slightly lopsided chimney appeared to be a giant chocolate flake, which blew out perfectly round rings of pink smoke. The aroma of the smoke gently rose up David's nose, and filled his lungs with the most delightful warmth. There was so much to imagine in this smell; a large English breakfast, lentil and ham soup and fresh home-made bread.

He found he had already entered the little front garden by a petite pink gate that looked like candy when he saw a small, stout lady open the cottage door and rush eagerly towards him. He noticed what a typical farmer's wife she looked, as she shuffled excitedly along the cobbled stone path between beds of luscious multicoloured flowers. She walked quickly, on tiny feet that just managed to support her rather overbearing frame. It was evident that she was as jolly as her rosy complexion gave her credit for, and her chuckles surrounded him with warmth. As he looked at her bright eyes, he felt further from Uncle Saul than ever.

David wondered if this fairy-tale cottage could also have been of his own imagining. Everything was so perfect and peaceful, with the exception of the rash cockerel, which was just quietening down.

Finally, the jolly farmer's wife reached him and took his hands.

'Well, well, well!' She cried in a high-pitched voice. 'You look like you think you're imagining things, and like you think this fancy cottage is also of your making. Well, let it be said quickly that it is a cottage of mine and my husband's imagining.' She tugged him up the garden path, and prac-tically ran to the front door and put David's fingers against it. 'And you can taste it... yes, go ahead, my dear!'

Here she left little time for a breath, but David just managed to give a satisfied 'Yum!' in response to his first enlightening taste.

She continued, 'I think it's the best edible cottage in the world, because – best of all – it can never be totally eaten. That's right! As soon as you eat it, it comes back again. Every sugary mouthful you take is replaced just as fast.'

With this, she brought him inside the house and he looked around in awe as she continued to jabber on. There was a welcoming fireplace in a cove of the room, where a simmering pot sat, and a round table laid out with knives and forks and tall pink chairs surrounding it. Above all, he admired the ceiling, which was held by low beams that smelt suspiciously of chocolate. The ceiling looked like light pink candy floss, in which was embedded sweets of all colours that glistened like treasures. David rubbed a part of a chocolate beam with his finger and licked it. It was beautifully intoxicating, so much that it left him feeling rather light-headed. He had quite forgotten that the farmer's wife was still chattering away to him until she laughed in delight at the effect the chocolate was having on him.

'What an invention – never-ending food! And it all started with a dream – a dream shared by me and my dear husband, Derek. And, as you can see, whatever my guest wishes for appears in my cooking pot.'

'So you can dream things to life in the Above World as well as in the tunnel?' David asked.

'Above World?' she cried in surprise. 'This is not the Above World at all; no sir! You can only get here from the tunnel; whatever you imagine from the tunnel, you can enter.'

'But if this isn't the Above World,' he asked, 'then how can the sun shine here?'

'Ah, bless me,' she chuckled, patting him on the head. 'You have to imagine that the sun is in the sky for it to be there at all. But once it's there, it stays there, and it will never set unless someone remembers to set it. Oh, the bother it can be putting the children to bed at night when they don't want to go to sleep. They make the sun appear again long after I've set it. I have to set it again and again on some nights.'

David laughed as he watched his food laying itself on the table before him. 'It sounds like a fun game to me. I never had such fun in our farmhouse.'

She peered down at David in a motherly way and lowered her voice. 'You are quite safe from Uncle Saul here.'

'You know him too?' David asked in amazement.

'Know him?' she gasped. 'Dear me, no! I have never even ventured into the Above World at all. I was born and bred here; in a world of my parents' making. Yet Above World messages travel ever so quickly to us Tunnel World folk. Now then, enjoy your lovely food.'

The food was every bit as good as David imagined. In fact, he enjoyed it so much that he forgot to stop imagining the food, so that it kept arriving on his already full plate. When he found himself absent-mindedly embarking on his third helping of bacon and sausages, fortunately his kind host informed him of this issue. And so, the eating done, David sat back in the pink chair feeling rather bloated, but very well nourished. He was then handed a glass of fresh orange juice, and it was the most refreshing juice he had ever tasted.

At this moment, the pot on the fireplace began to simmer, and he began to wonder how it was making food again all by itself, for he had certainly had his fill. The raised eyebrow from his host conveyed that she suspected he had a part to play, but a few seconds later, all questions were answered as the farmer himself entered into the scene with a merry whistle.

'So you brought the pink rings out of the chimney earlier, young lad?' he said jovially, scraping his huge boots on the mat at the door. 'Well, now it's my turn. That be right, Ellie?'

He gave his wife an embrace that swept her off her tiny feet, causing colour to rush to her cheeks.

'That be right, my Derek!' she said with a giggle, fanning herself with a fan that had only just appeared in mid air.

Derek gazed at her affectionately for a few seconds, then he turned to shake hands with David.

'So, you're David,' he said, seeming rather excited to have met him, 'the talk of the Tunnel World. But, of course, that was written about from the beginning.'

'What was written?' David asked him.

'The prophesy of old is written in the first ancient tunnel walls that were ever created...'

'You mean that there's a prophesy about *me*?' David asked in awe.

'Yes,' replied Derek. 'It tells us of a great musician who is from the Tunnel World line of ancient kings, but who would be born in the Above World. It says that he will free all dimensions from a creature of darkness, through his divinely gifted music.'

'Derek, do you really think he's the *One*?' Ellie interrupted.

'He bears all the signs,' went on Derek earnestly. 'Born in the Above World, and possessing a rare gift in music... and breaking free of his dungeon, and making his tunnel here. Few people from the Above World manage to enter the tunnel they have imagined, or come to believe in its existence.'

'All this time I lived in one world,' David murmured thoughtfully, 'not knowing that there were two dimensions to it. It feels like I have woken up, but I do not know fully into what, and I do not know where my future in this strange world lies.'

'Who knows their own future?' replied Derek, eyeing up his food as he sat down beside David. 'All I know is what I imagine to be the future.'

Meanwhile, Ellie stood ready with a bowl to catch Derek's soup, with a particular smile on her face.

'Oh!' Derek let out a raucous laugh. 'That was a close one! Thanks to Ellie, my food has not landed on the floor. I forgot to imagine a bowl, but you did it for me. Now that's what we call team work. Ha ha!'

David laughed at this simple mistake, wondering how long it would take for unaccustomed folk like him to get used to this radical way of life. Presently, he was stirred from his imaginings as Ellie tapped him on the shoulder.

'Now remember this,' she chirped. 'It all begins with dreams. What is your greatest dream? That will provide you with the next step in your own journey of discovery.'

David felt fresh desires welling up from within, and words poured out of his mouth like a torrent of water.

'I'd like to play music that influences everyone who hears it so much that they become better people. It will be music that heals every part of a person's mind, body and soul. The Master anointed me for this task when He met with me.'

Derek and Ellie were holding their breath in awe at the mention of the Master, as they looked down proudly at David.

'I think you have found the path to your future,' said Derek softly, 'for your future is with Him. In fact, your future *is* Him.'

As David left the lovely cottage some time later, Ellie pressed something warm into his hand. It looked like a large pink cake in the shape of a heart that shone out from his hand like a glowing lantern.

'Remember,' she whispered softly, 'you may eat this cake. Yet it can never be fully eaten, for it represents the love of the Master, which is eternal. But this is not a heart we have imagined. It was given to us by three visitors from the tunnels. Take it as a constant reminder of His love for you.'

On hearing these words, David was suddenly over-whelmed with a deep sense of healing power, and he gazed deeply into the heart as it shone back at him.

Derek's hand was on his shoulder. 'Return to us whenever you need to, son, for your path is never far from us. Our home is yours.'

'I shall return,' David promised, 'as surely as I first set foot here.'

'I should hope so!' replied Derek, winking. 'Now remember, you can use this heart as a light, and as protection against fear and all danger. It is the Master's love that you feed on, and His perfect Love casts out fear. Farewell, my dear son!'

David took a bite from the cake, and felt wonderfully reassured as he walked down the stony steps beside the cockerel's scarecrow perch to re-enter his tunnel.

The Grand Concert Hall

He was pleased to find that the walls of the passage were still glowing with supernatural light, and also that a wonderful melodic sound greeted him. The distant music of a violin and a harp were echoing round the walls, seeming to dance together.

'Oh, if I could get my hands on a harp of my own, the future would seem grand!' David spoke his wishes out loud.

The moment his voice echoed out to meet the sounds of the instruments, a strange change came across the tunnel – he saw that the walls were instantly filled with instruments, shining like silver and gold treasures in the dim light. The nearest instrument happened to be a harp. David ran to it and tenderly picked it up from its shelf. It was shining from its case, as if it had a light within, and on its frame it bore beautiful engravings that appeared to be in a foreign language. How he longed to play as he had heard his father play when he was young. This had been before his father had grown frail from his rare, fatal illness.

As if hearing his inner wish, the harp itself stepped out of its case and placed itself by his side, starting to play, and jogging his fingers with its strings. So David responded with great happiness, and as he did so, he saw his own name being scrawled on to the harp case in wonderful shiny golden writing. His heart leapt for joy and he let out a cry of wonder. How much freedom he found, as he plucked the harp's strings. He had always longed for a harp of his own.

Suddenly, all the instruments on the shelves started playing excitedly at once, until there was such a crescendo that David wished they would all stop. And so they did, just as he wished it, and at this moment he became aware of another musical sound; the echoes of an orchestra tuning up bounced around the walls.

'I don't think I was imagining that,' he said aloud. 'But how I would love to play in an orchestra! Yet how am I to carry all these instruments?'

The question was answered swiftly as the instruments started to pack themselves in their cases, and a huge trolley suddenly flew in which they all jumped on. David waited for a moment and then gingerly climbed on to the trolley to see what would happen. As soon as he did so, the trolley took off and they were transported down the tunnel at a terrifying speed, until David could bear it no more and cried out, 'Orchestra hall, come quickly for me!'

Sure enough, the trolley made a sharp turning to the right, and came to an abrupt halt. David and the instruments somehow managed to stay on the trolley in front of the grand archway at which they had arrived. It was beautifully decorated, with the same engravings of a foreign language as David had seen on his harp. It was the entrance to a grand, well-polished concert hall, in which they could see a large orchestra bustling around. Many of the players were already seated, but there was much movement due to new arrivals, who were rushing around to get ready. However, on looking more carefully at those unpacking their cases, he soon realised that they were not people at all, but instruments that were unpacking themselves.

'They must have come with *someone*,' David thought, and then he sighed aloud. 'What a relief! It looks like there are other latecomers, too. I had hoped that I wouldn't be the only one who was late.'

To his surprise, the trolley answered him in a sharp metallic tone, 'Why, of course, my lad! If you hadn't wished for it, it wouldn't have happened that way at all.'

In response, the instruments all giggled in their cases. David looked at the trolley in utter amazement. Well, he thought to himself, if things happen when I imagine it, then how did that trolley speak when I didn't imagine it could speak at all? He then started to wonder if someone else was imagining it for him, and soon enough he saw who he thought must be the conductor staring fixedly at him with a wry smile. He had a stern face and a long pointed nose, on which a pair of tiny spectacles were lightly perched. He also had a rather harsh voice.

'No time for delay, David! These other latecomers you have imagined hardly camouflage your own late arrival. They merely highlight the fact that you are the last one here, and they appear to require someone to give them direction, as they don't know how to organise themselves. They are clambering around like a pile of ninnies! Sort out this cacophony right away, or it will draw all pleasant music far away from here.'

At this moment, David was tipped rather ungracefully from the trolley onto a nearby seat, and his harp landed clumsily against his shoulder, mirroring his own inner tension. *I do think that perhaps I haven't imagined the conductor at all*, he thought. At this point, his thoughts were interrupted by a protest made by the large cello which had seated itself next to him.

'Hey!' it cried impertinently. 'I'm not an instrument. David has not imagined me.' As David examined the cello more closely, he realised that it was supported by a red-haired boy of his own age, who looked remarkably like himself.

'Hi David,' the boy said with a smile. 'My name's Nathan. It's great to meet you at last. I've imagined my own instruments, too. Problem is, it's hard to stop imagining them once you start!'

He pointed at the streams of music stands running in, carrying music cases with their strange metallic hands. Meanwhile, the conductor, who had been watching David rather suspiciously, screeched out, 'Order! I would appreciate it if you would stop conversing with your cello, David, and concentrate your energies on something useful... like imagining away this pile of music stands.'

'I am a boy, not a cello!' shouted Nathan, popping his head out from behind his cello. 'And the music stands are mine.'

Nathan's voice gave the conductor such a start that he jumped back, hitting himself in the head with his stick, and he fell off his platform. In response, the music stands started to laugh in a metallic chorus, and Nathan proceeded to go bright red. He had taken his imagining a little too far, as he could see in the conductor's fiercely bulging eyes and steaming face.

Nathan quickly suggested, in a tone of the utmost submission, 'I'll get them all to leave if you'd like, sir, so you'll know I'm not just a cello with a head.'

Taking in a deep breath to calm his rage, the conductor replied in a grave tone, 'I would be most obliged if you would do so, boy.'

Nathan shut his eyes tightly, and David noticed everyone else in the room doing the same, so he followed suit, to make the job easier. Together they imagined that the extra music stands were leaving the room, and the noise they made soon became a distant echo.

'Now!' the conductor called. 'As I already know who David is, may I learn your name, young man?'

'Nathan King,' replied Nathan.

A look of realisation came across the conductor's old, worn face. It was as if a parting in the clouds had occurred and a momentary glow of youth rested on his cheeks. His voice softened slightly towards his new pupil.

'You must be Ruben's lad. You have the same glow of red

hair. I remember tutoring him in the Above World, just before I discovered this place. What a fine cellist he was. I should have known that he had a Tunnel World gift – and to think his own son made it here. I guess that means Ruben is here himself now? Some never find this world, you know, even though they were meant to... For, to enter it, one must have an open and imaginative mind.'

He appeared to be visualising a world from the past. It was a memory that restored some more of his youthful glow. But soon, he became aware of himself again and returned to the present.

'Enough distraction.' His fierce voice returned. 'Tune up immediately! Unless the instruments have already done it themselves. And start playing... right away!'

'But what are we to play?' questioned David, in surprise.

'Play anything you like,' came the conductor's wild reply, as he started to jab at the air fiercely with his stick, as if expecting a sound to come out of it.

Then, all at once, the hall was filled with the most beautiful music. Sheets of music appeared on some stands as their owners played, whilst on David's and Nathan's stands there appeared nothing whatsoever. They found that they were able to play entirely by ear, and so finely tuned was David's ear that he continued to play melodies that surprised the conductor and captured the emotions of every person present. Soon everyone else stopped playing and listened. And as he played, he felt himself physically rising into the air for the first time. All he knew was that this song was a new break-through of worship to his Creator, and he danced high up around the angel figures in the ceiling, while he and his harp continued to be filled with warm melodies. Nathan joined him with rich harmonies on the cello, and became better by the second. It appeared that he too could defeat gravity, although he was more aware of it, and would often float back to the floor due to this awareness.

Soon, the conductor was heard tapping his stick on his stand, telling David to get off the ceiling with a rather nervous voice. It was evident that he had rarely seen anyone with this ceiling walking ability, if at all.

'Time to change tune,' he screeched, hoping that this would bring David back down to earth level; however, he was mistaken.

For David and the other players were so deeply engrossed in the music that they appeared to be in a sort of trance, and the conductor soon had to give up his efforts to restrain them. He quickly came to realise that David needed to be free in order to play to his full potential. As the playing continued, David found that he was singing words he did not understand; a new language seemed to flow from his tongue as if someone else was putting the words there. He wondered if it could be the language of the Master.

Meanwhile, all his other instruments had joined him and were playing themselves in mid air. So engrossed was he in composing melodies on each instrument simultaneously, that he did not notice the audience that entered the concert hall. People were coming from far and wide to listen to the music which they had heard from the tunnels; people from all over the world. The tunnels were also packed with people trying to get in to the hall. Many people who had illnesses left healed; those who came depressed left with a joyful, radiant glow on their faces, and all left singing wonderful songs of praise. Even after all the crowds had left, David continued to dance around the ceiling, feeling as happy as a skylark for some time. There, he drifted off into a peaceful sleep, floating on a rocking chair in mid air.

Tunnel World Academy of Music

It seemed a few minutes later when David heard Nathan's voice waking him. His rocking chair was already floating gently to the ground.

'Guess what, David? We've been enrolled in the greatest music school in the world – Tunnel World Academy of Music!'

'But how can I have been enrolled when I've been fast asleep?'

'I don't know,' Nathan replied. 'When I went to enrol, I found your name already on the list. I presume your father must have been here to enrol you.'

'No, he wasn't here,' David said quietly. 'He is dead.'

Nathan gulped audibly, and looked very downcast.

'But we were trying to find him... all this time...'

'You knew my father?'

'Yes,' replied Nathan slowly. 'I am your cousin, David. Your father, Joseph, is my father's brother.'

'You're my *cousin*?' cried David, welling up with joy.

'Yes,' replied Nathan. 'And my father and I have been looking for you and your father for a long time. Your father went missing in search of you down the tunnels a few years ago.'

'Wait,' David interrupted, 'you mean that my father found the tunnels?'

'Yes. He knew that you were alive somewhere, but as Saul had moved to a place in the middle of the mass of farmlands that no one had heard of, it was very hard to track you down. So he tried the tunnels in a desperate attempt to find you.'

'Wait a minute!' David interrupted again. 'You mean my father was still alive... after Uncle Saul had taken me in?!'

'He never really died,' was the unexpected answer.

'What?' David's mind was racing. 'But I saw him die. With my own eyes...'

'What I mean to say is,' Nathan went on, 'his apparent death was only temporary. We found a cure... although it took us time to find one.'

'So my father is still... alive?' He could barely speak the words.

'Unless he died again, yes!' answered Nathan. 'After Saul took you away, insisting that he would take good care of you, my father took your father's body to the cellar of our house, where they had been attempting to find a cure since your father had been poisoned.'

'You think someone poisoned him?'

'Well, it was like no illness mankind had ever encountered. All the symptoms were illogical and there was no apparent cause for them, other than a slow form of poisoning. Then, my father came across a new discovery that changed our lives forever. Whilst my father sat by Uncle Joseph, your father, in his months of suffering, they dreamed great things. After your father's death, my father discovered that their dreams were real. One day he stumbled across an underground tunnel in the cellar, which led him to the cure for your father's illness. And he learned that your father was not really dead, but asleep. He found a healing potion, and with one drop your father became as fresh as the dawn. We were celebrating all day and your father spoke only of you and how he wanted to find you. By that time, you had been living with Saul for two years already, and when we went to find his home, we discovered it burnt to the ground. We could only hope that you had not been inside when it happened.'

'The Master rescued me and took me out of the house,' David replied slowly.

'You've met the Master?' cried Nathan, in joy. 'I've met Him too. It was when we really started to search for answers and we prayed to him in desperation. I met my tunnel guide then, and he showed me the way to the Master. Then, we went on a search of all the farmlands, looking for signs of the vanished farmer. His story created quite a legend amongst the country folk; for all had heard of his foul temper and threats of burning down farmhouses. Some thought he was the cause of his wife's death, for he led her to drink in her misery. Children were told that they would meet Saul and his hounds if they stayed out too late, and that was normally enough persuasion for them to avoid the woods altogether after sunset. There were rumours that some children had seen a mysterious cloaked figure hovering in the woods on a moonlit night, moving towards them with deep, growling breath. These children were not all fortunate enough to escape, according to the stories.'

David stared vacantly at Nathan as he returned to the memory of the fire. He knew now that this had been Saul's attempt to take his own life, as well as David's. In a drugged-up and highly deluded state, in heavy mourning for the loss of his wife, Saul had somehow put the blame on David. However, after tying David up at the heavy wooden table, Saul fell asleep in the fumes, whilst several of his hounds whined around him. Finally, David saw them take Saul's coat sleeves in their teeth and drag him slowly out of the burning house. Finding himself totally alone in the furnace, David cried out at the top of his lungs to the heavens. And someone heard his cry. He felt someone untying his ropes, although he could see nothing. Then they took him in their arms and carried him out to safety. There, he found Saul waking up...

'I was with you in the flames.'

David could see the Master standing in front of him now, in the present, gazing at him with love in his eyes. He could feel His warm hand on his shoulder, and he knew in that moment that the Master had always been with him in the flames.

'My father is alive?' David murmured.

He found himself staring into his cousin's emerald-green eyes.

'Yes,' Nathan replied, seemingly unaware of the Master's visitation. 'And if he has died since, then we can soon revive him. All you have to do is *imagine* a curing potion that in every way counterbalances the one used to kill an individual.'

'But why would anyone want to kill my father?' David asked.

'I have no more ideas than you,' Nathan replied, looking quite lost. 'All I know is, it happened around the time Saul wanted to acquire some land, and your father led a petition and helped the other farmers to win a case against him. Your father was the mayor of the region, and had friends in high places. On a previous occasion Saul faced a prison sentence for vandalising local farmhouses and stealing hens. But your father, in his mercy, managed to lighten the sentence when Saul pleaded with him and promised he would change his wicked ways and his drinking habits. His behaviour only changed for the worse, as I am sure you must have experienced. David, what was it like – all those years you spent on the farm?'

'I don't like to talk about it really,' replied David, 'as I've only recently escaped. I got used to thinking about positive things. I tried to remember my father and how much he loved me, and tried to remember my mother, from what he'd told me. Do you know much about her?'

Nathan looked at him sadly. 'All I know is, she died soon after you were born. Uncle Joseph said an evil wind had blown her from a cliff into the sea, and she was never found. She had said she could hear singing in the waves, and that she wanted to know what it was. Your father found this on the shore – her own hand-embroidered shawl. I think you should have it.'

Nathan respectfully gave David a sea-green piece of material. It still had the pleasing smell of perfume, mixed with the fresh scent of the sea. His eyes filled with tears. He could feel his cousin's hand rest gently on his shoulder.

'Come, David. We must go to class.'

David's eyes never left the shawl as he followed his cousin into the next period of their shared life. He felt that this was the dawn of an exciting age of discovery. Together, they walked through a narrow corridor that was dimly lit by lamps that burned from coves in the walls. It felt very like the history museum he remembered entering with his father years ago. They came towards a group of young adults, who appeared to be waiting in front of an old, wooden door at the end of the corridor. They were talking about music and what subjects they hoped to be covering that term. As David and Nathan approached, the talking died down and the young adults turned to stare at them fixedly, as if trying to ascertain what these youngsters might be doing at the academy. They both felt a little uncertain as they joined the line of students. Fortunately, they did not have to endure the awkward silence for long, as a shrill voice from behind them commanded their attention.

'Form a straight line, class!'

She was a middle-aged lady of the utmost elegance. David noticed how prim and proper she was, as she peered down at them through little round spectacles, which made her look surprisingly like the conductor. David wondered if they may even be related. Yet, despite her forbidding appearance, his instincts told him that she was a very just and understanding lady. Somehow, he knew that if anyone gave them any trouble for being younger, she would soon give them cause to regret it.

She leaned in and whispered in David's ear, seeming to understand his thoughts:

'Quite right, David! And you two are not the only young students. There are the Bellini cousins, who are only two years your senior. And there will be a new girl coming later in the term who is your age. The five of you have been selected from all the young people in the world on the basis of your rare genius in music.'

David and Nathan, who overheard the last part of this, found themselves colouring slightly at this praise. Seeing this, the lady smiled and continued, 'And with your rare wisdom and gifts, you must assist the teachers here to add to the learning of your fellow students. My name is Miss Tree, and I will be your principal music tutor during your time at this academy. I teach the exceptional students.'

At this point, Miss Tree turned her attention towards two Italian-looking boys who had just arrived. They were whispering to each other and staring at David and Nathan.

'And if any student gives you less of a welcome than you deserve,' she raised her voice, 'they will have to contend with me.'

The Bellini cousins looked a little uncomfortable and coloured slightly. And with that, Miss Tree marched to the front of the line of students and opened the old door.

'Come in! Come in!' she called.

The Secret Room

And so, the lessons began. The first was called Musicolourgy, which was a general overview of the techniques of creating colours, or emotions, in music. Initially, David marvelled that, besides Miss Tree and the students, the room was completely empty. Surely they would have need for textbooks, or some sort of writing? But, to his surprise, none of the lessons involved any writing. All learning appeared to be 'off the page' and what was once an empty room soon appeared to be full of the creations of the entire class's imaginations. The Bellini cousins sat behind him and Nathan in class, and he would often hear them whispering spiteful things and smirking. Not too often, though, as Miss Tree's keen ear would soon pick them up and lines were consequently handed out. However, at break times, David and Nathan were not so fortunate as to avoid the cousin's sneers, and the Bellinis would do anything to torment them.

David and Nathan tried to decipher where their insecurities lay, and made every effort to help them in any way possible; such was their understanding and caring natures. They learned that both cousins, as well as being exceptionally talented, came from rich and successful Italian families. The leader of the duo was Leo and the other was Vinny. Their fathers dreamed of being even richer than they already were, and had become involved with a plot of great corruption that had led them to join the Mafia. David and Nathan had learned this information from Leo and Vinny themselves, as they used to threaten to set their family's mafia on them. On once such occasion, Leo and Vinny were just about to hit the Kings when the bells that hung in the academy's cathedral chimed to foretell the start of lessons, taking the Bellinis by surprise, and the Kings had escaped from their grips and rushed back to class.

For this reason, the Kings had taken to spending most of their time outside of lessons in one of the practice rooms, which they would lock themselves inside for the duration of break time. Here, they felt fully safe to be themselves and they would play music together and make up stories and act out plays of their own. At times, David felt like he was back in his haven, Selina's tree house. For like with Selina, he had a place of safety in his friendship with Nathan. And so, in this way, the two friends found in each other wonderful imaginative company, managing to avoid the taunts of the Bellini cousins for a good year.

Leo and Vinny could not find their hiding place, as it was a special room that no other students knew about. Miss Tree had entrusted the knowledge of the room, its whereabouts and its unusual access, to David as she felt he out of all the students may have the most need of it for his own protection. The room had a code by which individuals could enter it; they would have to speak in the Master Tongue. This was the foreign language that David had seen inscribed over the concert hall, and which he himself had automatically learned to speak in song. The words were: 'I am the gate; You must enter through Me.' When these words were spoken in the Master Tongue, a gate would form in the wall and then open. It would close behind those who entered, leaving a wall behind it, so that no one could know of its existence. Only Miss Tree and one other teacher knew – the conductor.

The conductor, as it turned out, was Miss Tree's elder brother, and he was also the headmaster of the academy, and although he was fearsome, he also had a heart of gold underneath his tough exterior. And the Kings came to like him very well. Sometimes he would turn up in their secret room and take them by surprise. But Miss Tree had a greater respect for their privacy, and never entered that room unless they requested it, for she knew they spent a lot of their time in there. The room was soundproof and they knew that they could make as much noise as they liked. On one occasion when they were in the midst of a particularly noisy scene which they were acting out with musical accompaniment, the headmaster made one of his unexpected visits. During this visit, he let them in on a secret, which he thought it would be wise to warn them about.

'There was one other, who had access to this room.' His shrill voice was down to a whisper. 'A former student of this school who turned away from healing music to sorcery and dark powers.'

David and Nathan listened in awe. They loved to hear stories of past students, but this seemed beyond anything they had heard so far.

'Yes, I remember him well, because he was, like your-selves, one of the most talented young people to enter this building. His name was Diago Morton, but after he left the academy he became known as Dragatorn. He could have used his powers for great good, but no. He strove for personal power. He did not care to help others. By the time he left this school, he had taken all the knowledge he needed, which he used to secure a dark future for himself. The last thing I heard, he came to an untimely end when he met his match; a man of great power in healing music came against him with the Master's love, and in that man's sacri-ficial death the sorcerer was reduced to nothing more than a mere shadow, lurking in the darkest night, hoping to find a weak-minded individual to possess.'

He paused, as if for dramatic effect. Then he raised his eyebrows, looking very eerie in the candlelight.

'That man who sacrificed himself was your father, David,' he went on.

'But Mr Tree, my father is alive,' David said quickly.

'How can that be?' the headmaster queried, a deep furrow forming on his brow. 'He took Dragatorn's poison, which he learned was destined for you, because of the prophecy. He had not yet entered the tunnel he had created, but he had learned of many things; he knew that poison could not be destroyed until it was drunk by one of the descendants of the Tunnel World kings, and his sacrifice did so much more than he could have imagined.'

'Mr Tree,' Nathan interrupted, 'there is indeed good reason to believe that my uncle, Joseph King, may still be alive. Before he succumbed to the poison, he and my father dreamed of a sort of antidote. As my uncle was dying, my father and I worked hard to imagine this potion into existence. When we saw my uncle come back to life, we realised that the potion we had brought into being may have been able to reverse death itself. But soon afterwards, my uncle disappeared in a tunnel search for David and neither of us have seen him since.'

'Well,' the headmaster replied, 'if what you say is true and David's father is, in fact, still alive, the fates of the whole of Tunnel World and Above World do not rest entirely on David alone.'

'Mr Tree,' David interrupted, 'what is this prophecy, and how does it involve me?'

'The prophecy of the tunnel guides of old,' answered the headmaster, with great reverence, 'was connected to the terrible curse that fell on the Tunnel World when one of its powerful guides turned his back on the Creator. Many have come to believe that this powerful guide is one and the same as Dragatorn. He lost his power when the Creator threw him from the Tunnel World. But man has given him access again – and we have, I suppose, been partly responsible with the training we gave him, for him to go on to become the terrible sorcerer he is today. The curse of Dragatorn is manifested in the pain that we see in the Above and the Tunnel World – although those who use their gift of imagining can limit its power. The prophecy was that the curse could be reversed by a musically gifted descendant of the line of the ancient kings, who reigned in the Tunnel World since the beginning of time. Your father's drinking of the poison has started to reverse that curse. But I sense much more has yet to happen to fully destroy it. That may be where you come in...'

'But if my father has destroyed the poison, does that mean that we are temporarily safe from Dragatorn?' questioned David.

'Most certainly not!' cried the headmaster. 'One more thing you should know about Dragatorn – he is highly inventive, and the moment one of his terrible schemes fails, be assured that he will be starting on a new plan. He knows about this room, not that he has any power to use it now – unless he finds a weak-minded individual.'

As he said this, he started to disappear from their sight, as if in a mist. He would often leave when he was saying something really important; such was his habit.

David and Nathan stared at each other in the candlelight, both feeling a shiver of fear.

'How does he disappear like that?' Nathan still seemed unnerved by it, although it had happened several times previously.

'More importantly,' David said, 'why would he not have told us that piece of important information before?'

'Perhaps he thinks it's of no risk to us,' replied Nathan. 'At least, I hope it isn't.'

'I've thought of something,' David said suddenly. 'If Dragatorn would have to speak the Master Tongue to get in here, surely he would rather avoid this place like the plague.

He would hate anything connected with the Master – all that is good.'

'That's a good point,' said Nathan with a smile, feeling a rising certainty that they really must be safe from harm. 'Otherwise, Miss Tree would never have let us in here, would she?'

'I'm sure you're right,' sighed David. 'I'm sure he would have better things to do than bother some school boys in their secret room, anyway. If power was really the main thing on his mind, that is. So my father knew about this place, even before he died... he knew about the prophecy. Maybe it *was* him who put my name on the enrolment list. But then why hasn't he come to find me?'

'Your name was engraved in old writing,' murmured Nathan thoughtfully, 'as if someone from centuries back had written it down. Maybe one of the prophets themselves had done it. The parchment on which the names were written looked rather decayed.'

'There are so many mysteries yet to uncover,' said David, rather jovially. 'What a strange adventure we find ourselves in!'

They were then interrupted by the cathedral bell, commanding them to return to lessons. Quickly, they got to their feet, and spoke the Master Tongue to reopen the door. They found themselves once again in the basement that had one set of winding stairs covered with cobwebs. They moved up it in their normal cautious fashion, checking that there were no eyes watching them from above. As usual, no one was lurking in the corridor, for this was the most secluded part of the school, and no students or teachers had any need to use these parts. However, on walking up another staircase they entered a corridor, at the end of which they came face to face with the Bellini cousins.

'There they are!' cried Leo, as they cornered them. 'Where've you been? If you don't tell us, we'll set the mafia on you. They know how to find hiding places.'

Before the Kings could respond, sharp hands appeared on Leo and Vinny's shoulders, shortly followed by the prim and proper voice of Miss Tree.

'Lessons, please! Unless you would prefer to have a detention.'

And so off they scuttled.

The rest of the year passed with considerable joy in learning and laughter. As the following year came, David began to share more with his friend about Selina, whom he missed dearly. Nathan realised that she must have been a very special friend to help David in all his troubled times, and he came to know her through what David told him. Nathan thought that Selina must be quite unlike most of the girls who he had met, as they appeared dull and boring and their pursuits lacked adventure. He told David that she would soon discover the Tunnel World, as she was so gifted and imaginative.

'Yes, but she would not come to this academy,' David sighed, 'for her gift was not musical. Yet her creative ability was very high, and she wrote wonderful stories.'

'Hey,' Nathan said suddenly, 'I wonder what happened to that girl who was supposed to be joining the academy later in our first year? Two school years have passed and she never came.'

'Perhaps she could not find the tunnel,' David replied.

'How would we have known about her down here, then?'

'Well, everyone knew about me. Maybe she's famous too?' David suggested.

'You're different,' his cousin said, smiling at him. 'There are no prophecies about her.'

Later that day, they were walking from the classroom to their secret room, with the Bellinis following close behind with their usual mafia threats, when they saw a girl of their age standing by Miss Tree's office with a large suitcase and several instruments. Two adults who must have been her parents stood beside her, talking to Miss Tree in amiable voices. On seeing Miss Tree, Leo and Vinny backed off, as they always did whenever they walked past her office – which was how they had never found the secret room, the staircase to which appeared near to her office. At this moment, Miss Tree looked up and saw David, and she leapt over to him in delight, her glasses nearly falling off her nose.

'And here are David and Nathan King,' she said brightly. 'They are both steady learners and uniquely talented students. They are cousins, so it's not surprising they have the same potential in their genes. Apart from you, Kiera, they are our youngest students at just twelve years of age. David and Nathan, I would like you to meet Kiera.'

David stepped forward and shook her hand. She took it warmly and smiled. She looked like she could have been from an Indian tribe from a distant land, as she was petite with slanting amber eyes, straight black hair and olive-coloured skin. She seemed to resemble her mother slightly more than her father; he had a very fair complexion and looked Scandinavian. She was, in fact, very beautiful, and Nathan seemed to shake a little at the knees on meeting her.

'P-pleased to meet you, Kiera,' whispered Nathan.

'Likewise,' Kiera replied, in a posh English accent that surprised the Kings. 'And I look forward to the three of us getting better acquainted.'

'It would be an honour to show you around,' continued Nathan, gaining more courage.

Kiera accepted instantly. 'I would most appreciate that.'

'Well!' Miss Tree beamed down at all three of them. 'I had better leave you to get to know each other.' Turning to Kiera's parents, she continued, 'And it's been a pleasure to meet you both, Mr and Mrs Berg. It is such a privilege to have Kiera with us at last. I appreciate that you had something important you had to see to first, Mr Berg, and that

Kiera has been learning all we have been teaching here in her own time. Thank you for contributing to the cultural music study, Mrs Berg.'

'Thank you for understanding, Miss Tree,' replied Mr Berg.

'Well, Kiera, it's time to say goodbye.'

'Father!' She thrust herself into his arms. 'It won't be long until we meet again.'

'Remember we are just a corridor away,' he whispered.

David and Nathan heard Kiera speak in another tongue as she hugged her mother goodbye. Then Kiera attempted to lift her cases, but Nathan quickly objected.

'Let the cases do it themselves,' he cried. 'Just imagine it. Did you imagine the cases?'

'No,' replied Kiera. 'They are real cases, so how can they move by themselves?'

'The same concept applies,' replied Nathan, in a knowledgeable manner, 'although it takes a little longer to master imagining real objects moving. David and I have been here for two years and we still have some difficulties.'

Kiera smiled in delight as she shut her eyes, and the cases moved up to her so that they were in a neat line, and then they turned and followed her down the corridor as Nathan and David directed her to the girls' dormitory. It appeared that she had no trouble learning a new trick.

Sometime later, the three met in the Academy common room.

'Settled in well?' Nathan grinned, still feeling a little awkward in the presence of a girl his age.

'Yes,' said Kiera with a smile, 'although it's so weird being the youngest. All the rest are eighteen years old at least. I'm so glad I didn't come here when I was ten. I wonder how you two managed.'

'Oh, it wasn't so bad.' Nathan was starting to portray a cooler image of himself than David had remembered him having at the start. 'We handled it because we had each other.' Seeing David's look, he added, 'Although the Bellini cousins have been an awful pain.'

'Bellini cousins?' Her eyes widened. 'Who are they?'

'Two Italian teenagers who think they can intimidate us.'

'Well, I'm sure the three of us can soon put a stop to *that*.' Kiera's pretty face looked fiercely indignant.

'There's no need for that,' went on Nathan. 'We have a secret room.'

'A secret room?' echoed Kiera.

'Yes,' David replied. 'No one else knows it's there – except the headmaster and Miss Tree. And one other – an old student who never uses it now.'

'Can you take me to it?' asked Kiera excitedly.

'Certainly,' answered Nathan.

And so the Kings took Kiera with them to the secret room for the first time. She was filled with deep awe as she entered the room, and they all sat down in silence, feeling that the sharing of this haven was somehow of great sacred value.

Kiera was the first to speak. 'Thank you for bringing me to your secret place. I feel very privileged.'

'We are pleased that we have found someone we can trust enough to share in this secret,' David said warmly. 'We both have good instincts about characters, and you certainly seem to be kosher.'

Kiera smiled. 'And likewise, I have a good instinct about characters and believe you two are also *kosher*.'

They all laughed and then Kiera went on, 'My father discovered the tunnels just over two years ago, so we are still getting used to the adjustment.'

'Would you tell us how he came to discover them?' asked David politely.

'Certainly! He met a man who claimed to be looking for his son. The man showed him a tunnel he had just discovered, and he seemed to be very pleased with it.'

'Kiera!' cried David. 'Could it be you've met my father?'

She gazed at him with tears in her eyes. 'When Miss Tree gave me your name, I did wonder if you were Joseph's son.' Her face had become sorrowful and David's heart sank as she continued, 'Your father, Joseph, came into the most unfortunate circumstance, for there was someone lurking in the tunnel. My father saw a cloaked figure devising a strange potion which gave off the most terrible fumes. The cloaked figure turned and saw them both and grabbed your father. There was a great struggle. Unfortunately, my father fainted in the fumes, and when he awoke, the cloaked potion maker and your father had gone. He was alone in the strange tunnel. He wished he could find your father, and in answer to his wish, he found himself in a sort of dungeon. He saw your father lying as if dead in a glass box, and by his side in another glass box lay a woman.'

'Could it have been my mother?' David exclaimed.

'She had honey-blonde hair, and her clothes were ragged and torn.'

'It could be her!' cried David. 'I must try to find them both.'

'But the creature will be there guarding them. My father only just managed to escape when the creature threatened him with a new, poisonous potion he had concocted. It told him that this potion was so deadly that no imagined healing potion could bring the victim back to life.'

Kiera stopped and looked at the others. David was thinking about the times Saul had kept such a constant watch on his whereabouts. Could he have known about the prophecy? The creature certainly must have known the prophecy and was attempting to destroy his father so that David would not discover his true life's purpose.

'Now the creature's potion is too strong to be counterbalanced, for the creature has *imagined* it to be so,' Kiera concluded.

'But surely the creature is missing something,' David

147

asserted, 'for though no other potion can bring my father and mother back to life, maybe something else can.'

'You mean the Master?' asked Nathan.

'Yes!' replied David. 'He has given me a gift and maybe this is the time for it to be used to its full potential. The headmaster told us that my father used his gift in music to manifest the love of the Master in order to fight Dragatorn (who I believe is one and the same as the creature your father encountered) and Dragatorn had met more than his match. I have seen people healed by the music I have played. Maybe, even though no potion can cure my parents, the Master's music still can.'

'That's it!' cried Kiera. 'Of course there is always hope.'

'David, I think you've got it,' agreed Nathan. 'And wouldn't it be weird if Dragatorn had stored your parents in Saul's dungeon? From what you've told me about your experiences there, it seems as good a place as any. I wonder if Saul imagined it into existence, being the tyrant that he is?'

'I thought that those who destroy dreams, like Saul, cannot imagine places into existence at all,' replied David.

No sooner had he spoken, than the whole room filled with an eerie laugh.

'Can't they?' a terrible voice said.

The candlelight was starting to dim all by itself. They all shuddered and drew closer together. A hooded shadow appeared and grew as it loomed over them. Then they could hear heavy footsteps slowly approaching. Soon they could smell the creature's foul breath.

'Have you ever tried extra strong mints?' Nathan muttered feebly.

His aim was to distract the creature with some of his wit, but the effect was momentary. The creature let out an evil laugh, which only filled more of the room with its foul scent, and then it clasped Nathan's arm in an iron grip. Meanwhile, the others worked hard trying to imagine a way of escape. But they were filled with such fear that they found it was nearly impossible to imagine anything at all. The dark creature continued to speak in a menacing tone, 'I am the fiend of your worst nightmares, and my servant has brought me back to life. I've got you now; you are mine.'

At this moment, David could feel a heat in his shirt pocket. The creature seemed to wince as this happened, and its eyes were drawn to stare fixedly at his pocket.

'What have you got in there?' it asked.

David gazed down and saw that a bright light was shining as if from his heart. Then he remembered the heart cake that Derek and Ellie, the farmer and his wife, had given him. Perfect love casts out fear.

The creature came and stood right in front of the children and screamed, 'None of you will see the light of day again, by the time I've finished with you! No daddy to rescue you this time, David.'

With this, the creature opened its mouth wide, and a terrible green gas poured out towards them. Suddenly, David felt an unnatural surge of inner confidence and took the heart out of his pocket. He held it up like a shield, between his face and the gas.

The creature cried out in surprise as he saw the heart, shining in all its boldness. A haunting melody filled the air, and then the heart broke in two. What looked like giant teardrops fell from its centre and a deep sigh rose up from its depths. All were motionless as they heard an eerie wailing echoing around the walls. The creature was twitching uncontrollably, and it stepped back from the children and covered its ears. A few moments later, an even greater light shone from the divided heart and they watched as it put itself back together again. The creature, still frozen in terror, let out a great growl. It seemed to become powerless against them and they noticed that it appeared to be picking up another presence in the room, which disturbed it greatly. It turned warily, sniffing the air and trembling. Then they could all hear the sounds of an orchestra, which brought out rays of sunlight from the heart.

David knew his imagination had returned because he was no longer full of fear. But then a lovely pure female voice that he had not imagined joined in with the music, and started to sing a song of praise in the Master Tongue. It was joined with a warm, mellow male voice which danced with the woman's voice, bouncing off the walls. In response, the creature cowered to the floor, appearing to be in pain as it clutched its chest. It howled in self-pity, then fled from the room and disappeared into a sort of green mist in the corridor. The three children stood staring at each other as the wonderful music continued, and the song brought merriment to their hearts.

It became apparent that the music was getting nearer. There was a harp playing and two voices singing from the corridor outside. They heard soft footsteps on the stairs and in an instant a tall, chestnut-haired man entered the room, followed by a woman with fair hair that flowed elegantly down to her waist. When David met the man's deep-blue eyes, he felt a strange electric spark, and he felt that he knew him at once. He wore a golden waistcoat that was covered with musical notes that actually danced around in response to the notes he was singing, and he played the harp with great vigour. When David looked at the woman, her sea-green eyes lit up with joy and she reached out her arms to him. They both stopped singing simultaneously as David ran into her arms, and she held him tenderly. He turned to the man, who threw his arms round him, and together they laughed so hard that they cried.

The Bellini Cousins' Discovery

'Father,' David whispered, 'you are alive!'

'Yes,' his father said, drying his tears of joy, 'and so is your mother.'

'But how did you both get out of the dungeon?'

'Your music awoke us both,' was her reply, 'when you first started to use your gift in the power of the Master. We found a cloak in the tunnel that turned into its surroundings and used that to escape from the creature. It became our haven. We hid from him for months in this way, imagining food to eat and water to drink, but soon we realised that all we really needed was the Master's music. This could turn the creature away, and it could combat its poison. And His music finally led us to you. We could hear a song with the words 'Perfect love casts out fear', and we saw a strange light in the shape of a heart leading us down the tunnel, and it took us straight to you.'

Nathan, who had been watching them all thoughtfully, said, 'The creature certainly fled when it heard the music getting nearer.'

'It's great to see you again, nephew!' cried out Joseph, and he scooped him up in his arms and gave him a big hug. Then Joseph took Kiera's hand and shook it enthusiastically.

'Well, Mr King,' she said, smiling, 'it's a pleasure to meet you at last. And at least we know what to do if the creature ever returns.'

'That creature reminded me of someone,' David

murmured. 'He seemed a little like… Uncle Saul.'

Joseph's face grew gravely serious.

'I feared for a long time that Saul was in league with the creature. I never agreed to him taking you to work on his farm, but your Uncle Ruben was not there at the time and I was so weak with the illness. I am so sorry for what you had to go through, David.'

'Don't worry, father,' David replied. 'Time has changed things for me now. The days on the farm are like another dimension, a distant dream. But whatever I went through was worth it, for it led to this reunion. It made me really value life and hold onto what is good.'

'I am glad we are together again now.' Joseph's eyes were brightened with tears, as he took David firmly in his arms. 'Didn't I tell you that nothing could separate us? Even time could not hold us apart for too long.'

'There is a lot to catch up on, my son,' whispered his mother, 'but we can begin now.'

'Yes, Maria.' His father gazed down at her affectionately. 'We will have all the time in the world now.'

David took out the shawl he had kept carefully folded in his trouser pocket and presented it to his mother. A lifetime of memories seemed to sweep across her face like a wave as she took it lovingly in her hands.

'When we awoke together in our glass boxes, we walked up into the kitchen of the house and met your old cook, Gretela, and discovered that we had been kept in Saul's farmhouse basement. She gave us her brother's address in Italy. She was planning on leaving the farm and moving over there. We also found out about your friends, the Woodmans. I am afraid that Saul had threatened to burn their house down. And one day he really managed to, but do not fear – Gretela said they all escaped the flames. When the firemen arrived, they found no one in the house. But we could not discover their whereabouts. No one knew anything.'

'Selina,' murmured David. 'I wonder if she found the tunnels too.'

'That would be the only logical explanation,' his mother continued, 'for no one in the Above World had seen them since. It was almost as if they were living undercover. But we are uncertain how to find them even in here. We did meet our tunnel guides whilst searching for the Woodmans, who told us that Saul and the creature were becoming one and the same. Perhaps that's why the creature reminded you of Saul.'

'But how could he have been able to transform himself into such a hideous creature of darkness?' David shuddered. 'Perhaps he has managed to imagine even greater things than we have – or even worse things, that is. At this academy, we are told that one thing we should never do is use our gifts merely for personal power and profit. It has to be about bringing good to others as well as ourselves. But giving over one's mind entirely to the powers of darkness is the worst thing anyone could do. Does this mean it is too late for Saul – is there no turning back now?'

'Only the Master can answer that question,' his mother replied. 'He can bring good out of anything. Whether Saul changes his dark path or not, is entirely up to him. Possessed by another power or not, he can still make the decision to turn back.'

His father looked grim. 'He seemed to have secured his destiny on the road of bitterness very early on. It would take a lot to convince him to change now.'

'Never underestimate the power of the Master,' his wife reminded him.

'Maria, you always have room for hope.' Joseph smiled at her lovingly. 'Always my strength in weakness!'

But David's mind was on something else. Selina. No wonder he had never been able to return to her house these past years. It was no longer there, or not as it was. Would they ever have a chance of meeting again? He did not know, but then he remembered something his guide had told him. He cried out, 'I will see Selina again. The guide told me I would see her, only not for a very long time.'

'Then see her you shall,' his father laughed. 'Remember, nothing is too far from the Master's grasp.'

'I told your father that,' winked his mother, and together they suddenly retrieved a harp each and started a merry tune. Soon all five of them were playing music together and the whole room was full of the sounds of a fine orchestra.

Later that day, Miss Tree noticed that the Kings and Kiera were finding it hard to concentrate in lessons, so she suggested that they took time out. Immediately, the Bellinis started to form a plan. As the three friends left the classroom, Vinny began to have what appeared to be a fit on the floor. As Miss Tree's attentions were turned entirely on Vinny, Leo slid out of the door behind the trio unnoticed. As they came to the secret room, and he heard them speaking in the Master Tongue, he smirked to himself. 'So this is their haven. Leo and I can just steal up on them and slip in behind them before they close the door.'

On his return to the lesson, he was handed lines to write for leaving the room without permission. But this did not bother him in the slightest. Miss Tree started to suspect that the cousins were scheming due to the glow of mischief clearly displayed on both their faces. As a result, she endeavoured to watch them carefully from that time on. However, the following day, they managed to follow the three friends to their favourite haunt by imagining a form of distraction for Miss Tree as they passed her office. A huge bird suddenly appeared in her room and she had some trouble trying to get it out of the window, and by the time she had realised that it was an imagined bird, Leo and Vinny were well out of sight.

Just as David, Nathan and Kiera entered the haven, to their horror, the Italian cousins shot through the closing gate. But this was not without consequence to the Bellinis –

for both took a sharp knock to the head from the closing gate, which did not seem to like intruders. As if this was not enough, Leo was unfortunate to receive a second injury – coming from a high kick given by Kiera, who turned out to be feistier that they had previously given her credit. And he only had this unexpected extra privilege because he was the first of the cousins to enter the room.

'How dare you!' she shouted at the slightly dazed Italian cousins, who were holding their heads in pain. 'We all knew what Vinny pretended to do. Miss Tree keeps us well informed.'

'I just got kicked... by a *girl*?!' snarled Leo in fury.

'Don't worry, Leo.' Vinny patted his arm loyally. 'I pay back anyone who shows disrespect to my cousin.'

'We are not unlike you, Leo,' David said. 'We stand by each other just as you stand by your family.'

'Are you threatening us?' Leo challenged him, still rubbing his sore chin. 'Do you really think you are a match for the Mafia? My father shall hear of this, girl. I won't hit you – but only because I was brought up to believe you shouldn't hit the weaker sex.'

Suddenly, he pushed David against the wall and wrenched his arm behind his back, and meanwhile, Vinny grabbed Nathan. David could feel pain shooting up his shoulder.

'You think just because you've grown a little taller, you can put up a fight?' Leo mocked him.

But then Vinny was heard crying out in pain. Leo turned to see him being pushed against the wall by Kiera and Nathan, with his hand behind his back.

'Hey!' Leo shouted, starting to feel a little outnumbered. 'If you insult my family, you insult me. If you don't release my cousin, then I am going to hurt David.'

'Vice versa!' shouted Kiera, pulling Vinny's arm more tightly.

But the three friends' faces fell when Leo pulled out a

knife. Instantly, they released Vinny. Vinny pinned Nathan down again and things were just about to get seriously nasty when two people suddenly entered the room. One of them ran to Leo, still holding his knife at David's throat, grabbed him and shouted, 'What do you think you are doing? You leave my son alone.'

Then came a voice of power: 'Get your hands off my nephew!'

It was David's mother, looking more like a ferocious warrior queen than the sweet-natured lady he had met previously. His father threw Leo's knife to the ground and held him against the wall, breathing heavily. Vinny did not know where to look, as he shuffled awkwardly from side to side. Maria's face changed in an instant from the warrior back to the caring mother as she gazed at them and her face filled with sorrow.

Nathan thought it was a good time to try humour. 'See?' he said to the cousins. 'Didn't we tell you that loyalty is very important in our family too? David's parents are quicker than a phone call away.'

Leo looked ashamed. 'I wasn't gonna use the knife. It was just for show.'

Vinny exhibited his family loyalty by seconding him. 'Yeah, I know Leo. And trust me – he never uses his knife unless he *has* to.'

Joseph released his tight hold on Leo, and looked both cousins up and down. They both avoided his eyes, which seemed to see right through them.

'You are only boys who want to be admired. You've been taught to win respect through violence. Your fathers did this, at the cost of all who were close to them. The way of the Mafia does not have to be your path too.'

Suddenly, their faces filled with pain. They had never before encountered a man who could read into their souls, and they did not particularly like the feeling. They could do nothing but shuffle from foot to foot, feeling like specimens lit up under a hot microscope. Leo could feel Maria's loving eyes burning into him too. What was this irrational love and where did it come from? They had just been attempting to harm their family. He looked over at Vinny and could see that he felt it too, but was not looking up to avoid the intensity of her sea-green eyes. Then she spoke in a voice that was as sweet as honey.

'There *is* love.'

Both Italian cousins looked noticeably touched on hearing these words. They started shaking, and David could see that their hearts had already begun to melt. He could feel the heart in his pocket pricking him with an electrical surge of heat, as it started to shine from him once again. In an instant, he found himself reaching for a harp that appeared in mid air and straight away a new song formed on his lips, one in another tongue. And this time, it was not the Master Tongue that he knew, but another he had never learned. The Master must have several languages, he thought. And he could see the effect of his song on Leo and Vinny. They could no longer control their emotions. Both started to sob lightly, and then they sank to the ground, covering their faces, as David continued to sing over them. Timeless moments later, Nathan and Kiera were helping them up to their feet.

'I'm sorry I kicked you, Leo,' Kiera said quickly.

Leo just gazed at David and said, 'I didn't know you knew Italian.'

Vinny was still crying, and he held out his hand to Nathan and gave him a hug. Nathan was a little speechless.

'You speak Italian?' Leo asked David. 'And you know my mother?'

Now it was David's turn to be surprised. 'You understood what I was singing? Was I singing in Italian? I've never spoken it before!'

Leo was completely astonished. 'You're joking?'

'The Master has given me His language, but I've never been given an earthly tongue before.'

'Excuse me?' chipped in Vinny. 'You talking English now?'

David laughed at the double meaning. 'Yes, I'm sorry. I guess you haven't met the Master yet.'

Vinny looked searchingly at Leo, who smiled back. 'I believe we have just now – thanks to *you*.'

Leo remembered what David had sung about. 'And to think that my mother was your cook. Your uncle sounds a nasty piece of work, though. In fact, if you introduced me to him, I'd like to do a few things to him! I am loyal to you now. Like family.'

David looked stunned. 'My uncle's cook, Gretela... is your mother?!'

'That's what you told me,' replied Leo. 'I suppose you didn't get an interpretation of the Italian tongue you were singing? She left my dad when he started to treat her bad. I've been looking for her for years. I would never tell dad where she was 'cos he'd probably punish her. You mentioned our uncle's address in Milan. So now I know where me and Vinny are headed for our holidays! David, I am indebted to you for this.'

Leo put out his hand and as David shook it, he found himself in a warm Italian hug.

'We are like family now,' Leo whispered.

Their bullies had become their close friends within the space of a few minutes.

And so, the seasons passed by smoothly and with much jollification. Miss Tree was astounded at the change in the Bellinis. They became helpful and motivated in a way she could never have envisioned. David's parents also became like new parents to the Bellinis, who turned to them often for advice. Much healing work was done in their lives, and the years passed by harmoniously. In fact, there was no sign of Saul or the creature. It seemed as if they were never going to return.

The Journey to Crossheart Island

Five years passed in this way, until the Kings and Kiera were eighteen. The time had come for them all to graduate from the Tunnel World Academy of Music. And this year, a long summer holiday awaited them. Leo and Vinny were going to see Gretela and were on the next plane to Italy on the last day of term. The Kings and Kiera had other exciting plans. Their parents had arranged for them all to go together on a boat expedition to the Micronesian islands, north of Australia, where Kiera's father, Elvin Berg, had met his wife Hanani on an exploration trip. In fact, one of these trips was the reason behind Kiera's delay in studying at the academy. Hanani was the sister of the chief of a tribe on Crossheart Island. The chief had given his sister in marriage to Elvin in return for him saving one of his sons from an enemy tribe who lived across the river. David and Nathan were filled with awe for Kiera after discovering that she was descended from a tribal chief. As it was, Nathan's admiration for Kiera had been growing over the years and David had noted a considerable change in their friendship. It was evident that they were courting and were undoubtedly destined for marriage. The day came for the expedition to begin. But before they came on-board, Maria took her son aside and said, 'David, you are going to meet some old friends on *The Gladstone*. I want you to be prepared. Selina is not with them. They will explain all.'

A few moments later, he was being greeted by Leah and

Eric Woodman, and then Samuel, all of whom looked delighted to see him.

'David, at last we meet again!' cried Eric.

'Where is Selina?' The question fell from his lips.

'When Saul burned down our house, we ran to the tunnel under the basement and there I met my guide. He instructed us all to imagine the same place in our minds and told us we would go straight there. We had all been to Gladstone on the east coast of Australia on holiday a year before, so we closed our eyes and thought of the beach. A moment later, we were there; but the tide was further in than we expected and we all landed in the ocean. That's when we were rescued by Elvin Berg! Then, we accompanied him on his expedition to Crossheart Island. Unfortunately, there was a terrible storm, and a strange green mist filled the air. Selina was washed overboard by a freak wave and we never saw her again. Some of the tribe said they had seen her being carried off by a strange shadow. We believe she is still alive somewhere. The tribe talk of a sorcerer who appears in a green mist. We think she may be with him. We are returning to find her.'

'So, there is a sorcerer on the island,' David said. 'I wonder if he could be the same one I met in the academy. Let's hope that this one doesn't like music either!'

Eric laughed. 'Yes, your parents have told me all about your gift – this came as no surprise to any of us.'

And so, on that bright summer's morning, on the east coast of Queensland, the large party set off from Gladstone on Elvin's large boat, *The Gladstone*. David had never been on a boat before and was delighted with the rhythm of the waves and the fresh sea air. Four mothers – Maria, Hanani, Leah and Michal (Nathan's mother) – were sitting on the deck watching the men – Elvin, Ruben, Eric and Joseph – manning the boat. Elvin steered the boat and Ruben was high up on the lookout post.

Suddenly, a loud voice spoke in David's ear. It was

Nathan's elder sister, Ruth. She was a bubbly girl, who never took her eyes off Samuel.

'What do you think of his painting, David?' she asked with a smile.

Samuel had been attempting to paint her portrait, but had only got as far as a light pencil sketch of her eyes.

'I thought it polite to wait until he had finished,' replied David, humorously.

'Oh, I haven't started yet,' Samuel murmured in an embarrassed fashion. 'I've spent so long mixing the paints, and trying out different colours.'

Meanwhile, Eric and Joseph were playing cards across the deck, and David could see that Eric's eyes were constantly on Samuel and Ruth, in some amusement. As Ruth followed his gaze, Samuel peered over his canvas to look at her for a few seconds. Eric was puffing at a large green pipe, and reminded David considerably of the Caterpillar in *Alice in Wonderland*. Joseph coughed from the smoke rings that came from Eric's pipe, and moved away a little.

'Oh, I am sorry for the smoke,' chirped Eric, 'I will puff in the other direction!'

'It's no trouble at all,' replied Joseph, with a beam. 'The wind blows it where it pleases at any rate, but the sea air is so fresh out here.'

'And I have the tendency to feel,' continued Eric, with a glint of mischief in his eyes, 'that *love* is in the air.'

They both looked at Samuel and Ruth with big grins, and Eric gave them a wink. Samuel disappeared behind his painting and Ruth kept her eyes on him, not saying a word.

To change the subject, Joseph quickly said to Eric, 'Well, I'm glad that Elvin is such a good sailor and navigator. If he hadn't managed to steer so skilfully around all those islands, we wouldn't have been able to play a decent game of cards.'

Nathan and Kiera had, so far, managed to avoid any remarks from Eric, who was focussing on his son. All of them were glad when the evening came, for it was accompanied by the telling of a special story which held all their attention, so there was no opportunity for Eric's mischievous remarks. It was Hanani who told the story, and Kiera translated it for the gathering:

'One day, Chief Lightfoot sat watching the sunset from the cliff overlooking the dark turquoise ocean. He was the ruler of the island that lay underneath the eternal sun, and he led a tribe that had lived there for many generations from ancient times.

'He waited for the sun to display its bright purple-red colours and to dip behind the vast ocean. He was a hunter, but not of any kind of animal or fish, for he loved vegetables and fruit. He had quick eyes that hunted out all dangers that might threaten the peace of his people. His nimble, slight frame enabled him to escape death like lightning. Predators, at that time, came in the form of wild animals, but soon another kind of predator would set foot on the island.

'Chief Lightfoot stayed on the clifftop by the shore, puffing his pipe and allowing the peace of the sunset to fill his whole being. He had a deep awareness of the spiritual realm, and often pondered deeply about his tribe's existence, and whether the force by which they were created would be revealed in more certain terms. Watching the sunset revealed to Lightfoot the glory of life itself, yet he desired a deeper wisdom and understanding of life and its purpose.

'Since he had become chief, his younger brother had displayed jealousy of his position. The people respected Lightfoot's judgment far above his brothers', and they considered his pearls of wisdom to be far more valuable than any of the precious stones on the island.

'Lightfoot would sit each evening watching the sunset, and each evening, he would give thanks to a higher being who made all things come into existence. He believed that this being must have the ultimate control. As he gave thanks once again, he started to notice a difference in the colours on the clouds ahead, as they turned from deep purple to a lighter orange that grew brighter and brighter. He gasped in astonishment, for it appeared that the sun which had just set was reappearing from the horizon as a shining light started to emerge. It became bigger and bigger, and as it did, Lightfoot began to perceive a figure in the centre of the light. As it came nearer to him, he realised that the figure was that of a great man, and that he was walking on the water.

'Lightfoot's heart was filled with hope and certainty from this moment. He thought that he was receiving the answer to his pondering. The figure of light approached him, and his radiance filled him with awe. He became overcome with the love he could feel from the light, and he fell to his knees. And as he did, a song of praise welled up from deep within his being. As he sang, he could see the kind eyes of the being, and he watched as the being stretched his arms out to him. He felt a great desire to run into the arms of this amazing person, but he also felt that the light was too bright for him in its beauty and perfection. However, in this light, he felt all his doubts pass away. All he could do was to throw himself face down and beg for forgiveness for not knowing the Great Chief of all creation sooner.

'As the Creator walked ever closer, Lightfoot started to wonder if it was his time to leave this world. Just as he felt his heart racing faster, and he prepared to breathe his last, the Creator stopped where sea met sand and stood gazing down at him. Lightfoot knew then that if the Creator had come any closer, he would surely have died. He sang out to Him in praise and wonder. In response, some of the light from the Creator danced up the cliff edge and surrounded Lightfoot with a sense of incredible love. He bathed in it, wishing he could take it back with him to give to his people. The Creator reached out His hands to him, and Lightfoot could see that there were deep scars in them. What was the meaning of such marks, that this divine being must carry them and reveal them to mankind?

'As Lightfoot looked into the scars, he could feel his inner pain and torment concerning his relationship with his brother being lifted like a heavy burden from his shoulders. In that instant, he understood the scars and he whispered to his Creator, "Your wounds heal me, for now I know life no longer ends with suffering, but that your suffering ends all pain and restores life again."

'Then the Creator spoke to Lightfoot, as Lightfoot bowed with his head to the ground. His voice was like a rushing waterfall as he said, "I am the Maker of all, and just as I created all and love all I have made, I also have paid the price to bring my children back to myself. For many have turned from Truth and live lives full of evil and pain, which is evil's consequence. I have come that you may have new life and wash clean your souls. And you, Lightfoot, must be my light to all the islands of this ocean, so that they may know me. Tell your tribe that I am the Eternal One and that if they worship me above all things, I can show them the best way to live. Cast aside their superstitious gods, and be allied to them no longer, and I will set your people free. I will anoint you with great wisdom and strength and they shall know joy they have never known before. Yet your brother will betray you and there will be division on the island. But if you cleave to me, unity will be restored. Do not fear, my faithful one, for I am with you until the end of the age, and beyond."

'At that moment, Lightfoot fell into a deep sleep, and when he awoke it was already morning and the Creator had gone. But in His place was a large, shining stone that looked pure and radiant as it was washed by the waves of the sea.

'In an instant, Lightfoot sprung to his feet and scrambled nimbly down the cliff to retrieve the treasure. He had dreamt of a pattern and a phrase which he felt inspired to carve onto the stone face. The stone was like the shape of a heart, which was also the shape of the island, as Lightfoot had learned in a vision that night. He had seen that the great river that fell from the waterfall by the once volcanic mountain also divided the island in two, and together with the lake that gathered beneath the waterfall, gave a cross shape in the centre, which was like a figure with arms outstretched.

'Sharpening a stone that lay on the shore, he scraped the shape of the being he had seen, with its arms outstretched to him, right in the middle of the stone, in the position of the river of the island. This stone would be a reminder of the unity of all people under one Creator. And across the arms of the figure he carved the words: "Creator's love lives in our hearts."

'By the time he had finished carving, Lightfoot was sweating underneath the heat of the rising sun, and he realised that it was time to return to his tribe. The tribe were used to him visiting the sunset, but he rarely stayed out until morning, and so they awaited his return with bated breath. He always quietened the youngest with his wise words. Lightfoot stood up and dragged the stone upwards to sit on his back. Then he struggled under its weight through the forest and by the streams. Several times he slipped, and the sharp bottom edge of the rock cut into his back. He felt the pain and he felt thirst, but all he could see was the bright imprint of the image of his Creator, filling him with great warmth. As he fell again, on a tree root, a strong ray of light shone through the trees, and he felt that the rock on his back was glowing supernaturally, and lighting up the darkest corners of the forest. He could also feel that the weight of his burden had been lifted.

'He came finally to the end of the forest, and moved into bright open land. He looked over the valley at his home village of mud houses. Children playing there had already seen him, and were crying out in joy. Women with babies tied around them in slings rushed out of their houses to meet him.

'He stumbled once more, and this time the large stone fell from his back onto the earth. As the light radiated from it, the gathering tribe marvelled at it, and gave loud exclamations when they saw the cuts on Lightfoot's back. They knew at once that this stone held significant meaning for their tribe. And so they waited for Lightfoot's story with bated breath. His wife and children ran to him and he drew them close. As they looked into his face, they shuddered, for it was glowing like the sun.

'After a long drink from a water jar, Lightfoot spoke to his people. The Creator, he told them, was the answer to all their questions. He was the Way, the Truth and the Life. He told them that the Creator dwelt in his heart and that he could dwell in their hearts also, and that he was going to worship the Creator for the rest of his life. The stone would stand as a reminder of that. And the island would now be known as Crossheart Island, for all the people would follow the Creator of their hearts.

'After he had finished speaking, huge applause rose from the excited crowd. On that day most of the tribe dedicated their hearts to their Creator and much celebration was heard on the island. It was such a victorious sound that he was sure he could hear the songs of heaven joining in. Lightfoot knew that the Creator was delighted with their expression of love to Him. But he was not aware that his brother planned to bring evil to the island, for a battle was already taking place in the heavenly realms, fighting for the complete freedom of this island, which had been bound by blindness for so long. Lightfoot's brother, who had watched the joyous gathering from a distance, decided to bow down to the stone as if it were a god. In doing so, he opened the door to evil on the island, and soon a sorcerer appeared from the ancient volcano and formed an alliance with the chief's rebellious brother.

166

'This displeased the Creator, whose light stayed ever present with Lightfoot, but darkness covered the chief's brother. Soon, the brother was banished to live across the river on the other side of the island, and he brought some tribe members with him, convincing them that there were more pleasures to enjoy on his side of the island. He promised that there would be no restrictions, such as the holy day Lightfoot had set in place every seven days, and he told his companions that those who lived under his rule could more or less do as they pleased. What these tribe members came to realise too late was that in going over to the other side of the island, they were straying from the Creator Himself, and they came to be under the control of the evil sorcerer's power, where they would live in terrible darkness and misery.

'Lightfoot was my father, and now my brother is chief of Crossheart Island in his place. He is still living at war with my uncle's tribe, who are now led by my father's nephew. The stone has been stolen from its place and hidden in the volcanic mountain. But all is not lost. We hope that on this mission we will not only find Selina, who was lost at the shore of the island, but also work to reconcile the two tribes and combat the forces of darkness through songs that remind them of Lightfoot's vision.'

Hanani looked around at all the listeners, who sat captivated in the lantern light with unblinking eyes. She drew in a deep breath, and sat back next to her daughter Kiera, who rested her head against her mother's shoulder. David and Nathan were mesmerised by the incredible tale that they had heard. They had been told that their trip was more than just a normal holiday, but had not perceived that it would turn out to be a great adventure. They both decided to spend as much time singing to the Creator as possible, and all the crew had their full support. For the days that followed, the crew prepared themselves in every way possible for what they may encounter on Crossheart Island.

Land Ahoy!

Then, one day, they heard the exciting words 'land ahoy!', and all the crew members crowded round to one side of the boat to gaze on the approaching cliffs.

The cliffs loomed over them like great entrance gates, and looked a little intimidating in the dusk sky. A spectacular waterfall poured from the rocks. After a while, there came soft splashing sounds. David looked out into the water and saw several long, thin boats heading in their direction.

A few moments later, he heard Elvin shouting, 'Prepare to turn the boat around! Savage tribe incoming!'

Eric started to quiver with great intensity. 'Next to the time Saul burnt our house down, this is the most scary moment of my life! I don't like the look of those spears they're shaking.'

'Silence, husband,' Leah hissed, 'and get to the sails, other-wise we shall all be killed.'

Elvin's voice was heard again. 'Duck!'

Everyone did, and just in time – arrows whizzed through the air and landed on deck. One narrowly missed Eric's head as Leah pulled him to the floor.

'Thanks, my dearest.' He smiled nervously. 'As usual, I am most indebted.'

'You're welcome,' she replied quietly.

Soon the arrow firing had died down but there was much shouting and what sounded like the clashing of spears. Elvin, Joseph and Ruben crawled to the far side of the boat that faced out to sea, and let themselves down to the water in a small boat. They took guns with them. Everyone waited, hardly able to breathe. Suddenly three gunshots were heard and they were followed by loud cries and wild splashes. After this, things quietened down and for some time nobody dared to raise their head.

Then, Elvin's voice rang out. 'It's all right, we are safe now!'

One by one, the group peered over the side of the boat to see Elvin, Ruben and Joseph standing on their boat surrounded by a large party of tribe members in canoes.

'These tribesmen are our friends!' shouted Elvin jubilantly. 'They helped rid us of the enemy tribe. We managed to wound one of them and they have fled to the other side of the island.'

He let out a cheer and the tribe members cheered in response, waving their spears above their heads and then thumping them against their canoes.

Ruth looked doubtfully at them. She asked Samuel nervously, 'Do you think that means they are safe?'

Samuel gave her a wry smile. 'I think if they weren't, they wouldn't be using those spears as percussion.'

David, Nathan and Kiera were surprised to see their own fathers attempting to do the same with their guns. Unfortunately, as they managed to sway their small boat considerably in so doing, they lost their balance and fell into the water. In response, the tribe cheered again, with big grins, whilst everyone on board *The Gladstone* laughed heartily.

Finally setting foot on the island, David was greeted by a young man who was much smaller than himself. He wore leaves that were woven together, as well as a wonderfully embroidered head adornment, and he was covered with decorative tribal markings. He stretched out his hand to David, clenching his fist against David's palm – as seemed to be the tribal greeting. Then he bowed to the ground. David was taken aback by this and proceeded to do the same, but the young man stopped him. He spoke in a language David recognised. It was the Master Tongue.

'You must not bow to *me*. For you are the one they prophesied about. You are of the line of the most ancient kings that came from another realm, an underground dimension. My grandfather, Lightfoot, learned of that realm in a vision. Come, I will take you to my father, Chief Lightray.'

Together, they walked under the giant waterfall, feeling some of the water drops on their foreheads, and headed down a winding path through a forest. Suddenly, they came to a clearing, and before them stood the volcanic mountain. David was surprised to see smoke of many colours puffing out of it.

'Do you think that volcano is safe?' asked Nathan.

'I'm more concerned about the sorcerer who lives within,' replied David.

'That volcano is supposed to be dormant,' said Kiera, 'but since the sorcerer came to the island, it has been doing a lot of smoking.'

Whilst she was speaking, young men came up to them and started drumming and dancing. And towards the centre of the dancing group stood the chief. He watched the visitors with a serene stillness, and David was filled with great respect for him. As they came to stand in front of him, he raised his hand and the drumbeat stopped. The chief held out his hand to Elvin, who took it, then bowed down to the ground. Then he held out his hand to Kiera and Hanani, whom he took in a deep embrace and the three of them laughed for joy. In a moment, he had lost all his solemnity. Then he walked to David. He appeared to be as filled with awe for David as David was for him. Instinctively, David bowed to the ground. He felt Chief Lightray's hand on his shoulders, raising him up so that they were standing very close, face to face.

To his amazement, Lightray then proceeded to do what his son had done earlier. He bowed in great respect to David, and then he turned and did the same to Nathan, and then again to Joseph and Ruben. When he arose from the ground, he beckoned some tribe members over, who placed decorative adornments on each of their heads. Then the chief turned again to David and placed his hand on his forehead. To David's delight, he started to sing a beautiful song in the Master Tongue, raising a hand to the starry skies above. David could actually see the words written on the night sky: 'You are chosen to bring peace to our brother tribes. You must walk a difficult path, but He trusts in you. Go in strength, for the Master is the Mighty Conqueror!'

David found himself shaking all over, and as Lightray continued to sing over him in great joy, he fell to the ground and went into a deep sleep. When he awoke, he could see the dawn had arrived so he got up. He was in a cosy mud hut and Nathan slept beside him. Their fathers slept on the other side of the hut. As he arose, he felt Nathan stir. He sat up, rubbing sleep-filled eyes.

'David, are you going?' he asked.

'Yes,' David replied. 'The Master came to me in a dream and told me what I must do.'

'What *we* must do,' corrected Nathan. 'You are not in this alone, David. We have been praying most of the night. The enemy tribe must be fought on your behalf as you go and face the sorcerer. And I am coming with you.'

David could hear the Master's voice in the sunlight, calling him to walk with Him.

'Come on, Nathan,' he said. 'You will come with me, but at the entrance to the volcano I must go on alone. You must keep singing at the entrance until I return.'

And so, they set off, walking towards the mountain as bright red and purple smoke steamed out of the top of it. Neither felt afraid, for they knew that the Master had told them both to go forth; they were the descendants of the kings who had first made a covenant with the Master and they knew His eternal promise and favour rested on them. As they drew closer to the mountain with the rising sun, both became aware of the evil presence emanating from the smoke, yet they remained fearless. Feeling as strong as warriors, they strode to the bottom of the mountain. Then they started to climb it. The fumes of smoke were surrounding them now. But they could hear the Master's breath, pushing away the smoke so that they were not intoxicated by it. As they climbed, they started to hear an aggressive chanting coming from the other side of the island. They could see men with spears running straight towards them.

'The chief knows that they will attack,' said Nathan, 'and he is ready.'

As if in response, the mountain started to rumble, and a great roar came up from within, causing flames of fiery lava to raise their fierce heads from the mountain top. David turned and could see the friendly tribe surrounding the enemy tribe and blocking their path to the mountain. War cries were heard and fighting started swiftly. Many were being injured and for a moment, David stopped and felt overwhelmed with sadness at the years of separation and enmity between these brother tribes. He felt Nathan's hand on his shoulder.

'We must not lose focus, or we will not be able to help these people.'

Feeling stronger again, David resumed his ascent. He found that the further they went, the harder the path became, and several times the two of them slipped. On one such occasion, Nathan tripped on a large stone and nearly fell clear over the side of the mountain, but David caught his hand and heaved him back to the path.

'I lost my concentration,' he said, breathing heavily. 'Thanks, David. I think you just saved my life.'

'And I think you have just found the stone!' marvelled David. 'The Master has told me I must take it up with us. He has said it must be *carried.*'

'Then let us take turns in carrying it,' suggested Nathan, eyeing up the size of the stone with some anxiety.

'Thank you for being with me, Nathan.'

He took his cousin's hand and Nathan's eyes filled with tears.

'Whatever we will go through, we are in this together, my friend,' Nathan replied.

Then, a little reluctantly, Nathan helped to lever the stone onto David's back. It was surprisingly light, but the further they walked under the rising sun, David could feel the stone really starting to bore into his back. When another great spout of lava shot out from the top of the volcano he started in fear, and lost his balance. As he landed, partly under the stone, he felt it cut into his back, and blood freely flowed. He lay panting on the ground as Nathan poured water on his wounds and gave him a drink. Then Nathan gently helped him to his feet, and took the heart-shaped stone onto himself.

'Not long to go now, my friend.'

David could not bear to see his friend stumbling under the weight of the stone, which seemed to grow in intensity the nearer they got to the mountain entrance. Several times, he had to catch him as he fell, and the stone cut into his back.

What seemed like hours later, they found themselves at the top of the mountain. Both of them were covered in cuts and their limbs were numb with exhaustion. They took a long drink together. Then Nathan transferred the heart stone to David.

'Here, I must go on alone,' David said.

Then Nathan saw a cello waiting for him, floating in mid air. At this moment, a fiery voice boomed from deep within the mountain.

'So, you have come!'

David peered into the mountain to see who had spoken,

but he could see very little due to the flowing lava smoke.

'Oh,' the voice continued, 'you won't be able to see me. I am in the lava and the lava is in me.'

Then it occurred to David. 'Why, of course! The lava is just *imagined*.'

Instinctively he reached for his harp and together he and Nathan began to play. In a few moments, the lava had vanished. David felt a strong longing to find Selina, and as he stood up, he found himself entering a tunnel that had suddenly emerged from the side of the mountain peak. As he moved soundlessly through the tunnel, with the stone on his back, and the harp following him in mid air, he began to hear the voice of a child, calling out his name. It was then that he saw a small figure crouching in the darkness before him.

'Hello, friend,' a familiar voice said. 'Welcome back to your tunnel.'

'My guide!' cried David in delight.

'You remember!' exclaimed the guide, clapping his hands together. 'And I should hope so too, as I have been with you all these years.'

Hearing the voice of the child echoing in the passage, the guide said quickly, 'Take out your cloak. It will hide you well. Your friend, Selina, lies deep within the mountain. She sleeps, but not totally unaware of this life. Sometimes her singing can be heard by the tribes of this island. You must face the sorcerer before you can set her free.'

David could sense that they were getting closer to Selina as the guide was speaking. At last, they entered into a sort of underground dungeon, which was full of enchantment. Ahead of them, in a strange green mist, was a glass box, in which a little girl lay. She had a deathly pale appearance.

'She has not aged a day since she was captured seven years ago,' the guide said.

As David approached the glass box, he felt a deep pain in

his heart. And then he realised the guide had gone. All he knew to do was to sing, and so he sang a special song over Selina, in the Master Tongue. It was a song that formed freshly on his lips like the morning dew. After singing for some time, he noticed a change come over Selina. A new light shone through her being and she woke up. In this instant, the box opened and she got up and stood beside David. Then, to his amazement, she started to grow before his eyes, and her clothes grew with her, as her features turned from those of a little girl to those of a young woman. Her hair, too, grew wondrously long and flowed down to her waist. She held onto him, trying to see who her rescuer was in the dim, misty light. It became evident that she could not see at all, for her sea-blue eyes stared right through him.

'Do not be afraid,' David told her. 'I am David.'

'David?' her sing-song voice sounded distant. 'I knew a David, once. He was a boy.'

Then David realised that he was covered with his cloak and quickly withdrew it to reveal himself to her. She gasped and scanned his face. But at this moment, they became aware of another presence entering the room. David quickly pulled his cloak around both of them, just as a hooded figure appeared in the entrance to the dungeon. Selina gasped again, but he gently took her hand, and drew her close to him.

'Show yourself to me like a man!' snarled a dark voice.

Seeing only one entrance to the dark place, David imagined another escape route, and sure enough, some light appeared beside them. However, just as they tried to slowly leave the room, the cloaked figure appeared between them and the exit.

'You can't escape me!' it said, with a foul laugh. 'Just because you are invisible, don't think that I can't see you. For I am the Sorcerer Dragatorn, and I see all!'

'Only the Master knows all,' David whispered to Selina.

175

The sorcerer sniffed the air and unleashed a dart of lightning at them, but they were protected by the cloak. He sensed that he had hit a hard object and grabbed hold of their cloak, removing it. David closed his eyes and started to imagine...

He found himself sitting on a ridge, with the heart stone, high up inside the mountain, some metres away from the sorcerer, who hovered on another ridge beneath him. Selina was floating through the top of the mountain, lying on colourful rings of smoke.

'Your powers of imagining have certainly grown,' cried out the sorcerer, 'beyond what I had previously reckoned. Think what great things we could achieve if we combined forces. My dominion would be complete, and you would rule, more powerful than any of your ancestors.'

'I will never join you,' cried David.

In response, the sorcerer screamed and sent forth another fiery stroke of lightning straight at David. The ledge he stood on crumbled instantly, and he fell many metres towards the lava as it rushed up at him. Suddenly, he found himself being caught and he turned and saw the white heart stone floating with him towards a nearby ledge. The lightning darts continued flying at him as he sat on the ledge, shielded by the stone. He quickly took hold of a harp he found hovering in mid air and started to play it in order to combat the lightning. The lightning soon turned into a stream of musical melodies and returned to its owner, who covered his ears in apparent agony. He could see the sorcerer's eyes of hate piercing into his soul, yet the more he felt his hate, the more he became overwhelmed by the Master's love. And as David continued to sing and play his harp, the sorcerer stopped unleashing his fury and listened for a while. He seemed to be slightly soothed by the playing.

However, this did not last long, as he suddenly took what looked like a spear of lightning and hurled it straight at

David. The stone took the bolt of lightning, but this time, it started to change form. It turned blood red, and blood started to drip from it into the mountain depths. David could feel a familiar warm sensation against his chest and turned to see that his heart cake was shining brightly, and he could hear crying sounds emanating from its depths. Almost in parallel, the sorcerer began to howl loudly: 'No! No! No!'

David knew that the love of the Master was destroying the fire of the sorcerer's hate.

'Who are you?' David called to him, with a tone of authority.

The sorcerer started to whimper.

'What is your name?' David repeated.

Suddenly, a great light shone from the heart stone, and a deep, warm voice spoke, filling the mountain with new life: 'Speak, and reveal yourself, for your time is up.'

Immediately, the sorcerer fell on his knees and shook all over. He pulled off his long garment and threw it down into the bottom of the mountain, where lava instantly dissolved it.

'I am Dragatorn,' he said feebly.

'No,' the voice said gently. 'What is your *real* name?'

'I am Saul,' he replied in a whisper.

He had turned into a frightened child. David watched as he became smaller and smaller before his eyes. The child was crying.

'Why did you leave me, father?'

David stepped onto the heart stone again, which took him to the ledge on which the little boy lay, sobbing. He reached out his hand and the boy took it.

'Are you my father?' he asked through tear-stained eyes.

'No.' David smiled tenderly at the young Saul. 'But I know someone who is far greater than any father you could imagine.'

'Can I meet him?' the child asked.

'Yes, as you have become like a child, you can meet with the Master. But He is already here. You have already met Him.'

'Father!' cried the child again, now more in anger. 'Why did you leave me?'

'Saul, Saul,' the voice came again, 'I never left you. You left me. But see how the years have eaten away the boy you were. You had to become a child again, that you might become the man you should be. These are but memories now, Saul. Memories that flicker in the flames. But this time, I want you to feel that I was there with you. I am always with you. Just as I was with David. I am eternal.'

Saul started crying again.

'Your earthly father may have deserted you, Saul. But I never could. Return to me, and I will give you back all that was taken from you. And much more.'

In this moment, David could see himself in the child that trembled before him, and without a word, he drew him to his chest, and felt the tears welling up. As they cried together, David could feel Saul's form changing, and when he released him, he could see a grown man with a new light in his eyes standing before him.

A new and victorious voice spoke from out of the depths: 'Saul, son of Benjamin, you have been given another chance.'

Saul began to sob again and he turned to David, and noticed the wounds on him.

'My nephew, I am sorry that I wounded you.'

David took his hand willingly.

'I have forgiven you for everything.'

A new song filled the air, a chorus from heaven that bounded across the mountain, and suddenly Saul and David found themselves dancing around together in mid air, above the lava. And in that instant, a bold, powerful light burst forth from the deep, swallowing the lava and pouring forth throughout the mountain and out of the top of it, filling them both with its eternal goodness. The light then lifted them up with it and carried them through the mountain-top entrance, where they met the light of the sun and Nathan, who was playing his cello. And behind Nathan, they met Selina, who was now sitting on the white stone. She jumped up and flung her arms around David and kissed him.

'Your work is complete! You have done the task the Master set,' she sang.

Then, together, they journeyed with light hearts down the mountain, entering into the light of a new dawn. And at the bottom of the mountain, many happy faces were there to greet them. There was the sound of drums and rejoicing as the two brother tribes reunited and embraced each other. David's mother was singing over some tribe members who appeared to be injured, and as he watched, he saw their injuries were slowly being healed. It was evident that the curse of the sorcerer had been lifted. David, Saul, Nathan and Selina joined in as they all sang as one voice in the Master Tongue.

> 'The Master reigns over this land,
> The curse of the darkness has gone.
> Peace has been sealed between men,
> And all has been forgiven.'

The cousins, Chief Lightray and the chief of the other side of the island, stood side by side, arm in arm, raising a drink to represent their new covenant.

And so, the Maker's purpose for these people on the island was complete, and he smiled down on them. There was much celebrating on the island for many days. The two tribes became one again, with Lightray as the chief, and the stone was restored to its rightful position.

*

Sometime later, the holidaymakers journeyed to their own land. Back in England, David and Selina would often return to their old haunt, the tree house – the only surviving remains of their previous life, as all else had surely been burnt down in the fire. There they would talk like old times, to their hearts' content. Sometimes, they would go and visit David's friends Derek and Ellie in the Tunnel World, who were always overjoyed at their arrival. So the two of them lived in complete happiness, as if they had never been apart. In fact, they became closer than ever before, and one day, they returned to Crossheart Island with their family and friends to celebrate their marriage union. Chief Lightray was delighted to conduct the wedding ceremony, and David and Selina proclaimed their love vows to the beat of drums. The party decided that they would settle there for the time being, and so Crossheart Island became their home. So they began to live out their days in this paradise land, learning from the wisdom of the chief and showing the tribe how to explore the Tunnel World in turn. Elvin often took the group on board *The Gladstone*, setting sail for other adventures across the Micronesian seas. As the years went by in much happiness, Chief Lightray constantly reminded his tribe of the meaning behind the stone. He told them that his father, Chief Lightfoot, had seen this day and smiled. And he was smiling down on them now, beside his Master, in the eternal skies.

The Third Tale

As Mr Friedman came to the finale of his second tale, he noticed a change had come over his musician, David. Looking as if he was still on that faraway island, David hummed quietly as he cradled his guitar on his lap, gazing into the flames of the log fire. Mr Friedman wondered if David was in fact joining in with the song of the character David as he had sung in the cellar and in the dimension of the Tunnel World, and suddenly realised how involved he himself had become in the telling of the tale.

'So,' Mr Friedman said. 'What was the Harpist's Haven?'

There was a silence and then some murmuring. Finally, Salomya put up her hand.

'It was Selina's tree house,' she said with great certainty.

'Indeed,' Mr Friedman agreed with a smile. 'Selina's tree house was one of David's havens during the story. And there were others… but there is one in particular of which I am thinking.'

Other hands went up quickly.

Little Judah cried, 'It was the Tunnel World.'

'And the secret room inside the academy,' added Ethan.

'Yes, yes,' said Mr Friedman.

'It was the harp itself. It was David's music, because he got really lost in it. And it protected him.'

This last comment came from one of the older ones at the back, Nehemiah. He was normally quiet, unless he had something important to say, and he often silenced the room with his rare wisdom. His father had been an alcoholic before his death, and it seemed that Nehemiah had gained insight from that early experience.

'So close!' cried Mr Friedman, pointing into the air. 'But think more personal, Nehemiah. It may have partly been the music he played, but think of the music source. Perhaps the Harpist's Haven was more of a *who* than a *what*.'

'The Master, of course!' As Nehemiah said these words, his eyes lit up, as did the glowing faces of all who were gathered there.

'That's the insight to this tale,' went on Mr Friedman, watching the excited expressions around him, 'and a message we must take with us. For in Him we can always find shelter and we can always live in His promise.'

'What promise?' questioned young Peter, frowning.

'The promise that He will never leave or forsake us.' Mr Friedman's eyes filled with tears. 'No matter who else may.'

The room was filled with a new sense of certainty as he spoke. David started to strum a few chords on his guitar, and the haunting melodies he sang led Mr Friedman very effectively into his third tale...

The Ministry of the Minstrel

It All Started with a Dream

Strange music accompanied a red dawn in a faraway land of another time. The sunrays struck the rooftops of a trading city filled with the clanging of iron gates and the crying of slaves. Deep within an impressive mansion in the darkest corner of a cellar was a hunchbacked circus child.

His life had become one of misery; he had been recently separated from the only love he had known – his mother. Together they had performed in an internationally renowned circus, not long after which they were each sold for a large sum due to their talents. However, the price to keep them together was too great and they were separated. Behind closed doors, his backstage world was a cruel cellar and a life of slavery.

His only companions were his music, his guitar and his voice. His mother had written in the sand one moonlit night under the stars and sung in the music of her tribe: 'You are my little minstrel and you were made to be His minstrel; in your song He will abide.'

They danced around the flames of the midnight fire chanting in the tongue of her people, and she held him closely in her arms. At first he heard her words in dull recognition, thinking it was to his father she referred. But afterwards he recalled where she had pointed when she sang; up to the stars and far beyond.

And now somehow she had been snatched from him, yet her song never left him. It filled his heart and was his only comfort; he longed for the time when it would set him free.

He wondered what purpose he had here, hunched and chained in a dark place, all alone. He sang for his freedom through the night, right until dawn.

*

And then the dream was gone. David lay awake in a hot sweat. He had had the same dream all night long and in his eyes he could feel tears that ran as if from a deep irrepressible well. The lamenting song of the enslaved circus boy rang in his ears.

He sat up and rubbed his eyes, trying to blink away the fresh tears. Over to the side of his bed sat piles of research papers and ancient books. His Cambridge University studies for his PhD thesis entitled *Evolution of the Minstrel* had turned into dreams that were invading his emotional privacy. The rest of the time he worked as an actor, and he partly lived off the funding he had been granted for his studies when he was out of work, along with a mysterious inheritance that had come his way recently from a distant relative he had never known.

In actor clothes he lived a varied life, mostly specialising in theatre of the Shakespearian kind, where he revelled in the comical aspects of the fools. These indeed were his speciality, alongside the occasional television period drama in which he was, rather unwillingly, cast in supporting roles. These were parts he had taken on his agent's advice, to avoid being typecast as the fool. Yet the fool did not suffer gladly when acting in period dramas for the camera; he found that all the shots, cuts and retakes repressed his flow of creativity and he was surprised he had managed to hold down any roles at all as he was often caught daydreaming on set. Of course, this only enhanced his view that life was all about theatre and theatre was all about comedy and making a mockery of life. However, he had begun to enjoy the contrast these television drama pieces gave to his true preference; they served the purpose of emphasising that he should be taking the path of comedy.

Yet in recent months a growing dissatisfaction had laid itself heavily on his soul as he tried to search for further meaning in comedy, and indeed in life itself. He was aware of the evolution of comedy, and had begun to observe its decadence, its surrender to the crude parts of life – as if it now pointed an unerring arrow at the meaninglessness of human existence. Or perhaps this grotesque new comedy was indeed nothing but a reflection of the degradation of the society in which he lived. In any case, he decided that the only way forward was to return to his origin.

As a comedian, he had decided to embark on a research project of his own in order to rediscover his lost roots. It was his hope that through returning to the past and the early entertainers of the world – as far back as the time of the court jester and wandering minstrel – he might discover some ancient wisdom that would shed light on his ever-searching and increasingly despairing heart and mind. And so his studies for the *Evolution of the Minstrel* had begun.

At the end of another long day of research he rested his eyes once more to sleep...

*

The sounds of slaves and market traders echoed through the walls of the circus boy's dungeon. The light rays were still trying to bring warmth to the cold stone building. And some-how he could feel that an external force was longing to reach him and bring him to life.

She would always search for him, he knew that. She would never let him go, for he was her minstrel and she was his, and would be to the end of time. He knew he would always be surrounded by the songs of his people, who were blessed by God. Thoughts of his mother filled him with faith and he knew that they could never long be apart.

As if in answer to his prayer, a great clanging sound announced the opening of his prison door. In came his master, towering above him and billowing with fat. His voice was deep and rough as it boomed around him, bouncing off the cold walls of his confinement.

'Market day today! You are going to fetch me a high price. Gather your instruments and your magic tricks and summon up whatever magic you can do. You'd better work hard for me, otherwise you'll be inside here all the longer.'

The circus boy jumped to his feet and grabbed his treasure chest (a heavy trunk full of his precious items, or 'treasures' as he liked to call them), and he ran behind his master as quickly as he could.

The fair was not far down the cobbled road, yet every step seemed sore beneath the morning sun's heat as he lifted the trunk with all his might, his hunched back straining under the weight. His master observed his hunch with some dissatisfaction.

'You folk are always deformed in some way. Still, it fetched me a slightly lower price, your back – tho' not much!'

And then his master cried, 'Make haste!'

They approached the fair, which was set up with stalls of freak shows, animals and strange puppets. The circus boy locked his jaws together and stumbled on. Then he felt himself being dragged backwards several paces as chains were placed around his wrists.

'Walk no further!' barked his master, as he hammered his chains into the earth. 'Your place is here – next to the Pig Child. It has been rumoured that royalty will pass this way today. And I'm sure we'll fetch a good price from them if you do your tricks well.' He paused, wrinkling his nose at the strange-looking child crouched alongside. 'Now, if you do what I paid good money for, you'll outshine all these... particularly this grotesque animal.'

He aimed this last sentence at the Pig Child, who was in fact a very large, muscular yet deformed child covered in a bright purple birthmark, who appeared to do nothing but grunt.

But as the circus boy looked at him, their eyes met and a strange, almost unearthly smile spread across the Pig Child's face. In his eyes there appeared an evil glimmer. The circus boy shuddered in fear and found himself feeling relieved that the Pig Child was held down with chains and could not attack him if he tried. Who would wish to buy him, he wondered. He could see the Pig Child's purpose as being little more than the guard dog of a mansion. Yet he felt such pity for him that for a few seconds he forgot his own purpose at the fair.

'Come, make haste!' his master snapped again in great irritation, and without warning he withdrew a whip from his belt and beat it across the sore on the circus boy's back. The pain was excruciating and the circus boy rolled on the ground in agony.

'Get up, slave!' his impatient master bellowed with yet more cutting cracks of the whip across the hunch of his back. He reeled in agony and wondered in sudden panic if he would ever get up again, for his back always caused him such trouble. This attack felt like the final straw; the straw that broke the camel's back.

'LAZY SLAVE! GET UP!'

Suddenly the whip lashes were coming down ten to the dozen and as he gazed up into sunlight he felt himself passing out. At that moment the chain-rattling of his neighbour, the Pig Child, reawakened his senses. In the commotion that followed, his master stopped lashing him as he beheld the Pig Child's behaviour in some bewilderment. The Pig Child was screaming as if in great agony; every muscle was in spasm on his deformed but mighty frame and his face was contorted as if beyond the severest extremities of pain. All of a sudden, the Pig Child ripped himself free of his chains that cut deep into his flesh. Then the monster was unleashed. In a roar of terrible wrath, he sprang upon the master with wild, bloodshot eyes and snarls that resembled the vengeance of hell. With two mighty blows, the master lay dead at his feet, his head pouring with dark red blood.

The circus boy cowered behind his rescuer in fear. Then he looked up at him in awe. The Pig Child turned around to face him, a great triumphant look gleaming in his eyes, and he gave a sort of victorious grunt. He reached forward and, seemingly effortlessly, pulled the circus boy's chains out of the ground so that he could move freely. Then he offered him his great hand. The circus boy took it with great uncertainty and trembling and then managed to stand.

At this moment there was the sound of trumpets, announcing the arrival of the king and queen. Along they floated in a golden carriage. The Pig Child became tense, and with one swipe he pushed the master's body into a ditch. He covered it with a cloak and placed a monkey's cage on top of it, so that no one would know that it was there.

The carriage stopped and its door opened. And that was when the circus boy saw her. She moved as gracefully as the wind, her long auburn hair flowing in bouncing waves down her back, followed by a trail of golden garments. Her crown sparkled like coral treasure on her head. Her eyes shone like emerald stars. The king moved close behind her almost as gracefully, his wonderfully handsome face filled with both delight and sadness as he viewed his surroundings. *That they should leave their comfortable carriage and set foot on lowly bloodstained ground like this*, thought the circus boy; *they are not the royalty I expected.*

These thoughts came to an abrupt end when the queen stopped right opposite him and turned to gaze directly into his face. He peered back at her as well as he could, squinting in the light that appeared to shine from her face. It was difficult to maintain eye contact with such a beautiful face. He was not aware that he was humming his mother's song. He saw her smile as her eyes filled with tears.

'This will be the one.' Her sing-song voice nourished his soul. 'The minstrel.'

The sound of this final word filled him with joy as he remembered the person who had last spoken it, and this confirmed that she surely could not be far away.

As he leaned forward to pick up his treasure chest, for the first time he saw the word 'minstrel' lit up in gold letters by the sun, as if newly engraved on its lid. Then he found himself being lifted up gently and placed in the golden carriage next to his treasure chest, opposite the king and queen, who were both smiling tenderly at him.

As they moved away to the clip-clopping of majestic royal hooves, he remembered his saviour, the Pig Child, and he quickly turned and peered out of the carriage window to see him staring longingly after them.

'We cannot take all the fair children,' the queen tried to reassure him, 'and we only wanted a minstrel. His path has another destiny to yours... yet you may meet again.'

She gestured to one of the servants that walked alongside the carriage as she spoke. He leaned into the window and she gave him a note, after which he quickly left the carriage and disappeared amongst the crowds at the fair. As the circus boy surveyed the queen's kind face, he somehow knew that the future of the Pig Child was in safe hands.

Later, as he found himself entering the castle, the circus boy was filled with new hope and purpose. And so his days in the court of the king and queen had begun.

*

David awoke, switched on his lamp and squinted at his clock. It was two o'clock in the morning. A nightingale was sitting outside his window, singing under the moonlight. As he listened to its song, he sunk back into dream-filled sleep...

*

The sunrays lit up a white castle set in a land of hills coloured like a patchwork quilt. In the castle courtyard, a young man with a hunchback sat playing music on a lyre. He was singing these words:

'Throughout my teenage years
I have played music on my lyre,
I have entertained with magic tricks.
The court jester has increased in wit,
Yet those with wit should not speak of it!
So I turn my wit to singing
About the flaws of human thinking.'

As the jester sang, the day turned into dusk, and so he picked up his lyre and entered into a tunnel that brought him underground to where his bed chamber lay. He lay on his bed, overhearing strange voices that echoed through the walls from another room.

'My dear wife, are we in agreement as to the way in which the deed must be done? My brother, the king, must not be given the slightest opportunity to suspect...'

'Yes, my husband. All shall be done as you command it.'

'If all goes as planned, he shall be dead by the end of the week!'

The jester gasped in horror. He knew that these evil plans must be divulged, and fast. He raced to the king and queen's courtroom and, finding them drinking a nightcap before heading to their bed chambers, he bowed low and brought out his lyre.

'Ah!' the king exclaimed jovially. 'The fine jester comes without being bid, my dear.'

'It seems he is eager to entertain us, or sing us a lullaby before we head to our chambers.' The queen smiled at him.

Seeing the jester's pale face, the king quickly said, 'Unless there is another reason for this late night visitation? Either way, young man, we would enjoy your playing as a part of our nightcap. So play away!'

The jester did not delay in starting his song. He knew it was the only way in which he could communicate the plan to his gracious owners. For it was not his place to speak without being called for. But singing... well, that was another thing. So he began his tale...

> 'As I lay in my rest chamber,
> The cat door stood ajar,
> And I heard voices from not too far;
> The king's sister-in-law and his brother,
> Telling of deeds of terror,
> They wanted the king's head,
> And claimed soon he would be dead.
> My being filled with dread,
> I could not rest on my bed,
> I normally sing of witty tales,
> But, my royal hosts, this once, I must FAIL.'

'JESTER!' cried the king, who had turned a little pale. 'Stop singing!'

The jester stopped straight away, his heart beating uncertainly. His master and mistress had always considered him as a valuable member of the court, as the bringer of wit and entertainment, yet his place there was clear; never before had he been demanded to give such a serious account. There could be awful penalties if this account was considered to be an offence of falsehood.

'Jester,' the king repeated, 'is this account true? This deed of which you sing – tell us plainly.'

'It is true, Your Majesty,' the jester whispered. 'Your servant overheard your own brother say these words.'

'Are you quite sure it was my brother and his wife?' questioned the king, leaning forward to search the jester's face.

'Yes,' the jester replied. 'Your Majesty, you know how they often sit in the Room of Tricks in the basement. Well, they have never realised that the walls around them have ears.'

'This is very grave.' The king looked mournful. 'Somehow, I sensed things were not right between us – and they have not been so for some time.'

'My lord!' cried the queen, who until this moment had scarcely been able to breathe. 'What shall be done?'

'Jester.' The king leaned towards him once again. 'You are esteemed by us, and by all in the court – the master of wit, the entertainer. Keep close watch on my brother and his wife, for I wish to know how this deed will take place.'

'Pardon my interruption, my lord,' the jester quickly said, 'but hadn't you better have them arrested straight away? Your life is at risk!'

The king did not show disapproval towards this objection, but only smiled warmly at the jester, and laid his hand on his shoulder gently. 'If I know my brother, he will carry out the deed on the day of our great anniversary, so that he can take my crown in front of the masses who will be gathered for the occasion. I want you to listen carefully in the meantime – and confirm that you have, indeed, framed the right plotters.'

The jester bowed low. 'Just as you will it, Your Majesty.'

No sooner had he left the king and queen's courtroom and entered the corridor that led to the basement did he feel a strong hand grab him. A black cloth was thrown over his head to silence his cries, and he felt himself being dragged down the stairs leading to the Room of Tricks.

A few moments later, the cloth was removed from his face, and he saw the furious faces of the king's brother and his wife.

'I think you will find that ALL the walls have ears, JESTER!' snapped the king's brother. 'Tell the king that you have been dishonest.'

'But,' the jester objected, 'if he thinks I have lied, that would be a punishable offence.'

'If you do not,' replied the king's brother sternly, 'you will die!'

The jester thought in desperation. He considered that the king would certainly be more merciful to him than his brother. In any case, he was bound to sense that something was greatly amiss. He hoped that the king would even strive to protect him, as it was evident that he had greater trust in the jester than his own brother.

'JESTER!' The king's brother was becoming red with rage. 'What have you to say?!'

'I...' The jester paused, then, drawing on an inner strength, continued with an air of great authority. 'I refuse to lie to the lord my king.'

'Then you shall die!' cried the king's brother. 'I am sure, as we are in the Room of Tricks – the place where you love to practise your silly games, or whatever it is you do – we can do some of our own magic, and make you disappear quite easily.'

'Wait!' cried the jester. 'The king will only suspect you all the more if you kill me. What good will it do?'

'Silence, jester,' he said in such a hushed tone that shivers of fear ran down the jester's spine. He knew that he would stop at nothing. The king's brother seized him by the neck and hissed, 'You will tell the king that it is not true. We will torture you here all night if necessary.'

'It is no good threatening me with torture. My mind is unaltered. Surely you heard the king say he already suspects you.'

'You will tell him it was a misunderstanding.'

'You don't know what you are saying! How can a plan to

kill him be a misunderstanding? Again I say; I cannot lie to my king.'

'In this case, you are no use to us. We will break your prying little neck, and cover your dead body and throw it in the river. No one will find it. The king will merely presume you have run away in a moment of mania. We will have the court doctor give a diagnosis of insanity. How does that sound?'

'PATHETIC!' the jester shouted.

'In that case, how does THIS sound? Hmmm?'

He drew out a gleaming knife that looked as cold as ice as it glimmered in the moonlight. The jester had to think fast. He pounced on the evil man, catching his arm just as he swung the knife in the air to deliver the fatal blow, and sank his teeth into the man's flesh. Then, as the king's brother recoiled in anguish, he fled to the cat flap that led to his room and scrambled through, with the fiend's wife trying to grab at his heels. He could hear the echo of their voices as he grabbed his precious treasure chest, and then ran off down a secret passageway that only he and the cat knew about.

'My lord! He escapes!'

'Well, don't just let him!'

Moments later, he had jumped onto the back of Lightspeed, the carter's faithful steed, and he raced off with horse and cart in the direction of the unknown wilderness. The moonlight caused shadows to flicker over him as he raced into the patchwork quilt of fields and copses.

And so, in one night, he had become a restless traveller on the road, an unemployed jester with just his treasure chest and a borrowed horse and cart to keep him company. He began to sing to himself of his recent loss.

'What was the gain, now it is lost?
With childhood dreams, now it is gone.
I moved onto greater things

Just to return to suffering.
I long for pearly gates, I long for old dreams,
Yet, if I turn back, I'll lose everything.
Where are you taking me, path of despair?
You must take me far from all I hold dear.'

Wishing he was back at the castle, several times he stopped his cart on the road and contemplated turning back, but he realised that his life was still under threat and even now he feared that he was being pursued.

*

Again David awoke feeling troubled, fearful that something was watching him from the window. Realising that it was only the nightingale, he allowed himself to close his eyes once again and slip back into a strange, fitful sleep...

*

And so the jester journeyed on. He had now been travelling for several days, and the days had turned to long nights filled with waking dreams of a perilous future and of life being snuffed out like a candle. At times he was certain he could see the king's brother not far behind him on the road. That night, when he stopped the cart for some rest, he began to have strange dreams as if he were half asleep and half awake, and he thought he could even feel an arrow piercing his heart as the nightmares became more and more real.

When he awoke from his fitful sleep and started a new day of travel, he became increasingly sombre. He missed being laughed at, smiled at and even cried at (some of the songs he had sung at the palace were rather thought-provoking and moving). Hearing these melancholic tunes in his mind as he rode on and on, he realised he had no idea where he was going and was now lost beyond ever returning to the palace.

It was here, in this mysterious wilderness, that his painful quest of self-discovery and search for identity began. What was his purpose without people to entertain? All of his life he had been laughed at one way or another, for better or for worse. Now he had no audience, just the trees, which seemed to mock him in the breeze. He had run out of food and was by this stage almost hallucinating through starvation.

I can see no way forward on this road of bleakness, he thought. *Everything has been snatched away from me and there is no one with whom I can share my sorrow. How can I make use of such a pointless existence?*

He stopped the cart, and slowly climbed out with a heavy heart.

The Mysterious Visitor

David awoke with a start. He wondered how long he had been asleep. The night's dreams still lay vividly before his eyes. Without a moment's pause he jotted down the whole tale in his bedside notebook. Then he remembered that he had a band rehearsal, so he got dressed, gathered his musical instruments and ran out of the house, burdened like a pack horse.

During the times when he was an actor at rest he also enjoyed other pursuits, which all helped to boost his work influence. He was a keen singer, songwriter and musician, touring the local pubs in Cambridge where he had played with his mother, Shaina Daly, who had been a well-known Irish folk singer. She had always been a great inspiration to him, encouraging him to fulfil all his dreams. David had also been inspired by a famous old comedian, Nehemiah Wiseman, whose routine always involved a song and dance. Since his childhood, he had researched and collected every article and detail he could find on Wiseman's exciting and often mysterious life. But there came a point where he could find out no more; Wiseman's performing life came to an abrupt end when he mysteriously disappeared from the showbiz world. It was rumoured that he had begun to live life as a hermit.

David continued to attempt to research the whereabouts of Wiseman, aware that he may be searching in vain, as the old comedian had probably long passed away. There was something in the way that Wiseman performed that he could recognise in himself; seeing his comedy hero on the screen sometimes felt like watching a mirror image. In fact, there was something of Wiseman that also mirrored David's own father, the father he had never known. His mother had only kept one photo, a faraway shot of his father standing on a beach holding a bottle of beer. His mother had only ever referred to him as a fool – and a drunkard. He had left her one day and never returned. That's all he knew. Certainly, there was a whole past in his own life he would need to unlock one day; he knew that, but for now his present studies were temporarily filling an empty space within him and he was bound on a course to eagerly pursue the *Evolution of the Minstrel* to its finale.

*

Many hours later, David had returned from his band rehearsal and was deep in thoughtful study once again. Already it was the end of another long day and he embraced the thought of sleep. He had started to turn his dream tales into a short novel entitled *The Ministry of the Minstrel,* and at times he brought the dreams into his studies as examples of the way of life of musicians and actors in old England. Indeed, his dreams were invading every part of his life so much that he yearned for them; he longed to journey once more with the minstrel jester and to find new discovery and hope on the lonely, seemingly endless road.

David rubbed his head slowly and allowed himself a long drink from his flask of coffee. The sun had long set, and out of the window he could see a moonlit glow on the lake in his lush garden. All was serene and still. Then a shadow passed over the shimmering moon reflection and the lake seemed to shiver in terror. David froze for a second, then arose from his seat and went towards the window. The shadow had vanished but in that instant there came a sharp knock at the door. He shuddered and his eyes flicked over to the grand-father clock as it chimed nine o'clock. On the ninth chime, he cautiously opened the great oak door with an eerie creak. Under the dim light of the porch lantern stood the cloaked figure of a hunched elderly man. He wore a black hat and supported himself with a gold-tipped cane. He stood still, watching and waiting for a few uncertain seconds. Then he tapped the golden cane quickly and coughed hoarsely.

'Sorry to disturb you at this time of night, mister,' the old man began in a deep, gravelly American voice. 'Have you got time for the company of an old man in the midst of your studies?'

'Forgive me,' said David, so taken aback he could not find the words, 'but have we met?'

'Yes... once upon a time,' replied the old man, 'tho' not recently, no!'

'And may I ask your name?' David enquired.

'Ah, sorry!' The old man chuckled, as if only for his own appreciation. 'I forgot... the dim light... let me step into the real light!'

And to David's dismay he hobbled straight into the hall, standing underneath the great chandelier with a look of expectancy. David moved closer to the stranger, studying his countenance, and felt for a moment as if he recognised the face between the lines, the soul in the deep-set eyes, the form underneath the sagging skin and the cheerful smile before him.

'Recognise me, mister?' The old man laughed and he tipped his hat as he continued, 'Maybe you don't yet. Give it time.'

With that, he placed his hat on the pinewood hatstand in the hall by the swirling staircase.

'Nice place you got here, David Daly.' He observed the high angel-decorated ceilings as he walked through the hall and into the spacious lounge towards the fireplace. 'Real nice.'

As the old man helped himself to a breadstick from a tall bowl placed on a glass table, David could feel his stomach knotting. This old man must be one of his eccentric fans.

'Look, I'm quite tired and I've been up to my eyeballs rehearsing and studying and...'

Here the old man interrupted, jabbing his finger out towards him.

'You study too hard. You know that! Every night – and yes I've been watching you – you sit here all alone in your study with your skyscraper-high ancient scrolls... I wonder whether you are really *living*.'

David felt some alarm rising in his stomach.

'You... you've been watching me?'

'Why, yes!' The old man chuckled as he caught the fearful look in David's eyes. 'Every night. Just this last week, that's all – your life really ain't all *that* interesting!'

He sat down in a ruby-red armchair, without waiting to be asked.

'Oh... and tea would be nice. No gin or brandy – I won't take to late-night drinking.'

David's head was reeling. He could not believe that this old man could possibly have the nerve to strut in with his gold-tipped cane and high hat without even introducing himself and treat the place as if it was his own. He would be putting his feet on the glass table next and asking for a foot bath and a shoe polish.

'Look,' said David again, with a rather sterner emphasis, 'it's getting late and I've no idea who you are. No offence intended, but I think you had better leave.'

The old man's face fell and in this instant David felt a pang of pain in his heart, and he could not understand it; he had been getting increasingly frustrated until this moment. He instinctively stepped forward, wanting to help, but he could see the old man's eyes had become sunken and now sullenly gazed off into the distance far beyond the lake, the sun in his eyes long gone.

David spoke in a kinder tone. 'If you'll just tell me who you are and how we met, I'm sure we can clear all this up.'

The old man stirred slightly, but there was no reply, just the sound of a lone dog howling in the distance.

David pressed him again. 'I thought I recognised you when I saw you... I just can't place where. You'll have to remind me.'

Slowly and against his will, David sat down on the sofa opposite the man, who still seemed paralysed. The man's eyes appeared to be scanning a time long past, as if trying to find resolution. But none came. Tears filled his misty hazel-grey eyes. David leaned forward and whispered gently, 'Please, sir... would you tell me?'

The old man turned and as he surveyed the young actor's face, life seemed to return to his own. Then he spoke.

'Yes. Tell you I must. But how and when, that's the question. David, you are right in thinking I've watched you. I've been studying you for some time – mainly in the theatres and on the screen. You triumphed in *Twelfth Night*; the clown Feste was at his most comical when you played him. The critics were marvelling – 'The Fool that Stole the Show' were the headlines. What a gift, and how well you've been mentored. But who is your mentor now?'

'Well.' David paused uncertainly. 'No one now... just my reading and my watching... I watch other actors and I continue to learn that way.'

'Do you, now?' mused the old man. 'Got any favourites?'

'Yes, there is one in particular,' David continued, lowering his voice as if he was about to share a deep secret with the stranger. 'I'm particularly fond of that old comedian – you know the one that was so popular all those years ago, who started the 'merging of the talents' as they called it, the minstrel-pupeteer-impersonator-jester-clown-dancer-musician-writer-genius. He jumped like an acrobat from one role to another with split-second comic timing.'

Here the old man laughed as if he had just gulped down a bellyful of ale and David had to steady him a little to keep him on his seat.

'Oh, yes!' He continued to chuckle. 'I bet I know the one you refer to... would that be Nehemiah Wiseman, by any chance? Born into a famous circus in Israel, then traded to a slave market, then rescued by royalty, then taken in by a wealthy American showbiz family – who happened to be his relatives – and then went on to become one of the greatest comedians?'

'Slavery?' cried David. 'I didn't know about that bit, or about the circus upbringing, come to mention it.'

'Yeah,' sighed the old man gingerly, 'the papers keep that bit pretty quiet – quite unlike them!'

'I'm sure if they had known about it that would have been world news,' went on David instantly.

'Naww,' replied the old man, 'not if someone pays 'em heaps to shut 'em up. Anyways, that would have ruined a reputation in those days... and there's a whole lot more to it than that besides.'

David stared fixedly at his increasingly fascinating guest.

'How do you know so much about Wiseman? I have researched him since I was a child, surely I would have known...'

'Never you mind!' chipped in the old man. 'What I know is for me to know and you to find out.'

Surprised, David leaned back tensely; he was beginning to find this mysterious old man rather frustrating again.

'Look here!' David suddenly piped up. 'You still haven't told me your name. I think that's the least you could do.'

'All right!' The old man raised his voice properly for the first time, wagging his gold-tipped cane. 'Keep yer hair on! This ain't gonna be easy for me, or for you, come ter mention it. But best be getting it over with.'

Here he paused; the young man listened. Both sat forward, one gripping his chair, the other his cane.

'I'm *him*!'

Another pause.

'I'm sorry, I don't follow.'

The old man sighed and muttered to himself, 'This is gonna be harder than I thought. David, look... I don't think you're gonna believe this but... I'm *him*.'

'What do you mean, you're *him*?'

The old man started to get flabbergasted.

'What does it take for the penny to drop? Who have we just been speaking about? With bated breath?'

'Nehemiah Wiseman?' replied David very slowly.

'You got it! Wow, I thought we'd be here all day – all night, actually. What do they teach 'em these days?'

'Nehemiah Wiseman?' David repeated.

'You said that before,' the old man replied. 'Gimme something new!'

'You're Nehemiah Wiseman?' David cried again, suddenly seeing the old man's features as if he was young again.

'Gosh, he's slow, isn't he?' Wiseman seemed to be making comments to the grandfather clock, which merely carried on ticking, quite oblivious.

'Mister, what did yer dad feed you as a kid, huh? Doughnuts?'

David felt his excitement momentarily sink at the mention of his father.

'No, actually. He didn't bother hanging around long enough to see what I ate... he was gone before you could say Nehemiah Wiseman.'

'Could you stop saying that name?' cried the old man, throwing his cane to the floor with a huge guffaw. 'It's getting kinda boring!'

David burst out laughing, and soon the two of them were chuckling heartily as if they were long-lost friends.

'I knew that I knew you.' David did not care how his words came out as he eagerly clasped both the old man's hands.

'Yeah, whatever,' replied Wiseman briskly. 'Now, when you gonna bring me that drink, sonny?'

David laughed once again; he could feel new warmth enter his being, casting away the loneliness of study in a cold room.

'What will it be? Brandy?' he asked.

The old man's laughing stopped.

'No, it better be a cuppa tea... seriously, I've gotta watch it at my age. I'm nearly eighty, you know.' He began a hacking cough, as if to demonstrate.

'I wouldn't have been able to tell – tho' I know your auto-biography well enough! Tea's on its way.'

David skipped happily to the marble kitchen. His dreams were coming true. From his childhood he had researched the life and disappearance of his hero, and now Wiseman had come knocking on his door! He could do with a mentor at this time – and he certainly welcomed a companion in the form of the older and wiser comedy genius.

He heard footsteps following him to the kitchen and turned to see Wiseman leaning on his cane.

'Your mother brought you up well; you got a good eye for decor.'

'A distant relative of hers left me this place in his will,' David replied. 'We never even met him.'

'Ah... did he now?' There was an awkward pause. 'Good thing he did. You say your father weren't so influential in your upkeep... just as well your mother's family was.'

'Yeah.' David paused, yet he could feel a new trust grow-ing for his companion. 'She doesn't say much about my father at all.'

'Not saying much is best when what's said is bad.' Wise-man paused, too, a flicker of regret surfacing around his brow, then passing on. 'Life is full of tricks – just stick with the good ones and you'll pull through. From what I heard about your father, he focussed on the bad when things got rough – he couldn't move with the changing times. Society grew up, moved on – he was old hat, he was dead to them...' For a moment his voice trailed off, then he seemed to recall something. 'David, remember my little proverb I used in my shows? "Only through discovering that one is a fool can one become a wise man." He had to learn how to wise up and he could only do that by facing who he was... and discovering that there was more to life than entertaining.'

David watched his misty eyes with great fascination.

'You speak of him as if you knew him. Did you ever meet my father?'

'Sure,' went on Wiseman. 'He was in showbiz too... for a time. We met in the movies I made. We became friends. He was a good man, your father – still is – despite what you may think.'

'I've only got my mother's words to go on,' said David quickly. 'She said he was a fool and a drunkard – but she never mentioned showbiz.'

'They all go off the rails,' sighed Wiseman in a strangely distant tone. 'I did, for a time.'

'Did you?' David enquired.

'Sure, that's why I quit, went and lived as a hermit. The pressure was too much. I took to the drink... but one day I walked into a church and got on my knees – yeah, I was desperate. Everyone around stuck their noses up; I reeked of beer. But then a strange thing happened. I could smell incense all over me, as if someone had poured oil over my head, but no one was anywhere near me. I think I'd scared them all away. The priest certainly wouldn't have touched me. And it was then... it was then I started to call on *His* name.'

'Whose name?' David asked.

'The name of my Father.'

'I don't know what you mean,' David said quickly.

'I know,' went on Wiseman, 'that's just it. But I hope you will understand in time – about the Father to whom I refer… not my earthly father but my Heavenly Father.'

At the mention of this name, David felt a deep pang once again in his heart, only this time it was deeper and more intense, and it brought tears to his eyes. For a moment he struggled to contain himself.

'W-well… I've been brought up a… Catholic,' stuttered David. 'Well, sort of… although I'm not really very religious. Anyway, I thought we were talking about my father, and you.'

He was not altogether comfortable and felt a change of subject was best. Wiseman took his cue willingly.

'Yeah, if you'll let me get to it. Anyway, what was I saying? Oh, yeah… I needed some breathing space. I needed to get away from it all. I fully understand your father – but that ain't no excuse for leaving a wife and child. How your mother coped I'll never know. How is she?'

'She's doing great, thanks. She lives across the way with my stepdad,' David replied. Then it came out of his mouth before he knew what he was saying, 'Do you know where my father is now?'

There was an uncomfortable pause. Wiseman softly tapped his cane.

'Sure,' he replied, in a quiet voice. 'Your father is… nearby.'

'Nearby?' David said hopefully. 'Will he be coming over to see…' he stopped suddenly. Wiseman was gazing steadily at him.

David went on, with some anger in his voice, 'I don't know why I'm even bothering to ask you that. If my father were interested, he would have come here to find me himself… and… and he wouldn't have left me in the first place.'

David could feel the hot steamy tears welling up and at that moment he also felt Wiseman's hand on his shoulder.

'Hey. Hey there... listen, sonny, that's partly what I came to tell you. Your father came with me so that he could see you.'

'Well, why isn't he here now?' muttered David.

Wiseman drew in a deep breath. 'I don't know. Maybe he's scared how you'd take to seeing a father you ain't seen for years. Most of us are scared when it comes to sons. Trust me. He wanted me to... test the water, as it were.' Wiseman paused, studying the deep furrow that had appeared in David's forehead. 'David, look – I've so much to tell you. But I think that's enough for tonight. It's late – how about we get some rest, huh? And talk about meeting your father tomorrow.'

The old man leaned on his cane and made as if to go.

'Hey!' David said quickly. 'You can't leave now! Anyway, you haven't had your tea.'

'I'll have it next time.' The old man turned round to look at him. 'It's great to see you... again.'

'Again?' David frowned. 'You said we'd met before. When was that? Was my father there?'

At this moment, the old man suddenly collapsed and fell to the floor, clutching his chest. In alarm, David fell to his knees beside him.

'What is it? Your heart?'

At first the old man did not respond; his face was clenched in pain. After a few moments, he opened misty, tear-filled eyes and gazed up into David's face, breathing unsteadily. Then David realised that he was sobbing, and in that second the face of the circus boy of his dreams came into his mind.

'My heart?' sobbed the old man. 'Yes, it is my heart. My heart is broken through years of loneliness and abandoned youth, abandoned dreams... friends... wife... *son*.'

He held his breath slowly and breathed out.

'David. I am your father.'

As he heard the words, David knew them to be true, as if he had known all along. And at once he picked up his father and held him close, as if he would never let him go.

'Please forgive me,' was all that his father could say for some time.

'For all those years I lost you, I forgive you, father. Because you've returned to me; I welcome you back because you came to find me.'

There was a timeless moment of a healing of hearts as the grandfather clock ticked on. Then there was celebration and laughing and singing until well gone midnight. And as the bird chorus started to call the dawn, the pair of them had just gone to sleep, both plunged into a dream world of song and adventure, and neither awoke until the next afternoon.

The Beginning of the Journey

Wiseman rested very well indeed and was still slumped down in the ruby-red armchair by the time David had written many more pages of *The Ministry of the Minstrel*, which had been further inspired by last night's dreams. In fact, so involved was he with his creative conducting of prose that when Wiseman awoke from his dream-filled sleep, he insisted that David read him the story from start to finish.

As they reached the end of the second dream, Wiseman raised his hand and requested, 'First, a cup of tea', after the drinking of which he sat back in his armchair, drew in a deep breath, raised his hand again and said, 'So the minstrel is lost and alone on the road without a friend in the world – sounds like someone I used to know. What comes next? Please tell me it gets better!'

And so David read him the following parts of the tale, as he had recorded it from the dream of the night before...

*

The wind howled around the lonely hills for miles. The sun was just setting on the horizon, and gradually all its vibrant colour faded.

The minstrel climbed out of the cart and took some rope with him. He knew that there were trees everywhere so he headed for the nearest one. Yet, just as he reached the roots of a tall, sturdy oak, he thought he caught a dash of light springing out from one of the boughs. He blinked in surprise and thought that he was hallucinating due to his hunger. But then, to his amazement, more sparkles of light shot out from one after another of the branches, and as he stood back to watch this strange firework exhibition, he started to hear music echoing from deep inside the old tree. He leaned forward and realised he was gazing into a strange withered old face that smiled back at him from deep within the oak. As he stared back in disbelief, the face lit up like a lamp and shone with such a glow that he was overwhelmed and was swept backwards off his feet.

He lay face down in the mud, and the strangest, warmest music flooded through his soul and drew him up to his knees. He looked longingly into the oak tree as he recognised the song of his mother and the music of her tribe. He wondered for a moment if his mother was actually in the tree, then before he knew it, a blinding light from a source outside of the tree came towards him and shone so brightly that he could not open his eyes. He stayed in that way for what seemed an age, and he could hear a deep, warm voice singing to him with a beauty that he had never known, as he lay in a sacred slumber:

'You are my son, the son of the King.
I am giving you a new name;
You are no longer court jester but healing minstrel,
For just as I am healing you with my song,
So you will minister to others with a new song,
And bring back my children's hearts to me, their Father.'

When he awoke, he felt as if his eyes had been replaced, for it was bright daylight and he seemed to see everything in a new light. Life felt full of meaning, for today he served a new master.

He realised that his purpose came in serving one master, and one alone; the True King. Then, to his joy, he realised

that his hunchback had gone and he fell down and worshipped the Creator of all.

So he set off on the road once again, with a light heart. He
also found that he had a new companion; an angel who rode
on top of his cart and who shone as radiantly as the midday
sun. With his new companion, he found that the journey
was no longer quite so lonely or tiring. Soon he approached
a little country village, and as he drew nearer to the village a
man came up to him.

'Hello, stranger. What are you hoping to sell?'

'Sell?' echoed the minstrel. 'No, I don't want to sell
anything. I'm here to sing.'

'Singing for money, no doubt?' questioned the cynic.

'Well, no,' replied the minstrel, 'I am here at my Master's
bidding. I'm just here to sing. Then I'll leave and travel elsewhere.'

The other man's eyes were full of amazement.

'Well, we haven't had a travelling minstrel in these parts
before... May I ask your name?'

'My name,' the minstrel thought for a second, 'is Minstrel.'

The other man laughed.

'Oh, come on! You must have a normal name. Minstrel is
what you do, not who you are.'

'True enough,' agreed Minstrel. 'It is what I was made to
do. And yet without this ministry I would very quickly lose
my sense of purpose. For I met with the Music Maker on the
road and he increased my gift and told me to serve him. So I
am His healing minstrel.'

'Music Maker?' queried the man, 'Well, where is he now?'

'He is here with me now,' replied Minstrel, who thought
that everyone could see the angel that travelled with him on
the roof of the cart. 'Can't you see his light?'

'I can see your cart,' replied the other man, 'but no one
else is in it.'

'I thought you may have found the light a bit bright,' said

Minstrel. 'It can be almost unbearable at times. Of course, he is a representative of the Music Maker, so he has to shine.'

'Well, come to mention it,' went on the man, 'the cart is a bit bright, as if there is a light shining from it. Is there a lantern inside?'

'No,' replied Minstrel. 'I have no need of a lantern when I have the Maker's light.'

There was an uncertain pause as the stranger continued to look Minstrel up and down, trying to discern his level of sanity, or his ability at magic trickery. But after a while of staring at the cart on which the angel sat, he seemed convinced by his own eyes and soon extended a warm hand to greet Minstrel's.

'My name's Sam,' he said. 'Pleased to welcome you to the neighbourhood. You can stay with me while you're here. My wife's cooking a good brew while we speak. Here, I'll lead your horse in for some hay.'

Minstrel got down from the cart and followed Sam into a cosy kitchen where a cauldron of soup was cooking on a log fire stove. A beautiful lady dressed in a stripy pinny stirred the pot gracefully and turned to greet him.

'Tabitha, this is Minstrel, a traveller here to stay for a short time.'

She nodded and smiled, then turned back to her cooking. In the corner of the kitchen Minstrel noticed a young man of about his age sitting over a board of paper, sketching. The young man had an unusually strong physique and was covered with a purple birth mark. It was not until Minstrel heard the man's deep absent-minded grunts that he had a sudden realisation. It was Pig Child! As he drew in a deep breath, the Pig Child stopped grunting and stared straight up at him. Minstrel walked cautiously towards him and reached out his hand.

'Remember me?'

Pig Child let out a deep growl at his approach, but just as

their eyes met, the penny seemed to drop and Pig Child smiled.

'You may be best leaving Pablo to himself,' Sam explained. 'We rescued him from a freak show fair; well, in truth, he was brought to our village by a servant of the queen herself. We offered to take him and we brought him up as our own, but he's never got over his experiences. All he likes to do is sit alone and draw.'

As he was speaking, Sam started to notice how Pablo had changed his expression and watched in awe as he shook hands with Minstrel. As their hands made contact, Pablo suddenly jumped up to his full height, which by now was very large; in fact, he seemed to have grown into a sort of mini giant. And to their amazement, Pablo took Minstrel in his arms and gave him an affectionate, crushing hug. When Minstrel was able to breathe again, he let out a hearty laugh.

'My friend! I never thought I'd see you again.'

Sam looked awestruck. 'He's never hugged anyone before – except me and Tabitha, although that took a long time. How did you two meet?'

'At the fair,' replied Minstrel. 'I was on display too – as a hunchback circus boy. I was rescued by royalty... leaving Pablo behind. I am so glad that he was brought to caring folk such as yourselves.'

'You had a hunchback?' queried Sam. 'You don't seem to have one any more. How did you lose it? I thought those things lasted for life.'

'The Music Maker healed me on the road,' replied Minstrel.

'I'd certainly like to know more about the Music Maker,' said Sam. 'He seems to be very real to you, although not to me. He's brought you safe so far, and healed your back... and your cart does glow quite brightly. I wouldn't mind coming with you on the road. Think of the adventures we'd have – the people, the places, the tales we'd tell...'

'But you have a wife and you are settled,' replied Minstrel. 'Do you really think the life of a restless traveller would be one for you?'

'Tabitha and I never had children,' explained Sam. 'We've adopted Pablo, but he could come with us.'

'Stories!' quipped Tabitha, with a knowing smile. 'Men will tell stories 'til the brew goes cold. Eat up, you dreaming men!'

And so Minstrel sat with his new-found friends round a wondrous broth and they ate and drank until they were merry. Then, later in the evening as the sun set, all the villagers gathered around the house to listen as Minstrel played his music and sang his life story and told them of wondrous visions of the future, of healings, of lands that were eternally sunny, where food and drink and celebration filled the air. And many that night were healed of all sorts of ailments, physical and emotional wounds.

At the end of the night when Minstrel had finished his last song, Sam and Tabitha came to him with one last request.

'Minstrel, your songs have healed so many in the village; as they came to you one by one, you sang a different special song over each of them. Our son is sick from a mortal wound inflicted in his infancy. Although he has come to find a father in me and a mother in Tabitha, I long that he would be healed of the wounds of abandonment and neglect. He has not uttered a word and keeps such pain within.'

'He needs to know the love of his true Father,' Minstrel began.

'But that will not be possible,' said Sam sadly, 'as he long passed away, killed by fellow thieves on the road – so Pablo's pictures tell us.'

'I am not talking of his earthly father,' went on Minstrel. 'Pablo needs to know his Heavenly Father's love, because only that love will set him free. I will sing for him now.'

And with that, Minstrel went over to the bed, which Pablo

was a little over-sized for, where he slept fitfully and fever-
ishly, and he sang a song that at first sounded like the tongue
of his mother, then changed to a tongue he had not heard
before. Pablo's eyes twitched and opened to stare straight
ahead and Minstrel could see a great light reflected in them.
All of a sudden, Pablo sat up and let out a kind of pig squeal,
and at this moment his deformed hoof-like hands became
normal human hands, and his purple skin darkened to
become a rich olive and glowed in revived health. Pablo was
sitting up in bed with a new eager and expectant glow on his
face.

'Thank you, Father!' he said, at first quietly, then again
and again more boldly.

He jumped out of the bed and began dancing around the
room and Minstrel joined him in song. Together they sang
and worshipped their Father until dawn. And as dawn
arrived, Minstrel took his treasure chest and carried it to his
cart where the angel sat, smiling at him.

'My work here is done. The Master is leading me on,' he
whispered.

'Surely not so soon!' cried Sam. 'You've blessed our village
so much in one night. Think what you could do if you stayed
for a week.'

'All your people have been healed,' replied Minstrel.
'Think how many more villages and towns and cities and
countries need the healing of the Father.'

Sam let him go, reluctantly, and said goodbye. Tabitha also
sadly waved him off beside a crying Pablo. Pablo had wanted
to come but Minstrel had told him that he needed further
rest there in the village to develop his speech, as the
surrounding villages would need to hear his story. It was
Minstrel's hope that one day the three of them would be
ready to join him on his travels.

And so the journey took him for a further day's travel,
well stocked up with food and drink from Sam's household.

217

Then the angel instructed Minstrel to stop at a new village. And once again he received a hearty welcome – news, it appeared, travelled faster than horse and cart – and most of the people were expecting him. And once again his Master touched everyone with His healing power through Minstrel's songs, and again Minstrel packed up his instruments and went on his way. Several villages went by in this way, and those lonely nights of travel on the road left Minstrel to pour out his soul time and again to his Master – and the angel, who listened in – of how he loved his new life but still felt a little in need of human companionship.

He felt the answer to his prayer would come as he entered the next village assigned for him. This, however, was certainly the most hostile village he had entered so far. The people were highly superstitious, and lucky charms were pasted all around its borders. Garlic also covered the site and as he entered children hissed at him in the streets, and their mothers would come out of their homes chanting strange things at him. He could only think that these people thought him to be some kind of evil magician or sorcerer. He rode in and parked his cart, however, knowing that against his better judgement his instruction from above was to stay in the village.

He sat in the middle of the village square by the statue of an enchanting lady adorned with shamrock leaves. Sensing that the very eyes of this amazing statue drew him in like a magnetic pull, he turned away from it and started to sing and play to the reticent ears of passers-by. Soon afterwards, a girl with a withered hand suddenly stretched it out in amazement and displayed its apparent healing to all who were nearby.

'Mother, look!'

'Quiet, child!' came a stern reply. 'It's dark magic... there will be a curse to follow.'

And suddenly a crowd had formed around Minstrel and before he knew it, his guitar was taken from him and thrown aside and he was being bound to a wooden stake in front of the statue. Someone lit a flame which set alight logs that lay beneath his feet, and then strange oppressive chanting started. He prayed for rescue without any panic in his soul, for he knew that rescue would come. And then, out of the corners of his eyes, he could see two figures step out from the crowd. They had their arms raised to heaven and looked different from the rest. They ran to his side, and suddenly several people pushed them right into the centre of the flames beside him. But as the flames rose up all three of their bodies, they did not burn, nor were there any cries of pain. For Minstrel knew that the angel stood right behind him in the centre of the heat and protected them.

A few moments later, water was thrown over the burning stake and many hands were unbinding Minstrel and his guitar was handed back to him, surprisingly still in one battered piece, and he was sat on a golden chair in the middle of the square. A great man in a cloak, the priest of the village, stood before him. And he said in a solemn voice: 'I see that you called on the name of our God and He answered you, and all three of you who stood in the flames were unharmed... But who was the fourth man we saw? He has vanished now.'

'Oh, that's an angel,' replied Minstrel, 'and he is still here; he only shows himself to whom God chooses.'

'As your God rescued you from the flames, I think He must be the same God we worship, only we have turned Him into something else... into superstition and lucky charms and idols. For this, we must repent.'

And with that, the priest summoned the elders of the village and instructed that everyone fast for a full day and bow down to the God of the heavens and the earth in full repentance. Then, after the day was up, Minstrel picked up his guitar and began to sing songs of jubilation. Many people that day were healed.

When the time came for him to continue his journey, the two who had been in the fire, a brother and sister called Thomas and Lavinia, requested that they travel with him, for the Master had told them in a dream that their lives, too, would be of travelling minstrels. With a glad heart, Minstrel agreed to take them along and it was with much rejoicing that they approached the next villages.

Minstrel found the other two to be great companions on the road and was just thinking of Sam, Tabitha and Pablo when word came from one of the villagers that they also were travelling around surrounding villages, singing and telling wonderful tales of healing. Minstrel hoped that soon their paths would cross once again. But for now, his two new young enthusiastic friends more than made up for the absence of the others. They had much to share and enjoy together. Lavinia was a keen harp player and storyteller and Thomas was a keen actor, and together they devised masked mini plays and gave much entertainment, which attracted the crowds in multitudes. And always in the quiet of the night, when all the village folk were relaxed, they would embrace the music of the Minstrel and his words and tunes healed their souls. The three would sing in remembrance of their time in the flames, knowing that the angel of the Lord encamped next to all who loved Him. At times they could even hear the angel joining in with the singing.

Things were going incredibly well until the group was met with opposition at their first town. They came full of joy, singing songs of all the Maker had done. However, on their joyful entrance, they heard whistles blowing and soon afterwards the marching of feet as a terrible army headed straight for them. The minstrels were halted abruptly in their tracks. They felt the angel stand up and take flight. This worried Minstrel exceedingly as he had come to take his angelic companion and protector for granted and could not envision the reason for his leaving their sides at a time like this, when such a threat advanced towards them. Minstrel could then think of nothing else but continuing to sing and as he did, the words came in a tongue from outside his dimension.

The army halted before them and its leader seemed to be staring in disbelief.

'You speak in a strange devilish language!' he barked. 'Do you know that going against the conduct of our city and playing music in the streets is a charge I can make for your immediate arrest?'

Minstrel stopped singing and stood up, as one possessed by an outer force.

'You have forty days,' the words fell from his mouth. 'Forty days to turn to God and away from the terrible laws which you impose on society. If you do not turn, you will be disempowered by a greater force, you will be defeated by God Himself.'

These words only angered the leader, who then ordered for their arrest and soon the three minstrels found themselves in chains and behind bars, on display to the town. Above their heads hung the sign: 'Death sentence in forty days for plotting to destroy the town.'

The days went by in hunger, then starvation. The captives were kept alive with a small amount of bread and water. Yet as Minstrel and his two friends sat in the light of the stars, they began to sing again of all that God had done, and the people of the town came silently to listen – the poor, the homeless, the lame and the blind – and their comforting presence uplifted the three.

Then the day came for the hanging – for that was their death sentence. But before the cock could crow and before the first rays of light hit the tops of the mountains, a trumpet blast could be heard. And then the sound of an army of hooves followed. Minstrel rubbed his eyes and looked longingly out towards the path on the nearest mountain and what he saw delighted his eyes – there the king's golden carriage approached, flanked by his greatest knights, leading a vast array of mighty warriors. Their jubilant marching song caused much unrest in the town as its inhabitants wearily arose, nursing hangovers from the night before. Minstrel saw the town leader emerge from his house holding his whistle, but as soon as he put the whistle to his lips, he froze and found he could not move.

In fact, as the king's army advanced, Minstrel observed that every individual who left their house that morning and gazed upon the victorious procession froze just like ice, and there they stood like solid statues, grotesque pictures of the life that once was.

And as Minstrel gazed at the ever-nearing royal golden carriage, he began to see a familiar figure sitting in its customary position on the roof of the carriage with its wings flexed, stretched out for action.

When the carriage entered the town it stopped at the bars behind which the minstrels were chained and the king stepped out and came to them. He quickly recognised the thin frame of the minstrel.

'I am sorry it took me so long to find you. But with the grace of God I am not too late. An angel appeared to me and directed me where to go… and here I am!'

The angel then broke the lock of the bars and Minstrel felt his chains fall off. The king extended his hand to help him to his feet.

'My son, to think I never realised.'

'Son?' queried Minstrel.

'Yes… I traced your origin to before the slave fair. You were a circus boy, the son of my first love, a circus lady. My parents banished you both from the region – and arranged my marriage to a Norwegian princess, who I learned to love. But we could not have children.'

'Do you know where my mother is?' asked Minstrel eagerly.

'Your mother was sold to a kind carpenter from across the seas, and so she has been taken back to the land of her ancestors, Israel.' Here the king paused. 'Of course, you may visit her anytime you like. But now I have found you, it is my greatest desire that you return to the castle with me, if that is your wish, and it is also my desire that one day you will sit on the throne as king.'

Then Minstrel remembered how his life had once been under threat.

'And what of your brother and his wife?' he asked cautiously.

'My brother and his wife – you were right – have acted traitorously and will be kept forever in chains.' The king looked around at Minstrel's companions. 'Your friends too will be welcome to join us in the castle. Tales of your ministry have reached the end of the land; you have raised up many more minstrels to do your work, the work of the Father, and you will continue to bless the world at the castle, as people will come from every corner of every kingdom to hear your divinely blessed music.'

And so the minstrels packed their cart and happily embarked on the journey home with the king and his men, leaving behind no living being – that is, all that had not frozen like ice – for the poor also packed their carts and journeyed with the king back to the castle at the prince's request, and all worshipped God as they went.

Time went by very happily within the castle walls, and out on the great lawns in the spring and summer, music and dancing was all that could be heard. At the king's request, many kings, princes, nobility and common people came to feast at his banquets and heard the heavenly music in his court, and all went away blessed and full of song.

However, after some time of living in this easy luxury, Minstrel and his friends felt uneasy and restless, and began to long once again for the road. So the travelling began again and led them to many more adventures, and Minstrel was reunited with his old friends Sam, Tabitha and Pablo. Then, further exploits took them to foreign countries abroad, where Minstrel was finally reunited with his mother. Together they wrote many songs of the tales of their lives, and she accompanied the six friends on their journeys, for she was still in her prime and did not seem to have aged in the slightest.

When all the years of merry youth had passed, the seven companions finally decided that they should rest from their travelling days and together they returned to the castle, where the king had grown old with grief at the recent death of his wife the queen, and wearily welcomed the prince and his friends. Minstrel's mother was received very warmly by the king and a few years later, they married.

Finally, Minstrel married Lavinia, for during their times on the road a special long-lasting friendship had developed. Together they had a son, Aaron, whom they taught the ways of the travelling minstrel.

Here in the courts of the king, Minstrel lived out his days, telling wondrous tales to the castle folk, and all who came to listen, until his father's death. And so Minstrel was crowned king over all the kingdom of which he had toured. Yet even as king, he continued to wear his jester clothes, as he did not wish to forget where he had come from. As his son grew older, he would take him on the roads in his old horse and cart, after it had been repaired, and together with his friends they went on many travelling adventures, continuing to touch the hearts of those around them wherever they went.

*

David had finished reading and he looked up at his father. Wiseman was gazing out of the window at the lake that had once been under moonlight and shadow, now reflecting a radiant sun in all its glory.

'I'm not sure how to end it,' David said slowly, 'or indeed if it does have an end... that's where last night's dream took the story and it does seem to have reached a conclusion. What do you think of it, father?'

The word *father* still seemed wonderful to say.

'Great, David... just great,' Wiseman answered absent-mindedly. 'What adventures they had! I was with them on their journeys. And these tales were all inspired by dreams?'

'Dreams and my own journey... and yours,' David replied.

'David, it sounds to me like you've found your purpose,' his father said. 'For me, it is too late... too late to live out my purpose for much longer in this life, anyway. For you, it is not too late.'

'What do you mean?' David asked. 'It's never too late. You've found your father too, who brought you back to me, so now I've found mine. I always thought if there was a God he would reveal himself one day – as a father.'

'Hey!' chirped up Wiseman. 'Let's not get the two of us confused! Earthly fathers sure make a lot more mistakes than our heavenly one, and they don't realise that there isn't time to make up for 'em.'

David sat closer to him. 'Your return has made up for it, father.'

'Well, at least I got to see my son one... last... time.' Wiseman's breathing was heavy.

'One last time?' David felt a lump in his throat.

'Son, I better be straight with you. I ain't no spring chicken. Truth is, doctor tells me I'm on my last legs.'

The music and laughter of the night before seemed to trail out of the window as a deathly silence took its place. David felt a cold chill.

'Father, no.' His mouth was dry, his voice almost inaudible. 'I've only just found you. You can't leave again.'

'Now, son,' his father replied. 'This frail old body ain't for keeps... trust me, that's a good thing. But one thing I told myself – I had to see my son before I die.'

Wiseman paused for more breath. David was silent.

'Truth is, I'd been looking for you for years – only managed to track you down 'cos you got famous. I got friends in high places, pulled a few strings... Now I've found you, I thought I'd spend my last days here with you – in this house I bought for you.'

David stirred and looked at him in surprise.

'Yes, you inherited it from me. It will be good to spend my last moments here, not in some dull hospital ward where you feel like you're already in the mortuary. I want to die feeling alive, not dead already.'

David had gone cold inside.

'*The Ministry of the Minstrel* ends happily,' he whispered. 'The king and his son live together for a long time.'

'Yes. it did end happily, but son, you know that wasn't the true end of the story. No, it gets even better. You see, I had a dream last night and the tale of my dream just so happens to bring an end to your story.'

And so Wiseman told David the rest of the story, as follows:

At the end of his days, Minstrel went on another journey. The angel carried him on his deathbed to a country far away, where everyone was singing, and there he found his True King, the Maker he had met on the roads. His King stood shining like the sun and in his hands were new clothes, which he presented to him.

'You have no need for your jester clothes any more. You've grown rather too big for them – in fact, you long outgrew them even on earth. Trade them for my clothes instead, garments of praise.'

'Was being a jester or a minstrel of no meaning?' queried Minstrel.

'No, just the opposite,' the king replied. 'It was of greater meaning than you've known. For I was a minstrel too, in my time; a parable storyteller, an actor of the old scriptures, a traveller, a healer, a miracle maker, a deliverer and a time breaker. I was also a king in many people's hearts. To the rulers I was a fool and a troublemaker. For the foolishness of God is wiser than man's wisdom. I chose the foolish things of the world to shame the wise, the weak things to shame the strong, the lowly things, the despised, the things that are not, to nullify the things that are, so that none can boast before me. I, too, wore your clothes for a time. But it's time to exchange them now, for clothes of a higher calling – the purpose which they served on earth has passed. They have linked you to this next life, where there is so much to be done and so much for us to enjoy together.'

So Minstrel put on his new garments and together they walked into the dawn of eternity amidst the celebrating songs of angels. And the further they walked together, the further behind him he left his adventures on earth, which became to him at first like a lingering shadow and then like a long-distant happy dream which he yearned for less and less.

*

David opened his eyes as if he had awakened from another dream. It seemed that his own dreams had reached their fulfilment. His father was smiling at him.

'That was my dream last night,' Wiseman said. 'And you know what, David? Just like Minstrel, that's my journey's end too. But it's not really the end is it, son? No, of course it's not the end. It's only the beginning!'

All was silent, except the old grandfather clock. Wiseman continued, 'Now the purpose met in this life leads us on to the next life. David, will you promise me one thing?'

'What's that, dad?'

'Promise me whatever you do, that you really live life to the full.'

'I promise I will.'

'Good. Time for my afternoon nap.'

And as his father closed his eyes to sleep, a faint song could be heard on his lips, one that David remembered hearing sung over him as a small boy:

> 'On the road again;
> A life of music and friends
> We're players in a minstrel band
> Travelling to untouched lands
> To heal them with our song.
> How much I long
> To be on the road again.'

The Fourth Tale

The third tale was told. Mr Friedman sat back with a look of some expectancy. As he gazed around him, he could see that all had been affected by the story. There was silence, and then a round of excited applause. And then, talking all at once. But the younger ones made way for David's voice, which boomed above the rest.

'Was that one for me?' He stood up, tears glowing in his eyes.

'Yes, David,' replied the storyteller, 'that one was. Especially for you. It was actually inspired by a series of dreams I had the last few nights. I had to write them down. I knew I had to call the main character David, just like the tale before it. No other name would fit. I am also sure that everyone else found a part to play in it, too.'

He looked around the room. All the little children nodded their heads, and they were smiling at him and David. A little girl put her hand up.

'Sir, I know that tale was written especially for David. It even had his name written on it. But I was also in the story.'

'Really, Lavender?'

'Yes, I was his wife, Lavinia,' she went on innocently, 'all grown up. That's what I'm going to look like when I'm older.'

'But how do you know what Lavinia looked like, Lavender?' Mia, the eldest girl gently asked her. 'Mr Friedman did not tell us what she looked like. He just said that she played the harp. So how do you know?'

Little Lavender put her nose in the air. 'I just *know*,' she said.

Meanwhile, Mrs Friedman had entered the room with a pot of steaming soup and was giving out bowls to the children, who licked their lips excitedly and beamed up at her. It was already late lunch time; the telling of the tales was always timeless, but that was expected on each Christmas Eve. It seemed that time froze for these magical storytelling occasions.

'And I was Thomas,' piped up little Tom. 'I want to do puppets when I grow up and wear masks and do plays.'

'I was Pablo,' said Peter, 'because I have a purple birth mark.'

'I wasn't in that one!' Judah cried out. 'And I was really, really certain that I would be in one story tonight.'

'And so you shall,' Mr Friedman said, laughing, 'and so you shall. Listen up, Judah, for the next one is for you.'

And the fourth tale was called...

Sailing Starlights

Surrounded

Guns were firing at the great tank as it lay on its side in a wasteland under the midday winter mist. It had been long deserted by the armies and had become a play station for local village boys. Only today it was the hideout of five immigrant brothers who had the police forces of several countries breathing down their necks.

'You have had your last warning. If you come out with your hands up and throw down your weapons, we will hold our fire.'

Reuben, the eldest brother, had been watching them from an opening high up in the tank. He climbed steadily down to meet the rest.

'They have poured petrol at the bottom of the tank and one of them is going to light a match. I will go and have words to settle the matter.'

'No, Reuben!' His brother Levi grabbed his arm. 'We are in this together. They will arrest you, and pin crimes on you which you never committed. All this long run will have been for nothing.'

The others all started ranting at once.

'Look how far we've got!' Amos, Levi's twin brother, cried. 'Don't tell me we are to be conquered by the Spanish police.'

'Remember where we've come from,' their younger brother, Joel, whispered. 'Think of our homes, and everything we stand for... all ended living out our days in a foreign prison.'

'I think we altered our course to that end. We did not need to start a life of crime.'

The last one to speak was Judah, the youngest of the brothers, the one who had least conformed to their new way of life and the only one that appeared to carry a conscience.

'Judah, this is not a time for you to say you were right all along!' Reuben cried. 'We are in this together, as Levi says. You may not have committed any crimes, but you were with us the whole way. You are not going to give up and hand yourself over.'

'I thought that's what you were doing anyway, Reuben,' interrupted Levi, letting go of his arm.

'No, Levi,' replied Reuben, 'I am going to *talk*. There's a big difference. I will talk whilst you leave. Towards the back entrance of the tank there is a kind of channel that goes underground. If I can distract them long enough, maybe you can dig a little way out to the forest right behind the tank and hide there. You can follow where they take me and rescue me at the right time. But now is the time to act.'

To Levi's dismay, Reuben jumped down out of one of the holes in the side of the tank. His voice could be heard from outside.

'It's OK, I am unarmed. I am alone.'

'Alone? We have reason to believe that there are four others inside.'

'No, the others unfortunately died last night in the train crash at the junction across the way. My brothers... all crushed in seconds! I am a broken man.'

'How come you weren't crushed too?'

'Oh, I went to use the lavatory. Fortunately for me the only one free was two train carriages away from the carriage that got hit. Oh, my dear brothers...'

'This is all very well, and could just be a good display of emotion from an excellent actor.'

'No! No, no… Why would I give myself up so easily? I am at the end of my tether. I am tired of running. As for acting, I cannot act to save my life. I've had a life of crime, all as a result of the bombing of my home and all that was dear to me. I had nothing except my brothers… and now… now they are gone.'

'Arrest him, officer, and take him away. We know all about him. Once he and his brothers were actors in their country, known as the Hypokrites. Apparently they used to perform in masks on the ruins of a giant amphitheatre near Nazareth in Israel. Yes, he was once an actor, but now he's a criminal. So don't believe a word he tells you!'

Then the same voice took command. 'Right! We know you're in there. Come out with your hands up and this whole thing will be over much more quickly.'

Meanwhile, Levi and three others had started digging a tunnel at the end of the channel whilst Judah kept watch.

'Oh! This is too much,' he heard Levi say. 'Why did we put him on watch? He won't fire a single shot and they'll get us. He's always been the weakest link. The runt of the litter. It's his fault we are all in this mess. If he hadn't repented of our crimes to that priest…'

'Be quiet, Levi!' Judah's closest brother Joel piped up. 'You know full well that our brother Judah has got us out of many scrapes – and don't forget he did actually save your life once. Now keep working!'

'This is your last warning! We will have to set fire to your safe haven. I will give you twenty seconds: twenty… nineteen…'

'Joel! Amos! We don't have enough time to dig! We are done for!'

'… fifteen… fourteen… thirteen… twelve… eleven… ten…'

Levi quickly gave up the shovel and screamed.

'I am coming out! Unarmed!'

And they heard him land with a huge thud on the earth beneath.

'Put your hands in the air!'

'I promise you that I am the last one left.'

'That's what your brother said.'

'I swear that no one else is in there. Reuben was just trying to protect me. He's always looked out for me. After the train crash, he's all I've got left. Please put us in the same cell.'

'Enough already! Put him in the van… Where is the van?'

'Er, we are sorry, sir – we managed to get it as far as the fence but there was no way in. It's a little walk away.'

'Well, get going!'

Judah, Amos and Joel were busy scraping away at the earth when, to their dismay, they heard someone trying to get in via one of the holes. Amos and Joel instantly turned and each fired a shot in a quick reflex action. The officer let out a cry, and fell wounded on the earth below.

'Officer Migdal! Help him quickly – he can't stay there in the petrol.'

The officer's name struck a painful chord deep in Judah's heart as he lay low, listening. Migdal had been the first to pursue the five brothers at the start of their life of crime in their homeland; the first witness on the scene, and like a true and relentless predator to the finish. Somehow Judah had known that Migdal would pursue them no matter where that led him.

As if to confirm Judah's thoughts, suddenly two armed officers appeared in two other holes and shot at Amos and Joel, who both fell and landed on the earth beneath, crying out in pain. So Judah was left alone inside the tank and he dug ferociously, praying with every movement that the sky would appear. Then to his horror, he could hear an officer coming closer. In a moment of inspiration, he lifted up a great lump of mud he had already dug free of the earth and set it up behind him like a wall, hiding behind it.

A few moments later he heard officer Migdal's voice outside.

'Looks like we've got our men.'

'Hold on, we've only got four. There was a fifth.'

'I couldn't see anyone else in there. The tank's empty. Maybe one of them did die in the train crash.'

Then Judah heard someone strike a match.

No! Please no! he thought.

In a moment, there was a massive explosion and everywhere beneath the tank was in flames. He resumed digging. When he began to see some light ahead the digging became much easier. Soon he found himself climbing out of the ground underneath a huge oak tree. Then he ran straight through the field into the mist.

'Well, I suppose that clears that up. If there was a fifth Barach brother, I guess he isn't there any more!'

'OK, well, we'd better all head to the van.'

'Yeah, which way is it?'

'Hey, that's funny. I thought it was across in that field. Seems to be no sign of it.'

'Oh, no!'

'What's the matter?'

'Someone's driving off with it onto the motorway!'

'The idiot! Doesn't he know we didn't come with all the cars because of the train incident? Most of them are otherwise occupied… Yes, hello sarge! Yes, the van's been taken. You'll need to send another one here right away.'

'What did I tell you, Reuben? Spanish police!' Levi muttered.

'Imagine that! The only time the police make a mistake and we don't have our weapons with us.' Reuben replied sombrely.

'That's enough from you two, thank you.'

Meanwhile, Judah was driving on the motorway in the

police van, with little clue as to where he was going. He drove for about a mile, and then it occurred to him that the police would probably not be far behind by now, looking for him. But it surprised him that there was no sound on the road of the all-too-familiar police sirens. About an hour went by in this way and, noticing that the petrol was exceptionally low in the tank, he pulled into a petrol station. It would be the first time that he would use stolen cash. His brothers had passed it to him from some bus passenger's bag but he had vowed never to use it; his life would never be one of crime, no matter what they said. Now, the time had come, for he was on his own, the only one of his brothers to escape the law. And now he would have to dodge the law to continue escaping it. He was just as bad as them, after all he had said to them. He felt like a real hypocrite now.

No sooner had he opened the petrol flap on the side of the police van than he began to hear police sirens sounding in the distance. In a moment of panic, he jumped up and as his eyes shot back and forth they fell on a van beside him. Noticing its driver wearily making his way to the kiosk to pay for his petrol, he quickly jumped in the van's open door, hoping to hide in the back. To his delight, he saw that the keys were still in the ignition, so shutting the door he turned the keys and sped off in the van, just as a police car entered the station. He did not turn and see the van driver return to the place where the van had been and collapse in a sudden faint. He did not know of the ambulance that later arrived to take him away. He just sped on the motorway from daylight until dusk, tapping at the radio tunes that were playing and watching fearfully out of the side mirror all the way. Sometime later, the news came on, reporting the mystery blackout of a young man at a petrol station. Judah managed to translate the report from the Spanish words he could make out:

'An English man has been taken to hospital after suffering

a mysterious blackout. Mr Joe Evans fainted at a petrol station just outside Portobello town around one o'clock this afternoon. Mr Evans is reported to be recovering well in hospital, with the exception of a loss of memory. If anyone knows anything more about the identity of this man, or of his business in Spain, police ask them to please come forward. Mr Evans cannot remember what he was doing at the petrol station and cannot, as of yet, identify the vehicle in which he is believed to have been travelling.'

The Heavenly Visitation

It was much later that he noticed the woman. She was asleep in the back of the van and had been silent until darkness came.

She stirred and murmured gently, in English, 'Are we nearly there yet?'

He jumped and stared back at her in disbelief, nearly swerving the van into a lorry on the motorway. He used his acting skills to regain himself and laughed jovially, replying in English, 'No, we are quite some miles away... you are best going back to sleep.'

To which she went straight back to sleep, completely oblivious.

A few hours later, she awoke again.

'I feel hungry and thirsty.'

Judah spied a muffin and a bottle of Fanta on the seat next to him, so he chucked them over at her. Unfortunately, the Fanta bottle hit her in the head.

'Joe!' she cried. 'Careful there – could have knocked me out!'

'Sorry,' was all he could feebly say.

After munching happily and taking a few noisy swigs from the bottle, she leaned into her seat and, to his relief, went straight back to sleep again. He had expected her to start a long conversation, but obviously her travels, wherever they had taken her, had made her feel even more tired than him.

After another hour, she reawoke.

'I really need a pee.'

'Very well,' he said, 'I will pull in at the next service station.'

And so, at the next service station he pulled in and she sleepily climbed out of the van without even looking at him. It was now his chance to drive on alone at last, undiscovered. But something held him there, rooted to the spot. Already the dusk had arrived and the sky was spotted with glowing stars. He noticed a nativity scene in the McCarthy's restaurant window in front of him, advertising an offer for a free nativity character in a children's meal. He leaned forward, frowning at the unusual nature of this offer. Normally he had noted that the McCarthy's chain offered characters from the latest cartoon or film in the cinema; it was odd to him that the West, being known in his area of the Middle East as the least God-fearing part of the world, would bring back a holy meaning to what had become a money-making yearly celebration.

As he was lost in his thoughts, he suddenly felt his entire soul shudder as if a divine presence pervaded his senses; for shining out at him in an array of heavenly gold, he saw the baby lying in the manger as if in a new light. Its presence for a moment felt so real, its face held a countenance of divine love and pure joy filled its amber-brown eyes and as he gazed more fixedly on it, he could have sworn a smile which had not been there before entered the face.

It was at this moment that a strange star appeared in the sky directly above him. He shivered as it actually started to move towards him and it came over to the nativity scene and shone brightly. He could feel his heart racing as the star became bigger and brighter, and continued to shine so dazzlingly that he had to put on a pair of sunglasses, which were resting on the car seat next to him, to cut out some of the light. He thought he must have been dreaming as the light continued to shine directly onto the nativity scene with such serenity that he felt certain that he was being visited by God Himself.

'Oh, God!' he whispered. 'If You are there, please forgive me for my part in my brother's crimes. I want to lead a new life. I want to know You more.'

As if in response to his prayer, for a moment he thought he could hear angel song. Then he saw the girl approaching the van, singing as she came. He quickly put on a big hat that also happened to be in the front seat and he pulled his collar up as high as it could go in an attempt to hide his thick beard. Then she opened the door and got in the back of the van.

'My goodness!' she cried. 'Where are we? Surely we are not in Portugal?'

'No, of course not!' he replied. 'Why would you think we were there?'

'Because I've just passed a sign saying 'Welcome to Portugal'! You were supposed to drive through France from Barcelona... Joe, why on earth are you talking in that funny accent? I'm being serious here.'

'Ooops!' He could not think of anything else to say. 'I think I forgot the turning. Don't worry; we'll turn straight back here.'

'This is like a really bad dream,' she said. 'Perhaps I'll wake up and find myself in England.'

'Hopefully,' he replied.

She looked over at him a little suspiciously. But to his surprise, she went straight back to sleep again and after some more hours of travel the dawn came, letting its sunbeams light up the motorway. Now Judah started to panic, for she would soon discover that he was not her friend. It also occurred to him that she may have been a hitchhiker who paid little attention to the appearances of those who gave her lifts, but then she called him Joe, which ironically was not unlike his real name, and which implied that she knew the person with whom she had travelled. He became so lost in his thoughts that he absent-mindedly started to sing in his own language, however, before he could bring his thoughts to a conclusion she suddenly sat up, and screamed loudly in his ears: 'You're not Joe!! Aaaah!!'

Judah could think of nothing but stuffing another muffin in her mouth, at which she gasped and then started to choke. Without hesitation, Judah quickly turned into a lay-by and pulled the van to a dramatic halt. He could see she was actually going purple, being unable to breathe and panicking. He dragged her out to the grass beside the road-side just as she passed out. Quickly, he managed to resuscitate her, feeling relieved that he could remember some first aid. A few moments later she awoke to find the stranger staring down at her and nearly screamed again. This time, he handed her a drink of water and she took it gratefully.

'You just saved my life,' she said, after a few sips.

'Yes,' he replied, 'after I choked you!'

'Thankyou,' she said, smiling.

'No problem.'

Then she asked suddenly, 'Where's Joe?'

'Joe... is just fine,' replied Judah quickly. 'I left him at the petrol station, where he was paying for petrol.'

A few moments later, she sat up to catch her breath. Now she was staring right at him, breathing a little unevenly.

'So who are you, and why are you stealing our van?' she asked.

For a moment he did not respond. He was starting to hear a strange music in his mind, melodies from his country far away in the Middle East seeming to call him back across the waters, and yet at the same time stirring him to go on. As he gazed up into the sky searching for an answer, the moon shone over them like a strange extraterrestrial force and the face of the baby in the manger penetrated straight through his soul and into his heart. And in this instant he knew that he must tell the truth and face his shadowed past, no matter what the cost.

He could feel her eyes watching him as if they were burning through the back of his head as he sat crouched over, his face in his hands. Somehow he felt that she would accept him and his strange tale. The waves of the trauma that had hit his home town of Nazareth those years before filled his mind and seemed to overwhelm him; the sounds of mourning, the crying of children in the streets, and the weeping of women who had lost their loved ones. Slowly he gazed up at her with his dark over-shadowed eyes and she felt the magnetic pull of his gaze as he began to speak.

'I am Judah, and I come from Israel. Once there was singing on our streets. Now my home is as a desert land, with no plants, no livestock and few inhabitants. Most of the land was blown up in the bombs planted by our terrorist neighbours. Fortunately for my four brothers and I, we happened to be touring with our latest show, for the first time taking our stories to areas outside of Nazareth and beyond Galilee when the bombs were dropped. Yes, I was once in a family theatre company; we called ourselves the Hypokrites, taking our name from our predecessors, those who performed in the giant amphitheatre in a city once known as Sepphoris, built by Herod the Great when Yeshua was a boy...'

At the mention of the name Yeshua, his voice suddenly seemed to hold great reverence and he paused before continuing. 'I haven't previously considered that, in fact, Yeshua himself may well have seen the Hypokrites in action as a boy; his home town was none other than mine, Nazareth, which overlooks the theatre – now in ruins – which we used for our plays... anyway, I talk too much of history. Believe it or not, now I am a criminal on the run with my brothers but once, as I tell you, we were actors, accomplished in our artistic trade, with many supporters and followers. Like our namesake, we traditionally wore masks to tell tales of virtue and morality. Now it seems that most of us are learning the lessons of our own tales years later, or perhaps not all are learning their lessons.' His voice became tense. 'But we were desperate; there was no food. We returned to find our homes had gone and our families and friends...'

Here Judah trailed off and breathed unsteadily, the flashbacks coming ever clearer, and once again he could hear the music getting louder as the moonlight grew stronger. For a moment he considered that the moonlight was actually healing him of his traumas but his thoughts were interrupted by the voice of the girl. She had moved closer to him as he spoke and he noticed that the moon shone directly over her head like a halo.

'I heard you mention the name Yeshua,' she began slowly. 'Does that mean something to you?'

'No,' he replied, with a broken voice. 'No... not until tonight.'

'Tonight?'

'Yes, on the road, after you had left the van, I had a sort of experience like none I have ever had. I equate it to that of a vision. A star, a truly bright healing star, descended on the nativity scene before me which I saw through a window. It seemed to tell me all I needed to know in the brief moment I had with it. It acted like a divine source and was a great comfort to me. It did not show me the way on from here, but since seeing it I feel a great sense of well-being and purpose and I've started to feel new wings lifting me up and stirring me to go ever west, to the coastline... this is where I have been driving to, and this I know will lead me to my destiny.'

For a moment he was surprised as he spoke, for the words seemed to tumble from another dimension. Suddenly, he could feel her clutching his arm and as he looked into her eyes he felt the same spirit of adventure and faith encapsulated within them.

'Then to the coast we must go.' Her words soothed him. 'I was told by an angel in my dream to travel west with a stranger, and that I must trust in God and an amazing future will follow.'

'You dreamt of an angel?' Judah marvelled. 'This must be a sign.'

'Well, he looked like an angel,' she replied, 'for he shone like a star, and he was bound for the ocean, which he passed into and then disappeared.'

'What is your name?' asked Judah.

'I am Selene,' she replied. 'I have been touring with a theatre company from England called Sailing Starlights around Europe for the last seven months and we have just come to the end of our tour.'

'And does your company have a spiritual ethos?' he asked quietly.

'Yes, we are followers of Yeshua.' Selene's reply showed that she too revered this name.

There was silence as the two considered the strange events that had drawn them together, and for a moment Selene thought she could hear the music playing from Judah's homeland, stirring her heart to move on. To their horror, they also both started to hear the sound of a siren.

'We must get up and go,' Judah said quickly.

The van sped off down the motorway and to their surprise the siren faded out; as it happened, the police car was on the other side of the motorway to them. For some time they travelled with bated breath to the coast, and when the sign for Porto appeared they were able to relax a little.

'But, what now?' Selene asked him.

'I do not know,' Judah replied. 'I didn't think that far ahead. We just wait for a sign, I suppose…'

They got out of the van and walked to the edge of the port, searching for an answer in the waters, but none came. Judah noticed how brightly the ocean glimmered under the moonlight and felt a strange sense of peace. In this instant they could hear the sounds of sirens once again and Selene shuddered. But Judah remained calm and mesmerised as he watched the rhythm of the waters. They seemed to be calling to him.

'Judah, they're coming.' Selene's anxiety penetrated his soul for a second. 'What shall we do?'

The sirens came closer and next they could see seven cars surrounding the port and drawing ever closer. Then there came the sound of a familiar voice through a loud speaker. It was Officer Migdal.

'Judah Barach, this is the police! You are surrounded.'

Judah did not move; his eyes rested longingly on the lapping waters.

'Judah, throw your weapons to the ground and release the hostage!'

Selene clutched his arm, and whispered, 'It may be best to give yourself up. Perhaps that's what this was all about.'

Judah shook his head slowly, still gazing into the shimmering waves.

'Put your hands in the air!' barked Midgal from the loudspeaker.

Judah slowly put his hands in the air. Selene sighed sadly, but as he continued to lift his hands, she started to hear a quiet mourning song passing from his mouth, and she realised his eyes were closed in prayer. At this moment the moon shone ever more brightly over him and then the tides of the sea started to change. Several police officers were running over to where they were with their guns raised, but the scene that followed caused them to freeze in their tracks. For as Judah sang to the heavens, the seas began to part from the point where he was standing. To the complete bewilderment of all the onlookers, the shores turned into two walls of water with a sandy path in the middle. And at the front of the sandy path stood a great shining figure with a sceptre, in a small, ancient-looking boat.

Judah and Selene found themselves moving gracefully towards the figure of light and they did not realise what they were doing until they had sat down in the boat with the strange being, which shone so brightly that they could hardly see. Neither could they see much of what occurred next, for the being pushed his sceptre into the front of the boat, and the whole vessel lit up. At this moment a huge cave entrance appeared beneath them and before they knew it, the boat had dropped into it. Then they felt as if they were falling down a never-ending hole through the bottom of the ocean. The sensation caused them to lose their senses as strange dreams filled their minds.

Journey to the Atlantic Ridge

When they awoke, they found themselves in a dimly lit underwater tunnel, where they could hear the sound of water lapping the boat, and a distant echo of a haunting song. The figure stood tall in front of them, and he steered the boat silently.

A fair amount of time passed in this way, Judah and Selene staring watchfully and rather fearfully at the mysterious companion in front of them. And after some contemplation, Judah felt pressed to speak; for all they knew, they could have been travelling through the depths of the earth with no hope of return. Yet at the same time, he could feel the strange magnetic pull of the waters and wanted for nothing more than to be taken to the place where somehow he knew his purpose would be complete.

'Where are we going?' he asked.

'We are destined to enter the underground beside the Atlantic Ridge,' was the deep, whispered reply. Then all was silent.

Judah wondered whether it would be too bold to ask further questions; perhaps their guide was not particularly talkative. Nonetheless, he considered a little light on the matter would help them.

'Why are you taking us there?'

'You have been summoned by my Master, the Last Nephilim King of the Moon World,' was the solemn reply, and then more silence.

'What for?' Judah asked quickly.

'That,' replied the being, this time turning round to stare closely in Judah's face, which gave him a shudder, 'you must discover for yourself.'

'Who are you?' Selene found her voice at last.

At this question, their companion looked into her eyes just as he had done with Judah and she felt a jolt of electricity pass through her.

'Hmmm.' He paused. 'Stronger magnetic pull than expected.'

'I'm sorry?' she asked, confused.

'Interesting,' the great being murmured to himself, then he responded. 'My name is Helios, servant to my master, King Sol of the Moon World and watchman over earth. His sister, the Princess Luna, unfortunately is recently deceased, rest her moonbeam.' He touched his chest in remembrance. 'She was the musician in the courts, and the main communicator between Moon World and earth. Now we have had to travel down here as a last resort; there are no other Nephilim left, only their descendants, and most of them reside by the Atlantic Ridge. This tribe from ancient times have recently called on us for help in finding the last Moon King.'

'So now that King Sol has come to earth, how can he help the tribe?' asked Judah, thinking that he may still be dreaming.

'There is little he can do now, for he is dying,' Helios said mournfully, touching his heart again. 'He must find the last king descendant, the last heir from his family line, and pass his moonlight on to him, or there will be no hope for earth. The waters will create havoc without the moon's power to guide them and soon will come the very end of the age... before its appointed time.'

'So how can we help with that?' questioned Selene. 'We were born and bred on earth and have no supernatural powers.'

'You must see yourself again in the mirror on a moonlit night,' answered their guide. 'Have you not seen a halo that surrounds your friend's head?' He addressed this question to Judah.

Judah remembered their conversation on the roadside under moonlight.

'Why, yes,' he replied. 'So what are you suggesting? That Selene is descended from your people, the... er... Moon Folk?'

'Indeed,' answered the being, turning to face him fully this time, which really unsettled Judah as his eyes glowed like balls of fire and had an intense, magnetic pull. 'And likewise, Judah, you often catch the moon. Have you not felt the pull of the waters?'

'Yes, tonight,' replied Judah, 'but never so strongly, until I saw a strange star.'

'That star,' went on the strange being, 'was me. I called to you.'

For a moment the two humans drew in a breath of awe.

'But now that my sceptre has hit the waters,' his deep voice continued with a sense of urgency, 'the Sea Dragon has awoken and we have little time left to accomplish our task.'

'Sea Dragon?' asked Selene. 'That sounds a bit like an old myth.'

'You're in a "myth" story, earthling,' was his reply, 'so you will need to get used to it.'

'Don't you think all of this is a bit hard to believe?' Judah chipped in. 'And yet here it is, a myth happening before our eyes, and we still think we're dreaming.' Then he addressed their guide, 'Excuse me, Mr... *Helios*, but what were you saying about a dragon?'

'*Sea* Dragon,' Helios corrected him, 'by the name of Poseidon – or that is how he is known amongst Moon Folk (of course, here he may be known by another name). Yes, as his Greek name suggests, he is the god of the sea and of earthquakes, but he dwells within the lava of the Atlantic Ridge and can change form in a second, and often shoots lava out at those who dare to trespass too close. He was once one of us, a Nephilim, but he lost his power when he chose to play with fire instead of filling himself with the Great Light. So he was cast down to the flames in a solitary existence, and he will be snuffed out with the end of the world.'

'I... I shouldn't like to meet him in these waters,' said Selene, shivering suddenly. 'You said we were headed towards the Atlantic Ridge, didn't you? Is there any particular reason why we must travel that way? Perhaps a route far around it would be more appropriate, if we are heading to the Americas or thereabouts?'

'An alternative route,' replied Helios sternly, 'would not be an option. Towards the Atlantic Ridge is where we are headed – and I say towards, but not right into it, for that would be a fool's errand and we would be destroyed by the lava, so that would be of no use at all. No, we must fulfil our mission in this way.'

'But why?' questioned Selene again.

Helios's tone of voice was becoming more impatient by the second. 'We are going there because that is where we must meet with the tribe, the last living descendants of the Nephilim (with the exception of yourselves, of course), as that is where they reside – in the caves at the bottom of the ocean by the Atlantic Ridge...'

This time it was Judah's turn to interrupt. 'Are you telling us that there is a tribe of humans who actually live underwater by the Atlantic Ridge at the bottom of the ocean?!'

'Yes.' This was Helios's shortest answer yet, and now it appeared that the time for questions had ended as almost straight away there came the most terrible noise. A great wailing echoed up through the waters, causing giant ripples to surround the boat. Helios stopped steering with his sceptre and put his finger to his lips. There was an eerie silence. The sceptre began to dim a little and for a second, Selene and Judah were worried it would go out. Judah thought that perhaps this was Helios's intention, so that they might not be seen by the preying eyes of the predator within the ocean depths.

'It's him,' whispered Helios almost inaudibly. 'He has risen and can sense our presence. But do not fear,' he said, seeing the look in Selene's eyes, 'for I am here to protect you. Just remember the name of the Creator at all times.'

As the word 'Creator' was spoken there was a terrible tremor in the waters and then there followed a great scream that filled their minds with a feeling of growing torment and despair.

Helios moved towards them and they could feel his light glowing warmly into their faces.

'Whatever lies he tries to fill you with, do your best to fight it,' he said quietly. 'You have not experienced this type of battle before but you will be given strength. I have fore-seen it.'

At this moment, Judah could feel a throbbing in his head. Two blazing red eyes entered his mind and he felt afraid. He began to feel like backing down, despite the waters that ever drew him, and he tried to push the image away from his mind, but to no avail; the eyes only glared stronger. Meanwhile, Selene could see a beautiful siren beckoning her into the sea. She felt no pain, just a longing to meet the friend who lured her with enchanting song, and she knew all she had to do was get up and dive in, away from the screams of the monster and away from all sound, to dwell in silence... forever.

The splash happened before Judah knew how to stop her. She heard Judah's cry and then Helios's voice singing in a strange tongue as she was met by the blinding light of the sceptre and found herself drifting down, down to the bottom of the ocean floor. There all seemed peaceful, and she felt her eyes close calmly as she seemed to drift off into a new world of dreams, leaving the screaming ocean far behind.

The Nephilim – Human Tribe

It seemed timeless moments later that she found herself under a blazing sun surrounded by many silhouettes dancing around her, chanting strange things. She blinked under the sunlight and tried to sit up, and found that a person at her side shaded her from the sun with a giant leaf. It was a small child with beautiful suntanned skin and decorative tribal markings painted over its little face. She could not identify the gender of the child but knew it to be of sweet nature by its innocent smile.

The tribe continued singing, chanting and dancing around her, then the drumming came to an abrupt halt. One of the tribe members approached her, holding out a container of purple liquid. It was steaming and its intense odour made her retch. It was the strangest smell she had ever encountered, and it made her think of too much fire and everything that burns the stomach. If this was their method of healing, she did not think much of it. Nonetheless, feeling somewhat pressurised not to offend these people, she took hold of the container, which resembled a giant coconut, and took a small sip of the liquid.

What followed, much as she had suspected, was a fiery sensation flooding her gut and the sudden overwhelming desire to find cool water, and to find it fast. She jerked to her feet and rushed around the huge rock face on which they all stood, trying to find a glimpse of a nearby lake. Almost as if in telepathic response, a bold-looking young man wearing

255

a great golden headpiece stood up and presented her with a smaller coconut. Without even looking inside, she grabbed it and poured it into her mouth, swallowing down the liquid – which turned out to be water – in a few great gulps. There was much laughter in response to this and as she looked around in some indignation she realised that she must have been the source of much entertainment to this gathering. Perhaps this was a tribal ceremony to welcome visitors – or ridicule them. Some welcome. She could have sworn that they had taken the purple liquid straight from the lava of the Atlantic Ridge, where the Sea Dragon dwelt, and she did not consider this the best place to find a healing lotion. Then she remembered what had just happened to her and considered that maybe this treatment was given to those who had nearly drowned at sea and needed a fiery awakening; a definite way to tell that they were truly revived!

'I see,' she said slowly, mostly to herself.

The bold-looking man who had given her the water smiled at her and gave her a good pelting on the back as he laughed, causing her to cough considerably.

'Well, really,' Selene cried out, 'there's no need for that. You've practically re-killed me already!'

He stopped, as if able to understand some of her words. Then he spoke to her in a quiet, solemn voice and waited for her response. At first she could not understand him, but then she suddenly had the impression of words falling into her mind from the sky. She felt the words: 'Do not be so afraid, moon-white girl. We are your shelter from Poseidon. Helios has placed you here as our honoured guest.'

As she nodded at him in understanding, he smiled warmly and let out a great whoop of joy. He raised his hands up high, letting out another great cheer, and the rest of the tribe did the same. Then they all began to sing again, this time accompanied by beautiful stringed and woodwind instruments. As the chorus was repeated many times, the words started to sink into Selene's mind and soothe her heart, filling her with a sense of well-being, that all would work out for Judah and Helios in their adventurous task. She lay back smiling on the ground and let the words minister to her.

'Fear not, Moon People, for your king has come,
Sent by the Creator above to renew all love.
All wrongs will be put to right and all enduring good
    will live on
Evermore and evermore into the eternity of new Moon
    and new Sun.'

As she sank into the chorus of new hopeful song, she prayed for the mission to be accomplished through the day and through the night that followed, alongside her new friends, the Moon Tribe. She noticed that in their dance the men folk appeared to be preparing for battle, and sure enough, soon afterwards they were seen collecting special weapons which shone like the moon and then heading down a great tunnel to the underground beneath, still singing the victorious song.

The Last Nephilim King

When Selene dived from the boat, the sound of her splash drew Judah suddenly away from the red eyes blazing in his head and back to the present. He cried out her name to no avail, so instead he called on the name of Yeshua. Then he heard Helios sing in his own mysterious tongue; the waters immediately calmed and the crying of the ocean rogue quietened in an instant. In the still that followed, the sceptre began to shine brightly over the waters and Judah squinted, feeling great delight at the beautiful scenery that lay ahead. On a majestic mountain stood an ancient castle, and a waterfall gushed out from the mountainside, sparkling like jewels. He was so taken by the view that he temporarily forgot about Selene altogether. But then the sound of the glorious singing which welcomed them into the heavenly rock city reminded him and he questioned Helios.

'What about Selene?'

'She has been taken to a place where the sea beast will not know to look,' Helios replied, 'to the island above the waters where this tribe also dwells. For there is a special rainbow of protection over these people, both above and below the ocean beside the Atlantic Ridge. Even though sometimes the practices of these people can be a little strange and not altogether displaying complete reliance on the Creator to sustain all their needs, He watches faithfully over them due to a covenant made with them long ago, when man had only newly been born – long after *our* creation, of course...'

'What practices do they partake in which Yeshua might disagree with?' asked Judah inquisitively.

'You use the *name*.' Helios suddenly seemed to warm to his companion considerably, and he laid his sceptre aside and sat alongside Judah as the boat appeared to drift by itself into the shore. 'I heard you use it when the girl jumped overboard. How long have you known Him by this name? You are wise to use it, for there is great power in it.'

'Tonight has been a strange night,' replied Judah, 'a night of change. One minute I was running from the law, and now I am on another mission altogether with a new purpose. The moment I saw your star, I was snatched from one dimension to another. I wish that I had all my brothers with me and that they could see all this... but they are to be imprisoned, for a long time.'

'Perhaps you will find the means of freeing them.' Helios spoke as if his mind was faraway. 'But you must talk with Yeshua about that.'

Suddenly he came back to the present. 'Anyway, I'm forgetting myself. You asked about the practices of these folk...' Here he stepped out of the boat onto a glimmering rock surface and held out his hand to assist Judah. 'Well, for example, I dare say that our dear friend has been confronted with the "welcome a stranger whom we have rescued from death's door" tradition, which, unfortunately for her, I believe, involves drinking the boiled water which they collect at great risk from the lava pools by the Atlantic Ridge. They heat up a sort of fruit cocktail especially for such occasions – perhaps as a way of imbuing more life into their visitors. We all know never to play with fire and sometimes I think they quite forget this rule. Never mind, I am sure that she is more than fully recovered as a result! Anyway, enough talk. Now is the time to meet the King of the Nephilim.'

As Helios spoke, they entered a passageway that led to a

great golden door, on the top of which was inscribed an ancient text.

Helios read it out loud: 'Open and Shine for the Nephilim King.'

As he said this phrase, the great door creaked boldly and began to turn on its hinges, letting a great light into the passage. Judah had to shade his eyes as he went through. As his eyes adjusted to the light, he started to notice things around him. Scattered everywhere were glowing golden roses and he noticed that they swayed as if they had a life of their own. A strange music echoed through the grand hall and he started to connect the sounds of the music with the light source itself. At the front of the hall, there lay a great being in what looked like an immense, golden bed made of glass. Judah was reminded of Father Time as he approached the being, who was dressed in a translucent white mantel and had a great silvery beard that hung on his chest like a glorious garment. His arms were folded and one of his hands bore a great golden ring from which musical sparkles of light shot out, rather like fireworks. At their approach, his lids flickered and his muscles tensed. Then there came a great booming voice.

'My son approaches.'

Helios stopped and signalled for Judah to go up to the great king alone. Every footstep began to feel lead heavy and his heart was in his throat as he sensed that he was drawing near to a great ancient being. Soon his legs were trembling so much that he could go no further, and his eyes could hardly see in the light.

'Come closer,' called the great voice, seeming to understand his fear.

Judah bravely obeyed but found that he was so overwhelmed by the strong presence before him that his knees caved in and he fell on the floor, bowing before the king.

'No!' the voice cried. 'You must not bow before me. I am

merely one of the Creator's servants. You must come to me that I may impart my power to you. That is all.'

As Judah gazed up into the kind, wise face, he felt that the light became easier on his eyes and as he took the great ringed hand that reached out to him, his legs steadied.

'Now, Judah.' The voice was becoming fainter as the light around it started to fade. 'Last son of the Nephilim King, you are here to receive your crown, and with it all the responsibility that I had as the king and the watchman of the earth. You will take power and light, which I must impart to you...'

'But wait a minute.' Judah was surprised he was able to interrupt. 'There are four others. Surely the eldest brother is due the crown.'

'Wrong,' was the certain reply of King Sol, 'for it is Nephilim tradition that the youngest son becomes king. Such was my duty, and the duty of my father before me. We have a history that you must know before I pass on my life to you. The least is first, and the first least. You have seen that you are the least corruptible of your brothers and for a good reason – the Nephilim King must be strong and incorruptible to lead others on the way of light. We have a higher calling than man. We are his watchers and messengers, and we must stay close to the light. The moon gets its light from the sun, yet in ancient times there was another light source which made the moon shine magnificently and lit the way on a dreary misty night. There were once people of light who sang and shone amidst the moon's craters and who lived and breathed of the light which they shone. Their purpose was to serve the Creator and be the watchmen of earth.

'Yet one day, their watching grew in intensity and their attention drew them nearer to the earth, until they were pulled in by its gravity and they settled and married the daughters of men. Some of these men were of the tribe of Judah, a people of future kings. Others were called the Anak, who lived in neighbouring countries and were the giants and heroes of old, and who have now died out. And a group of travellers, who were of the tribe of Judah's Nephilim of ancient times, were drawn by the waters to reside by the Atlantic Ridge, where they came to settle – the tribe that lives there today.

'One by one, the male Moon Folk deserted their people – for there were no young females left amongst them – and they settled with earth folk, gradually losing their power and their lifespan until there was only one King Nephilim left – a king and his faithful servant. The king's sons had deserted him for earthly lives and had long since died. He decided that he would wait until later earth times – and so he waited alone with the shining stars and their constellations, patterns formed by his Great Father above, as his aid until the time was right, and a signal from the last Nephilim humans, of the tribe of Judah on earth, was given (a prayer for the revival of the last king). And so the Nephilim King came down to earth, ancient and dying, to rest on the island beneath the waters of a certain ancient tribe of the human Nephilim. On the way to this island, the king's servant, Helios, caught sight of the last king of the bloodline under moonlight by a nativity scene and when the last king was taken on a course he could not control, where moonlight shimmered and oceans roared and the moon drew the tides in unexpected directions, the old Nephilim King's dying breath passed on the moonlight to Judah and King Judah alone, and with it the power of the Nephilim granted by the Creator of the Great Light.'

With these words the great King Sol breathed his last, placing his hands on Judah's face and pouring his breath straight into the last king's mouth. Judah could feel a great warmth fill his body, as if a flame had been ignited inside, but this was in no way a similar experience to Selene's lava drink, for this was a feeling that made him feel alive and enlightened all over. It was as if he was becoming aware of parts of himself that he had not noticed before, like being woken up and feeling a lightness of spirit. Suddenly his heart burned with a passion to do the Creator's will and to protect His people with his newfound light.

After some minutes spent with his head bowed in awe of his new life within, King Judah slowly opened his eyes and found to his surprise that the great King Sol had completely disappeared, and that in his place lay the white mantel and a sceptre beside it, and lying on top of the cloak was the golden ring, still erupting with sparkles of light. Judah took the great mantel and threw it around his shoulders, and he placed the ring on his finger. Then he saw his reflection in a great golden mirror that hung on the wall and noticed that somehow a crown had already been placed on his head and he marvelled at how much he shone. Suddenly there was a hand tugging on his mantel.

'Your Majesty, King Judah.' He turned to see his companion, Helios, smiling into his face with pleasure. 'I must accompany you now to the Upper Island on the Atlantic Ridge to meet your future bride, Princess Selene. Standing too long in front of one's reflection is not advisable for great kings of light, for they must share that light with others no sooner than they are given it. After all, it is given in order to be given away.' Then Helios bowed to him and said, 'Your Majesty... Shall we?'

Helios extended his arm warmly to the king, who took it, and together they moved gracefully down the marble stairs which Judah could now see as clearly as the golden angels that adorned the ceiling. He realised that the angels appeared to be moving their wings as he advanced with Helios towards the great doors, and all of a sudden, they were greeted by a wonderful angelic trumpet blaze and a chorus of happy voices proclaiming:

'Long live King Judah, the last Nephilim King!
May his reign prepare the way for the coming of the
Creator King!'

*

Meanwhile, Selene had almost forgotten her life before the
island as her mind was filled with new adventures and
wonders. She had become so much at one with the tribe that
she was highly favoured in the chief's eyes, who happened to
be the bold man who had handed her the drinking water. As
he already had a wife, he had not immediately considered
the proposition of a second. However, on reading some of
their old scriptures one lazy sunny day, it had come to his
attention that some of the Israelites of old had taken for
themselves more than one wife at a time, and indeed up to
five or more women, (if one included concubines and
servants who bore children for the leaders of the household).
And so these scriptures inspired the chief to act accordingly.

However, the chief, despite his boldness, was actually
rather a cautious romantic; he knew he broke the tradition
of the chiefs who had ruled before him and who only
believed in marrying one wife. And as a cautious romantic
he became very keen to impress the woman he wished to
pursue as a wife. He attempted all sorts of fine displays to
woo her heart, but none of them altered her opinion of him
in the slightest. Despite the fact that she had settled in and
had developed a deep love for the people, she had always
resented her initial treatment by the tribe, under his leadership, when they had forced her to drink the lava water, and
she had come to the unmoving conclusion that the chief
followed some senseless practices and that he was a bit of an
idiot for doing so. Nothing and no one could persuade her
otherwise. Although the tribe had told her stories of his
bravery and sound leadership, she needed further conviction
that he was actually at all wise and no love token could

possibly lead her into admiring him.

And so, after a series of failed attempts to gain her love and affection, the chief took to sulking, sitting day after day in the shade of the cedars, or grunting in the shadows, until finally he decided that the best way to make his princess into a queen was to treat her in the way he considered a queen should be treated. Early every morning, he would make strange cooing noises outside her hut and wake her up, which was not a great way to start to the day. As soon as she popped her head out of the entrance to her hut, struggling to open her eyes, and identified the source of the noise, she simply withdrew into her hut, though not before throwing a coconut or other such hard objects out at him, causing him to take evasive action to avoid injury.

The next thing he tried was the red-carpet treatment. Several musicians crowded round to serenade her as she emerged from her hut, whilst the chief bowed low and fanned the lady with a giant leaf before sitting her down on his own throne and singing to her. The only problem with this was that the chief could not sing to save his life and his voice was in fact so shrill that the princess had to put her fingers in her ears. When the hint was not taken and the singing did not stop (the chief had ensured that he had his eyes closed to 'set the mood', as advised by his trusted servant), the princess had no choice but to tiptoe from the scene as fast as her dainty legs could carry her.

Eventually, the chief understood that she was not the slightest bit interested in taking his hand. But then things got worse. He brashly decided that if she was not willing to comply, then he would make it happen by force. He was a strong-willed chief and had come to the throne far too early in life due to the premature death of his uncle, who had no children and had left the throne to his foolish nephew. The chief had got used to getting his own way, and although he was generally a person of good temperament, occasionally he forgot the meaning of good leadership when settling his own affairs.

And so Princess Selene was in the middle of an enforced ceremony of betrothal to the hasty chief when King Judah arrived to rescue her. He shone like the moon and struck awe into the hearts of all who were gathered there on the great rock. In an instant Princess Selene felt herself being lifted up by a greater force, and then she became clothed with a pure bridal gown and a golden crown suddenly shone from her head. She reached out with joy towards her well-timed rescuer, and took the glowing hands of Judah. Then, a voice from above said:

'Today, King Judah and Queen Selene are united in holy marriage under the blessing of the Creator, in the hearing of the tribe.

'Now arise, King Judah, and face the coming battle, for the dragon of the deep does not easily give up the fight, and he comes in many forms.'

Then the Sea Dragon made his presence known. The ocean screams reverberated right up to the surface and out splashed a great claw, which indented the island, causing it to smoke. All who stood there backed away with a great gasp. A deep laughing was heard, gurgling in the ocean depths. A terrible face arose from the waves and nostrils that breathed fire ignited several bushes near the shore with green flames. Then Judah recognised the blazing red eyes and knew right then that he must conquer the beast. They no longer paralysed him with fear, for now he had the weapons to combat the fiend. Selene pressed close to him in fear, but as his light encompassed her, she began to feel warm inside and suddenly knew that Yeshua was with them.

The dragon bellowed again and this time he filled the whole ocean with a raging fire, green and red, the flames dancing around wildly as if they had been released from a great prison.

'Poseidon,' commanded the king boldly, 'you have no place here. Back to the depths with you!'

Poseidon recoiled his long spiny neck on hearing this voice, and spat out green fluid, but Judah quickly realised that his eyes were blind, and therefore he could not see who spoke or the light that surrounded him.

'Who dares to challenge me?' the bitter voice demanded. 'Under what authority do you command me to return to the depths?'

'I have no authority of my own,' began Judah, not fazed by the dragon's sneers, 'but I come in the name of Yeshua.'

At the sound of this name, the dragon winced and shut his foul eyes tight. 'Do not mention that name here, earthling. You are no match for me and so you cling to another name. You have no weapons of your own; you have not the light source. That alone, given by the Creator to his Nephilim, can give me battle. This is my domain; I am the god of the ocean and of the earthquakes on the ocean floor. I have been given a land of lava and a bed of fire and water, and one day the whole earth will be dissolved into it. So be gone, earthling, back to the earth from where you came, which soon will be no more!'

And with that, the dragon Poseidon let loose his fiery breath into the air until the tribe started to choke on the poisonous fumes. Poseidon's laughter rose high above the land and Judah knew that the time had come to combat the dragon. He raised his sceptre and shouted out at Poseidon, 'Creature! Your time here has come to an end, and your reign in the underworld will end with the earth. You are blinded to truth as you are to the light. For I am King Judah, the last king of the Nephilim and I stand with the light source, the power granted me by the Creator to use in the name of Yeshua!'

As Judah's voice rang out in the dragon's ears, a greater light shone from his sceptre directly into Poseidon's eyes, and the dragon fell back into the sea and wailed in a loud penetrating tone which disturbed the tribe greatly, but Judah continued to speak boldly, 'And so, in the name of Yeshua I command you to be gone! Go and return to the world of the deep, and dwell there in hot flames under lock and key until the time is set for your destruction.'

As he spoke, Judah found that the great shining sceptre which he held had become a giant key, and he knew his mission; to take the dragon back to his dungeon. The dragon sank slowly back into the sea of green flames and Judah left Selene to rest on the island, then he rose up in the air – for the light enabled him to fly – and he grabbed the dragon by the throat. Poseidon struggled and roared and snapped at him, but it could do him no damage, for the dragon was afraid of the great piercing light that had penetrated into his eyes, which were burning with pain. Together they journeyed, struggling, far down into the deep through streams of lava, which could not scorch Judah, for he was wrapped in light like a warm blanket of protection, until finally they met the solid lava base of the Atlantic Ridge. Here Judah used his sceptre to forge a metallic structure from out of the lava, much to the horror of the dragon, who was kept at bay by the light source. At the sound of the chink of metal and the awareness of the expanding barred form that surrounded him, the dragon lay in a defeated heap, quivering with each blow. Finally, the structure was complete, and the dragon was powerless within it. Then, the lock was completed to fit the key, which shone in Judah's hand, and soon the prison cell was locked.

The Return to the Origin

A surprise awaited Judah on his return to the Upper Island. A group of familiar police officers had arrived, still searching for the convict on the run. The whole tribe had been surrounded and the foolish chief was attempting to make merry and play tricks on the officers, who were not in the mood for games.

'Aha! Judah Barach!' Officer Migdal confronted Judah, but his victorious expression quickly fell as he beheld the spectacle of light that stood before him. 'What the...'

'You wanted me, officer?' questioned Judah in a matter-of-fact voice, as if to convey that he wore this bright attire every day.

'Well,' continued Migdal, who for a moment had seemed quite speechless, 'I do declare that you have become this tribe's chief.'

'Correct!' replied Judah. 'And a little more than that. But I can only leave that to your imagination, which I am afraid would limit the whole scene somewhat. Are you here to take me away, Officer Migdal?'

Migdal was obviously puzzling over the scene he was witnessing. 'Well, yes, that is what I would like to do. Will you... er... hand yourself over?'

'Certainly, officer,' replied Judah with a smile. 'I must let an officer of the law do his job correctly. After all, I am a convict under your law, although I don't suppose that covers these islands, does it?'

He reached out his hands, which were immediately hand-cuffed.

'Don't think that by joining this tribe you've got out of trouble,' grunted Migdal a little fiercely. 'Believe me, you are under the same law as your four brothers, all neatly locked away in their cells for the crimes which they have committed.'

'Yes, what you say is true,' replied Judah, 'although I have no memory of committing the crimes they did.'

'I suppose being an accessory to the crime doesn't come into it, then?' queried the officer, leaning forward into Judah's face as if trying to discern the source of his light. 'Yes, I've already heard from their own lips that you are innocent. The only one who never committed a crime – except for the van you stole, owned by the Sailing Starlights Theatre Company, and not to mention the girl you took hostage, who I see has become equally acquainted with this tribe as she seems to have become... with you...'

Here Selene spoke up. 'I am in this just as much as Judah. I was with him every step of the way, almost from the moment he took the van.'

'I guess you'd have no choice in that, sweet cakes,' retorted Migdal sarcastically, 'as he was driving the whole way!'

'I think we've done enough talking, haven't we officer?' piped up another police officer, who had been regarding the garments Judah and Selene were wearing with some admiration. 'Hadn't we better follow orders and take them away?'

At that moment, a great voice called from the heavens, causing all the present company to fall to their knees on the ground:

'You take orders from those above you, who do not see the full picture. I command a higher order and I am sending King Judah to another realm, beyond that of mankind's experience. Yes, they have the authority I have allowed them to wield, but have they really lived and breathed of the eternal light that it radiates from? My son has a new mission, to watch and guard the earth with his queen and their descendants, amidst their new tribe, and the chief of this tribe will be their servant alongside Judah's servant, Helios. For the first will be last and the last will be first.'

By this point, the officers were quaking in their boots. None could speak and all gazed up to the skies with their hands shielding their faces from the light.

The great voice spoke again:

'The authority granted to you was given by me. You have done your duty. Now Migdal, lay down your arms against Judah, for you also are of his tribe, and you must become his counsellor in the other realm. Yes, you also are a descendant of the Nephilim, and of the tribe of Judah, just as Judah himself is. The rest of you men of arms, return to Spain, where you must tell your colleagues and those in prison of what you have seen, and at the right time, the four Barach brothers will be released from prison and will join their youngest brother, the Nephilim King, up in the heavenly lights, to walk on the moon and to live and breathe of my eternal light like their ancestors before them.'

As the voice from the heavens spoke, the light that surrounded Judah and Selene gathered the tribe together and they were lifted high into the sky. With great wonder and surprise, Migdal found himself also being lifted upwards. The 'men of arms' were left crouching below staring up at them in awe as they turned into glowing starlights, and then became specks of light against a darkening sky as they headed for the moon.

From that day, they were referred to as the Sailing Starlights, and there were many tales about them on earth, which some believed and others disregarded as myth. The tales reached the ears of the four brothers, who were repentant of their crimes and who longed to see life in a new light. And sometime afterwards, they did.

King Judah, with his wife Queen Selene, together with all the Nephilim tribe, began their watch over the earth, and lived a life of warmth and joyous light right up until the end of the world, when all peoples came to join them and live forever with the eternal light.

The Fifth Tale

Mr Friedman sat back and gave a sigh of relief. David was plucking the strings of his guitar and singing a mysterious and haunting song which emphasised the eerie glow that the candles gave, making the company feel as if they were surrounded by the music of the Moon Folk.

'These tales are using more energy than they used to,' panted Mr Friedman, patting David on the shoulder. 'Anyone up for more of Mrs Friedman's lovely broth?'

'Yes, please!' Up went all the hands.

Mrs Friedman was waiting to serve them all once again.

'Thank you, Evelyn.' Mr Friedman proceeded to compliment his wife on her soup. 'This truly gets better every year, my dear! Mmm, tomato and basil – my favourite.'

'That was an adventurous tale.' Judah was still mesmerised as they passed the bowls around. 'And I think that you maybe had a dream about that one, too?'

Mr Friedman pondered as he took a long sip of the warm soup.

'Now then, Judah, this story was partly inspired by my dreams, and by a verse of scripture that has often puzzled me about the origin of the Nephilim – but remember this is Mr Friedman's make-believe fairy tale. As with all the other stories, there are elements of truth in it, but you have to decide what you believe the whole truth to be.

'"Sailing Starlights" was truly inspired by you and your family. Yes, I saw the land you came from in a dream, and the disasters and the bombing. But I have also seen far beyond that; this tale tells you something of what can come out of pain, the good things that can come out of the bad by seeking for truth and life in a world of despair.'

'Really?' questioned Judah. Then he thought about it. 'Actually, already I can find one good thing – I came to live here! And in the story I went to live on the moon.'

'Yes, you did, in *that* dimension,' Mr Friedman continued. 'However, you may not necessarily go and live on the moon in *this* dimension.'

'Oh.' Judah looked somewhat disappointed.

'Your life will be so much greater than that,' went on Mr Friedman in an encouraging tone. 'You don't need to run away from this world. You are not on the run from the police. But we are all in a battle; an invisible battle. And we all need you to take your position in the great fight against darkness, and to pierce it with the light of truth that I have told you all about. You may think you have one set path in life, but believe me, God's always got much better plans than you could possibly imagine. So hang on in there, Judah, my son. You are going to be all right. Much more than all right, actually. Because one day, you are going to be ruling and reigning with Him.'

'Him?' repeated Judah in awe, his whole countenance lighting up like a glowing flame. 'Wow!'

A little girl leaned in and studied his face. 'Yes. I can see it now.'

'See what?' questioned Judah, puzzled.

'Your face,' she said, smiling. 'It's a moonbeam!'

'Really?' he replied, then he studied her for a second. 'Come to mention it, your face is glowing too, Selene!'

'That's because I was the girl in the story,' Selene said proudly.

Mr Friedman laughed. 'You kids are just great. Timeless characters. How much your Heavenly Father delights in you.

Now, listen up. As we explored how God sees our lives so differently to how we do, that leads me on to the theme of the fifth tale. This tale is for one or more of the older ones. It's called...

The Hermits of
Rosendale House

The Spotlight

The months had passed by in silence. The more the seasons turned, the more the hermit sheltered. She lived within a safe cave she had discovered and fitted out herself.

Inside, on the cave walls she drew the stories of her life. She hung wind chimes around as musical decoration and hummed as she worked to the melodies of a little silver music box. The music box bore the engraving of a fine rose in full bloom. It had been her discovery on first entering the cave and it was her prime trophy. She had no idea of how it came to be there. To her, it represented love, truth and happiness – all that was good – and it gave her much pleasure as it played a haunting folk tune from far across the seas.

The hermit also had a special collection of varnished vases. In each vase stood a rose which she had found, or picked after dusk from the neighbouring cottage gardens. She only chose one rose from each garden; the one in fullest bloom. When the petals began to wilt, she would take the rose and crush it, then make it into perfume with other special ingredients, which she would give to the gypsies who lived across the hill.

The hermit had neatly lined up her vase collection on a glass table that, together with the vases, echoed a pattern of rainbows throughout the cave when the sun shone through.

She loved the feelings of adventure and fun which flooded through her soul as she gazed upon the works of art she had created. She knew that she was gifted in the arts and she followed the lives of other artistes quite closely; in fact, the life of one artiste was of particular interest to her. On market days, she would wrap a golden shawl around her head and wear sunglasses so that she would not have to look people in the eyes as she walked to the village to survey the newspaper stalls. If the particular artiste she followed appeared in the paper, she would buy it, then tear out the article and picture and stick it in her scrapbook, for later reading by candlelight. This article collection, second to the silver music box, was also her trophy, and she knew more of this artiste than anyone else, more even than the paparazzi who followed her life so closely. The article collection had only begun in recent months, since the artiste had mysteriously disappeared and become a missing person, so that she was well out of reach of even the 'all-seeing' paparazzi. The newspaper articles were full of vain searches for this much-loved celebrity or would reveal rare sightings of her, which turned out to be false. The paper's pictures showed her red carpet appearances and told of her latest acting triumphs.

Today the hermit looked forward to reading a recent article from yesterday's paper which she had not managed to read yet because she had fallen asleep to the sound of her music box the night before. And so, as was her tradition, by candlelight she read the words:

Mia Herman: The Mystery Continues...

It is now seven months since singer-actress Mia Herman's disappearance, and there is still no trace of her whereabouts. Far-fetched rumour has it that she has begun to live the life of a hermit in a cave in a remote part of the Highlands of Scotland, where she entertains mountain goats and sings with the birds. Yet in the light of events leading up to her mysterious disappearance, even such mythical tales may need to be taken with something other than just a pinch of salt.

Just weeks before Mia left her thatched cottage in Buckinghamshire, never to return, a neighbour has claimed to have witnessed her late one night helping herself to another neighbour's roses. Other such odd behavioural changes had been noted; Mia developed a sudden obsession with wig shopping, whilst undergoing a complete clear-out in her wardrobe, as her close friend and confidante, Alice Butler, commented: 'It was as if she was getting ready to leave and go somewhere. She became more distant towards me as the visitations of the paparazzi increased and just before she went missing she had stopped sharing anything.'

The rumour of Mia becoming a hermit in Scotland began when inhabitants of the Highlands started to notice that roses were going missing from their gardens. Furthermore, there have been sightings of a lady dressed in a golden shawl and wearing dark glasses, even when there is little sunlight, at a village market in the Highlands behaving rather furtively. It is well known that Mia Herman's trade symbol was the rose, since her movie *Russian Rose*, a story depicting life for early Ashkenazi Jewish travellers attempting to settle in a hostile England. In this tale, Mia's heroic character, Rosa Sharman, has the nickname Rose of Sharon, a symbolic image found in the Jewish holy book, the Tenach, which is thought by some theologians to refer to the Messiah.

In any case, whether or not the disappearance of Scotland's roses is due to Mia, it is evident that the golden-shawl lady is beginning to attract great intrigue from the Highlands' inhabitants. As a result of this, an investigation will be underway shortly and daily updates will be available in the *Daily Entertainer* or online at our new website: www. missingcelebrities.news.org

Sandra Parish
Celebrity reporter, *Daily Entertainer*

Slowly and cautiously, the hermit stuck the article into her scrapbook, making sure that she did not crease the picture, which revealed half of Mia's finely sculpted face and half of a blooming rose. Then she retrieved a black wig and a hat from a table at the back of the cave and set them neatly on her head. After some puzzling at the reflection in the looking glass before her, she picked up some black eyeliner and painted a moustache above her upper lip with skill and expert precision.

When she was fully satisfied with the dark young face staring back at her with an earnest expression, she got up and left the cave, making her way with new assertive steps to the local market to find the latest article in the *Daily Entertainer*.

Little did she expect to find a sea of faces in wait for her, not to mention members of the paparazzi, but the actress was prepared for her task. She knew that as long as she could hide behind her new disguise, she would not feel afraid. However, if her cover was blown... well, she could not plan that far ahead. For this reason, she was entirely taken aback when three paparazzi members practically flung themselves in her path as she entered the bubbling market and the flashes of camera light filled her with terror and alarm. Perhaps they were just taking pictures of every person who came into the market that day.

'That's right!' called a photographer to another passer-by. 'All people coming to the market get a shot! Particularly those who come at the time when Mia Herman is scheduled to arrive. Keep smiling!'

She had just found the paper she wanted, when a hand grabbed her shoulder and a voice shouted, 'Hey, what if this man's seen Mia? Let's ask him.'

She felt a pain in her throat, as if the hand that had grasped her was tightening its grip on her vocal chords. She quickly coughed and said in her lowest whisper, 'Oh no, I haven't seen her. To be honest, I think it's all a lot of nonsense.'

'Nonsense?' challenged the man with the tight grip. 'Well, more than one local has seen the lady in the golden shawl who wears sunglasses even in the rain! Are you a regular here?'

'I am not,' she replied quickly, considering that admitting to her own regular appearance at the market would only lead to more questions, and puzzlement from the market people who may not have recalled seeing a dark-haired man with a moustache and a hat.

'Well then, you can't say if you've seen Mia or not!' cried the man, loosening his grip slowly. 'Hey, mister, you sound like you've got a bad cold; I'd recommend you take one of these throat sweets.' He handed one to her, which she took promptly, nodding. 'And get yourself inside, away from the cold. It seems to be our destiny to stand out here freezing our butts off as if we are laying in wait for the king. Celebrities! Can't live with them–,' the man attempted a humorous wink as he nudged her, '–can't live without them!'

Just as she felt the nudge, she realised that her cover was at risk of being blown. Already she had felt her hand smudge the hand-drawn moustache as she put the throat sweet rather too quickly into her mouth. But the nudge at her elbow pressed her hand much harder against her upper lip and she noticed the man's expression start to change.

'Hey, are you a lady-man?!' he cried suddenly, and started to beckon the rest of the group over. 'This one will be worth a few photos, crew!'

She could feel the old panic setting in.

'No, please!' she said in a rather louder whisper than she had intended, her voice getting higher by the minute. 'I can't stand photos. I really think I'd better be getting off now.'

'A lady who dresses as a man is *camera shy*?' cried the man, laughing loudly, whilst taking half a dozen shots. 'Hey, wait a minute! This lady-man might be our girl!'

At this moment there was such a commotion that she felt

herself being pushed right to the ground. Her wig and hat fell off and her long chestnut-red hair flowed out, and she could feel people pressing in on her from all sides. Her vision went blurred as her breathing grew from bad to worse. In a few moments, she was convinced she was going to pass out. Then, all of a sudden the commotion was broken into by a loud voice. It was a great, rich voice that spoke with authority. She could only just make out the words: 'What has this society come to?! Aside! Stand aside! I command you, in the name of the king!'

The Music Box

Moments later, she was being lifted by strong arms and she felt herself being placed onto a seat. She realised she was in a carriage as she could hear the rhythm of horses hooves, speeding her away from the place of peril. When she opened her eyes, she looked up to see a kind young man watching her with thoughtful eyes. He said nothing, but she felt that his presence was comforting and her breathing became calmer. The journey was short and soon they were pulling up at a great manor house set within ancient ivy-covered stone walls. A rusty, cobwebbed sign naming the manor 'Rosendale House' swung noisily in the breeze.

'I hope that you have recovered?' His voice was soft but tentative. 'Perhaps you would like a drink by a warm fire?'

'No, thank you,' she said quickly, 'but I appreciated your help at the market. You have been very kind. Good day!'

She flung open the carriage door and jumped out of the carriage, fearful that they were being followed.

'Wait!' he called. 'Can I not take you to your home?'

'No, thank you!' she called. 'I know my way from here.'

And with that, she darted behind the carriage into the trees by the lane and ran across the woods towards the hills. He leaned out of the carriage and tried to watch the direction she went, his brow furrowed in deep concern. All he could do was hope that she had returned safely to a home with a warm fire, far away from the riot at the market. He could not envision what would precipitate such barbaric behaviour from a group of photographers and normally well-meaning citizens. But then, he was almost completely out of touch with modern-day fetishes and had not followed the papers as closely as most.

Slowly, he closed the carriage door and called 'Homeward bound, Sidney!', at which the driver cracked the whip and drew the carriage into the courtyard of Rosendale House.

The young man continued to consider the unusual events of the day, and the strangely timid, beautiful lady he had just encountered. He remained deep in thought some time after entering the manor, so much so that his father noted the change in his temperament but said nothing of it. His old father sat puffing his pipe and musing over a crossword, tapping to the Rachmaninoff concerto that played on a scratched record.

Soon there came an interruption to his thoughts – the sound of cars racing up the drive. His servant, Sidney the driver, came rushing to meet him and bowed.

'Master Hosea, the lady whom you rescued has returned,' he said breathlessly, 'followed by the rabble we rescued her from.'

'What?' Hosea got to his feet. 'I will have no more of this,' he said adamantly. 'They have some explaining to do, but first we must remove them from the manor right away!'

'Yes, sir.' Sidney bowed low as his master marched swiftly across the hall, beckoning to several servants and giving instructions. Hosea headed for the main door, followed by five servants. There was the sound of boots on stone as a small army of uniformed guards ran to the main door, rifles in their hands. In response to all this, Hosea's elderly father stirred; he complained that the vibrations were destroying his listening and he pounded his fists on his marble table in an agitated manner.

Moments later he sat up in surprise as he beheld a young, graceful woman standing before him. She looked sorrowful and her face was downcast, gazing longingly at a silver music box that she held in her hands. In fact, she looked so miserable that the old man straightaway was moved deeply in his heart and felt pity for her. Yet he was struck dumb as he began to recognise the music box she held. It was an item he had not seen since the passing of his wife and one he had longed to see again.

'Dear child,' he began, but found he could not speak further, for the music box started to play a tune on its own.

'Sir,' she said in time with the music, without looking up, her eyes heavy with burdens she could not bear, 'would you be looking for a gardener?'

At the sound of the word *gardener*, his eyes filled with tears. His wife had loved to tend to the garden. Since her departure, however, the gardens had become so overgrown that ivy decorated the bushes on which roses once grew.

He thought for a moment. 'Well, you have come to the right place, for the gardens here have been long forgotten. I will set you to work straight away, and see what you're made of. If I like your work, you may return.'

'Thank you, sir.' Her reply was meek and submissive, as she bowed low. 'I will prove to be a good worker.'

'Hosea, of course, has been in a dark world of his own.' The old man appeared to be talking to himself rather than to her. 'He hasn't been right since she went, and he dwells in the basement most of the time, although today he went past the market; the first time he's left the house since...' His voice trailed off.

Suddenly she became aware of another presence. At the door stood Hosea, breathing heavily.

'So you have returned?' he addressed her in a friendly manner. 'Do not worry about that incessant rabble. My men have dealt with them. They will *not* be returning.'

'What rabble?' coughed his father.

'Paparazzi, father,' his son replied. 'Chased this poor lady right into our courtyard. What they want, I could not say.'

'Paparazzi, you say?' inquired the old man. 'Who is he?'

'Greedy photographers who chase well-known folk as if they are hunting game,' Hosea replied steadily.

'Ah,' the old man went on. 'Well, he isn't going to come in here. I'll use a stick if I have to. It's been put to good use before and I am happy to use it again.' He clutched a golden cane which leant against his chair and shook it wildly.

Hosea was unaffected by this display as he stretched his legs and sat down by the fire.

'Lady, what is your name?'

'Mia,' she said slowly, clenching her teeth. 'Mia... Herman.'

'Mia Herman,' he repeated. 'No, I'm sure I have never heard of you. Then again, I have been out of touch with the modern world for quite some time, living as a hermit. Do sit down.'

Mia walked over to a large armchair by a golden lamp stand and rested in it rather tensely.

'The girl would like to do our gardening,' the old man said. 'I do think our garden is in need of some kind of order.'

'Indeed,' the young man whispered, thoughtfully. 'It is a mirror of our shadowed lives, father.' He paused as memories flickered in his pond-blue eyes, then he looked at Mia. 'Well, at least it could be a safe pursuit while we wait for those fiends of yours to leave the streets. A carriage will deliver you to your house each day when you have finished work. Do you live far?'

'Not far,' she answered, barely looking at his eyes. 'I am happy to walk, as it is no distance.'

'Oh, we can't risk those dogs catching you again,' Hosea replied. 'Do you know why they pursue you?'

Mia paused uncertainly. 'I... I think they've mistaken me for someone else... someone famous.'

'Being famous certainly has its consequences,' Hosea went on. 'Fortunately, we've been protected here in the country, but we were so pursued by the press, years ago. Now that's all died down. But the paparazzi... well, they're something else. Another breed altogether.'

Mia looked at him properly for the first time. She wanted to ask the reason for his previous experience of news photographers, but she felt that she needed to maintain a low profile through silence, unless questions were asked of her. She had not intended to return here, but the threat of the paparazzi finding her in her secret lodgings had filled her with terror. She had grabbed the object dearest to her and run across the hills as she heard their cars approaching. The music box began to play again as if in response to her thoughts. Hosea glanced over to it, and his eyes widened quickly in surprise. For a moment, he too was speechless.

'Where,' he began, in a tone of awe, 'did you get that?'

'I found it over the hills,' she replied softly.

He got up and moved towards it and reached out his hand.

'May I?' he whispered and she gave it to him a little reluctantly.

He held it tenderly in his hands, letting it play to him for a moment, and she heard him hum the tune as if he had hummed it many times before.

'This was my mother's,' he breathed, without raising his gaze. 'She kept some treasures in a cave in the hills. My father gave this music box to her; it was a family heirloom, passed down generation after generation. It has a twin: my father's. He gave it to me after my mother's passing. This one plays the harmony notes. Together they are complete.'

Mia frowned as small tears filled her eyes. Her precious treasure was not hers to keep at all. She knew it must be returned to its rightful owner. He saw her tears and held out the silver box to her.

'You can keep it safe for me if you like,' he said kindly.

'I see that you have taken to it. These boxes are special; they seem to reveal the tender hearts of their possessors.'

Mia was touched by this act of kindness. 'Thank you, sir.'

Caught on Camera

That sunny day was spent in divine happiness. Mia worked to the sound of the music box, alongside the servants of the manor. Together they pulled up the ivy that had taken reign over the ground and covered all the foliage. Bit by bit, bushes started appearing and after a full day's work, the land was significantly more attractive than it had been when they began. They knew it would be some time to wait before the blooming of new rose bushes which, it was hoped, would be ready for the master's birthday the following spring.

The servants were all warming themselves by the fire and chatting merrily. One of the scullery maids addressed Mia.

'You've captured Master Hosea's heart,' she said lightly. 'The master rarely comes up from his study in the basement. We've barely seen him upstairs in the house, except some nights when he sits with his father in the hall.'

'He is still grieving his mother's death,' suggested Mia.

'Yes, that and a lost love,' sighed the maid. 'He was in love with a girl before his mother passed on. She fell for another and broke his heart. He has become more like a recluse every day since. A hermit in his own house.'

'Yes, broken hearts can try to mend themselves in strange ways,' mused Mia, almost forgetting herself.

'You sound like you speak from experience.'

'Yes, I do,' Mia replied. 'I know what broken love can do. It can change everything. It can make you want to run away and start over again somewhere else, where no one knows you.'

The maid frowned at this. 'That sounds a bit dramatic. This man you speak of, he must have really got under your skin. Perhaps he was too possessive?'

'Yes,' said Mia quietly. 'He treated me rather like a display mannequin on a shelf. I came to realise I was just one of many mannequins.'

'He doesn't sound like he's worth the time of day,' cut in the maid. 'You'll be much better off here... with Master Hosea.' Here she winked and smiled, before she got on with her duty, carrying a silver tray into the next room.

Mia realised that she had better sneak out, now that dark was gathering. She did not want the master to see her go, for fear that he would send Sidney to take her with the carriage and then her cover would be blown. So she waited until the attention of the other servants was occupied and slipped out of the back door, walking amongst the previously ivy-choked rose bushes until she came to the courtyard, where she moved silently through the shadows and out of the main gate, which had been left slightly ajar. She moved quickly into the dark lane and out towards the cave in the hill. She did not know that the master had seen her, or that he followed her very closely as she walked in the chilly night air.

Moments later she was entering her haven, and lighting a candle. The nights were starting to become colder and for the first time she wished for a warm room with a log fire in the manor. But she knew how to make fire outside the cave. The only issue was being seen from neighbouring hills. She gathered the wood and was just about to light a match when she felt a heavy arm on her shoulder. She shuddered in fear.

'Smile for the cameras, Mia!' The familiar voice of the man who had called her a lady-man caused her heart to race.

Then there followed flashing lights, as a crowd of photographers surrounded her, seeming to chant like a wild tribe. She needed her music box. She needed to run away but she did not know where to run. She knelt down on the ground, crying in fear as they continued to taunt her. The flashbacks were returning, of the time he had ridiculed her in public and boldly claimed, 'Look at her! She's no more to me than a doll. Only destined for the cameras. I've made her what she is!'

As she sunk to the ground, her terrible thoughts were interrupted once again by a deep, resounding voice.

'Leave her be! She is not an animal.'

There was the sound of gunfire, and in an instant the crowd quietened. Panicked shouting followed as footsteps were heard running away down the hill.

'Let's get out of here!'

The wild sounds of male voices full of fear echoed through the hills and gradually faded into silence. She lay with her hands covering her face, in a crumpled heap. She could sense him standing behind her, not far away. Then, she felt him kneeling down beside her and without a word he took her in his arms and held her close to his heart to quieten her sobbing. She drew near to him, allowing his embrace. His heartbeat seemed to be racing to the rhythm of 'I am here, I am here', and she felt great comfort as she rested in his arms. He was silent and she liked that. A few minutes later, he lifted her up and carried her across the hill to the carriage which awaited them on the roadside.

They sat in the carriage in silence, and it was not until they approached Rosendale House that he spoke.

'Mia, Rosendale is your new home now. The servants are collecting your belongings from the cave as we speak.'

She was silent, but her eyes shone with gratitude.

*

Time passed in her new abode very happily and the season turned to the coldness of winter. Mia did not wish for the cave now, but delighted in warm foot baths and log fires to her heart's content.

And the master was pleased with her efforts in the garden. It was becoming a magical Christmas scene, as the statues were being uncovered and the springs had come alive again. There was one new item in the garden, one which enchanted Hosea and his father considerably; an archway of roses which had been designed and planted by Mia and which gave the garden a wonderful spiritual touch. Mia was deeply proud of it. The master came to see the servants whilst they worked more often now, and he particularly doted on Mia, who was gaining confidence the longer she lived at Rosendale House.

One day, Mia received a message that the master wished for her to join him in his basement study. She left her duties and found him sitting with his back to her, poring over a book with great interest. In an instant she recognised it; her own scrapbook of articles and pictures. It had gone missing and she had assumed that one of the paparazzi members had grabbed it. But here it lay in the huge dusty study of a manor lord. He turned on hearing her approach.

'Mia,' he addressed her with a slightly distant tone, 'I think Sidney forgot to give you this.' He handed her the book.

'Thank you, sir,' she replied and curtseyed.

'Mia, why didn't you tell me?' The question surprised her a little, and she could hear the hurt behind his voice. 'I thought you could be open with me now.'

Mia shifted uncomfortably. 'It's my old life. I thought I could move on from it.'

He looked at her for a moment, and then addressed her in a slightly warmer way.

'Mia, I fully understand the distance you need from this. I know about your lover and the way he treated you. It's all written down here. But surely if you want me to protect you adequately, you owe it to me to let me know that you are hunted by the media because of who you are... even if you don't feel you are *her* any more.'

'I'm sorry, sir,' she replied. 'I thought you would treat me differently. I just want a normal life, and this life is so... *so* much more than any I could have dreamed of.'

He was moved by her deep gratitude and he turned to face her fully, with eyes that were filled with tenderness.

'I understand, Mia. Like me, you became a hermit to escape from the old life. You must recognise that we are not so very different. I, too, was hunted. As the son of the king's sister, my life was on display, until we were left alone. I suppose they got bored with us. Quite a relief, really. But like you, Mia, I have a broken heart. I just wanted you to know that you have a safe place here and that you can tell me things, whatever is on your mind, and I will listen. You can always... trust me.'

She knew she could. 'Yes, sir. I know you to only be a trustworthy and very kind man. I promise I will not keep any secrets from you again.'

'Thank you, Mia.' He smiled softly; how she loved that smile, and she had noticed that he had been smiling much more often lately. 'Thank you for coming.'

He held out his hand to her and she took it as he arose. For a moment they were standing close together and she could feel a small sparkle of electricity flooding her body with fresh warmth and joy. She curtseyed as he let go of her hand.

'Good day, sir,' she said softly.

'Mia,' he whispered, 'you can call me Hosea. "Sir" means that you don't know me as well as you do.'

'Very well, Master Hosea.' She curtseyed again and left quickly, aware that she was smiling more brightly than ever.

He grinned to himself as she left. Each day since her arrival he had watched her working and longed to invite her in, just to spend more time in her presence. He always felt that a sunbeam shone out of her soul and when he was with her, the past seemed to be healed and his grieving seemed to fade away. He was glad that the servants had mislaid the scrapbook, for this had initiated her first visit to the study, and at last it felt like her light had penetrated even into the darkest part of the house.

The Rose of Sharon

Hosea's light thoughts were interrupted by the sound of hounds in the hall upstairs. Normally he gave the orders for their release, but evidently his father had got there first. On his entrance to the hall, he found a great commotion. Servants were running around in panic and several tall men, the bodyguards of the manor, were blowing whistles to get the hounds to heel. And in the middle of it all stood his father, waving his cane around his head and barking out orders.

'May I ask, in the king's name, what is going on?' shouted Hosea above the din.

He marched to his father's side and held him by the shoulders. His father's defiant face softened on seeing his son.

'Ah, Hosea,' he sighed. 'I am afraid she has gone.'

'What do you mean, gone?' Hosea cried.

'The girl, Mia,' his father continued, 'has been taken.'

'Taken?' Hosea's voice was hoarse. 'Taken where? Taken by whom?'

But before his father could finish, Hosea was already running out of the front door.

'They don't know who they're dealing with!' His raving voice could be heard in the courtyard. 'This is the last time they will see her. Sidney, follow their cars.'

Meanwhile, Mia, who had been gagged and blindfolded, sat in terror in the back of the car she had been thrown into. She could hear the familiar heavy breathing of the man she so feared. The fiend, her old, twisted lover, had returned out of jealousy on hearing that she was living a happy life in a manor with a lord, a hero who protected her from harm. She knew all too well that he would stop at nothing to gain the prize he had lost. Rosendale House now seemed like a distant fairy tale. She sat with every muscle clenched, her eyes tightly shut, as she felt his poisonous breath on her neck.

'So you thought you could have eyes for him, did you?' he snarled. 'You thought you could forget all about me – the one who gave you fame and fortune. You threw it all in my face when you left. You are not going to be allowed to leave my house again.'

He turned away from her for a second.

'Yes, here he comes again, the knight in shining armour to rescue you in his golden carriage… Ha! What good can a carriage do when it can't keep up with cars?'

She did not reply but went back into her silent world, praying under her breath. A few minutes later she heard him gasp, a rare sound to come from the foolhardy man she had known. He gripped her arms until it hurt.

'Would you believe it?' His voice sounded a little uncertain. 'He's left the carriage and is riding the horse right at us… and he's holding a rifle!'

Gunshots were heard, and immediately there was panic in the car as the driver swerved until the car came to an abrupt stop. There was the sound of smoke hissing, and Mia knew that everyone was scrambling to get out of the car. His hold only grew tighter. A moment later she could hear his voice, the voice of her rescuer, and it filled her with a sense of calm. She guessed that as he spoke he held a rifle to her tormenter's head, for he became so limp that it was as if he was paralysed. He let go of her and she jumped away from him and desperately tried to find the door handle.

'How dare you hold my employee hostage?' came the voice of authority. 'I've heard of you, Byron Jackall. And so

will the whole world – when they see you banged up in jail
for your crimes. Now get out of the car, quickly!'
    She felt Byron being removed from her side, and she
sighed in relief. A few moments later, kind hands were
unbinding her wrists and her blindfold and gag were
removed. Hosea's kind face shone upon her like the warm
light of day and she flung herself onto him with deep gratitude, and rested her head on his chest. Softly he kissed her
forehead and lifted her up in his strong arms. They walked
again to the carriage and there she came face to face with her
kidnapper, bound and gagged. A shudder of fear entered her,
but it could not remain this time, for she suddenly realised
what a sorry state he looked and she could only feel pity. The
man who had bullied her throughout her acting career and
who even attempted to grab her back again now faced a
complete loss of power in his life; the consequences of a
terrible life of crime.

*

Mia sat in the hall as servants tended to her wounds; her
struggle with the men who came to take her had been fierce.
So special to her was the new life she had found that they
discovered she was a creature of considerable strength and
new resilience, one that could not easily be captured. It had
taken two men to hold her down whilst her evil ex-lover
had roughly bound her. In those moments, she had come to
believe that she would not see the light of day again. Yet her
hero had returned.
    Hosea stayed by her side for a few hours in which she rested
and he cheered her with amusing tales of his adventurous
dealings with the media. And all the time, he planned in his
mind what he would do to combat any future confrontations
with the paparazzi. He had already instructed Sidney to over-
see the construction of an electric fence to be put up around
the walls. The gate would be constantly guarded by several

armed men who would take on night shifts. The hounds would be on hand for any trespasser to the manor; the master himself would be armed at all times and Mia's bedroom quarters would be guarded constantly. Yet, Hosea also had other personal plans regarding Mia.

One day, Mia was out in the garden trimming the hedges when she found a mysterious note attached to one of them. It read: 'Find me under the rose arch.' Mia followed the instruction and there on a glass table lay a rolled-up parchment within a ring that bore a carved blooming rose. She picked it up and opened the letter. It was a reference to an old scripture found in the Tenach, the Jewish holy book, written by the prophet Hosea. It read as follows:

'Dearest Mia,
I am taking you back into the wilderness where we had our first date, and I'll court you. I'll give you bouquets of roses. The question is this: will you be my Rose of Sharon?'

She smiled as her eyes filled with tears. She pressed the letter to her face and placed the rose ring on her wedding finger. A perfect fit. Then she saw him, standing by the vines, beaming in delight. He held out his hands to her and she ran to meet him in great joy. As he took her hands, he asked her, 'Does that mean yes?'

'Yes!' she cried. 'I long for nothing more than this.'

'So, we are to be married?'

'Yes, if you'll have me.' She laughed.

'That I will.' He laughed and shed tears of joy as he took her into his arms. 'That I will.'

To the sound of two music boxes playing side by side, she walked up the aisle in the manor chapel. Most of the members of the paparazzi who heard of the wedding thought better of attending, and those who attempted to were later reported to have been sent to hospital, recovering from the effects of electric shocks.

Later the newly-weds set aside time to invite guests to enjoy their feast; namely the homeless in the streets and those who lived as hermits. Much was reported about the rays of hope which Hosea and Mia spread across the land. So many stories were told of the life that they brought to others that these tales reached the ears of Mia's old tormenter in prison, Byron Jackall, who was paying the price for a life of injustice. On hearing the tales, even he started to see life in a new light.

Soon, Hosea and Mia's mission became that of hospitality; for they began to see that the manor, with its vast size, could be put to good use in providing shelter for the homeless and it also became a place where strangers could come and share their troubles. And so they lived many happy years in Rosendale House, to the sound of new children playing and where the roses ever bloomed and grew straight up towards the skies.

The Sixth Tale

The fifth tale was finished, and the children all applauded. Mia was sitting apart from the rest, looking thoughtful.

'I can see you have been touched by the tale, Mia,' Mr Friedman commented. 'Would you like to tell us what you thought?'

She was still for a moment; her eyes seemed to stare right through the fire as it crackled, remembering a past she was grateful to leave behind her.

'I never want to be alone again, and I am glad you found me when you did,' she said, but then she added with a wry smile, 'But Master Hosea sounded like a very nice man!'

The other adolescents laughed along with her, then a cheeky youth sitting amongst them whispered, 'He's a real live character, too!'

'Shhh!' she replied.

Mr Friedman knew they were referring to his own son, with whom they had grown up, and of whom Mia seemed to be especially fond.

'My son will be coming by this evening to pay us a visit.' He chuckled as a few more quiet titters were heard. 'I am afraid time is short and the little ones will need to be tucked up now. The final tales are for the adolescents, who can stay up later. Now, younger ones, get up and follow my sister, Mrs Jarman, who will tuck you up and sing you a song with Mr Jarman before you close your eyes.'

Eli Jarman and his wife Edita had already entered the room and were waiting with expectant smiles.

The younger ones seemed to accept this without complaint, for they knew that one day their time would come for the older tales. Slowly, they got up one by one, and followed Eli and Edita Jarman upstairs, where their beds had been warmed by hot water bottles, and a small gift waited on each of their pillows. Eli and Edita acted as teachers, as well as the aunty and uncle at the home, of which Mr Friedman was the director. Eveyln, his wife, was the nurse and provider of all their needs. The other member of the household was Mr Michaelson, the mysterious butler who served Mr Friedman. There was a rumour going around the youngest children that he was really an angel and that he could appear and disappear whenever he wanted. One child even believed that she had seen him flying in front of the house when there was a thunderstorm, as if to protect them all from being struck by lightning. Such stories had spread round the children like a fire that no words could put out.

The children got in to bed weary, but filled with excitement from the fireside tales which they had heard. Then, they were slowly lulled to sleep by the Jarmans' lullabies.

Meanwhile, the adolescents stirred restlessly, and moved closer to Mr Friedman, wondering what to expect next.

'Now then, teenagers.' He immediately got into setting the scene of his next piece of theatre. 'Cast your mind back to not so very long ago, when you believed in fairy tales. Now, you may think; why did I send the little ones to bed so soon? You'd better wait and find out, for this is really rather a dark fairy tale; a reminder of the real world of darkness, and how easy it is to get entangled in it before you know it. It's also a reminder that when you seek truth and courage, you will surely find them, and strength will be given you to regain what was lost.'

He gave them the title of the sixth tale…

Parallel Existence

Song of a Siren

There was once a little girl,
Who locked herself away safe inside.
On the outside she lived a dream,
Of song and sunshine in her smiles.
Living like a princess, singing like a siren,
She made for herself a parallel universe
Which was her reality, safe yet dispersed.
On the outside she was everyone's dream,
Pop princess, face of the magazines.
No one knew what was really inside,
The deep intense mess she had to hide,
Until one day when she had to confide
In the newspapers that showed her true light,
And the only way to go was down,
Safely tucked away in the underground,
Away from the glitz, glamour and fame,
To turn off the voices shouting her name.
A life of stability she had to find,
But only when she was at one with her mind,
And it was then she turned to the siren within,
Suppressed by the crowd that pushed it in,
Hidden from the mirrors, clinging to childhood treasures;
A music box played, frozen in time,
Floating away to rest on the sea bed,
Like a sweet fairy tale playing in her head.
But now she was locked away from her crowds,
Forced to search within and rediscover who she was,
And one night she was visited by her inner siren.
A ringing sound arrested her mind and the spell was
    broken,
And the siren shined with light that sent music through
    her soul,
Reviving her with words of truth; reality she had never
    known,

307

Highlighting how the world of fame had made her heart
  grow old,
Helping her to find the treasures of youth and years of
  gold,
And finally on the ocean floor, she surrendered her
  parallel life,
To the song that made her spirit soar to the eternal light.

The Barista Palace

Princess Ruby Twining-Stone was the youngest resident of Twining-Stone Palace, which had come to be known far and wide as the Barista Palace due to the most unusual invention of all time that dwelt deep within its underground chambers.

Ruby's father, Prince Ebedgar, second son of the late King Malcolm, was in fact its inventor. He was a fairly eccentric character, who did not live as a typical prince in luxury, but who, with his trusty family, ran the hugely successful Barista Business within the palace, which attracted the multitudes worldwide.

If one were to stumble across the invention itself in the dark, one might not think its small metallic frame was much to behold, but whenever it was actively at work, one would realise that there was more involved in this little construction than originally meets the eye. The invention was named the Reader of Inner Needs and it would do exactly this for all visitors to the palace, reading their physical states and emotional levels through the chemicals it detected in their bodies. It then supplied a chemical balance to add to a drink made specifically for each individual. The machine was also set so that no person could take a drink that had not been created for them. And in this way, the business ran smoothly and was viewed as a sort of magic potion healing centre for all who came to visit.

As for the ingredients themselves, they were collected during Prince Ebedgar's famous visit to the Wangalanga

Islands, historically documented as man's first step into these previously uncharted magic forest islands, which were literally made up of ancient trees that grew straight up from the ocean. These rare trees held a strange sort of fossilised ingredient that was said to possess untold healing power for all illnesses that mankind had ever met. Ebedgar had been delighted at the prospect of putting his invention into practice using such rare ingredients.

From that time, the Barista Palace grew and flourished like no other had before, blessing all who entered. The visitors enjoyed different aspects of this relaxing environment. Some enjoyed lying back on the reclining chairs (which moved into a position that fit an individual's posture and back perfectly) whilst surveying the marble ceilings and inhaling the intoxicating air. Others enjoyed the strange and haunting music entwined with birdsong, and the sounds of the animal kingdom of the Wangalanga Islands, which had been taken from recordings made during the prince's travels, whilst others still came to meditate in the chapel, a warm and picturesque place filled with huge padded couches, cushions and foot baths.

There were many tales of how visitors were changed through entering the Barista Palace. Many people who came alone would end up meeting their soulmate, and many others would find faith in those healing walls. There were even a few stories of people who were healed from terrible diseases and saved from death.

And yet, the biggest mystery of the Barista Palace was not the wonderful invention, or the properties of the drinks themselves. It was the Baristas who served the drinks and took care of the general maintenance of the Barista Palace, who held the greatest air of mystery. As previously mentioned, the Twining-Stone family were behind the running and upkeep of the Barista Palace, but none of the guests knew anything about where the other strange-looking

Baristas who assisted the family had come from. The Twining-Stone family were the only ones who really knew what they were. Most assumed they were the family's servants, but they were much more to the Twining-Stones than that. Ruby's father had found them just before his discovery of the Wangalanga Islands, and it was, in fact, through them that he came across the strange magical forests in the waters at all.

The Baristas had first been seen at the tops of the trees, flying like sparkles of light in the starry midnight sky. Prince Ebedgar had cried out in awe of these strange winged creatures, initially claiming that they were far more impressive than England's birds. Soon afterwards, however, he had come to realise that they were not birds at all, but were little winged people. They even spoke English perfectly, and appeared to be able to pick up any tongue at the drop of a hat. Great imitators, indeed, but they possessed so much more than what met the eye or ear. For they possessed healing powers, which Ruby's father told her kept the special properties in the fruits, nuts and cocoa beans of the trees of their island active, and which they would use when they met any individual with a need. They also acted as counsellors, and many people worked through emotional conflicts whilst sipping the Baristas' drinks. Some Baristas seemed to be particularly anointed in song, and these were the minstrels who sang healing and joy into the hearts of their guests in the Barista Chapel.

It became clearer in time to Ebedgar that these Baristas were really God's own angels, sent to earth with one main mission, and that was to direct mankind to the ingredients with the most powerful healing properties on earth so that by drinking of these substances, people would turn their hearts to worship their Creator. The reason that only the Twining-Stones knew about the true identity of the Baristas is that Prince Ebedgar reasoned that no one else would believe him if he told the full story of his famous visit to the islands. But he had not predicted that a few would have certainly believed such a heavenly tale after visiting the palace and experiencing dramatic faith conversions.

On the front of the palace was written on a placard in huge golden letters 'The Palace of Light that Conquers All Darkness', as Prince Ebedgar had been instructed to write by the angels. Indeed, some dark fiends had tried to conquer the palace, and failed. These fiends sought the throne and had tried to overthrow Ebedgar's elder brother King Mica, who also lived in the palace, a man who had married but had never had children. But the Baristas were quick in their defence, and as they carted these fiends off to jail they quoted the words of the placard in jubilant song into the pained ears of the defeated. There had not been any such attack since, but the plotter of these crimes, whose identity had not been uncovered, and who had sent his servants to attempt to do his foul work, started to come up with a new and terrible plan. This plan conjured up all the forces of the kingdom of darkness, and he sat in his stony castle waiting for the moment when he could strike the Barista Palace again. Although he did not know the true identity of the angels, he knew that they possessed strange powers and he planned to capture them and take them for his own – but not until he had stolen the most vulnerable member of the Twining-Stone family, who he would take as hostage to demand a great ransom.

Ruby Twining-Stone had mostly enjoyed childhood, although she had needed to grow up fast in the limelight of the newspapers. The world often tried to invade her own happy, carefree existence, and particularly since her father's strange invention, she had felt the pangs of fame like an ever-burning hot furnace. She had tried to shut it out, but it grew so much, with news of their miraculous Barista Business spreading across the world seemingly at light speed, that she had finally given in and bowed to its whims. Soon she was known not merely as a princess, but also as a great singer. She had quickly become a sort of world icon, and would regularly give concerts in the Barista Palace. Her songs would reach the top of the charts and every detail of the teenage life of the 'Pop Princess' was plastered across magazines in every shop in the kingdom. Any other normal teenager would have been overwhelmed by the measure of attention she received. Sometimes, she felt that she would actually cave in if she had to take any more, and often opted for a retreat from the imposing world of fame. There was no better place than deep within the underground of the Barista Palace itself, where its healing fumes emanated across all levels of the stone floors and where the songs of the angels embraced her. She knew that as long as she remained in this palace she would be safe. For she also knew that she had a sensitive nature, and at times before her father's discovery of the machine and of the angels and their healing trees she had been prone to thoughts of self doubt and low esteem, despite her happy, even if a little eccentric, upbringing. She knew she had come to rely heavily on the work in the palace. This world would always be there for her, and would win against the other imposing parallel world outside, which was scary and where there was no protection from the *darkness* the angels had warned her about. They had told her not to stray too far away from the rays of light that emanated from the palace.

As a child she had a close friend, Ethan Hartley, the only child of her father's third cousin, Lord Hadrach Hartley, who played with her in the labyrinth outside the palace courts in the summer. In the middle of the labyrinth there was a fountain, which had been brought back to life by the angels and now held a rare property that healed the heart of whoever drank from it; and the heart it healed was the heart of the soul, and its emotions. A poorly spiritual heart was said to be the cause of most of the body's and mind's sicknesses, and once healed could transform a person's entire well-being. But of course, those who drank of the fountain had to believe that they would be healed, and many were cynical of the water and the life that dwelt within it. And furthermore, once one's heart had become sickly or cold, it was very difficult for anyone to help that person believe that they could be cured.

A strange thing occurred on the day of Princess Ruby's and Ethan Hartley's shared twelfth birthday, and it was a day Ruby would never forget. Ethan left the palace to go fishing with his father in the afternoon and neither ever returned. They had no other immediate family – Ethan's mother had died in childbirth and the father and son lived alone in a great mansion some miles from the palace. The newspapers were full of the search for the missing Lord Hartley and his son, and how all attempts to trace them ended in vain. This event in Ruby's life had weakened her emotions considerably, but her father told her she had to carry on living life without her dearest friend Ethan. It also made Ebedgar more cautious concerning his own daughter's activities, so much so that she often felt quite smothered by him and her mother, Princess Claudette.

Ruby was an only child, as her parents had married late in life and were not able to have more children. Ebedgar had never been one for settling down, to his parents' dismay, and his life was all about inventions and adventures overseas, until he happened to come across Princess Claudette, widow of the late Duke Rene le Belle, during a swim in a lake whilst on a holiday trip to a neighbouring country. After admitting that he could never envision meeting such beauty in his life again, and after a considerable period of pining, he finally arranged for the wedding to take place, and the bond between the two nations was sealed.

As the only child of such a love bond, Ruby was a very

special gift to her parents. She felt their parental guidance to be quite overwhelming at times, and although there were often other children in the palace, she could not by any means have a normal childhood. Sometimes, as she sat in the middle of the labyrinth she would gaze fondly into the fountain that healed sick hearts and wonder if she did need some healing. But the fountain had become to her like a sacred and untouchable supply of water and she considered that it could only work on the severest of cases and should be saved for such. Her heart was not in as much need as some. In her library, she had read stories of heartbreak and despair beyond anything she was sure she could ever experience. Little did she know how much she really needed her heart to be cured, even in those early years. And so she lived in her parallel existence, putting her smile on and singing her songs to impress the crowds. She did not know that something terrible was about to change everything, and strip her completely bare and put her in a place where she would have to face reality; a place where she would have to learn to breathe all over again.

The Parallel Dimension

It was the day of Ruby's eighteenth birthday and there was a grand masquerade ball held in the Barista Palace in her honour. Guests came from far and wide in wonderful masks of all varieties and there was even a competition for the best dressed, judged by the princess. The evening started with dancing, and Princess Ruby chose all the people she wished to dance with; much to her mother's dismay, she danced more with those whose masks she liked best, not caring about their gender or being influenced by who may be behind the mask. Often her mother asked her who she had danced with and she would reply that it was a monkey or a tidal wave or a starry sky. She loved the pictures before her. It was like a sea of fairy tales and as she drank of the wine and danced throughout the night, she started to feel a little light-headed. Finally, her mother took her aside and sat her down, fanning her.

'My dear child, you must not overdo it, or you will be in no fit state to attend to your fine guests. *We* know who is behind the masks, but *you* must pay attention. For at the end of the night, you are to guess the ones we select. And one of these may well be your potential suitor.'

'Oh mother, can't I just enjoy the night? I love the dancing.'

'And dance again you shall, but not before the meal and the competition. You shall get one more choice of who to dance with, and it is my hope that you shall choose a decent young *man*!'

'Why should I be "snapped up" on my eighteenth birth-day? You and father married when you were in your forties!'

'Hush now! You know well that your Uncle Mica has no children and that you are next in line after your father for the throne. We have a duty to follow, one we have been bound by for many generations. Remember, you are the role model of the youth of this nation. Now you must rise up to accept it!'

'Don't think you need to remind me of that, mother.'

At this moment the trumpets sounded and the guests were all seated, after which many varieties of food and drinks were brought out by the Baristas, who dazzled many with their speedy delivery, and made some blink twice at their beating wings. Then came the time for the competition. There were seven masked men lined up for the princess to question, in order that she would select the one she liked the best as a dance partner. Ruby rolled her eyes at her mother and made a face, which was mostly hidden behind her mask. She had chosen to wear a mask of the labyrinth, with the healing fountain at the centre. Her dress was covered in embroidered stars and was made of dark blue velvet. She had stunned the guests that night as she made her first appear-ance, floating graciously down the marble stairs.

As she surveyed the line-up of potentials before her, she was drawn in particular to the mask of a winged bird in flight, but the closer she looked at the bird, the more she realised that it was like one of the angels at the palace, and for this reason, she viewed the wearer of this mask favourably. She also felt a strange magnetic pull towards him. The other masks were of warriors and knights, which she also loved reading about, but there was nothing like the supernatural to win the princess's young heart. She was also enchanted by the voice of her preferred dance partner; it seemed like a voice she had heard before in a long-distant dream.

As they drew nearer to each other for their dance, he whispered into her ear.

'I bet you will never guess who I am. So I will tell you, but you must promise not to tell anyone else that you know my true identity.'

She nodded, feeling excited by his air of mystery. She noticed that his voice held a rare resonance, and she felt drawn in by it, as she continued to listen.

'I am Lord Molech Goyim, the only son of the late King Malcolm's brother-in-law.' Ruby certainly would never have guessed who he was, for she knew very little about Lord Goyim indeed, other than that he had come to a regal function early on in her life, and he was a great deal older than herself, which was somewhat of a disappointment. However, she saw her mother was beaming at her expectantly, and trying to subtly nod at her whenever the lord's back was turned. So she felt confined to stay with him for the evening. Yet as he continued to speak with her, she could not help feeling rather captivated, and hoped that when he withdrew the mask his countenance would be pleasing.

'My lord, it is a wonder to speak with someone I have never properly met before, and I am dazzled by your angel mask, but may I have the pleasure of seeing your face?'

'I promise that you will see me in my true form by the end of this night, princess. That, I can hold my word to.'

She noticed that he seemed to play games and do all he could to keep his cover, and she often felt tempted to remove the mask, but as he continuously pointed out, this was a masked ball, and it would be quite against the rules. As she became more impatient, he leaned closer and said softly, 'If you really desire to see me in my true form, then meet me at the centre of the labyrinth by the fountain on the stroke of midnight.'

She felt excitement filling her heart at this mysterious invitation. Yet she still did not wish to be disappointed, and wondered if the moonlight would be bright enough to enable her to detect his true features clearly. Still, she loved his voice, and surely that was a good sign in itself. She could not wait until that moment when the truth would be told. Having read so many fairy tales, she was sure that a good suitor would have a handsome face, so she braced herself for that moment, temporarily forgetting the tale of Beauty and the Beast, and the fact that beauty is only skin deep.

She kept glancing at the clock as the time ticked by. The dancing continued, but now she had to be occupied with all her guests.

'Ruby, have you worked out the identity of your potential suitor?' asked Cameron, her second cousin and confidante.

'He had to tell me himself, I was that slow!' she said, laughing. 'It is the Lord Goyim. I hardly know who he is.'

'Lord Goyim?!' cried Cameron. 'Is he not the one that is most estranged to our family? He lives miles away, and no one knows where. Well, I suppose it's nice he made the effort to turn up. But Ruby, is he not well into his forties by now?'

'Well, he has a nice voice,' Ruby replied slowly, 'and he is going to remove his mask by the fountain at midnight tonight.'

Suddenly, Ruby remembered the last words he had said, and she repeated them to her friend: 'But remember to be there on the stroke of midnight. Do not be there after the stroke of midnight, for I will not be there.'

'Ooh,' breathed Cameron. 'Hasn't he got an air of mystery?'

'I quite like that,' replied Ruby. 'It's what makes him different to the rest.'

'Careful, cousin,' interrupted Cameron. 'You are speaking as if you actually know him. He's not one of the men in your dream novels, you know. I'd be careful, if I were you. He might steal you off into the night. I shall accompany you to make sure he doesn't try anything untoward.'

'Cameron!' objected Ruby. 'You are starting to sound like my mother. How she wraps me up in cotton wool...'

'But it's for good reason,' went on Cameron. 'You are a princess and you need protection. The angels won't always be there. They are not omnipresent. They won't be in the labyrinth at that time as they are looking after the guests. So tonight I will be your angel.'

'I couldn't ask for a better angel,' Ruby said and smiled, and together they linked arms and slowly headed for the outer archway. It was nearly time for her midnight meeting. They breathed in the cool night air, admiring the stars that twinkled. Suddenly, a din from within the palace drew their attention.

Cameron backed away from the entrance.

'Oh dear!' she exclaimed. 'I forgot, I was asked to be a judge at the mask competition and I have to prepare the prizes. You must come soon too, to make the final judgement...'

'But it's nearly twelve o'clock!' cried Ruby.

'Very well, meet your man. But be quick! He should be inside too if he wants to get a prize.'

And with that, Cameron hurried back inside. Ruby was abandoned by her angel. In truth, she was relieved. The last thing she really wanted was a chaperone. Quickly, she headed towards the labyrinth. Once she was inside, she started to hear a strange song. What could her dance partner have planned? At first she wondered if he had called upon one of the minstrels to sing, for the voice she heard seemed to be luring her in. For a moment she shuddered, as she wondered who this strange singer was and she thought that the labyrinth had become strangely dark. It was two minutes to twelve, so she picked up her skirts and moved more briskly. Finally, she reached the centre of the maze and stood by the fountain, gazing into it. She was alone. Perhaps he was standing in one of the nearby bushes. An eerie wind rushed by and she started to feel a shiver of unearthly fear. She had not been wise coming here, knowing so little about him. She should have asked her parents more about him. But surely they would not have invited him to the ball if they had not trusted him. Quickly she brushed those illogical thoughts aside. Just as she did, the clock started to chime twelve, and as it did, she realised that she was not standing by the fountain at all, but by a lake with a strange dark statue standing in its centre.

How funny, she thought, *I have never seen this lake in the labyrinth before. Oh dear, I had better look for the fountain.*

Too late, for the clock came to strike its twelfth chime all too quickly, and as it did, she saw the dark statue start to move towards her. She cried out in terror as it stepped from the lake and took her by the shoulders. Suddenly she heard his voice.

'Do not be afraid. It is me!'

She sighed in relief as she heard the voice that she liked.

'How did you do that? Are you a magician?'

'Maybe I am, of sorts,' was his amused reply. 'And now, princess, for the unveiling. You must remove my mask.'

Slowly he placed her hands upon his mask. As he did, she felt an electric current surging through her hands and she jumped back in alarm.

'What is it?' he asked, laughing. 'Are you too scared to do it?'

'No!' she cried. 'It's just that the mask is so hot.'

He placed her hands back on his mask and once again she felt its current, but this time it burnt her hands. She cried out but he kept her hands on his mask, and only laughed louder.

'Stop it! Stop it!' she cried out, feeling as if her hands were full of flames.

'Do it! Do it!' he shouted. 'Lift off the mask now!'

As she struggled to pull her hands away from him, she

realised that she had no choice but to lift that wretched mask off his face. Suddenly, she saw it had changed from an angel to a dragon, and she screamed as she struggled to lift it away. And then she was face to face with her suitor, and all she could see were flames pouring out of his face. The laughing grew ever louder and she felt herself being drawn into that face. The burning sensation filled her whole body as she was sucked into a deathly parallel existence. She felt all she knew becoming a dim recollection, a little like a childhood fairy tale, as her surroundings faded into a mist and disappeared.

Her eyes began to adjust to a strange, dark environment, and she found herself in a small room at the top of a dark tower. She could see hills far away from out of her high window. All seemed so peaceful. Then she realised she was not alone. He stood beside her, and she gasped in awe, for he was so beautiful. He looked much younger than she had expected, and his face was strangely pale and held an unearthly glow. She could not help gazing deep into his dark, handsome eyes, which had an almost purple glow in their centre. And all the time, he drew her in with such a wonderful song that she suddenly longed for nothing else but to be with him and spend the rest of her days in his castle with him and him alone...

The Heart Tremor

The days that followed in the Barista Palace were very difficult, and there was much mourning in the courts as many guests came to pay their respects to the late princess. In the labyrinth, far away from the fountain at the centre, Prince Ebedgar and his wife Claudette had discovered what they believed to be proof of their daughter Ruby's death. They knew the dark statue to be the same one they had found on Lord Hartley and his son Ethan's disappearance six years earlier, though they had never had the heart to inform their daughter of the omen and what it meant. Ebedgar knew of events that he could not tell his daughter for fear of troubling her mind and filling it with nightmares, for he knew what a vivid imagination she had. But now, he regretted this sidestepping more than anything else in his life. Prince Ebedgar knew of Lord Goyim and his schemes. He certainly had not invited him to the masquerade ball and had not realised when this old fiend had crossed the threshold of his palace. He knew that Lord Goyim had dabbled in sorcery but he had not realised what a powerful sorcerer he had become. When he asked the angels why they had not stopped him, they explained to him:

'We tried to distract him from his task, but by midnight, we became detained by powerful principalities that guarded the labyrinth. These evil fiends could get no closer to the palace. We do not know who gave them permission to set foot as close as they did, but we fought a fierce battle with them until just after twelve, when we defeated them, and rushed forth into the labyrinth, where we discovered we were too late to rescue your daughter from the evil clutches of Lord Goyim. But do not fear, all is not lost...'

'My daughter is dead!' cried Ebedgar. 'How can you say all is not lost?'

'She is not dead,' replied the chief minstrel angel. 'Not in *this* dimension, anyway.'

'What do you mean *this dimension*?' demanded the prince.

'She has been sucked into another parallel existence,' replied the minstrel angel. 'She lives with him, but she does not see him as being evil. She believes all is well, and she has forgotten everything from this world and her previous existence.'

'She is really alive then?' cried Princess Claudette.

'Yes, she lives,' the angel said with a smile, 'as if in the world of the dead. And we will do our utmost to get her back... only it may take time.'

*

So, Ruby lived a new life, unaware of what came before, although it still echoed in her recollection like a dim fairy tale, and at night she would hear strange music and dream she was singing in front of the multitudes. She was known as Miss Ruby Stone, and she was a maid in the castle of Lord Goyim, a servant to his every wish, and completely unaware of her royal heritage, for these truths had been swept from her mind from the moment her hands had been burned by the sorcerer's mask.

She worked hard. The duties of a maid in the castle were many and varied, but as Ruby was the personal favourite of Lord Goyim, she would often be requested at the table after the evening meal had been served for some 'light entertainment'. Lord Goyim loved to hear her sing, but only as long as she sang songs for him and him alone. He even composed songs for her to learn and sing before all of the residents at evening concerts. Ruby felt that she dearly loved her master, but deep within she knew that something was not quite right, and that this existence held a dark mystery that she could never quite comprehend. She was not held prisoner in the castle by any means, as her master knew her to be deluded by the spell he had placed upon her at the masquerade ball, and there was no way in which this spell could be broken or shifted, unless she were to meet someone who was beloved to her from her previous existence, who may trigger old feelings of affection.

The reason the lord had removed Ethan Hartley from Ruby's life early on was that he felt that, as a close friend of hers, as well as a relative, he was a potential suitor for Ruby in later life. Lord Goyim saw that by marrying Ruby himself, as heir to the throne after her uncle's and father's death, he could have complete rulership over the kingdom and then his terrible powers would have no limit, even with the magical Baristas at the palace. By giving the throne to him and his wife, mankind would have vowed to hand over the land to him, and no man or angel could go against that permission without seeking higher assistance. But the Creator, Lord Goyim reasoned, seemed to allow some territories of his creation to be governed by the power of evil. How long He would allow this kind of treachery, however, Lord Goyim did not wish to consider. His main aim was to strike while the iron was hot, and terrorise the world as much as he could in whatever time he was able to do so.

Lord Goyim's descent into such treachery was partially understood by those who knew of him. All his ancestors were power seekers and aimed to marry to gain positions that were influential. This was the reason why his father had married into royalty, and he in turn had passed on his evil gift of sorcery to his son on his deathbed, a gift that seemed to grow in power with each generation.

What very few people knew was that as a young man, Molech Goyim had suffered terrible heartbreak that was seemingly beyond all cure. He had been jilted at the altar by a dazzling beauty who had stolen his heart, without ever giving him hers in return. She had found a more profitable suitor; one who was always admired in the public eye, and who could offer her more money to spend on stunning dresses and carriages. Therefore, she no longer held any interest in Lord Goyim's isolated existence in his old dusty mansion, with his pet dog, Pooch. This heartbreak weakened the lord's mind so much that he became a willing participator in the darkest form of magic, which he would turn to in order to bring some control and comfort into what he considered to be a helpless, despairing existence. And it was to this dark magic that he surrendered his mind, and eventually his heart, perhaps in some desperate attempt to make it whole.

Later on, Goyim became infatuated with Princess Claudette, sometime before her marriage to Prince Ebedgar, although she was older than him. During her first visit to the country, Goyim had surveyed her brunette beauty with untold rapture, and had promptly offered her his hand in marriage. She, however, could not summon up even the remotest form of interest in him, viewing him only as an aloof and untrustworthy outsider of the family who dabbled in foolish magic. At this stage, his abilities in magic were not as strong, and his attempt to invade the Barista Palace to take the lives of those in line for the throne and to steal Princess Claudette ended before it had properly begun, due to intervention from the Baristas.

And so, Lord Goyim's heart, which was becoming increasingly vile and corrupt, came to turn itself entirely over to evil. Goyim did not know of the miraculous healing properties of the Fountain of Life, at the centre of the labyrinth. In fact, his father warned him against going anywhere near it, for he felt troubled in his spirit if he ever stepped near it himself, and he therefore believed that something very untoward and untouchable must have lain within its centre; perhaps a terrible creature that possessed power beyond their own dimension of existence, like an angel of fire or, worse still, the Creator Himself. The lake in the labyrinth where he had met Ruby on the night of the masquerade ball was merely an illusion formed by a trick of sorcery. His magic song had, in fact, caused the labyrinth to move around as Ruby had entered into its zigzagging paths, taking her far away from the Fountain of Life. Little did Lord Goyim know, but had he ventured into the Fountain of Life after the heartbreak of his youth, he would have saved himself all the corruption that followed.

Back in the present, everything was going fairly smoothly, and Ruby was quite settled in this seemingly carefree existence, that is, until the day a stranger came to call at the door of the great castle.

The stranger was a young man in his early twenties, who had a rough appearance and a grubby hat which he clutched in his mud-stained fingers. He asked to be presented to the lord of the castle for the prospect of possible employment, and the butler, on viewing his disposition, advised him to expect a short consultation with the master.

Nervously, the young man stood, waiting to be summoned from the hallway. The stuffed wolves surrounding him cast fear into him. They all faced him and seemed to snarl at his humble presence. He thought perhaps he had better turn and embrace the lonely road he and his father had been travelling on, but his father's health was vastly failing and any accommodation by a warm log fire was welcome, even in a dusty, wolf-haunted mansion. Before his thoughts could continue, a sharp voice summoned him to the main hall, where the master sat. He entered quickly and stood before the lord. He gasped in wonder at the great stature and noble appearance of the man. Smoke rings filled the room as Lord Goyim puffed on a silver pipe. He was laughing in apparent disbelief to himself as he surveyed the humble young man.

'So, you have come.' His voice was cold.

'Please.' The young man bowed low. 'My name is…'

'Yes, I know your name, boy,' snarled Lord Goyim, 'and I don't believe that you could possibly have come even within a ten-mile radius of this place without…'

'You know my name?' cried the young man, almost forgetting himself. 'A poor humble carter? How?'

The lord stopped himself from replying, and became deep in thought. He muttered to himself, 'he must not know.'

Presently, the lord decided he needed to test something, so he spoke in a slightly kinder tone of voice, if it could be called kind. 'Young man, may I ask what you *think* your name is?'

'It is Ethan Hartley that addresses his lordship.'

'What?' The lord forgot his powers for a moment, breaking out in a sweat. 'The magic did not go that deep? How can he know his full name – yet not his identity? Of course, my princess must keep part of her name, if she must indeed be my princess one day…'

Lord Goyim did not care that the young carter could hear his words, for he knew that they would be incomprehensible to him. In truth, Ethan considered that perhaps the lord had lost his marbles and patiently waited for his permission to resume discussing the nature of his visit.

'So!' The lord finally raised his right hand. 'You have come seeking employment.'

Before Ethan had time to reply, the lord answered his question for him.

'No, we have no need for a carter. We have plenty of servants in this house. Good day!'

Ethan felt a little crushed, but in truth, this was little more than he had expected, and he bowed low to the ground before he left the hall with a sigh. Watching him go, Lord Goyim made a note to do a special spell to avoid him ever crossing the threshold of his territory again. But then again, he knew that there would be no need for any future visit, so he decided to give his spells a rest for the time being, as they consumed a great deal of his energy.

Ruby was cleaning the top tower window when she saw the young carter leaving the main castle door for his horse and cart, and in a flash his head turned and his eyes gazed on her face with wonder. A strange electric current flew between them and all of a sudden she felt a painful chill deep inside her heart. The other maid who was beside her caught her just in time.

When she awoke, she found herself in bed, supported by the other maid and the stranger was by her side, mopping her brow.

'Perhaps you work too hard!' he said and smiled.

His voice captivated her heart, and she felt it skip a beat.

'I feel like I have known you somewhere before,' she murmured. 'Maybe in a distant dream.'

Her voice seemed to stir his heart similarly within his chest.

'You have probably seen me when you came to the market to buy your master's food. I certainly saw you in the crowds. I thought I knew your face. I have seen you walking through the streets of Camden for the last two years.'

Here the other maid chuckled, but the sound of the master's voice called her attention. She started in fear and jumped to her feet, and rushed from the room, whispering, 'I will convey your condolences for your absence from the lord's presence today.'

Ruby strained to sit up in bed.

'No, Rose, I am quite all right. I shall present myself to him as I always do, or else he will not be pleased.'

But Ethan stopped her. 'You are unwell. Please rest here.

329

I must go to see to my father in the cart shortly. But promise you will rest and stay here.'

'No, I am quite fine now. I don't know what happened earlier. It has never happened before. Not quite like that. I remember you in the market place. I think you may have helped me once before. But I am in good health now.'

It was at this moment that a severe cry penetrated up the tower stairs. He saw her face fill with alarm.

'He calls for me. I must not keep him waiting. I must not try his patience. I *never* try his patience. I want things to be in harmony... I must go!'

And before he could stop her, she had gone.

Ethan sighed, and knew in his heart something was not right. As there was little else he could do for the time being, he walked downstairs sadly and went to the cart to see to his father. But alas, when he reached the place where his cart had been, it was nowhere to be seen.

'Father!' he cried.

'He can't hear you,' the voice of Lord Goyim said, but Ethan could see no one. 'He has been sent to the other realm, and there you will be sent too.'

Suddenly, flashes of lightning came straight towards him and he burned so much that he thought his insides were going to explode. When he opened his eyes, he found that he was well dressed and that he was seated opposite his father, also in new rich garments. They were sat on great armchairs with golden decoration in the middle of a vast hall where a log fire burned. All at once, a clear memory from his childhood returned to him and he knew this to be his house. His father was no longer coughing, but beaming in his old good health.

'Father!' he cried. 'We have returned!'

The Sword in the Heart

'Returned, yes,' replied his father, 'but from where? Have we just had a strange dream?'

Ethan paused as the events of the day almost seemed to vanish from before his eyes. 'There was a castle… and there was a girl, a beautiful young maid… I forget her name.'

'Oh, yes!' His father chuckled. 'You certainly have been dreaming, haven't you my son?'

'But it all seemed so real,' muttered Ethan, trying desperately to remember. However, any meaning that had come from his previous existence and short acquaintance with the beautiful maid was becoming harder to grasp.

'Some things just cannot be explained,' he contemplated.

'Fetch the maid!' his father cried. 'Time for our afternoon tea, remember?'

'But there was a lord,' went on Ethan thoughtfully, 'and there was lightning.'

'Now the lightning I remember,' his father replied, sobering up slightly as he leaned forward to survey the warm countryside view from their grand window. 'Yet all seems calm out there today. Quite pleasant, actually.'

'The lord was an evil man,' murmured Ethan.

'Goodness, this dream of yours certainly calls for some waking up!' cried the old man. 'Summon the maid, Ethan.'

'Yes, very well, father,' replied Ethan a little reluctantly, but then he had an idea. 'Let's see if this works… MAID!'

There was no reply, just a faint breeze and the sound of

the branches tapping against the mansion.

'MAID! MAID!' echoed his father.

Again, no response. It was then that they noticed how thick the cobwebs had grown on the high ceilings and how there was a distinct lack of the patter of footsteps of scullery maids and the jovial chatter that once filled the air.

'Something's seriously wrong,' his father puzzled.

'Yes, I know father,' replied Ethan, 'and I must get to the bottom of it.'

He fixed his eyes on his father's face, trying to stir a memory, but there was not the slightest flicker from his conscious mind. His father, meanwhile, quickly slipped into a pleasant sort of unconsciousness, demonstrated by a gentle snore. As he watched his father's slumber, still deep in thought, suddenly his fingers found a piece of paper in his trouser pocket. There were mysterious writings inscribed on it, which at first he could not comprehend. The words were written in such a strange, rough scrawl he could barely read them. Through the dried mud and what could have been rain or tear stains, he read the following words, which stirred him deeply:

Isolation

No matter who I'm with, I feel trapped.
No company is right for me.
Everywhere I tread is someone else's turf.
I move from place to place like a restless traveller,
An outsider who walks like a free man but is locked in
    inside,
A prisoner who is moved from barred room to barred room,
Chained to a strange lock and key.
Just as a lock is chained to its key, so a key is its servant.
But who am I serving?
What is required for both to be free?

One would lose purpose without the other.
If I ever get out of this prison, what purpose will be mine?
Branded a prisoner since birth, I cannot see life with blind
    eyes that never learnt to see freedom.
But what is knowing freedom without knowing chains?
Without suffering's resolve, how is freedom gained?

I have a future vision of a parallel existence:

I've left the prison walls; the gates are open wide.
I'm free, yet I look behind; there's still a prisoner inside,
And I see prisoners roaming, still under lock and key,
And it dawns that I'm no less a prisoner than they.
I'm imprisoned in a mind that has lost its memory,
Imprisoned to the road; the journey takes me on.
I just sit and enjoy the ride and fill the country with song.
In this strange existence, I try to embrace the day,
And we share the joys and trials that come along the way.

Whose words were these? The writer may have come from a
completely different class to him, yet his writings struck a
very familiar chord; the feeling of needing to break free. But
from what? The previous dream he and his father appeared
to have returned from, and which seemed to have lasted for
an eternity, was drawing ever nearer to him. And soon he
realised that this writing was none other than his own - even
though he knew his handwriting usually displayed the style
of an educated class. He remembered the social conditioning
of his regal upbringing, as if from yesterday, yet he also knew
that he had just come back from somewhere so far removed
from this reality and he longed to remember that part of who
he was. This had surely been his parallel existence; the life of
a poor man. The paper had been found in no pocket but his
own, after all. The faces of a poor carter and his sickly father
flashed before his mind. And then he saw *her* face, as he

moved through the market place, offering lifts in his cart to members of higher classes. He saw her vanish, and suddenly she was lying in his arms on the cobbled stones of Camden, seeming to be in a sort of fit. One of the washerwomen threw a bucket of water over her beautiful face, and she sat up with a start. She was clearly seeing a nightmare before her eyes and all she could murmur was, 'I must return to him... I must return to him.'

A few moments later, Ethan had jumped to his feet and stirred his father from his sleep, who was somewhat reluctant to be awoken. Nonetheless, his father understood the urgency behind his son's voice and in a few moments they were mounting the old cart that stood in the stable, with its faithful old horse, which had also been flung from the other dimension, and they were making steady speed in the direction of the Barista Palace. Suddenly, within a matter of minutes, things were becoming crystal clear.

'He thinks he can outdo us by lurking in another dimension, with his stolen hostage,' he cried out to his bewildered father, 'but when I summon the angels, there will be hell to pay! He made a big mistake in returning me to this dimension, because all has come back to me and I remember the boy that I was, and the man that I have now become.'

*

Soon after Ruby had been summoned by her master, she entered the hall feeling a little confused and feverish. For some time her master surveyed her through the smoke coming from his pipe with a certain amount of dissatisfaction. Then he instructed the other servants to leave them alone. Presently he addressed her.

'I hope, Ruby, that you have come to see me as a good master.'

'Oh, yes!' she replied straight away. 'I have come to appreciate you more than I can say.'

'Good,' he continued, seeming slightly more pleased, 'and I hope that you are happy here in my castle, where I have provided for your every need.'

'You have been more than good to me,' was her reply. 'I could not ask for a better master.'

'So it would seem,' he said quietly, his voice reverting to an eerie whisper. 'And yet, I would hope that you have begun to see me as more than a master.'

'Indeed I have,' she responded eagerly, wondering why she could feel a strange grip of fear around her throat. 'I see you as much more than a master. You have my heart, my lord.'

As the word 'heart' came out of her mouth, she felt as if her words had been specially polished and performed many times before, and she wondered how this could be. Yet she smiled in apparent pleasure at her master, and although the tension in her voice had made him start a little at first, he seemed to be a little more convinced by the smile. And soon he let her go back to her duties, however, following her every movement with slightly more watchful eyes.

Ruby started to forget about the enchanting stranger she had met, who had drawn her back to a distant world she had once known. Yet when she settled down to sleep that night, strange songs filled her head and she could not understand the words which they spoke into her soul. She knew all was not as it had been, since the electricity had passed between her and the stranger's eyes. She had a vision of a music box held by a little girl. The girl was singing to its melody, and somehow she knew this girl to be her closest friend and the song she sang was a song they had often sung together. She often found that when she had this dream, she would start sleepwalking around the castle. She would wake up after opening the castle door and find herself leaning against the courtyard gates, her face pressed against the bars, yearning to be released. These gates were kept locked at night, but they started to symbolise a lot more to her than mere physical separation from the other world she longed to know. She knew she would not always be able to hide this growing desire from her master.

Meanwhile, Lord Goyim, trying to counteract the force which he feared would start to undo his power over the princess, composed an evil song and he set a spell so that it kept playing in her bed chamber day and night. As she tried to sleep at night, she was oppressed by the chanting and started to long to escape from this enchanted place. As the eerie music continued, however, it only seemed that her inner music became stronger and at night the face of the young carter flashed before her eyes. Sometimes he spoke to her in a different tongue, which she came to understand, and he told her his name was Ethan and that he was preparing to battle with the forces of darkness in the name of the Creator. As she heard his name, she felt a parallel life begin to reawaken. He told her she was a captive and that the Great King of all was planning for her release. Becoming increasingly aware of her captivity, Princess Ruby started to write down new songs; songs about release. One such song came from her late-night experiences, being surrounded by unearthly music that invaded her bed chamber. This was, against her will, starting to become like normal background noise that she feared one day she would be so accustomed to that she would no longer be able to hear it. It was a constant, negative drone and the lyrics filled her mind with lies. In order to counteract the curses she was hearing, she jotted down this narrative song of the old life which she had begun to remember:

Back to the Music

When I was a child, I played music in which I lived and
    thrived,

336

And as I got older, my music gave me wings to fly.
I was alone in this world, seldom shared;
A place where I could put most of my cares.
There was no other place to turn;
Music was my first love, my coping mechanism,
And once bitten, twice shy, I would retreat to my world,
When danger or pain passed me by.
But gradually over the years, my music opened out,
So I shared with others the comfort music can bring,
The way it can shelter you under its wing,
And in a parallel existence, newborn I emerged,
Small and vulnerable in a thorn-filled world,
No sugar coating, no protective womb to hold me in,
I arrived at the surface of the pool I had been kept in,
Thinking I'd found love and a world of adventure,
Thinking I could soar into a bright new future.
But soon the highs became too high,
The lows were beyond my experience,
This new life became too much for my sight, touch and
    hearing,
And so, slowly I withdrew back to the world of my making,
To re-embrace the music so that I could live within,
And just as I began, as a child, to play,
I returned to my inner music and came back to life again.

She laid her pen down slowly on the table and then she
became aware of his presence, standing at the door. His
breathing was heavy and unsteady. She could see his eyes, lit
up like glowing lanterns in the dim moonlight. Then she
recalled that he always came here, at the same time every
night. But for the first time, on this night she was awake.

He started to sing, and she flinched inside. But her body
moved towards him, against her will.

'Give me your whole heart, give me your whole soul,'
were his words, and his hands were outstretched. She

walked to him, feeling her heart hurting inside as she took his hands. And then he led her slowly down the stairs. She tried to keep her song in her head, but felt that her thoughts were being held down by an unseen force. A few minutes later, they were entering a dark dungeon. And at the corner of the dungeon, there lay a great red beast, snoring in deep sleep, and breathing out smoke as it slept. When she saw that it was a dragon, her being filled with fear, and then she remembered that she had felt this way every previous night as they had walked the castle dungeons.

'And now,' Lord Goyim said, 'it is the night when our souls will be legally bound. For I already have your heart; now I take your soul and you are mine for all time, my wife and soulmate, to rule over my kingdom with me, under my command.'

At this moment, he opened a trapdoor, which appeared to have been guarded by the dragon. The dragon arose, roaring, with flames spitting from his mouth. Immediately, Lord Goyim addressed the beast with authority.

'Quiet, Pooch!' he screamed. 'Submit to me! Sleep, sleep, sleep again. Or else, all of the castle will be woken, and there is no need for them to witness this ceremony.'

The dragon snarled a little, and suddenly reminded Ruby of a dog as it reluctantly obeyed its master, and settled back down to sleep. Lord Goyim reached in through the trapdoor and lifted out a heavy glass box. Ruby shuddered within, but tried to remain calm on her exterior, for what she saw in the glass box shocked her senses. There stood two beating hearts, side by side. And she knew at once that one of the hearts was her own, but she did not know to whom the other heart belonged. She clutched her chest, wondering how she lived without a heart in her body, and started to feel a little faint.

'My princess!' His tone was suddenly wary. 'What causes such a reaction to the sight we have always witnessed these past months? Have you not seen your own heart before?

How true it beats, for it is true to mine! And yet, tonight, it seems to waver and skip beats.'

Sure enough, the heart in the case began to tremble.

'What? What is this sight? Princess, have you something to tell me, because I certainly need some explanation for this!'

'My lord,' she tried to answer with a sweet, controlled voice, like one in a trance, 'I cannot explain the actions of my heart. Perhaps it is happy to see us again.'

'Silence!' His eyes looked straight into hers in deep suspicion. 'You will not lie to me. You have been unfaithful. What were you writing in your room as I came to you?'

'A song,' she replied coolly.

'A song to your lover, the young carter?' he snarled.

'No, a song to my own heart,' she replied, 'to reawaken the music deep in my soul. That must be the reason for this trembling of my heart.'

'No!' He seemed to feel some pain, and as he did, she noticed the other heart in the glass box begin to writhe and bleed.

She felt pain for him and tried to touch his shoulder. He pushed her hand away fiercely. He appeared to be crying.

'How could you write a song for *anyone* other than me? That you could write for another heart...'

'But master, it was for *my* heart.'

'Silence, maid! This is unfaithfulness, and should not go unpunished... After all I have given you... I have given you my heart; you should not want for anything else. You have become selfish, and for this you will pay the consequences.'

'No, master!' She started crying. 'You know how devoted I have always been.'

'Until now!' he snapped, but then as he watched her, his tone became strangely warm again. 'Yet even now, I will give you one last chance to prove you will be faithful again. You will now prove yourself to me by giving me your hand in marriage.'

Suddenly, the face of Ethan flashed before her eyes. She could hear his voice wailing, as certainly as if he stood in the dungeon beside them. Lord Goyim seemed to hear it too, and he started.

'How could he have got back in here? I sent him back... back to the other realm. How?'

At this moment, she felt her eyes being led to a sword which hung on the wall behind the sleeping dragon, and she knew what she wanted to do. She ran to it and swept it from the wall, but it proved too heavy for her to lift and she fell, the flat of the blade hitting her head. In her moment of haziness, she felt the sword being lifted from her by the lord as he sang a strange chant, and to her horror she watched, paralysed, as he raised the heavy sword and pierced it into her heart, where it lay in the glass box. She clutched her chest in pain, watching the heart bleeding, and started to think that this was the end of her existence. She lay on the floor, her whole body in strange spasms as she felt the life draining from her. Words started to fill her mind as she gasped for air. They were words Ethan had spoken to her in her dreams and they gave her new strength. She cried out, 'I will never marry you! Not unless you make my heart like a heart of stone!'

'A heart of *stone*?' he mocked her. 'But surely that is your destiny, to have a heart of stone, just like your namesake – Miss... Ruby... *Stone*!'

His laughter filled the air. As she watched her bleeding heart, she noticed a change come over it. For as the lord chanted, surely enough, it became hardened and turned from ruby red into a cold, white stone. At this moment, Ruby lost all consciousness and her existence from this moment became as an endless sleep. But even in this existence, she could hear an inner siren singing over her, and telling her to keep her courage high. The siren seemed familiar to her, and after a while she knew it to be the face of her friend Cameron. Her face became like her guardian angel through the long watches of the eternal night. Sometimes, in her dream-filled sleep, she also saw a great king of light coming to her rescue in a golden chariot, driven by winged horses and singing the song of dawn.

The Quest to Save the Princess

Back in the Barista Palace many prayers of thanksgiving were being raised, for the return of Lord Hartley and his son Ethan was an event to rejoice over. On hearing that Ethan had recently met their daughter in the other realm, Prince Ebedgar and his wife Claudette were greatly encouraged. Together they arranged for a non-stop prayer and praise service in the chapel. The Baristas never needed to sleep, so they were set on duty there to pray to the Creator for the release of Princess Ruby, and of all the other captives under the power of Lord Goyim and the forces of darkness.

There were two Baristas constantly on guard by the Fountain of Life in the labyrinth, although the true entrance to the other dimension was still unknown and the Baristas knew that no principalities of darkness would really go near to the Fountain of Life. They realised that Lord Goyim must have made a temporary imitation of the fountain through his sorcery, before taking Princess Ruby captive and they constantly patrolled every part of the huge labyrinth, looking for any suspect signs. None were revealed, and it was thought that maybe the evil lord would not use the same point of entrance more than once. But none were certain on what had given him authoritative access to these grounds, in the spiritual realm (except for his father's own marriage into royalty, where his wedding ceremony was conducted within the labyrinth).

Cameron, Ruby's closest friend, had a vision that Ethan

would have a major part to play in the deliverance of the lost princess. She had also dreamt that she was giving a music box that played worship music to her friend, and that this music comforted her and kept her closer to their parallel realm. All at the palace were greatly encouraged by her dreams, but even more so by the often detailed and informative dreams of Ethan Hartley. Ethan's dreams were becoming a major guide in the prayer meetings of the palace folk. He was convinced that in his dreams he had actually managed to enter the dungeon of the castle of Lord Goyim, and he described the events he had seen. He had even come to realise that his presence there was not unfelt by the others, and that he may not be entirely powerless in that realm. However, he knew also that when he had directed Princess Ruby to the sword by the dragon, he was still unable to help her to attack Lord Goyim with it. Somehow, Goyim's power was too strong in that realm, even though he was unable to foresee that Ethan would gain entrance to his kingdom.

As a result of the nightmarish event, where Ethan had witnessed Ruby's 'death', or descent into unearthly sleep, and where he had seen the sword turn her heart to stone, he had found his new mission. That mission was to rescue the lost princess, through training as a warrior who would give strong combat to Goyim and the forces of darkness. He knew the only sure way to do this was to get closer to the Almighty One, who would equip him for this task. So Ethan began praying and fasting and day by day, he entered into the presence of his Master, as led by the angels in the chapel. Ethan had come to know his Creator personally on his recent return to the palace, where he had received a vision. It was a vision of a great, wildly beating heart which filled the chapel with ceaseless rhythm and inexpressible passion. Ethan would hear this heartbeat whenever he felt downhearted and also when he felt he was drawing nearer to his

Creator, and his desire to come to know his Creator better was getting stronger every day. He and his father remembered the place where they had been enchanted by the evil lord; they had seen a dark statue by the river in a side entrance to the labyrinth, but the angels had purified that place all those years ago, and had fought with other principalities there, overthrowing them. There was no need to guard the rivers now that those who had once been captured there had been delivered. As time went on, Ethan and his father both grew in spiritual strength, alongside Prince Ebedgar and Princess Claudette, who also fasted and prayed for the time when they would be commanded to go forth into the other realm.

But then, one day, as Ethan and his father were praying in the chapel, a strange thought occurred to Ethan and he voiced it aloud.

'What if the other realm is more accessible than we think?'

'What do you mean, son?'

'What if Lord Goyim is hiding right under our noses and we never knew it? What if all this time, he has been as close as home itself?'

'What makes you say these things? Anyway, I never was sure that we should be seeking to find Goyim. Surely our Creator is the one to present us with the day and place of battle. Perhaps we should not be seeking Lord Goyim in the kingdom of darkness.'

'We must, as directed, go forth into darkness, father, if we are to reclaim ground that has been stolen from us. Under the Creator's direction, of course. Man would be foolish to go in his own strength and knowledge alone! The Baristas will accompany us, when the time is right, and so we will never be alone, not with His divine power at work in us. But my point is something quite different... I have been thinking that on my entrance to different parts of Goyim's castle in my dreams, there are aspects of it that are not unlike our own mansion at home.'

'What is similar about it?' questioned his father. 'I only have your word to go on, as I have never set foot inside his castle, although I'd imagine it to be an awful, cold, deathly sort of place.'

'That it is, father,' replied his son. 'But if you were to turn it around, and imagine that the stuffed wolves that put fear into me were really something else altogether, like... like the angel statues in our hall, and that the main dining hall where we so often sat with the fire had exactly the same layout as Goyim's smoke-filled hall when I visited him that time. In fact, all the dimensions in the house are the same, it's just their content that is quite different.'

'What is the relevance of this, even if it were so?'

'Father,' went on Ethan, 'I remember you telling me years ago that Lord Goyim was turned out of his house by the late king, but we never found out the reason for this. Now we know it could have been due to him turning to evil ways. Could it have been our very house that was once his? You remember that you moved into it before I was born, from the old cottage in Camden.'

'Yes, that dear old cottage was sorely missed, but not for long, once we got used to our lives of luxury.'

'Indeed. Well, father, consider this; as a sorcerer, would Lord Goyim ever really *leave* his residence, or would he continue to live there in a different dimension?'

Here, Lord Hartley shifted rather uncomfortably in his seat. 'My son, are you saying that the lord has lived with us all this time?'

'Not *with* us,' Ethan replied, 'I think he has lived in another dimension of the house we have. He must have built a replica... and if this were true, it also means that we need to proclaim full ownership of our house, and we need to reclaim the stolen ground if we also wish to enter his domain properly and rescue Princess Ruby.'

'My son, what has inspired these thoughts? That is, how can you really be sure that what you say is correct?'

'It was the uncanny nature of the resemblance of his castle to our house, and when we were returned to this dimension, where else best to arrive but straight into our own house? Besides, I have felt this has been revealed to me through these prayer times with the Creator. I must tell the others.'

And after the others had heard the tale, the angels counselled Ethan and his father with this advice:

'As rightful owners of the mansion, it is up to you to do battle with the other kingdom, from the mansion itself. Two angels will go forth and assist you. The rest of us will stay back in the palace, supporting you in prayer as you step out in faith. Yet, we must wait on the Creator for the desired time for battle.'

*

In Lord Goyim's castle, Ruby slept fitfully where she lay in her bed chamber, the highest room of the tower. The music of the lord continued to surround her and her dreams were filled with her longing to be free. Once, she dreamt of a princess writing on the walls of her tower, and as she did, the pen cut into the walls so that they bled. She began to realise that the walls were really the soul of the princess, and she longed to free the girl from the bondage in which she lived. In other, better dreams, she would see her own personal siren rise up from within and sing songs of comfort deep into her being, in the places where the soul's flesh had been cut. But night after night, he would come and chant over her, and she wished she had a method to fight his power. Until finally, she began to rise in strength against him, even while she was in the deepest of sleep.

In a dream the face of Ethan flashed before her, and he told her he had new weapons to fight the forces of darkness.

She had a vision of Ethan returning to his mansion with his father, and there they found the log fire in their hall already lit. Yet on seeing it, they immediately put it out with water that radiated through the room in a supernatural way. The fire roared and turned green. Then she knew that their room had also been under enchantment. The second after the fire was put out, the two figures were seen disappearing as they stood at the chimney where the fire once was. They were followed by two winged creatures, who carried shining swords and shields.

*

Ethan and his father, sure enough, had found a method not only to fight the evil lord's power, but also to gain access to his domain again, by defying his own entrance guards. Ethan had realised that fire and heat were what the lord used to move from one dimension to another. He remembered how the lord had made the labyrinth bushes burn so that Ethan and his father would attempt to put them out using the water of the river. But little did the lord realise what would happen if the water used against his fires was that of the Fountain of Life. So, before they had set off to their home, Ethan and Lord Hartley had taken containers full of the fountain's water, and as well as this, Ebedgar had released his wonderful invention from the Barista Palace so that, combined with the water, it might liberate, deliver and minister to the residents of the castle. These were two good weapons, but the two men also brought with them their own swords in the Hartley family name. After having sprinkled their armour with the pure water, they felt better equipped to fight in the spiritual realm. And two minstrel angels came with them as their guides and protectors.

As they entered Lord Goyim's castle via the fireplace, they noticed that the dark room was strangely silent. It was late at night; he would be up in the tower, as Ethan had dreamed, singing over the princess in her unnatural sleep. He knew the way they had to go and the deed that must be done, and without delay, they set off to the dungeon, where they would have to confront the dragon that guarded the trapdoor, under which two hearts lay. As they entered into the hall by the castle door, Lord Hartley and his son saw the wolves savagely glaring at them in the moonlight. Of course, they were stuffed and could not move, but occasionally Lord Hartley was convinced he could see their eyes or nostrils twitching. Not long after this, their cages began to rattle and a strange howling filled the air.

'We must make haste!' cried Ethan. 'It must be Lord Goyim's alarm to alert him of intruders. Quick!'

In a few seconds, there was the sound of quick footsteps and a great voice howled as they ran to find the door to the underground.

'Who goes there? Who *dares* to trespass on *my* domain?'

On hearing no answer, Lord Goyim ran down the spiral staircase and found no one in the hall, but the wolves were still howling and baring their teeth.

'Quiet, my pets!' he soothed them. 'You have done your duty.'

He picked up his trailing cloak and became as silent as the darkness, as he moved from room to room.

Meanwhile, the others had found the door to the dungeon and were moving slowly across to the trapdoor where the dragon lay. It slept as usual, snoring like a dog. Ethan headed straight towards it, his jaw clenched and his sword in hand, ready for attack. Slowly, his father shifted the dragon's claws from the trapdoor beneath them and Ethan got the invention machine in place right by the dragon's nose. As Ethan lifted the trapdoor up and reached in to fetch the glass box with the hearts, the dragon awoke as predicted and roared violently, blasting flames out of its nose and mouth. Oddly, at this moment, the machine picked up that the dragon was in need of a dose of dog food, and this is what popped out of the machine, right at the dragon's feet. Taken aback, the dragon sniffed at the food in some suspicion, but then straight away licked its lips and gave a sigh of satisfaction, before finally gulping down the meal whole. To their amazement, as the dragon digested its much appreciated food, it started to change in appearance. They watched as it turned slowly into the form of a small dog and began to yap incessantly at the intruders in some indignation.

'Wow!' cried Ethan. 'Would you have guessed that the dragon was Lord Goyim's pet, Pooch, the little yappy dog he was once famous for? He won't be impressed we've turned his mighty dragon into this harmless little yapper!'

'No, he won't be impressed at all.' A deadly voice echoed around the dungeons, but they could see no one.

'Or, perhaps,' the voice continued, starting to laugh, 'he will be impressed if he turns each one of you into a dragon and burns the silly machine that reverses the spell!'

The machine started to make a strange dark-chocolate milkshake drink, but the cup was picked up by an invisible hand and thrown across the room, whilst the laughing continued.

'So, the machine may know what the dark lord needs to drink, but the dark lord knows that if he drinks of the chocolate, he will himself become a reformed character and the dark lord does not want that to happen now, does he?'

Suddenly one of the angels was dragged upwards and a battle was started in mid air. However, the lord, evidently, had found much more than he had bargained for, as all could hear from his loud groans of frustration. Even whilst the angel seemed to be winning, to speed things up the second angel joined in, and the dark lord was outnumbered. Meanwhile, Ethan opened the glass box and found the stone heart, with the sword that pierced it still inside it, next to the beating heart of Lord Goyim, which appeared to be writhing in agony.

'Don't you think I can summon all the forces of darkness to battle with you? Only two angels; for I see now that is what you are. How can you withstand a whole swarm of us?'

At this moment, Lord Goyim raised his voice and chanted in an unknown tongue and the others could hear the wolves from the glass cases upstairs howling, and then to their horror, padded footsteps could be heard running down the stairs and entering through the dungeon door.

'Brace yourselves for the big fight!' Ethan cried, swinging his sword high, and his father did the same.

Suddenly, foul fangs were upon them, launching through the air and tearing through flesh. There was a long, bloody, gruelling fight, where the wolves were flung from one wall to the other, but never seemed to get tired, or to die of their injuries. Finally, one of the angels winged down to them and grabbed hold of several wolves and shouted, 'Ethan, the heart! You must stab Lord Goyim's heart now, before it is too late!'

Ethan dashed another wolf to the wall, and before its return, he took the writhing heart and plunged the sword deep into it, with the utmost vigour.

As this happened, Lord Goyim suddenly became visible to their eyes, and he screamed out in pain, writhing on the floor at their feet. The wolves all whined and lay down as if mortally wounded. Even at this time, he couldn't help sneering at them:

'You'll never get her back. My power cannot be undone. For my sword lies in the stone heart. Her heart will always be like a stone! And it will always belong to *me*!'

'Do not listen to his lies,' one of the minstrel angels told Ethan. 'The sword is not really his; it is an imitation of one of your own, kept in your basement. Just follow my instructions. We are going to sing a song of revival over the stone, and as we do, you must remove your sword from the stone and take ownership and authority over it in so doing.'

As the minstrels started to sing, Ethan stood up and touched the handle of the sword, but it immediately burned his hands.

'Ow!' he cried. 'It's too hot! I cannot!'

'You must,' the angels pressed him. 'We will call on the Creator and He will hear us. Use your water!'

So Ethan held the sword in his burning hands and screamed out to his Creator as the sword scalded through his skin, and he tugged and tugged. Meanwhile, his father threw on all the water they had brought with them, calling on the name of the Great King. Feeling a current of electricity going through his entire body, Ethan fell to the ground. There was the sound of hissing, and he knew that his hands were smoking just as much as the sword was. But then he watched as a change came over the stone. The sword finally fell from it, and the stone turned back into a heart again, healthy and beating like a revived organ, and then it disappeared.

'It has returned to its rightful place,' one of the angels reassured him, smiling. 'The job has been done. Now we must return to the Fountain of Life, where your hands will be cured, and where we must release the evil lord's heart. If nothing else can change him from his wicked ways, maybe this can.'

'But I thought he was dead,' stammered Ethan.

'No, he is far from dead,' replied the angel. 'Although, of course, he has not really been living for a number of years. Let us return.'

The angels helped Ethan to his feet, and held up both his arms.

'Well done, good and mighty warrior!'

Meanwhile, the princess, who lay in deep enchanted sleep, had a vision of a king of light. He had eyes that burned like fire; pure fire, unlike the enchanted fire of Lord Goyim. At first it was too bright for her to look, but somehow she knew that she must look at the purest, most beautiful light in the world, and as she gazed in His eyes, she knew herself to be purified, inside and out. Suddenly she felt a new heart beating within.

'My heart has been returned!'

'Yes,' He said gently, 'yet your heart must also be fully restored and renewed in my light.'

She felt Him reach into her heart and she watched as He performed a kind of heart surgery which filled her whole being with a new golden glow. Then He breathed over her with a healing song that she felt waking her soul. A few moments later, she got to her feet and He led her down the ever lightening spiral staircase to the underground where the others stood, as if frozen in time.

'All time has been reversed, and brought back to the present,' the King told her, softly, 'It is as if the enchantment never ever happened. Walk in my light.'

Then, He was gone and she was gazing on the triumphant warriors. She saw Ethan lift his sword from the heart of stone with much pain. She heard the angels counsel him, and raise up his scalded hands. And a few moments later, Ethan looked up and could see Princess Ruby had just entered the room. Tears glistened in her eyes.

'You came for me!' she said, the sound of victory in her voice.

'Of course,' he said. 'Just as I said I would, Princess.'

Palace of Eternal Song

As Ethan looked around him, he could see that the surroundings had changed back into his own mansion, and that the dungeon was now really his dusty old basement.

One of the angels carried Lord Goyim and flew ahead of them as they travelled back to the Barista Palace by horse and cart.

They were greeted in tremendous excitement by all at the palace, and Prince Ebedgar and Claudette threw their arms round their long-lost daughter with much joy. Ebedgar was also particularly glad to have his machine back again, safe and sound.

The heart of Lord Goyim was thrown into the Fountain of Life. As this happened, a deep groan filled the palace walls, and none had been heard like it before or since. From this moment, Lord Goyim became a mute, living like a servant in the palace, where he enjoyed the company of his pet, Pooch. The princess always ensured that she filled his bed chambers with positive praise melodies that would help him to sleep at night. Whether or not the lord was grateful for this regular rendition, none could say at first, for he could not talk of his feelings on the subject, and tended to lie low, avoiding all social interaction. He seemed contented enough, however, and in time did manage to delight the Baristas with the occasional smile – though some residents at the palace were not too convinced that he could possibly have become such a reformed character, and wished him to be forever under lock and key in the basement; not surprisingly, given his sordid history.

Soon after this followed a momentous occasion; the marriage of Ethan Hartley to his bride, Princess Ruby. ('As they were always destined to wed,' Prince Ebedgar muttered with tear-filled eyes, 'and the Lord Goyim could do nothing to stop it! Ha!')

And so, our story of parallel existences draws naturally to its close, but not without a final glimpse of the life of Princess Ruby Twining-Stone. For, as already seen, in the time when Ethan had taken the sword from the stone, she had felt the Creator give her a new heart, and this heart was one that beat with true richness, like it had never beaten before. She came to realise that as Ethan had taken the scalds of the sword and his father had poured water over him, water had also poured into the heart of stone and given it everlasting life. So now the heart pumped and beat, and the years went by, yet still it pumped and beat as healthily and youthfully as ever. And so Ruby lived on, alongside her husband and family (who drank of the Fountain of Life), and they all continued to live far beyond the end of this dimension of human existence.

As for Lord Goyim, he also gained eternal life, due to the water that had washed his heart, and in this one action, the generational curse of his ancestry was broken and he was free from his own enchantment. In time his speech was returned to him, along with great joy like he had never known. And so, Molech Goyim became a man in his true identity; as a son of the Creator King, living forever more in peace and joy with his family in the Barista Palace.

So as not to forget the past, which was starting to become like a distant mist, Princess Ruby wrote these songs, and many others, which she sung forever more in the courts of the palace:

354

Background Noise

There is a dull, constant droning like the firing on a distant
    battle line,
A throbbing in my temple of vengeance that won't lay
    down its arms.
There's a relentless crowd that's ever storming the castle;
For long, long ago, its gate was broken down.
There's a princess who sits unmoving, tired by tears of wait-
    ing;
Her writing covers the walls, cutting the flesh of her soul.
Once, long ago, her restless heart was aching;
Now it is buried in ruin and snow.

There's a voice far quieter than the still in the storm;
A voice that when you hear it makes you suddenly feel
    strong,
To find the truth amidst the lies; to know all fear has gone,
To override the background noise and turn it into song.

Deep within the castle a sword lies in a stone,
Faithfully waiting for its master's return,
For light to dawn and bring it to life once again,
To turn back the stone to the heart it once pierced.
And the crowds still drone and thunder, filling her temples
    with fear,
Drowning out the music that echoed in her early years.
For once her courts were filled with songs of divine joy,
But in time they were drowned out by background noise.

Yet as time rotated a strange light appeared;
A light that had not been sighted for many light years.
Like a glorious eagle it rose from outer space,
And entered the land at a light-speed pace.
She shielded her eyes; at first it was too bright,
But then she became bold and let it set her mind alight,

And in the centre, she saw a King of Light.
All background noise subsided as He filled her mind.
In the sacred silence, she felt her pierced heart;
As light flooded her castle, she heard the sword and stone
    part.
She felt a new heart beating as she watched the gold
    sunrise,
With the King who soared with the eagle over the skies.

There's a voice far quieter than the still in the storm;
A voice that when you hear it makes you suddenly feel
    strong,
To find the truth amidst the lies; to know all fear has
    gone,
To override the background noise and turn it into song.

Daughter of the King

Once upon a time, there was a princess in a tower,
Entrapped within a fortress ruin, enslaved by a spell.
The source of her enchantment lay within an evil song
That only captivated hearts with what is wrong.
A creature kept her prisoner there, infested with such
    greed;
He sought to glorify himself, so turned to tyranny.
The princess he imprisoned there was true heir to the
    throne,
Beloved daughter of the true and only king.

And so, she dwelt in chains, her song was silenced by a
    cruel mask.
She lived within a world of death, where mocking shadows
    danced,
And though she tried she could not cry towards the moon
    at night,

For she thought nothing could bring rescue from her
   plight.

Then one day, a new world sang to her and made the dark
   night flee;
A prince was singing by her tower His song of victory;
'I have come to take your chains; your pain will fall on me,
When you surrender your whole self, you will be free.'

The princess heard these words just like a light unto her
   soul;
She threw her chains down at His feet and He climbed
   them up the wall.
He lowered her to freedom as He put her chains on Him,
And sang, 'Meet me in the east when the Sun is risen.'

Her voice again caused thousands to bow before the throne,
With songs of awe and wonder of the love the king had
   shown:

'I'm your daughter, oh Mighty King;
You are greater than everything.
I'll raise my voice; let endless praises ring
To the Lord of lords, to the King of kings.
Loving Father, hear the praise I bring,
For you gave your Son as an offering;
He took my chains, my pain fell on Him,
Now He's lifted high, crowned as King of kings.'

The Seventh Tale

The sound of a guitar strumming melodious chords filled the room as the fire crackled in the grate. They could almost see smoke rings rising from the flames and disappearing, and several of the boys and girls had to blink twice at them. Mr Friedman looked around to see the impact his story had had on them all. David stared straight back at him, smiling, for he had played a big part in the tale. His guitar-playing had accompanied Mr Friedman's singing, creating an enchanting atmosphere that set the scenes as they were being told. He leaned forward to congratulate David.

'Hey, David, I think you and me make a great duo. Perhaps we'll go far; the storyteller and the musician! Talking of which, I'm thinking of holding some public performances. Your gift in music will be essential to that, as will the acting skills of a few of us…'

The teenagers were all sitting back in their seats, looking relaxed and almost ready to sleep. Yet at times in the telling, Mr Friedman had noticed that some of them were sitting rather tensely in their seats, gripping their chairs. In particular, he had noticed Ruby doing so, for she knew this tale was for her.

'So, Ruby, how did you find it?'

'Dear Mr Friedman, you know me so well!' she marvelled. 'I totally see myself as a trapped princess. Not here, I mean. This is a wonderful house. But I always long for my knight in shining armour to come.'

'I can be your knight,' said Ethan, her close friend.

'I know,' she said softly. 'You're lovely. But what I mean is, I want *God* to come himself and rescue me from… *myself*! As a little girl I used to have nightmares about my past experiences. The way that evil lord sang over Princess Ruby made me think of all the lies that I've allowed to invade my thoughts over the years. They had become to me like background noise. Only since coming here have they started to go away. But I need more of His light to fill me. Mr Friedman, have you another story for us?'

Before Mr Friedman had the chance to answer, his son came in, shivering from his time out in the snow. Yet, Mr Friedman noticed that he had a warm, rosy glow on his dark, handsome face.

'Sorry I'm late, Dad,' he said, settling down next to Mia. 'The carol singing went on longer than expected, because it drew up quite a crowd! We were also given free mulled wine at the end. I really liked that bit.'

'That's all right, son.' His father beamed up at him. 'That's funny, but you are actually right on cue. The next tale I'm about to tell may even have you in it.'

Then he went on, 'This final tale is one with a difference. It should draw the other tales together, and in fact should round up our whole experience here very nicely… Listen up. This tale is one for the open-minded, for it is one of a highly mysterious nature. Brace yourselves, for you will be transported across a multitude of dimensions.'

And he gave them the title of his final and seventh tale. It was…

The Last Port of Call

The Mysterious Butler

Manfred wearily made his way up the stony steps, fighting against the gale-force wind. The mansion loomed like a giant monster before him, and looked terrifying when lit up by the forked lightning. Reaching the porch, clutching onto his large satchel, he sighed and shivered in the chilly night air. He rang the bell and the sound brought strange comfort to his soul. Not a minute passed before the door was opened. A sturdy butler stood before him, a man who held the look of complete integrity on his old, furrowed brow. And he smiled in the way a father might. Manfred felt instantly at home.

'Best be coming out of the wind, sir,' the butler suggested, without even asking his name. 'We've been expecting you.'

Eager to be out of the chill, Manfred stepped inside, and the door closed behind him with a mighty, booming thud. He blinked in the eerie candlelight, noticing the absence of electric lights, and then he became aware of rosy warmth surrounding him, and turned, expecting to see a glowing log fire in the sitting room. Yet, to his surprise, none existed. Where, then, did the warm glow come from? His questions were brought to a pause by the elderly butler, who addressed him whilst taking his coat and hat.

'It's been a long road, sir.'

It was more of a statement than a question. Manfred just nodded weakly in sheer bewilderment.

'You say you were expecting me?'

'Of course. We hoped you'd get the message. Either way,

you came, and you are here.'

The butler had a solemn tone. He showed him to a chair decorated with golden trees. Manfred observed a grand piano in a corner adorned with the same intricate pattern.

'Message?' Manfred frowned as he sat back in the chair.

'Obviously you did not.' The butler bowed slightly. 'A drink, sir?'

'Ah, yes!' replied Manfred eagerly. 'Brandy, please.'

For a moment he thought he was seeing things incorrectly, and he stared at the butler in disbelief, for suddenly a tray appeared in the butler's hand, bearing two glasses and a bottle. He was sure the tray had not been there before. The butler handed him a glass of brandy.

'Is the owner of the house at home?' questioned Manfred.

'The owner has sadly passed away.' The butler bowed his head solemnly. 'Natural causes. He died a happy man in peaceful sleep. But not before he passed on a message. He was a friend of the man who would have been your last host, in the house next door. You probably struggled to find the house.'

'Well.' Manfred gasped for breath. 'I struggled indeed. There *was* no house.'

'You may have noticed the cliff edge is rather close to this garden wall,' went on the butler. 'Lost in the sea is that man's house, who would have been your host. Your *last port of call*. Unfortunate.'

'I'd say!' cried Manfred. 'Is the poor old chap all right?'

'Lost at sea,' replied the butler. 'No one has seen him since the fall.'

'Great Scot!' exclaimed Manfred. 'When did this terrible tragedy occur?'

'Last night,' was the butler's reply.

'But wouldn't he have been expecting it? I mean, surely the cliff erosion was gradual enough to give him time to move elsewhere. Surely there was *some* warning.'

'He didn't see the signs,' replied the butler, 'so set in his ways was he. Deaf as a doorpost, outside and in. His whole life, he had dreamed of a house by the sea. That was his entire dream. That was what he lived for.'

'Yet the other hosts that I have met on my quest had all found some deeper meaning in life,' Manfred said, more to himself than the butler, and lost in his thoughts, he continued, 'I went from host to host to find the meaning of life, and each of them had a different story, but I could not depict its meaning. I feel like I'm back at square one – and this is the last port of call!'

'The last port of call it may be,' replied the butler, 'but with it comes the beginning of discovery. What did you notice about all the hosts with whom you stayed?'

Manfred thought for a moment. 'Well, they all seemed frightfully familiar. I felt as if I'd met each one before – at a different stage of life. Not to mention that they did all look quite similar, too!'

'Similar?' repeated the butler. 'Like the same person?'

'I shouldn't think so, no!' replied Manfred quickly. 'Although, that would be awfully hard to say – as they were all such different ages. The first host was a boy in his late teens. In fact, each host I stayed with was a bit older than the last. They all took such an interest in my quest of discovery, each claiming that they, too, had been on such a quest – and they all told me pretty much the same thing.'

'Which was?' queried the butler.

'They talked of an eternal gate,' replied Manfred. 'Now, this is all rather surreal, so just bear with me... they had all been through this gate, and it had brought them here.'

'And where did they find this eternal gate?' asked the butler.

'Well, you'd have to believe in religion to accept this story...'

'Religion?' interrupted the butler. 'Or just life outside of the box... beyond the gate?'

Manfred looked at him closely for a second. He noticed that the butler's voice had started to echo, and that a strange glow emanated from his face. For a moment, he was stopped in his tracks, but feeling a strong sort of courage, he soon continued.

'The gate comes from the stories about the beginning of time. It existed in the forest where God once walked with man. Apparently, in the times before man's rebellion, he had access to the gate. According to my hosts, it represented eternal life, and all that is good. Before man walked away from God, he had no need for anything else.'

'Why would man want to walk away from such a blessing?' the butler asked suddenly.

'I can only assume that something more tempting came along,' said Manfred, shrugging, 'although I can hardly imagine what!'

'Something very profound must have enticed him away from all that he knew to be good, perhaps?' suggested the butler. 'Something he had not even considered before, that offered an alternative, equally wonderful life, and that also offered complete independence from God.'

'But what could possibly have seemed better?'

'That which *seems* better very often isn't,' replied the butler. 'We are all tempted off the track by lies that blind us to truth. Anyhow, what else do you know about this eternal gate?'

Manfred was pleased that the butler, as with his previous hosts, appeared to have an open mind when it came to discussing subjects that most of the men he encountered considered to be anti-social taboos.

'Well, what I've learned from each one of my hosts is that when mankind enters the gate now, he will be granted eternal life once again. The only thing is finding it. The forest, I am sure, is hard enough to find. And apparently once you are inside it, it can become as spacious as the entire world itself – though I dare say no one's taken the trouble to measure it – and there's no certain way of finding the gate. The instruction my hosts gave was that I merely *look* for it. Well, that's a little vague, if you ask me...'

The butler had been watching Manfred with deep interest for some time.

'Manfred, do you believe in dimensions?'

'Dimensions?' Manfred muttered. He could not see what they had to do with anything.

'What if there is a gate that you have access to, but you don't yet know it? What I mean to say is – there may be a gate that rewrites your story before it has even been rough drafted...'

'All right, so now I'm really confused.' Manfred frowned deeply.

'What if the gate took you beyond the realms of time altogether, and enabled you to see your life, and how you would or *could* become, from another dimension? What if it brought you to the multiple dimensions of your own character, in all the stages of its life – past, present and future – all at once?'

Manfred drew in a deep breath and froze as all of a sudden, the faces of each of his hosts flashed before his eyes.

'Wait a minute,' he whispered. 'Are you actually suggesting that all of the hosts I have stayed with are... in fact... other dimensions of ME?'

'Precisely,' the butler replied, and Manfred could feel a shiver creeping down his spine.

Presently, the butler spoke again.

'Before the fall, the gate did not need to show us how to live. But now that is what the gate will do – when we find it.'

'But I haven't found the gate,' went on Manfred.

'Yes you have,' replied the butler. 'You just haven't walked through it yet. Not in this dimension, anyway. The other dimensions of you have walked part way through – one foot in, one foot out. They rely on you to complete the circle. The thing with the gate is you have to be wholehearted to seek it and follow its truth – otherwise, you may forget how to find it again.'

'How do you know I've found the gate?' questioned Manfred.

'You wouldn't be talking to me – or the other seven hosts – about it if you hadn't. You wouldn't have found us, without first embarking on a quest of discovery.'

'But... but...' Manfred felt confused. 'I got the address of my first host from a tramp when I was walking the streets, at my wits' end. And it all started from there, house after house passing me on to the next stage. I'll never know who that tramp was.'

'That tramp was you, from another dimension,' replied the butler. 'He hasn't quite approached the gate yet. I gave him the address he gave you. He gave a good gift away. He is still searching for truth in an alcohol bottle. But the gate is never far away. Sometimes he actually sees it – inside the bottle glass...'

'But how did all these dimensions of me meet here, on *my* world?'

'Your soul called out from the depths of time and space as you walked the streets. You knew you had to search your soul – so deeply that it would take your shattered pieces right from the borderlines of space to help you to complete your quest.'

Manfred gazed at the butler in awe.

'Who *are* you?'

'I am your guide. I am, in fact, your guardian angel.'

The Eternal Gate

'My... guardian angel?' Manfred whispered. The butler's face glowed in the dim candlelight. 'Yes,' he said, 'I had to travel against time, at light speed across space with God's mighty aid, to find every part of you that would help you put the missing pieces of your soul together. Of course, time and dimension are no problem for God, who made them all.'

'But why are there only seven chosen hosts?' Manfred questioned.

'Seven is a complete number. They were the ones closest to the truth out of all the dimensions. But actually, your hosts would have been nine in number if you had started your quest a little sooner (including the recently deceased, and the man lost at sea). These represented the nine lives you could have had a chance to live, but you make the number ten, because you have been offered eternal life. For the grace of the gate counteracts the earthly law of nine lives.'

'You mean, I have been offered eternal life?'

'Yes,' the angel replied, 'for this gift was given even before the beginning of time to all mankind. They just needed to receive it.'

At this moment, Manfred noticed that a change had come across the sitting room. The chair on which he sat, which was engraved with golden trees, started to grow up into a sort of stump, and branches poured out of it. The room filled with birdsong, and the grand piano in the corner floated on

369

a giant lily pad in the middle of a luscious lake, which bathed his feet with refreshing crystal-clear water.

Suddenly the butler appeared in his true angelic form; glowing like the sun, in a long garment out of which great wings sprouted, and he floated to the piano and began to play a melody that was so beautiful it could not have been recaptured or written down. As this melody played, trees sprung up all around, and what was once a sitting room became a grand and majestic forest. And there, from out of the open lid on the piano, grew a beautiful gate, tall and shimmering like silver stars. As Manfred gazed upon it, he started to feel he had seen it before, in a dream perhaps, and the more he looked, the more he felt he actually knew the gate. It seemed to behold the countenance of a divine person, and its presence was timeless, like that of an eternal king.

He felt the stump on which he still sat raise him up to his feet. And at this moment, the gate started to open. The angel sang words he understood to mean:

> *'Now is the time to enter the gate*
> *You have the power to change your fate*
> *Do not look back, or it will be too late*
> *Now is the time to enter the gate.'*

So, Manfred walked into the lake, towards the gate. But just as he did, he felt a strange current come over the waters, as if a great beast at the bottom of the lake stirred angrily. Suddenly, a great howling emerged from the waters and at this moment, great waves appeared and lifted up above his head, and came crashing down on him. Then a terrible wind appeared and drew him straight into the eye of a storm. He felt powerless but tried to continue swimming towards the gate. The waves threw themselves all over him, and he began to feel he was losing his senses. He considered turning back and running for his life, but he could hear the words the angel was still singing, '*Do not look back, or it will be too late!*' So he tried to battle on, but finally weakened as he felt a strange creature dragging him down beneath the pounding waves to the water bed.

He cried out, 'Save me, Lord!'

At this moment, he felt a strong hand grip his arm and pull him up to the surface.

A great voice cried, 'PEACE!'

And in a flash, the storm subsided.

Manfred found himself to be floating on a boat, guided by the angel, heading straight for the gate.

'Well done for not looking back,' said the angel with a smile.

A moment later, they were walking through the gate together, and much wondrous singing filled the air.

Then the great voice spoke again: 'Those who enter through the gate will be saved.'

As soon as Manfred passed through the gate, he felt a lightening of his spirit and a new joy rose in his soul. He was in a beautiful labyrinth garden, full of fruit trees of every variety, and vines bursting forth from the hedges. A majestic castle stood ahead of them, shining as bright as the sun. In one part of the garden, he saw an elderly man hunched over a glass of wine, which he sipped delicately and with much enjoyment. The man looked up at their approach.

'Aha! I see you've brought my guest, Michaelson. Good show! Shame about the house, but at least this castle with a lovely view of the sea more than makes up for that. How are you, Manfred?'

'Great,' Manfred replied. He saw the resemblance to himself in the old man. 'I'm glad we get to meet at last.'

'I'm afraid I wouldn't have done a great job at directing you to the gate – not like some of the others, anyway. Almost to the end, I was still rather too obsessed with my own little world...'

'Aren't we all?' said Manfred, laughing.

The old Manfred's face dropped, and he looked at his younger form very seriously.

'No, no!' he cried. 'We all need to guard against becoming selfish old men who are so set in their ways that it's too late to change them. I had the chance of a new life – even whilst I lived on earth – but I feared change. Michaelson had tried to warn me of the awaiting peril, but I only paid heed to his message when I fell into those terrible waters. Still, I ended up in the right place... but YOU!' Here he jabbed his finger out at him. 'I hope you shall be nothing like me. You still have years left. Whatever you do, don't get a house by the cliff edge – well, not too close, anyway! No, you must live your life wholeheartedly. You must be the link between these two worlds. You must learn not to live as I lived. Yes, life is great for me here, but you don't know of the inheritance I missed. Of course, you still have the opportunity of entering into that inheritance on earth... and, if you store up the right sort of treasure, you'll be richly rewarded in this world, too!'

Manfred smiled a little uncertainly.

'I would enjoy such an inheritance, if only I knew what it was.'

'You will, when you get there,' the old timer replied. 'It's the people you'll touch – that's the big part of your inheritance. It is in helping others that you will live your life to the full, and in doing this, your life will be complete.'

Manfred gazed across at the angel, who smiled back.

'If I may inform you, sir,' Michaelson said, bowing, 'I believe we are finished here.'

'Certainly,' replied Manfred, who shook hands with the old man as they parted. It was strange because he could not feel the man's hand at all; then he recalled that he had never shaken hands with any of his hosts.

'Just as I thought!' the old timer said with a merry wink.

Together Manfred and Michaelson walked to the gate, as the old man waved them goodbye with another hearty chuckle. In a few moments, Manfred was sitting back in his golden decorated chair, and all the room was back as it was before – the only difference was that the angel, Michaelson, was no longer there. It was morning, and the sunlight crept in through cracks in the blinds.

'Must have taken all night – or perhaps it was a dream,' Manfred considered.

At this moment, there was a rapid knock at the door. He considered who he would expect to see, in some anticipation, as he rose to answer it. And as he opened the door, there before him stood a small boy holding a silver key.

'I meant to give this to the butler, sir,' he piped in a high clear voice. 'It's the key to the house. The old man always used to let me come and go as I liked.'

'Ah, yes,' replied Manfred, instantly feeling some fatherly affection for the little lad, as he peered kindly down at him. 'And what's your name?'

'Mannie!' squealed the boy excitedly.

'Well then, Mannie,' went on Manfred, 'a friend of our late friend is also a friend of mine. And if he let you use the key, then so shall I.'

'But old Manfred instructed me to hand in the key. Because I shall be going so very far away, and I won't have any use for it any more.'

'Oh, yes?' said Manfred softly.

'Yes, far, far away,' went on the boy. 'Besides, he also left a message – that the house was a part of your inheritance. He said there would be lots of other little boys coming to stay and that you'd need plenty of helpers. Perhaps you'll need a servant and a butler.'

'Oh!' cried out Manfred, with a delighted laugh. 'I know there's one thing I certainly won't need – and that's a butler!'

'Oh, yes,' said the smiling boy, 'Michaelson will always be

with you – just as he is with me, as I journey back to where I come from…'

'Yes, indeed. Mannie, I have heard it said that some have entertained angels without knowing it… well, it appears that I have been entertained by an angel without knowing it!'

Mannie let out a ripple of laughter and jumped around delightedly from foot to foot.

'Well, I must leave, for you are all right now. Goodbye, sir!'

'Goodbye, little Man.' Manfred leaned down and patted the little boy's head. 'Go forth with light speed and live your life to the full.' Then he whispered, 'And remember that the gate is only a breath away!'

Mannie chuckled with more delight, and jumped up and hugged Manfred (a hug which Manfred could not feel, but which touched his soul). Then Mannie turned and ran down the garden. As Manfred watched him scuttling away down the path that led to the sea, he noticed how in the distance the waters had advanced, and how as the boy followed them he became a silhouette, like a mere shadow of life that once was, before finally disappearing into the mist. In this sweet encounter, Manfred clung to the hope of new life that was just beginning to dawn with the rising day.

A Time for Dreams

Having reached the end of this thought-provoking tale, Mr Friedman noticed that all the adolescents sat with their mouths wide open. Possibly, the multitude of dimensions was a rather imaginative and even a slightly mind-boggling tale to be telling at this time of night, he considered.

'Dad, that was different,' whispered his son.

'Thanks, Mannie,' he said, 'I'll take that as a compliment. And guess who that was about?'

'Well, I suppose with a name like Mannie, it must have been me.' Mannie chuckled, and took this opportunity to wink at Mia, who smiled.

'Yes, partly,' his father replied with a mysterious smile.

'Partly?' echoed his son.

'Partly,' repeated his father, 'for that tale was about you, son. But it was also about me. You were all the orphans that Manfred was going to take into his home, which I guess you worked out. And I was none other than the main character, Manfred himself. Of course, only my son knows that Manfred Friedman is my full name. But now, you all have the luxury of knowing this. So there you have it, folks; that story was all about my own life, from the beginning of my discovery to what you see now.'

'Really?' Lots of faces were staring in awe as Ethan asked, 'Every part? What about the angel? And the whole house changing? And the hosts?'

Manfred laughed. 'I am so glad that, although you have

become "of age", Ethan, you have not left your wondrous imagination behind. But you may still be surprised to hear that the story is true. The angel butler, of course, is my butler Mr Michaelson. This tale was told in his absence tonight, in order that he would be with us in spirit – for tonight he visits an old friend; the butler to a lord who resides in the castle further up the coast. As you know, he has always been an angel in this household. Have you never wondered how all those gifts appeared just when you needed them? It is evident that he is immortal, in his ability to survive the storms of life. But, of course, I do not mean to take the credit away from God's mighty hand, as He has been our constant protector and the true provider for all our needs.

'It is actually quite true that I had a trip to heaven and back, as I literally died in a storm that threw me over the cliff edge into the sea when I first came to inherit this house. I was clinically dead for three days, and I had a vision of such beauty – just like the vision of the castle by the sea beyond the gate, as described in our tale – that when I returned to earth, I promised my God that I would do all the things He would ask of me, and honour Him right until my second dying day. And that is the origin of the orphanage you see before you today.'

'That's an awesome story!' cried Mia. 'You should tell that story to every orphan that comes to this home.'

'Indeed, I will,' agreed Manfred, 'Every one who enters the orphanage shall hear it.'

'I prefer not to see it as an orphanage,' Ruby said thoughtfully. 'It feels like a real home. I think if there is anywhere that would echo heaven on earth, it's right here.'

'You know, Ruby,' said Manfred, suddenly finding that he had to push back the tears, 'hearing you say that is better than any Christmas present I could ever wish for. Of course, having you all as my children is much more than I could ever have imagined.'

'What about me, dad?' joked Mannie, with another grin at Mia.

'You will always be my first son.' His father looked at him tenderly for a moment, then, without warning, he grabbed him and pulled him into a great hug.

'Oh no, Dad!' Mannie was laughing loudly. 'I wasn't asking for that! Not the Father Hug!'

'Oh yes, Mannie,' his father cried out for joy, 'I think you were! I think you were asking for the Father Hug. You are never too old for it, you know. Hug! Hug! Hug!'

The rest of the children all laughed around them, and soon each one was tackled with the Father Hug in its fullest measure. Much joy was heard in the fireplace lounge long after the little ones were deep in their dream-filled sleep. Then, as the older children were starting to feel a little sleepy, Eli and Edita returned to summon them away to bed.

Last but not least, the four of them – Manfred, Evelyn, Eli and Edita – finally gathered around the fire to draw the evening to a close. They shared the merry tales of the day over a heart-warming nightcap, before turning in to their own bed chambers, where they readily embraced dreams of their own.

The snow fell softly outside, bringing a truly magical white Christmas to the large family when they woke to carol singing at dawn, when much merriment and many more wonders awaited them. And, as the large family turned to embrace the new year, taking the adventurous tales they had heard with them, they waited with great expectation for next Christmas's instalment of magical adventures...